GRAVE AFFAIR

Nina Green

Pendragon Press Limited

A Grave Affair

Published in the UK by:
Pendragon Press Limited
Testa Teres House, Copse Road
Fleetwood, Lancs., FY7 7NY
Tel: (01253) 772788. Fax: (01253) 773359

ISBN 0 9530538 1 4

Printed in the UK by:
Dinefwr Press Ltd.
Rawlings Road, Llandybie
Carmarthenshire, SA18 3YD

For my husband Jim
to honour the memory of our mothers
Emily and Gladys

Oh what can ail thee, knight-at-arms
Alone and palely loitering.

Keats: *La Belle Dame sans Merci*

PROLOGUE

~

. . . Meantime, across the moors
had come young Porphyro,
with heart on fire for Madeline

Eve of St. Agnes

Tonight her beauty was enhanced by danger. He paused in the
doorway of the bed chamber; her flesh sang with the bloom of
youth and sheen of voluptuousness. A draught from the gallery
caused the torch in a nearby wall sconce to flare, sending light
flickering across his armour and burnishing it with flecks of gold.
The dipping of shadows caused his hand to automatically move to
his sword hilt. He looked both ways along the gallery, but seeing
and hearing nothing suspicious, closed the door and turned the
key in the lock.

She was lying across the bed, her mane of chestnut hair cascading
over naked shoulders and breasts. As he advanced he saw how her
limbs, loose and heavy with desire, appeared to bruise the crumpled
coverlets of fur, velvet and sensuous satin. Sections of a felled oak
burned and crackled in the stone fireplace, beating back the chill that
crept from the castle walls. His senses swam; the heat intensified
the heady scents of cedar and sandalwood that rose from a silver
censer, precious oils brought back by St. Clair from his last crusade.
He forced thoughts of her husband aside and moistened his lips
with the tip of his tongue. The flames had flushed the alabaster
globes of her buttocks with rose, and deepened the shadow that
lurked between waist and hip to the purple of crushed mulberries.

She watched his approach in silence, but her sensuous lips parted
in a smile of welcome. "Antony," she breathed reaching for him,
her eyes slanted like those of a cat. Even now whilst in the grip of
fever, he was struck by his foolhardiness, his powerlessness against

this forbidden passion, so he maintained an arrogant stance as he unbuckled his sword belt.

But now he was about to die. His tongue thrust greedily between her lips and his body arched and bucked as though of its own volition. In turn her limbs encircled his and her small white teeth nipped at his shoulder, urging him to still greater passion. Then she was weeping and tossing her head on the white satin pillow. He moaned aloud as though in anguish. "Madeline . . ." then again and louder, and at the last exultantly as a conqueror might on thrusting his standard into virgin soil. He shuddered then and lay still in her arms, dying the petit-mort.

Madeline allowed her body to relax and become limp again, luxuriating in the delicious sense of languor. He lay with his head on her breast like a sleeping child, and she shifted slightly beneath the weight of his love. Tenderly she stroked the dark locks of hair. Always when it was over she told herself this must be the very last time, yet knowing it would not be so. It was worth the risk: this loving that over-rode everything from guilt to wifely duty. She stretched her legs luxuriously. This was the first time they had dared to make love in her chamber; usually the sky was their roof, the mossy earth their bed. But tonight Justin St. Clair was away at his border lands. She looked up at the rampant unicorn depicted in the wall-tapestry beyond the bed, then smiled down at her lover's spent body.

As though sensing her triumph, his muscles tensed as he coiled and pushed himself up in a fluid motion, resting on his knees and imprisoning her with a hand on either shoulder. His thighs gripped her flanks as though he were riding a spirited mare, and she moaned softly as he increased the pressure. He kissed her eyelids, then ran his tongue lightly over their sensitive skin and felt her respond. He rose above her, his shadow leaping grotesquely up the wall, then paused like that, momentarily disconcerted by guilt. That he, Sir Anthony Chase, one of King Edward's most favoured knights, should have broken his vows of chivalry. She opened her cat-like eyes and smiled. Lowering his head he pressed his lips to hers and knew himself to be lost.

ONE

~

Jo Cavanagh eyed her agent with something approaching belligerence. "Blake Durante is a bastard, I tell you." She felt a pang of guilt at her disloyalty, then recalled the previous night's row, the way he had stormed from the flat thus denying her the chance to justify her decision.

Louise Costello crossed one long, glossy and elegant leg over the other and murmured: "But such an attractive one."

"One I can do without." The irony in Jo's voice didn't quite match the sadness that lurked in her widely-set eyes. She looked past the other woman to the plate glass window, beyond which snarled-up traffic seethed and London basked in the dusty sunlight of an Indian summer. And let's not forget, Jo thought with a touch of annoyance, that Louise is biased in his favour, given that she and Blake had once had a bit of a thing. The tiny stab of jealousy caught her unawares.

Louise watched her for a moment, a tiny frown creasing her well-preserved and flawlessly made-up face. With a graceful movement she eased herself off the corner of the desk upon which she had been perching, and crossed to a drinks cabinet set against the wall, her high heels sinking into the deep pile of the carpet as she walked. "Join me," she said, returning with two double gin and tonics and handing one to Jo. "So tell me Jo: what went wrong? I thought you and Blake were becoming a permanent fixture," she added, returning to her former perch, the ice in her glass clinking with the sudden movement.

Jo shrugged and took a sip of her gin before replying. "In a way that's the problem."

Louise spread her hands in a theatrical gesture. "A dishy guy like Blake falls hard for you and it's a problem?"

"He wants children," Jo said flatly.

"Marriage first, presumably? – although I know it's not necessarily in that order these days."

"Yes, marriage comes first with Blake." Jo sighed and pushed back her chestnut coloured curls with a gesture that showed her agitation. The image of a tall man with broad shoulders, dark hair and dramatic good looks that gave away his Italian descent surged from the back of her mind to accuse her and challenge her independence. Leaning forward, she placed her glass on the coffee table then sat back again. The white leather of the settee sighed softly like a living breathing thing as she shifted her weight.

"And?"

Jo shrugged and stood up, pacing the room like a caged cat, aware of Louise's shrewd eyes following her movements. She's worrying in case I accept, wondering how much return she's going to get for her investment, Jo thought cynically. But then who could blame her? she added in fairness. The last book had been a huge success but a lot of hard work had preceded it: a novel based on the life of Wittgenstein wasn't an easy package to market. The combination of off-beat philosopher and hitherto mid-league author must have been an agent's nightmare. But her angle had saved it: the Freudian interpretation of Wittgenstein's eccentricity; of suppressed sexuality that smouldered beneath his supposed hatred of women. It had worked, and earned her new fame and respect. A double-edged sword though. At least that was how Blake had seen it. Touring book shops, media studios and lecture halls hadn't done much for their togetherness. Louise didn't see it that way of course. She would now be coolly calculating the effect of marriage and kids on her protegee's career. No need to make her suffer any longer. "I'm not ready for it," Jo stated laconically.

If Louise Costello felt a surge of relief at this revelation, she hid it admirably beneath her smooth sophisticated exterior. "So why the push, honey?" Suddenly her expression changed, and she tapped her glass with long red-laquered nails making the crystal ring. "You're not pregnant?"

"No way." Jo picked up her drink, finished it and putting the empty glass down crossed to the window. The flush to her normally pale translucent skin signalled her anger and indignation. She turned to stand with her back to the window, vaguely aware of the hum and surge outside. A drive and power-buzz that she wanted to share, a high-powered slice of life. The only problem was her inability to totally believe in her good fortune; the fear that 'they' would one day suss her out, realise that her success was only a fluke, that she wasn't as clever and gifted as they thought. She couldn't be; her talent, if any, was for following up a gut feeling, relied on hunches rather than a distinguished academic career. So she had to work harder at it than most. And here was Blake asking her to stop just as the momentum gathered, to choose between him and her career. "He's given me an ultimatum," she said tersely.

Louise skewed round to face her. "So: marry me now or- what?"

"He'll move out of the flat and take an overseas commission," Jo finished for her.

"He's still in the Conflict Resolution business then?"

Jo nodded. "It's so unfair! I mean, can you see him giving up *his* goddam job with the U.N. if I wanted to suddenly settle down and have two point five kids?" She tossed back her hair again, so that sunlight caught the movement and imparted flashes of rich chestnut as she moved back to the table and picked up her bag. "Anyway, I can't do it. It's emotional blackmail."

"Chill out, Jo; we're all guilty, when we want something real bad."

"I suppose. But anyway it's history now; I've made my decision."

"Shame. Of course, it's a bad moment to take time out —"

"Tell me!" Jo exclaimed, hitching the strap of the bag higher on her shoulder. "I get my first break and Blake wants me bare foot and pregnant in the kitchen!"

Louise grinned. "Hey come on honey, isn't that just a weeny bit over the top?"

Jo shrugged theatrically and camped it up. "His grandmother was a big Italian momma, remember – with a swarm of bambinos swinging on her apron! It's in the blood, that sort of thing."

Louise waved her levity aside with an airy gesture. "But you could have a bambino and *still write.*"

"Yes, but not *live it.* Not with one ear cocked for 'Baby'," Jo mimicked with a grimace. "And what about my lectures? Not to mention research. No thanks, I can do without the broken-nights-and-house-bound handicap! Besides, it's the principle of it."

"Principles are pretty cold comfort on winter nights."

"And now you're sounding like Blake."

Whose side was Louise on anyway? Jo thought indignantly, then half-grinned as realisation struck: her agent obviously knew her too damned well! Basic psychology really: opposition only stiffened resolve. Like when she was a kid and her parents urged her to do something, and she would dig in her heels and refuse. Clever bitch. Louise was still protecting her investment.

"So how's the new one coming along?" Louise asked with a smooth change of gear as she levered herself off the desk and followed Jo to the door.

"Okay." Despite her down-beat mood, Jo's face became animated. "It's grabbing me this one. I thought nothing could after Wittgenstein." Her face took on a closed expression as she recalled the fascination, the total absorption and even obsession with this man who had given away his inherited fortune and rejected the snobbery and ritual of Cambridge. But now there was a 'new man' in her life, an enigma to unravel and attempt to solve. Ruskin. Was it true that his marriage to Effie was never consummated? And why had he seemed to encourage her relationship with John Everett Millais, stood by whilst they eloped? And then that later tragic love affair, the focus of the new book: "It's such a sad and poignant story, Ruskin and his Rose," she said aloud, and a trifle defensively given Louise's sceptical expression.

"H'mm." Louise gave her a look that said she was now wearing her business hat, was once again the hard-nosed agent confronted with a difficult subject and recalcitrant author. "Similar angle?"

Jo nodded. "Has to be I think, if it's to have wide appeal."

Louise visibly relaxed. "Absolutely. Victorian repression/obsession with sex?"

Jo nodded. "And sublimation of sexual passion, in Ruskin's case. But he was a sensitive and gifted man, nothing like the dry stick his critics would have us believe. And Rose La Toûche was a victim of her time as much as of madness."

"Yes, well let's hope you can persuade your own critics, Jo."

"I shall," Jo retorted, opening the door. Her smile of confidence gave no sign of the sudden stab of anxiety, the old fear of failure.

Louise touched her lightly on the arm. "If you need a bolt-hole until Blake has been to collect his things, you're welcome to my cottage in the Lakes."

Jo paused on the threshold. Louise could be brash and bitchy at times, but she could also, as now, display great kindness and sensitivity. She had been dreading just that scenario: watching Blake dismantle their life together, packing it up into bags before taking it through the door. "Thanks, Louise. I may just take you up on that one."

"No problem. Call me."

"I will."

As she left the office Jo hoped it would not be necessary, and that Blake would have already gone.

As Jo pushed her way through the lunchtime throng of stressed-out workers and idling tourists to her usual eating place, her mood had taken a downward turn. A quick glance round showed her that most of the regulars were seated there, but no Blake. She smiled at a young woman with a blond bob, an editorial assistant from the publishing house on the next block, and nodded at her male companion from the publicity department, before sitting down at one of the smaller tables away from the crush.

After picking desultorily at her dressed artichoke she pushed aside the plate. What the hell, she thought, picking up the menu and scanning the dessert section, given the stress of the split with Blake, added to the particular time of month, this wasn't the moment to be worrying about calories and junk food. Give in to the hormonal urges, she thought with a half-smile, making her choice and preparing to pander herself. The peach melba when it came, dripping chocolate sauce in dark runnels over ruffles of whipped cream, afforded a brief and wicked buzz, but after eating her way through roughly half she pushed it aside, nauseated and annoyed by her weakness. She ignored the bronzed and athletic looking guy at an adjacent table who had been watching her, and who grinned as he caught her eye.

Black coffee restored her taste buds and self-respect. She was into a second cup as the shadow loomed over her shoulder. She knew who it was even before swivelling round to look. "Hello Blake," she said coolly, turning back to her coffee without betraying the smallest sign of the adrenalin-shot that had surged through her system.

"Hi, Jo."

There was a strained look around his eyes, she noticed with a pang.

He placed a cup of coffee on the table, sat down on the chair opposite Jo and regarded her gravely. "You look tired," he observed.

"It's warm," she retorted unneccesarily, given the perspiring faces around them, and the damp patches on the shirt-front of the man who had grinned at her and who now studiously looked away. Blake Durante, even when off-duty, gave the impression of authority and a man not-to-be-messed-with.

He shrugged. "Enjoy it – it's not often we get an Indian summer like this one."

"No, 'Jack' will be whorling our windows before we know it." *Oh God, we sound like polite strangers,* she agonised, searching his face then dropping her gaze as theirs eyes made contact. She played with her coffee spoon, trying not to dwell on the hurt she saw in his eyes, or the pain in her own tight chest.

He was watching her with keenness, his expression solemn. "Been visiting your publisher?"

"Agent," she corrected, responding eagerly to this mundane and innocuous turn in the conversation.

"How is Louise?"

"Fine."

"Does she know about us?"

"What, exactly?"

An expression of irritation flitted across Blake Durante's tanned features, and his dark eyes deepened to almost black. "That we've split," he said deliberately, and in a voice that rebuked her evasion.

Jo fiddled with her spoon. "Why should she?"

"Oh, she's fond of you and once had a thing about me." He grinned, obviously making an effort to keep things light.

"Which makes her one in about a hundred females in the London area alone," Jo quipped with a brittle smile. She inwardly cringed: it sounded childish even in her own ears. In Blake's too, judging by his quizzical look and obvious silence.

"Don't let's fight." He placed a hand over hers, the sunburned skin a perfect foil for the gold watch she had bought him last Christmas. Seeing it brought back that perfect day: cavorting like kids in the snow once the presents had been opened, the laughter as they pulled crackers over dinner, then later cognac and intimacy before a blazing log fire. A lump rose in her throat. Christ this was awful. Could she go through with it?

His eyes were seeking hers, forcing her to connect. "Have you thought about what I said, Jo?" he asked softly, leaning closer across the table to guard against eavesdroppers.

She swallowed hard, forcing herself to recall what was at stake here, that he was seeking to place his own wants above her needs. "Nothing's changed, Blake," she said quietly.

"I see." He withdrew his hand.

"Why the push?" Jo asked, unconsciously echoing Louise's words. "Just give me a little more time. Ask me again in the New Year."

Blake sighed and looked away. "Then at Easter, then Christmas, then again at the next New Year. No Jo. I've had enough," he said turning back to give her a direct look. "I'm all screwed up. Don't know where I stand. You see, if you can't commit now, I don't believe you ever will."

Jo made a deprecatory sound and shook her head in disbelief. "That's rich! It's exactly what I thought when you were busy screwing my agent! The colour in his cheeks heightened as he dropped his gaze, and she knew her long-held suspicions were correct. "Commitment wasn't exactly your top priority then," she added.

He held out a hand in a gesture of appeal. "I hardly knew you then, Jo. We weren't an item."

"How convenient." She pushed aside her cup and reaching for her bag, prepared to rise.

"I only saw her a couple of times –," Blake started to say, but Jo cut in angrily:

"You mean '*bedded*'?"

"Come on, Jo. It meant nothing. It ended as soon as I realised how I felt about you."

"Just like now? You decide you want to settle down and Bingo! – I'm expected to drop my life and start living yours? It's so bloody unfair!"

He studied her in silence for a moment, then appeared to make up his mind. "Fair or not – it's commit or break time Jo."

Her eyes sought his. "So you won't wait?"

"I can't stick around anymore just to be hurt at the end."

"What end, Blake? It's in your head." It was Jo's turn to be irritated and unknowingly she had raised her voice slightly.

Blake was already looking uncomfortable. He was wearing the look that said 'keep this up and I'm off'; the look that infuriated Jo, the look that just lately initiated one of their frequent and debilitating rows. He glanced round looking embarrassed, then turning back to her repeated: "I'm sorry Jo. It's Commit or Break time."

When she remained silent he pushed aside his coffee cup and rose to his feet. "I'm busy until the weekend. Okay if I collect my stuff then?"

She couldn't look at him. "Sure."

He paused at her shoulder, looked down at her with a look that brought a knife-like pain to her chest. "I'll be off Sunday night. I'll be away for a while I expect."

"Where this time?"

"Bosnia. Carl Bildt has been pulled out over the U.N. withdrawal issue. They need another mediator to open negotiations between Presidents Keradzic and Milosevic to try for agreement on Bosnian boundaries."

Jo's eyes flew to his. "But that could be dangerous."

He shrugged. "It solves your problem, Jo; I'll be out of your hair."

Before she could turn and protest, Blake had gone.

The flat was empty – and felt it. Wearily she threw down her bag and after opening a window, made her way to the kitchen and the 'fridge. Several mouthfuls of orange juice straight from the carton refreshed and soothed her dry and dusty throat. Pouring the remainder into a glass she closed the fridge door, wandered back into the sitting room and sank down onto the settee. The laughter of children playing, a dustbin lid being replaced and the cooing of pigeons filtered in from outside. Ordinary sounds of ordinary lives being played out. She sighed. Why couldn't she and Blake live peacefully together? Why should their lives be torn apart by conflict?

Her gaze slowly swept the room as she sipped the orange juice. It was all here: the picture they had bought from a street artist in Paris, the Venetian vase, the Tiffany Lamp, the fisherman's lantern from Greece; all the 'finds' and mementos that had gone into making their home, a rosary of memories evoking nostalgia and pain with each image. Putting down her glass, she picked up the photograph from the coffee table. A bronzed Blake smiled up at her from a sunlit garden during a visit to her parents' home in Wiltshire. Looking at it now brought back the fullness of those lips, their softness against her own, their sweetness on her body, and she laid her head in her hands then and wept. She couldn't be here on Sunday. Couldn't watch him dismantling their life, sharing out the pieces like the spoils of war.

War. He was going to Bosnia. He may not return. *What am I doing?* she asked herself wildly, filled with sudden panic. But she couldn't give in to ultimatums either. If he loved her as much as he said, he wouldn't walk out when she refused his unreasonable demands. Anger crept in, a welcome predator of grief. Well she wasn't going to be here for the final torture. She would take Louise up on her offer of the cottage.

Rubbing her damp cheeks with the back of her hand she suddenly sat upright. Being stressed-out at the time, it hadn't occurred to her that this was the ideal solution in every way. Apart from giving her respite from the trauma with Blake, it would provide the perfect opportunity to visit and research Brantwood on the shores of Coniston Water, the house where Ruskin had spent the latter part of his life. She would have to go at some stage during the writing of her biographical novel – so why not now when it served a dual purpose?

She had no idea what the quaintly-named Twilight Cottage was like, or where it was situated, other than 'somewhere in West Cumbria'. But then that had been the whole idea. Nobody was *meant* to know. Louise had acquired it at the height of her affair with the man she affectionately referred to as her 'Scottish Laird'. A well-heeled landowner with a large estate in Ayrshire and a couple of Western Isles to his name, she had met him in London during a major debate on Scottish devolution. Whereas Louise, after two marriages and as many divorces, was free as air – her laird was not. Tucked away in his ancestral castle he had a formidable wife and four children of varying ages to carry on the family honour; the latter, Louise had told her in a moment of gin-induced levity and confidentiality, being his religion and therefore ruling out divorce.

So the cottage had been used as a 'half-way house' rendez-vous, with Louise flying up to Carlisle whenever the opportunity arose. Jo grinned to herself. The cottage wasn't in use much these days, not since the arrival on the scene of the Texas ranch owner who had become Louise's latest 'rave'. The smile faded and she rose to her feet as a devastating thought struck. Had Louise ever taken Blake there, to her love nest in the Lakes? Fiery colour flooded her cheeks as anger surged through her, that and a double sense of betrayal: Blake and Louise had both deceived her about their fling, so there was no reason to suppose they hadn't spent an illicit weekend there. She couldn't, Jo decided marching into the bathroom and turning on the shower, even think of taking up Louise's offer.

The shower soaped and rinsed away her anger, and a simple meal of soup and garlic bread, followed by a couple of gin and tonics, induced a mood of nostalgia and melancholy. She crossed to the window. Despite the warmth of the day, night was closing in with an autumnal chill. Where children had laughed and played earlier, the square below was now quiet and sedate, the province of adults strolling home from restaurant or bistro, or hurrying from a business or charity meeting, breath rising in little white clouds as the temperature fell. The couples walking hand in hand, heads turned to each other, and cocooned in the warmth of their own magic world, made her ache with sadness. A lump rose in her throat as she watched two lovers pause to kiss beneath one of the square's maple trees, its leaves flaming in the light of the street lamp and stirring in the light breeze. Oh, Blake, why can't we get it together, she thought, leaning her forehead against the cold glass.

I can't stay here, she resolved anew, drawing the curtains before turning from the window. Blake would remove his clothes and belongings at weekend, and along with them the last vestiges of his presence, then the flat would feel emptier than ever. Where to go was now the question. Perhaps, she mused, her condemnation of Louise had been a bit hasty. After all, she must have been hurt when the affair was abruptly ended. Given that Louise had a soft spot for Blake even now, her feelings for him at the time must have been pretty intense. And, Jo reasoned sinking onto the settee, if Louise had taken Blake to the cottage, she would surely not be bitch enough to volunteer it's use. Maybe the best course would be to confront her, have her confirm it. But there was another aspect to all this: Louise Costello was a damn fine agent, one of the best, and there was no good to be had from leaving her over something that was history. So, Jo reasoned, maybe the best way forward was to be adult about it and not betray any jealousy, or even that she knew about the affair. She stood up and paced the room, aware of what she was steadily talking herself into.

Actually, she thought turning on the television, flicking idly through the channels then switching it off again, if she decided to accept after all, there was no reason why she shouldn't over-winter at the cottage to write the book. It was perfect: peace and solitude in which to write, and a rich research ground within easy reach. And Louise would probably be glad to have someone in there keeping the cottage aired, rather than slowly decaying from lack of use. She hesitated a moment, then picked up the telephone and dialled Louise's number.

"I can pick up the key Friday then?" Jo reiterated. "Okay, fine, thanks. I really appreciate this Louise. But I can't stay there over the winter without paying rent," Jo was saying, winding the telephone flex around her finger as she talked.

Louise gave one of her deep and characteristic laughs; Jo heard the chink of ice on glass as she spoke: "You'll be doing me a favour. Stop the rot, and all that."

"Okay, thanks, it's very good of you Louise." Jo hesitated, undecided about whether to raise the question of Blake and the cottage, but then she shrugged. What the hell, they were all adults here weren't they? And, sobering thought, if it came to that, she and Blake were now history too, so in the end what did it matter?

Louise's voice when she spoke sounded faintly puzzled. "What is it? Something bothering you Jo?"

"No, nothing. Just overwhelmed by your kindness," she ad libbed to excuse the gap in the conversation.

"Well hold on there, Jo! You might not be so grateful when you get there."

"Why, do I have to work by candlelight and draw water from the well?" Jo quipped.

"Not exactly. But it is rather out in the wilds."

"That'll suit me fine. I'm going there to work, remember?"

"Okay," it was Louise's turn to hesitate, then she added, "but there's just one other thing . . ."

"Yes?"

"The area is supposed to be haunted!"

Jo laughed. "Oh, by whom?"

But with another throaty laugh and a "Take care, Jo," the line went dead and Louise had gone.

She had intended doing a couple of hours work on the Ruskin book before going to bed, but decided she was too weary for mental activity. The confrontation with Blake and the subsequent soul-searching had drained her, she realised, and decided to make a start on the packing instead. It would need some care, now that she was to be away for at least a couple of months. Besides, the sooner she left and the better; Blake might come earlier than he had said. So the evening passed reasonably enough, despite frequent glances at the clock, and buzzing along the nerves when the telephone rang, but it was only one of her friends. At last it was time for bed, and she carried a milky drink and a book into the bedroom.

Could I possibly be wrong? she agonised, surveying herself in the dressing table mirror. The face reflected there was paler than usual, the muscles around the mouth tense. The eyes that stared back at her had a strained look, and faint purple smudges beneath the bottom lid. *You're letting him go; is that what you really want?* she asked herself, assailed by doubts. But she couldn't give up her independence either. With a sigh she picked up a brush and rhythmically stroked her hair, deriving a simple comfort from watching the auburn curls spring back in shining coils. Soothed, she climbed into bed and switched off the light.

After tossing and turning for several minutes she sat up, switched on the lamp again and reached for the bedside 'phone. Her hand wavered a second or so before picking up the receiver. Another moment of hesitation before dialling Blake's number. The ringing-out tone droned on and on as though mocking her weakness. That he might not answer had never crossed her mind. Irrational anger stirred: anger at Blake for not being there, for being unable to appreciate her gesture, and for being unaware of her need.

Where was he anyway at this time of night? She peered at the bedside clock, her eyes as yet unaccustomed to the light, and saw that it was not quite eleven. Even so, he was hardly sitting at home mourning his loss, she thought banging down the receiver.

Well Blake Durante you've missed your chance, she consoled herself, nursing her injured pride whilst waiting for sleep. Her humiliation wasn't helped by the too-late realisation that she had not first dialled the blocking code to withhold her number, and that he would therefore know she had called. But what did it matter? she thought wearily, what did any of it matter any more. Determined to put him out of her mind, she amused herself instead by thinking about Louise and her strange remark about the vicinity of Twilight Cottage. Okay, so it was just a joke, but even so it was an odd thing to say, that the place was haunted. At last sleep came, bringing crazy dreams in which Blake pursued her with a wedding bouquet, and wide-sheeted ghosts barred her way as she tried to escape.

TWO

~

The red Rover coupé looked as though it might actually groan as Jo piled in a second carton containing books, tapes and computer discs. By contrast her clothes and personal things were kept to a single suitcase and hold-all, which she reflected, clearly said something about her priorities. Perhaps Blake had a point; maybe she was obsessional about her work, but surely that was the only way to guarantee results: total absorption.

Thoughts of Blake shadowed her eyes with sadness. He hadn't telephoned, or attempted any form of contact, but to be fair didn't know either about her visit to Twilight Cottage, or that she would soon be out of reach. Any minute now she would be on her way, and tomorrow or the day after he would arrive at an empty flat to collect his things before embarking on his own journey to Bosnia. Suddenly it hit her: *this really is the end.* Loneliness washed over her, and a reluctance to leave before his arrival. It was hard to go, knowing he was coming – but harder to stay. Knowing Blake, he would not be willing to compromise, would still make the same demands – ones that she was equally unwilling to meet. They would be stuck at the same *impasse* and cause each other more hurt. *You're running away.* Ignoring the small voice in her head, she checked that her lap top computer was secure, slammed shut the rear door and with a last look at the flat, climbed into the driving seat.

She paused before closing the door, uncertain about whether or not she had heard it. No mistake, the telephone was shrilling from inside her flat. She hesitated a moment: if it was Blake, maybe it was better to drive away instead of risking further distress. On the other hand, it would plague her, the not knowing. She eased herself out again, lost precious seconds pausing to glance at her watch which told her it was just after nine. The shrilling continued. The dash to the front door and the fumbling in her bag for her key seemed to take an age. In her haste she dropped it and swore with frustration. It must stop any moment now; but the ringing still summoned her, demanding her presence. At last she was inside and running for the telephone. As she picked up the receiver the ringing stopped and the line went dead.

Number unobtainable read the message on the screen of the display 'phone. Was it Blake? And if so, had he been calling from a hotel – or somewhere else, somewhere he shouldn't? The stab of jealousy came as a shock. An unwelcome image of Blake, face and chest flushed from love-making, sitting up in bed next to some tousled-headed woman flashed into mind. She dismissed it, pulled herself up; if there was somebody else on the scene, he would scarcely have asked her to marry him. Besides, she had relinquished the right to be jealous.

Still breathless with anxiety and the dash from the car, she sat down and leaned her head against the back of the armchair until calm was restored. She could check out his home number; he might just be playing games, not wanting her to know his whereabouts. But she didn't want to appear to be chasing. Minutes passed in indecision. "Oh what the hell, this is ridiculous." She reached for the telephone and dialled Blake's number. She let it ring for a full minute, then none the wiser, replaced the receiver and left the flat.

And now she was leaving behind the M6 where she had stopped off for lunch at the Forton services, to zip along a duel carriageway flanked by grey inhospitable hills. The warmth and softness of the southern Indian summer had gradually been replaced by overcast skies and cooler weather in the midlands, then the hard edge of the chill had become more pronounced the further north she travelled. Even the grass had a colder look about it, she thought with a sideways glance at the blue-green fields. On leaving London she had felt a distinct sense of relief mingled with her sadness, but now doubts began to creep in at the enormity of what she was doing. This wasn't the time to play the wimp, she decided, ramming an Enya tape into the player and turning up the volume.

An hour later and she was passing through the southern lakes, motoring along a sunlit valley speckled with cloud shadow and spectacular in autumn red and gold. Jo began to relax, to mentally plot the course of the new book, deciding on the point at which to start Ruskin's story, and where to end it. But the pale sun proved transient and fragile, slipping in and out of banks of cumulus that loomed over the mountains, which were closer now and directly ahead. The valley road wound through a flat glacial valley now palely lit, now dappled, now plunged into menacing shadow. Speculation about the novel was left behind as the narrow road began to steeply climb, requiring all her attention.

Do people really live out here? she wondered, spotting the occasional smudge of white walls against gunmetal rock as farmhouse or cottage came into view then was lost in the wilderness. The foothills through which she passed were grimmer and higher, the countryside more remote, and mountains, huge with menace, hunched the horizon like slumbering mammoths. I *must be mad,* she thought, surveying the wasteland with something approaching horror. Although her speed had already dropped to below twenty miles an hour, the car had to crawl now up ever steeper gradients and round hairpin bends that wouldn't have disgraced a roller coaster. To make things worse, the sun was blotted out completely and armies of nimbus rolled in from the west. She groaned aloud as raindrops the size of crow-droppings spattered the windscreen and road ahead.

Will I get off here in one piece? Jo peered anxiously through the rain-lashed windscreen and rammed the stick into first gear. Another vivid flash split a sky that boiled with suppressed fury. That morning had seen her safe and warm in London; now she was caught in a freak storm, over a thousand feet up on the worst road in Britain. Daylight had dipped into shades of grey and bruising purple, and the car was still climbing. She ducked automatically as thunder reverberated against the wall of rock that flanked the mountain pass. To her left gaped a heart-stopping drop to the valley bottom. She chewed her lip and prayed that nobody was coming the other way; the road was single-track with passing places that were perilously close to the edge.

The Rover bucked and skewed like a living thing as she hauled on the steering wheel and narrowly rounded another hairpin bend. London may be enjoying an Indian summer, but here in the North it was more like premature winter. She gasped involuntarily as a blue flash zigzagged across the fells like a giant strobe, briefly illuminating the crags and gullies of a forsaken landscape. Far below a silvery beck snaked across the valley floor: a streak of earthed lightning. Another hairpin bend. The car banked steeply, the angle causing the nose to block the windscreen, so that the only things visible were bonnet and boiling sky as she revved hard into the three-in-one gradient.

Climbing higher now into the mass of cumulus that towered over the fells and wrapped them in a grey shroud. Another blue flash split the gloom. The crash of thunder came almost immediately and the air reeked of sulphur. The cannonade rolled and boomed around the surrounding crags, terrifying in its intensity.

She shrank back in the seat whilst struggling to hold the car on the clutch. Rain sluiced across the windscreen and bounced off again in torrents of spray, rendering visibility almost zero. The wipers, even at full speed, made little headway. A cry escaped her as the nearside tyre glanced off a rock and the steering wheel spun out of her grasp. As she regained control, another flash flooded the valley below with unearthly light. In the strobe-glare the barren peaks shuddered, stark and satanic. "Come on, come on, damn you!" she cried, forcing the car up and on and round yet another hairpin bend. Thunder crashed overhead as with a squealing of tyres, the Rover crested the summit.

All around stretched a treeless bleakness and wilderness: a moon-scape straight from a Sci-fi film. The car seemed to stop and draw breath before launching into the break-neck descent.

Lightning shivered and crackled across the sky. In that second she saw it: a figure shrouded in cloud-shadow blocking the road. She was going to hit him, couldn't miss. Unconsciously in that split second her mind registered the form as male. Her foot hit the brake. In desperation she tugged at the wheel. The shadow loomed closer; the car shuddered on impact. Her scream filled her ears as her foot pumped the brake. Sick with panic she peered through the streaming windscreen; the figure had disappeared. Tyres squealed and the Rover's rear end skewed round as it went into a skid. Jo screamed again as the front wheels spun crazily over the edge. Lightning flickered, lending the scene a surreal and nightmare aspect. Half-crazed with fear she wrestled with wheel and road, wondering whom she had maimed or killed. Then rational thought ceased as the car pitched forward. In wide-eyed disbelief she watched the nose dip and felt the body lurch as the vehicle plunged off-road. Downhill it ran, bumping and swaying across the uneven and rock-strewn ground.

Her cries locked in her throat and the breath was knocked from her body. Every bone was jarred, every nerve screamed and pain ripped holes in her courage. Thunder boomed drowning her cries. It seemed nothing could stop her headlong flight to the valley floor and probable death. She gasped as a sudden jolt brought the car to a shuddering halt. The side of her head made contact with the door. The lightning stopped as somebody threw the switch and the world went black.

But there was light at the end of this long dark tunnel in which she found herself. A circle the size of the full moon. She must reach it, stretch and free herself and rise towards it. No pain, no discomfort, no fear, just a pulling sensation, as though she were being drawn from her body like a cork from a bottle of wine. Rising, rising, then her body resisting at the last, but the pull is inexorable. Then with a slight jerking sensation she was out, and looking down on the car which listed at an angle. A metal animal, came the incongruous thought, in the throes of death. The front end had run partially onto the outcrop which had halted the deadly plunge. One wheel was still abortively spinning. Dispassionately she noted her own body slumped in the driving seat, a thin trickle of blood staining one white cheek. Yet no mangled corpse sprawled on the road. There was no sign of her victim, of the figure she thought to have crushed beneath her wheels.

The scene below faded and all thought ceased. Now there was only feeling, a womb-like darkness and softness that enfolded and muffled her senses. Above her the light pulsated like a giant star, whilst the circle was growing larger and increasing in brightness. Wind rushed past as she spiralled upwards, through the tunnel towards that window on Life. There was no time for thought or fear. Like a sperm threshing its way to the womb she swam through the darkness towards the glow. The circle pulsed and expanded as she hurtled towards it, drawn by a terrible need. Then the cold and dark of the tunnel were left behind as she burst forth into light, warmth and incredible peace.

It was as if she had awakened for the very first time, as though the window on her senses had been washed and cleansed of the grime and smears accumulated in earthly living. Air was no longer an abstract thing, but a living entity that whispered enchantments and minutely caressed her skin with warmth, giving rise to ripples of near-ecstasy. The atmosphere itself shimmered like one huge rainbow, the colours of the spectrum luminous and vibrant with the clarity of jewels, a Pre-Raphaelite palette magically brought to life.

The ambience changed: her flesh prickled with the growing awareness that she was not alone. He came to her through the haze and standing before her, held out his hand. His hair was the bronzed black of dying bracken, his eyes green as the emerald set in his gold ring. He did not speak yet was calling her to him, laying claim to her allegiance. His need crackled across the space, that and something else, something sinister that she couldn't define. His energy streamed forth to enfold her psyche. Shock waves pulsed through her being, and she reeled beneath the impact of emotion: a love, a desire, a yearning never before encountered. Like a flood tide dammed for centuries then released, the torrent swept over her, threatening to drown her soul. He was drawing her into himself, her essence blending with his in a shuddering climax. Still he spoke no words aloud, yet she understood, heard them in her mind. *I love you; I will love you forever.* The hand with the ring stroked her hair. Bliss, sorrow, ecstasy and fear – every emotion she had ever known coursed through her like an electric current, but with an intensity that scorched and stunned.

She was melting, fusing, the edges of her personality becoming blurred. But then something was pulling her back, willing her to return to her body in the car. There was a rending, the coldness of separation and loss of bereavement. She was drawing back from the brink. Then the pain of shock: a spasm of fear that shot through her being like twenty thousand volts. The love, yearning and passion had turned to cold green fury, a rage that blazed and consumed her with ice-fire, threatening her very existence. The pull was becoming irresistible. She was drawn from him, arms outstretched, their fingertips touching then losing contact. His eyes blazed hatred, and vengeance streamed around her in a vortex of energy. Whirling, whirling away from him, further and further into the darkness, until his face is just a dim memory. But his words still reached her, searing her mind, echoing down the tunnel and round and round inside her head.

I love you. I shall kill you; but I shall love you forever.

Out of the tunnel and into her body with a sickening jolt.

THREE

~

A blackbird ceased its trilling and watched from the branches of a rowan whose leaves, like the rest of the foliage in St. Bridget's churchyard, hung limp and perfectly still. In fact the stillness was oppressive. The yews which surrounded the ancient church of weather-worn and pitted granite stood stiffly to attention, dark sentinels seeming to watch and wait, as did the fells that hemmed-in the glacial valley. Spiders paused in spinning their webs between wall and sandstone buttress, and the shufflings of creatures through autumn leaves were now silenced. The only noticeable sound other than the grumble and slap of the nearby river coursing over its bedrock, was the sharp flinty ring of spade on stone.

It was, Seth Rigby mused as he wondered what his shovel had struck, as though everything were holding its breath. Leaning on his spade he bent down and picked up the obstruction. A piece of masonary, he saw, turning it over to look. He brushed off the loose dirt with one calloused hand, then picked at the encrusted earth with black-rimmed nails and peered myopically at the revealed surface. Nothing much of interest, not to the likes of him any way, and if no-one knew then nobody would miss it. They did say the church and graveyard rested on an ancient site, he admitted; but who wanted arty-farty archaeologists and the like disturbing the village dead? A can of worms that one. He'd seen it happen over at Kirkthwaite when he used to live there. That little lot had ended with demented relatives threatening to lynch the vicar. With a gesture of disdain he flung the fragment over his shoulder and carried on working.

Ten minutes later he paused in digging the oblong trench in

which he was standing to peer at the brassy sky. Taking a grubby handkerchief from his pocket he mopped his forehead. It was warm work digging a grave. Thirsty too. There was a flask of tea on the tractor seat, but judging by that sky he had best get on. A storm threatened and no mistake. He coughed and spat on the newly turned earth, "begging your pardon Maud, and no disrespect intended," he said apologetically into thin air; "and anyhow, my mouth's so dry I can scarce spit threepenny bits." Not that there were any of those around these days, he reflected with a pang of nostagia, applying his spade to the rich, iron-red earth. The present generation had probably never seen one. It was all this decimal nonsense today. Progress, so they say. He sniffed in disgust and heaved a shovelful of soil onto the heap at the brink of the grave. "Reckon you're best out of it, Maud," he said aloud. "But then, it's alright for us that's still livin' to say that; don't suppose you'd see it that way."

He paused to swipe at a bluebottle that buzzed around his head.

He'd known Maud Bickley since he could remember; had sat next to her at the village school, but then had taken a shine to the Birkstead boy, what was his name now? Ah, yes, Thomas. He half-smiled at his memories. She had been a bonny lass then. Not like now, shrivelled with age and marbled by death. Ah well, comes to us all in the end, he thought philosophically, and ruthlessly pushed aside the image of a wax-like Maud in her satin-lined coffin. He applied himself to his digging with renewed vigour, as though seeking in physical effort a reminder of his own quickness, and a talisman against his own inevitable demise.

Still, a nice spot for Maud to lie, Seth comforted himself as memories moistened his eye. Just here, where the sward ran gently down to the old postern gate and the sweep of river beyond. You could hear the falls from here too; the water dashed down between mossed boulders into the rocky basin beneath. He put his head to one side, listening; today even their roar seemed muted. He rested on his shovel a moment whilst recalling Sunday afternoon picnics of long ago. She hadn't been in a hurry to go, hadn't Maud. 'Hang on to the last' had been her motto. Seth grinned to himself as he resumed work: here by the gate would suit her fine, like she was waiting to make her escape!

A dipping of the light made him look up at the sky again, this time with consternation. Banks of cumulus were piling in from the west, subduing daylight to deepening shades of violet-grey. He pushed his cap back and scratched his head, suddenly wishing himself back home, with his Janice nagging him to take off his dirty boots. Because something didn't feel right, nothing he could put his finger on, but it made the back of his neck tingle just the same. The surrounding fells were melting back into the gloom, but a solitary shaft of sunlight streamed down the valley and struck him where he stood in the grave. He shook his head to rid of it fancies, and put his twitchiness down to the task at hand and the pending storm.

The failing light hadn't deterred the bluebottles. He brushed one from his sleeve with a slight feeling of revulsion. They hovered above his head, their monotonous drone grating along his nerves. A bit late in the year for Beezlebub he thought with a grin of bravado, taking another swipe at the air. His spade struck something unyielding again and he bent to pick it up. Another piece of masonary, and another. He threw them over his shoulder to join the first. The bottom of the trench, he now noticed, was oozing water. An underground tributary of the river, he shouldn't wonder. Raindrops the size of fifty-pence pieces were spattering the water that seeped through the freshly-dug earth.

As he turned up his collar and climbed from the trench, the first rumblings of thunder echoed around the hills. It was raining stair-rods now, with that peculiar suddeness characteristic of a brewing storm. Damn: he'd been hoping to get the thing finished today. Great splashes spatterered the soil and splashed his legs as he stamped the mud from his wellington boots. Another roll of thunder grumbled, and closer this time. Cursing under his breath he picked up his shovel and hurried towards the tractor. Old Maud would have to wait a mite longer, he thought smiling grimly as he clambered onto the seat. Good job the funeral wasn't till Monday.

As he turned to look back at the newly-dug grave, a flash of lightning shuddered across the darkened and rain-lashed sky. Beneath that flickering and blue'ish light, the scene took on a sinister quality. The squat stone church seemed to Seth like a malignant animal set to pounce, and the lancet windows, shining and inky black, watched him like dead-men's eyes. "I've had enough of this place for one day," he muttered eying the yew trees with dislike. Shoulder to shoulder they seemed intent on closing ranks to prevent his exit. Another flash of lightning crackled and hurriedly he started the tractor. *The chug-chug-throb* of its engine was familiar and a comfort. The giant tyres churned up earth and the body listed and swayed as the tractor lurched out of the graveyard and lumbered onto the lane.

As it rumbled away from river and graveyard, Seth glanced over his shoulder and peered at the church through the driving rain. He stared harder and almost stalled the engine, then shook his head and laughed aloud. Silly old bugger, he said in self-mockery, clucking his tongue against the roof of his mouth; as if folk wouldn't have more sense in this weather. He was still smiling as the tractor trundled past the overgrown track that led to Twilight Cottage.

For a moment there, he could have sworn there was someone standing by Maud's grave.

FOUR

~

From the doorway of the nursery wing Justin St. Clair watched his
wife as she played with their six month old son. The mesh of evening sunlight and whirling dust motes filtered in through the ivy at
the high lancet window and tangled in her hair. Its gloss and
colour brought to mind the chestnuts that littered the forest floor
beyond the castle. A crack opened along his heart and oozed blood.
So real was the sensation that his hand went to his broad chest and
he felt a physical pain. In future autumns young William would
run excitedly into the woods searching for chestnuts to play the
game of 'conquer'. But his young mother would not be there to
watch.

The poignancy of that thought was intensified by Madeline's
throaty laughter, as William grabbed a lock of her hair and tugged
it free of her silver fillet. St. Clair's dark brown eyes turned almost
black, heavy brows met over the aquiline nose, and his lips compressed in a cruel line as he imagined those neatly-coiffed tresses
loosed from their combs and spreading in fiery abandon, and saw
the thick coils tumbling over her milky breasts, breasts exposed for
the lips and hands of her lover. The bile rose to his throat and spilled
into his mouth, so that the soft sweep of lash on her cheek as she
looked down at the child, for once failed to move him. Did she
really imagine he did not know? Fury consumed him, leaving his
love for her blackened and shrivelled like a fragment of parchment
tossed into the flames. His fists clenched into balls and at that
moment he felt he could murder her on the spot. But no: he must
deceive her just as she deceived him. He stitched a tender expression
into place on his battle-scarred features. His shadow fell across

Madeline; the infant stopped gurgling and laughing. She turned, fear momentarily darkening the lustre of her eyes. Seeing his smile she relaxed, and sweeping William into her arms rose from her knees to greet her husband.

Bitch! Lying, adulterous bitch, he thought as he bent his head to kiss her cheek.

Jo staggered along the road and almost fell as she looked about her in a daze. A shadow flickered across her mind like a silhouette of the silent screen. She clutched at the memory; it slipped from her grasp leaving her anxious and confused. Lightning flickered faintly over the distant coast, and was followed after a while by the slight rumble of thunder; the storm had moved on and the deluge had almost stopped. *Storm,* that was it. *Car. Crash.* Little by little the scene was re-run in her mind: the car hurtling out of control and off-road, bumping and swaying down the treacherous incline. She pressed a hand over her mouth, holding back the nausea and panic as pieces of the jigsaw clicked into place. She turned her attention back to the road: a black mamba writhing down the fellside and glistening with runnels of water. *Oh, no!* Her mind exploded into awareness. *The man.* The man who had stepped out in front of the car. Dear God, he had to be here somewhere. The man she had run over and either maimed or killed.

She paced the side of the road, feverishly searching. A low rumble which she thought at first must be thunder but wasn't, made her stop and listen. A car appeared at the crest of the pass. She raised her arm, her movements clumsy and lacking co-ordination. Water coursed down her face and her body was wracked by shivers. Feeling still that she moved through a nightmare, Jo ran one hand distractedly through her saturated hair. Vaguely she was aware of the vehicle stopping, of a man climbing out. He turned up the collar of his jacket against the persistent but lighter rain. Thunder growled faintly from the barren Scafell range; the storm had now truly passed over. *Where was the body?* She stopped pacing and waited for him to advance, but her gaze still probed the road and hillside beyond.

"Is that your car? Are you hurt?"

Jo stared at the man who was firing questions at her in anything but a friendly manner. Somewhere in the depths of her shocked mind it occurred to her that she could be at risk, up here on her own and miles from civilisation; but relief that someone, *anyone*, had come was her over-riding emotion. "Yes – my car." She shook her head: "And no – I'm not hurt." She tried to keep her voice steady and took another deep breath to ward off lingering faintness. "But the man? At least, I thought-," she saw he was frowning at her and knew he was doubting her rationality. Making an effort to clear her mind and control her emotions she said with a semblance of calm: "I saw a shadow on the road, thought I had hit someone."

He looked around him again with a puzzled air. "There's no-one. No signs even." He indicated the surface of the road with a sweep of his arm.

"Please, could you –?" she pleaded, and made a vague gesture with her hand.

He stared intently into her face, then as though he had seen something there to convince him, he shrugged and climbing down the nearside bank, began a systematic search of the troughs and gullies at either side of the road.

Jo waited for him to reappear, her stomach knotted and her legs threatening to give way. Why had she ever left London for this god-forsaken place? Barren grey crags streaked with strands of white water loomed on all sides, and the lower slopes were cloaked in the slimy brownish-black of dead and sodden bracken. Never had she set foot in such an inhospitable landscape. There was not even a tree let alone a dwelling to tame the wildness. Panic and anger twisted her judgement and brought her close to tears: it was all Blake's fault; he should never have left. She shuddered as lightning flickered in the distance, bringing back memories she had suppressed. For a breath-stopping moment she was back in that tunnel whirling towards –, but she couldn't think about that right now. Her stomach leapt as the man reappeared and clambered back onto the road, his hair plastered to his head and his shoes caked in mud. She waited, knotting her hands and not daring to breathe.

"Nothing," he called, shaking his head so that raindrops sprayed onto the shoulders of his already saturated jacket. Jo let go her breath and felt a surge of relief. Her limbs began to shake uncontrollably. "Thank you. Thank you so much for searching," she called fervently, feeling her body go weak. *So what had happened?* she fretted. But watching him walk back to her, she decided that as her worst fears were apparently groundless, she would have to worry about that later. For the moment her chief concerns were practical ones: her car was out of action and she was stranded in strange territory. *But at least she hadn't killed or maimed anyone.*

That awareness allowed her to take more interest in the stranger, and her present situation. At a guess he was in his early thirties. He was wearing an Arran sweater beneath a brown cord jacket, and had a sensitive look about him, when not scowling with displeasure. As there was nothing predatory about him, she decided he was probably worthy of her trust. Of course there were no guarantees, but she could spot a male on the hunt at a hundred paces. From his manner, he was seeing her rather as a nuisance he could well do without. This was borne out by the habit he had of briefly closing his eyes as though she was a child who had said something stupid and he was struggling to keep his patience.

He reached her side and peered closely at her face. "You *are* hurt."

She saw the concern in his weathered, rain-streaked features.

"No really, I'm perfectly alright," she protested.

"You've hit your head."

It was almost an accusation. "It's nothing." She put her hand to her face and felt the stickiness of blood. It couldn't be serious, she told herself, or she would be bleeding more profusely.

"You can't know that; you need a check-out. You could be concussed. And you're not exactly going to drive off there, are you?" he said caustically, jerking his thumb at the outcrop below as he stamped mud from his feet.

"I suppose not." She stared back at the car, then down at the valley bottom and looked away quickly as dizziness overcame her. Not for the first time since clambering out of the Rover, she realised that it had been a near thing.

"I fainted, that's all. Look, could I ask you to telephone the R.A.C.?" she said trying to sound brisk and in control.

"I'll take you to the medical centre – then deal with your car," he said firmly.

"It's really not necessary," she started to protest, but he closed his eyes again in that charactistic gesture of impatience and halted her with one up-held hand. "My way – or not at all."

Taking one look at his implacable face, Jo gave up the argument and followed him to his car.

He handled the descent of three-in-one gradients and hairpin bends with the confidence and near-contempt of one familiar with the pass, and from this Jo deduced he lived in the locality. Her attitude was rather less blasé; her knuckles turned white as – forbearing to grip the dashboard for fear of ridicule – her hands surreptitiously gripped the sides of the seat. She breathed a sigh of relief as they levelled out and sped though a valley littered with boulders and threaded with a white-water river which surged and writhed parallel with their course. By now he had told her his name was Colin Gilmour – she had only admitted to 'Jo' – and that he was a sculptor on his way back from an exhibition at Carlisle. It seemed the three peices he submitted had been sold, and he had come away with several commissions.

"You must be good," Jo commented, feeling marginally more at ease with her tetchy rescuer.

"Not bad."

Having delivered this laconic reply, he turned his attention back to the winding road.

Jo glanced quickly around the car, but on this occasion her writer's habit of observation yielded little of significance. A box of tissues in the glove compartment were white and of standard size, thus giving no clues to gender. The same was true of a tortoiseshell comb in the depression next to the hand brake. But then as they passed a farmhouse with light streaming from its unshaded windows, her companion opened a small drawer in the dash. He took out a packet of chewing gum and slammed it shut again, but not before she had seen the bottle of *L'Eau d'Issey*. It belonged, Jo guessed, to a woman who liked the great outdoors and country life-style, felt close to nature, but also had uncompromising good taste. Intrigued, she wondered if Colin Gilmour would let on that there was a woman in his life.

At this point he turned his head and gave her a brief scrutiny. "You alright?"

Jo nodded, forcing herself to ignore the nausea and the throbbing inside her head. "Fine."

He pulled into a passing place to allow a tractor to pass. The driver nodded and raised a hand in greeting and Jo was reassured: he was obviously known in the valley and not shy of being seen in her company, all of which indicated that he was above board.

"H'mm." He grunted and pulled away again, then turned his head to mutter: "You look bloody pale."

Jo said nothing, and declining the offer of chewing gum, stared straight ahead and concentrated on holding herself together.

"Tourist?" he prodded some five minutes later as they wound through a valley flanked by high fells.

"Sort of."

He snorted. "Well are you or not?"

"I'm supposed to be spending the winter at a cottage somewhere round here." Jo inclined her head to look around, then winced as pain seared her temple. The road was still only one car width, but at least, she noticed with relief, there was the odd farmhouse or cottage nestling amongst the trees to give a semblance of civilisation. Some of the panic and sense of being locked in a nightmare was fading. Unfortunately, so was the daylight, briefly restored after the storm but now drawing in as autumn nights will. She ought to find out where this damned cottage was and not leave it until she returned in the dark. She shifted on her seat and extracted from her jacket pocket the rough map and directions left for her, along with the key, at reception by Louise, who had been called unexpectedly out of the office. "Here it is: Twilight Cottage – and from what I can make out, it's near a St. Bridget's church. Perhaps you know it?"

He gave a short laugh. "I should. I live next door as you might say."

Jo turned to stare at him as the nightmare feeling returned.

He returned her look and frowned. "What is it?"

She stroked her forehead with a hand that was still shaking. "I don't think I can handle this – I mean, such an incredible coincidence."

He switched off the window wipers as the rain finally ceased and the wipers dragged squeaking across the windows. "Not really," he said mildly, and as though amused by her reaction. "The only sane person who would be on that pass at this time of day, and in a storm, would be someone who lived in the valley. As to being your neighbour – in this part of the world that means I live in the next cottage – which is something like half a mile away!"

"I see." Jo was conscious of a feeling of foolishness, but also of relief, having begun to think she had stepped out of reality and into a horror film. Obviously the incident and the bang on the head had affected her more than she had realised.

"Lighten up a bit," he advised with an expression of impatience. "Push your seat back and relax." He placed a cassette in the deck and the sound of *Clannad* filled the ensuing silence.

Jo leaned back, closed her eyes – and furious at her own weakness – squeezed back the tears. Obviously Colin Gilmour had little time for emotionally intense females.

It was growing dark by the time the car turned onto a main road and he braked outside a telephone kiosk. "I'll just have to do an 'E.T.' and 'phone home'," he said with a flash of rueful humour. "Finola will have Mountain Rescue out if I don't!"

"Your wife?" Jo probed, pulling herself upright but wincing at the movement.

"Girlfriend. We share the cottage."

Jo felt smug on recalling the *L'Eau d'Issey*. "I see," she said, relieved that he was being open about his involvement. "Are we going much further?" she asked as he got out of the car. He ducked his head and spoke through the open window. "About eight miles. It won't take long now that we're on the coast road."

"I thought we were going to the nearest clinic?"

"It is the nearest," he said wryly. He started to walk away from the car then turned as though on an after-thought. "You'll probably get on well with Finola; she goes on a bit too," he said with a grin, disappearing into the telephone kiosk. Even had he waited, Jo felt too weary and traumatised to retaliate. She began to feel a certain sympathy for the unknown Finola.

Before long they were pulling off the road at a sign which read: *The Cumberland Cottage Hospital*. The building at the end of the drive was a two storey Victorian half-timbered house set in spacious and well-laid out grounds that like the house itself were effectively floodlit "But it's a hospital," Jo protested, getting out of the car. "Albeit it doesn't look like one."

"If I'd said so you wouldn't have come," he said shortly, locking up and leading the way to the front entrance. "And," he said severely over his shoulder, "you don't mess about with a knock on the head."

"But is there a Casualty Department?" Jo looked dubiously at the unclinical-looking façade.

"It's not an A & E Hospital as such, but they'll not turn us away."

"You've really been very kind; I feel like an ungrateful wretch."

"So you should." He gave her a mocking look before mounting the steps and pushing open the double doors.

"Why are you going to so much trouble for a stranger?" she asked curiously. He frowned and gave her an odd look as he held the door for her to enter. "Because that's the way we do things here."

He shook his head as she passed as though he found it a strange question.

The receptionist had taken Jo's details and a nurse led them to a waiting area prior to being seen by a doctor. Jo had given Colin

Gilmour her 'Recovery' card at his request, and he had promised to make the necessary arrangements for the car and empty it of her belongings. He had also requested the key to Twilight Cottage. Initially Jo declined, until he explained that Finola would deposit her luggage there, and leave essentials like milk and coffee. When she gratefully accepted and handed over the key, he left her with his address and telephone number.

"You'll be okay then?"

"Of course. And thank you again, Mr. Gilmour."

"Colin. We're going to be neighbours remember."

"Okay Colin, thanks, and apologise to Finola for me."

"No problem. Don't forget: call us when you are ready to leave, and myself or Finola will come and take you to Twilight Cottage."

"It's very good of you, but I can't let you do any more. And it could be late; I'm sure the receptionist will arrange a taxi for me."

"I was thinking more of tomorrow morning; it's likely they'll want to keep you in overnight for observation."

"Oh, but I can't stay –," she protested, starting to rise.

"You'll do whatever they say, Jo," he said firmly, pushing her down again on her seat.

His manner left much to be desired Jo thought watching him leave, but she couldn't fault his kindness.

FIVE

~

She was missing Blake. Lying on a trolley in a hospital cubicle hundreds of miles from home was a lonely experience, and given the circumstances, one that didn't do much for her confidence. Images flashed across a screen in her mind: billows of black cloud surging across the sky in slow-motion, zig-zags of lightning crackling with power and eerie blue light. Then the figure in the road, her foot on the brake and the spinning of wheels. As she waited alone to see the doctor, Jo relived her terror as the car bumped and lurched down the slope, and as it came to rest on the outcrop, felt again the jolt that jarred her body. *Enough*. The door had to be shut on that other memory; she would think about that later. Sweat beaded her forehead as she fought for control. If only Blake were here to put his arms around her and make her feel safe again. If only she hadn't let him go. But now it was too late.

"Miss Cavanagh?"

Jo turned her head as the curtain was pulled back. A woman of about thirty stood in the opening of the cubicle. She was wearing a white coat and had the obligatory stethoscope slung around her slim shoulders. "I'm Dr. Cahill," she said entering before Jo could respond, "Josie Cavanagh," she said with a thoughtful expression whilst consulting the notes on the clipboard at the end of the trolley. "Not the author by any chance?"

Jo nodded, amazed that anyone in this outpost of civilisation had even heard of her. "That's me."

"I read the one about Wittgenstein. It's good, excellent in fact."

"Thanks."

"Holidaying in the Lakes?"

"Sort of," Jo said evasively.

"Recharging the batteries ready for the next book?"

Jo returned her smile. "Something like that. At least, that was the idea," she said ruefully.

Dr. Cahill unhooked the stethoscope from her neck. "Okay, let's take a look at you, shall we?"

A nurse entered and turning, swished the floral curtain across the rail.

Dr. Cahill smiled and wound up the tube and bulb of the sphygmomanometer and replaced it on the instrument trolley. "You'll live," she pronounced, then spoke in a low voice to the nurse who wrote on a sheet of paper resting on a buff-coloured folder: "no sign of fracture on palpation, haemorrhage nil, ditto traumatic shock. B.P. 130 over 80, Temp. 98.9, both pupils react equally to light. Observation ward, regular diet." she intoned, then waited until the nurse had finished writing. "Give ward five a ring please and see if they have a bed." The nurse nodded and left, and Dr. Cahill turned back to Jo. "There's no apparent serious injury, but for tonight I'd like to keep you under observation."

Jo grimaced. "Is that really necessary?"

"A wise precaution. You're one lucky lady."

"I guess so," Jo capitulated. If she were honest, the thought of tackling the unknown cottage in the cold and dark and in her present condition was far from alluring.

"How are you feeling now?"

"A little confused."

"That's normal after an accident."

Jo coughed awkwardly. She had been determined to say nothing about what happened *after* hitting her head, but she wanted some answers, and here was the opportunity. Wise not to mention *him*, otherwise Dr. Cahill would think her some kind of freak; selective confession was in order here. "I mean, in a more specific way than that," she began tentatively, "something that happened back there at the car."

Dr. Cahill held up a cautionary finger as the nurse popped her head round the curtain.

"I've just spoken to staff nurse Johnson, ward five," the nurse reported.

"They have a bed?"

"You can send your patient up when you're ready, doctor."

"Fine. Thanks." Dr. Cahill turned back to Jo as the nurse disappeared.

"So tell me – whilst I take the weight off my feet for a couple of minutes," she added, sitting down on a nearby tubular chair.

"And then I was spinning through this dark tunnel towards the light," Jo concluded.

Dr. Cahill looked thoughtful and weighed the end of the stethoscope in her palm. "But you hadn't actually hit anyone?"

"No. Mr. Gilmour searched both sides of the road. There was nothing."

"Right. But the really important thing here is that under the storm conditions – reduced visibility and plenty of stress – you believed you had killed someone. That trauma could easily have triggered the out-of-body experience. That and the blow to the head. In fact, what you have just described sounds very much like an N.D.E."

"N.D.E?"

"Near Death Experience. Strictly speaking It's not supposed to be part of my vocabulary! But I've heard too many first-hand reports to entirely discount the phenomenon."

Jo had been slowly shaking her head as she listened; now she massaged the base of her neck. "But it was nothing – didn't even need stitching."

Dr. Cahill shrugged. "It happens." She grinned suddenly. "Don't worry, you're not about to die! But tell me, on coming round where you immediately aware you had hit your head ?"

Jo frowned. "No, actually I wasn't. Not until Mr. Gilmour saw the blood and drew my attention to it."

Dr. Cahill nodded. "That fits. Sometimes the victim of a very minor head injury appears to be dead. He or she becomes completely paralysed and lax with no palpable pulse and no breathing. Yet within seconds the person then gets up, makes a complete recovery and may not even be able to remember the impact of the blow or even what led to it. This transient state of retrograde amnesia is thought to be due to a momentary cessation of the brain's activity. An example of true concussion. It's unusual, but as I said, it does happen. Which is why I'm keeping you overnight. It's standard procedure, just to ensure that no damage to the brain has occurred." Dr. Cahill rose to her feet. "However in your case I'm sure it's just a formality."

"Thanks. I was worried," Jo confessed, "but I feel better about it now."

"Good. Anything more you want to ask, I'll be examining you again in the morning before your discharge."

"You've been very kind," Jo said with gratitude. "Of course I've read about these things –,"

"But it's different when it actually happens to yourself," Dr. Cahill finished for her.

"Do you believe such experiences are a glimpse of another dimension?" Jo asked, curious.

"Who knows? The popular explanation in my profession of course is that it's due to the release of endorphins in the brain – to render the trauma of death more bearable." Dr. Cahill moved to the curtain.

"What do you believe, doctor?"

She smiled. "I'm not sure. Nurse will take you up to the ward now. You can have biscuits and a warm milky drink, but then try to get some sleep."

"I will. And thanks again."

Jo watched her leave and heard her call to the nurse.

The relief at having shared at least part of that bizarre experience, and receiving a possible explanation for it, was intense. It wasn't until 'lights out' and she was lying between crisp white sheets on a bed in a side ward, that Jo allowed herself to reflect on that other aspect. What she had thought was a figure on the road could easily, as Dr Cahill had intimated, have been a trick of the mist and failing light. But there was no explanation she could think of for that other man; the one who had been waiting at the far end of the tunnel. Or for the intensity of emotion, and the feeling that it was *real*. By the light of the muted ward lamps, she watched a nurse walk silently past the windows then the glass door then disappear from sight.

She tried to remember what he looked like, recall his image; then as the fudged edges began to solidify into a figure, and green eyes blazed with anger, brought down the curtain on memory. A delusion of course, but why? Where had it come from and what was the trigger? Then she recalled Louise's last remark on the telephone. *The area is supposed to be haunted.* That was it, had to be. She had been psychologically set for the experience. Without her being aware of it, the suggestion had taken root in her subconscious. Given her nervous state after breaking up with Blake, and the onslaught of the storm whilst driving over the worst road in Britain, there was plenty of reason for her mind to play tricks. Yes, that had to be it. With Louise being out of the office, there had been no chance to ask her about it. But she would ask Colin Gilmour tomorrow if there was a local legend. No, on second thoughts best to forget about it.

Primed by a joke. How Blake would laugh. If she could tell him, but she couldn't; because Blake was about to leave the country – and her life. It didn't help to know it was her own fault. Had he called at the flat yet? Would he leave her a message? She pictured him wandering round the rooms, selecting this, discarding that and pausing perhaps in front of the photograph taken in the Wiltshire garden before walking out. Silent tears wetted her cheeks. He may have already left the country, be on a flight to Bosnia. She closed her eyes and tried to sleep. Then as though triggered by heightened emotions, flashes of memory returned. It seemed all too real again; she was back in that dark tunnel whirling towards the light. A glimpse of a man, arms outstretched and waiting. And then she knew it was some crazy delusion. Because he was wearing what looked like a surplice, with a hawk emblazoned across his chest.

As she drifted closer to sleep, she heard the words again inside her head.

I will kill you; but I will love you forever, forever, forever.

SIX

~

Seth's knuckles whitened as he rested his hands either side of his knife and fork. If only she would she shut up about it. He glared at his wife's back then down at the checked table cloth, striving to push down the rising tide of anger. He was being unreasonable, and knew it, yet was helpless against the intense irritation that was as bad as a hornet sting. It prickled along his spine and made him want to scratch inside his head, which in itself was a ridiculous thought but nonetheless it fitted the bill. He watched Janice Rigby scoop up a second egg from the pan and slide it expertly onto the plate next to the tomatoes and field mushrooms. "And you were tossing and turning all night; even after you went back to sleep. Kept *me* awake you did. I told you not to be eating that cheese just before you went to bed," she scolded on, but without rancour.

Pulling the lid down on the Aga she wiped her strong capable hands on her pinafore and picked up the plate. Hands that had eased many a calf and lamb out of its mother, Seth recalled watching her, consumed by guilt at his hostile feelings. "There, get that down you – and then get out from under my feet," she fussed putting the plate down in front of him on the farmhouse table. Nonetheless she gave him an affectionate pat on the shoulder.

Seth eyed the plate with initial pleasure, but then his gaze was transfixed by the glistening black gills of the mushrooms.

"Don't let it go cold after me cooking it for you."

Nasty and black, unnatural-looking things, he thought, eyeing them as though for the first time. From deep within the earth; they had been dug up too. They also had their life-force beneath the ground where it couldn't be seen: a network spreading in thread-like strands, like a web waiting to catch and ensnare. These also grew in dark unwholesome places. Why had he not seen it before?

"D'you hear, Seth? You'll have it cold, lad."

Seth tried to look at Janice but was mesmerised by the earth-black and bone-white fungus. To do with magic and fairies and curses and things. Like other things lately, best left buried. These even had fresh soil clinging to them, like the earth at the bottom of Maud's grave. He poked at one with his fork. The three holes made by the prongs oozed inky fluid which spread as the gills broke down and turned to slime. He poked again with his fork then threw it down in disgust. Nothing here but rotting flesh. He peered closer and felt his own flesh crawl as he saw the wriggling maggot. Plump and cadaver-pale it squirmed across his plate, leaving a trail in the glutinous black mess.

"What is it? What's the matter?" Janice demanded hovering at his shoulder.

"This!" he pushed the plate of food across the table towards her. "How long have you kept them?"

"Why I gathered them myself – fresh this morning!"

"Couldn't have! You must be blind woman!" Jumping up Seth pushed back his chair and strode from the kitchen.

Janice Rigby picked up the plate and peered closely at it. Shaking her head, she crossed the kitchen and scraped the sausage and bacon into the dog's dish. It wasn't like Seth, wasn't this. And for the life of her, she couldn't see cause for complaint. Frowning, she scraped the perfectly good mushrooms into the compost bin beneath the sink.

Seth rubbed the back of his neck with a calloused hand and stared into the grave. It still dogged him, whatever it was that had left the churchyard with him the day of the storm. It clung to his back, sticky, black and sinister, like the belladonna plaster his father used to wear for his lumbago. Not that it could be seen, but it was there, and stronger here by the grave. He shook his head and stuck out his lower lip. He was beginning to think he had been wrong, this was no fit place to put poor Maud. It looked unhealthy down there. He peered closer and watched the water seeping in, turning red earth to mud: red with oxides, red with blood. He leaned closer. There they were again, the maggots that had got into the mushrooms. Plump and opaque they wriggled and writhed in an obscene heap. White against red. White maggots, white bone, protruding through the earth where the subterranean stream had broken it down, an arm outstretched, bony fist clenched in defiance of death.

A strangled sound escaped Seth's throat. He closed his eyes, clenching his eyelids tight to shut out the sight. Seconds later he screwed up courage and opening them again, blinked in disbelief. He was going off his head, must be. Either that or he'd best ease up on the home-made scrumpy. There was nothing at the base of the neatly-dug trench; nothing but water, earth and a fat pink earthworm thrashing its tail to and fro. No maggots, no blood, no bones. Picking up his shovel he walked to the gate, muttering as he went. The grave was finished alright, but it was still no place to put Maud.

SEVEN

~

Jo stepped into the taxi with mingled feelings of relief and trepidation. It was good to be discharged from hospital, but the unknown lay ahead. Earlier that morning Dr. Cahill had examined her for a second time and pronounced herself satisfied that no permanent damage had been sustained in the crash. An obliging receptionist had telephoned a car hire company operating from the nearest town of Beckdale and now, Jo thought forcing herself to relax back on her seat, for good or ill she was on her way.

An hour or so later the hospital and civilisation were left well behind, and she recognised the valley road along which Colin Gilmour had brought her the previous evening. *Was it only yesterday?* It seemed an age ago. The driver, whose tutting and mumbling had begun on being shown Louise's rough drawing and increased with every subsequent mile, grumbled aloud to himself as they turned into a narrow unmetalled lane with ruts and hollows that could double as golf course bunkers. His heavy sighs also increased as they reached the overgrown opening on the left which, according to Louise's map, led to Twilight Cottage. Obviously, Jo thought, neither he nor his well-polished vehicle were accustomed to plying their trade in a rural wilderness. Suddenly the car lurched to a halt and the driver swivelled round, hooking his arm over the back of the seat to peer belligerently at her. "Enough's enough lady!" he protested with a marked Cumbrian accent, "You should be hiring a tractor for this job!"

Jo knew a moment of panic. She had handed the key to the cottage over to Colin Gilmour, and if he let her down, and this wimp of a driver drove off, she could find herself stranded. "It can't be much further. Please keep going. I'll make it worth your while," she promised.

"That's as maybe – but what about my suspension?" he complained.

Jo, torn by an urge to swear and a desire to laugh, especially given the man's 'Michelin-man' well cushioned body, fought for control. "You'll need to turn anyway," she pointed out, taking comfort from the fact that he had not switched off the ignition and the engine was still ticking over. This, she figured, was more of a protest calculated to increase his compensation, than an out and out refusal to continue. "The lane's so narrow you'll probably do more damage if you were to attempt to back out."

"Likely." He glared at her, then without another word turned back to the wheel and to Jo's relief, put the car into gear.

Jo gripped the dashboard as the taxi bumped and swayed along the rutted track for a half mile or so. The further they progressed the more alarmed she became; having forgotten how far north she had travelled, the almost leafless trees came as a shock. On either side gnarled and sinister blackthorn leaned, forming a spiny arch that scraped the roof of the car as it passed beneath, eliciting more grumbles and tutting sounds from her reluctant driver. Ancient oaks sprawled and twisted across the way, their naked boughs mossed and encrusted with lichens, whilst a tangle of evergreens added to the gloom: glossy-leaved holly, prickly juniper and dark stunted yew – escapees no doubt from the nearby churchyard. The holly brought forth a string of muttered expletives as it scraped the sides of the car. Boughs latticed the grey sky and between, the air had that translucent bluish quality peculiar to Cumbria, and which in the past had lured Turner to the Lakes. The thought brought to mind Ruskin and her book. The prospect of work was reassuring; work would give structure to this crazy chaos.

She gasped involuntarily as the car dipped in a deeper than usual rut. After much revving and cursing it was righted again and they lurched on.

"You planning on staying here alone?" the driver asked with a look of horror as they reached the cottage which stood in a clearing.

"I'm not the nervous sort." Which seemed the only possible reply. Jo opened the car door and climbed out, she breathed appreciatively of the damp-earth and pine-scented air and stood looking at Twilight Cottage. Low, built of stone and with whitewashed walls it gave the impression of sturdiness and permanence. The roof was covered with green Westmorland slates, each the thickness of a man's finger. Smoke, she saw with relief, was rising lazily from the chimney: Colin Gilmour must have kept his promise. A telephone wire to the house boosted her confidence further. But then Louise would never have contemplated staying here for a minute without a life-line to London, she thought with a grin.

Gesturing to the driver to wait, she walked to the front door and tried to lift the latch. Stiff with damp and misuse, it at first resisted but then the door swung open. Okay, so she had admittance; from here she was on her own. Excited and fearful in turns, she took money from her purse, walked back to the car and paid off the driver. After thanking her for the generous tip, he shook his head dolefully at her folly, manoeuvred the car in a three point turn and drove off. Jo watched the vehicle dipping and swaying in the ruts until it disappeared around the first bend. The sound of the engine grew fainter and fainter until it finally ceased.

As she stood there alone, the trees seemed to hem her in, cutting her off from civilisation.

A sweep of loneliness overwhelmed her as she turned back to Twilight Cottage. Here she was in the middle of nowhere with no friends, no permanent home – and no Blake, then she instantly despised her weakness. It stemmed from not having a car, she rationalised, pushing the door wide and stepping inside. The car was her passport to freedom, and once it was repaired and parked outside the front door, this awful sense of insecurity would pass. In the meantime, there was nothing for it but to make the best of the situation.

The short hall had three doors leading off it: two to the left and one to the right; she closed the front door and opened the one on the right.

The sitting room in which she now found herself had a low beamed ceiling, and a fire had been banked-up in the grate so that it smouldered rather than blazed. A blackened piece of timber resembling half a tree trunk formed a mantelpiece over the stone fireplace, and an antique clock ticked ponderously at its centre. Several boxes containing her books and documents, she saw with relief, had been stacked by a rosewood writing bureau inlaid with mother-of-pearl. Her lap-top computer had been placed on a table which also held a couple of *Country Life* magazines. Jo noted with approval that Louise had not been tempted to go over the top with china knick-knacks, chintz and horse brasses. The walls were painted white and the room simply furnished: a squashy-looking settee heaped with tapestry and patchwork cushions, a fireside chair and footstool and a small bookcase. It was an ideal place in which to work, with no clutter and few distractions.

But then, she thought with a wry smile as she walked over to one of the two Georgian-paned windows, Louise had hardly had interior design on her mind when she took this cottage. An image arose of Louise and 'her laird' before the fire, sharing a bottle of wine in cosy intimacy. She pictured them tossing cushions onto the floor, removing each others clothes, spending their nights and possibly days too in tenderness, laughter and passion. Thoughts of Blake followed, and the smile died as her loneliness increased. But there was no point in looking back, and viewed from here rather than a hospital bed, and with the prospect of work ahead, any regrets seemed easier to bear.

The prospect from the window offered something by way of consolation. It overlooked a wild garden of ancient apple and cherry trees, gnarled by age and mottled with mosses and lichens. Beyond them reared a stand of massive pines, adding to the seclusion and in winter they would provide shelter from icy northern winds. Closer to the cottage rustic fencing hosted a tangle of clematis and rambling roses, both now bare but promising a colourful summer. A beck tumbled down a sloping green which mocked the term 'lawn' and veered off at the corner of the cottage. The window latch, reluctant with damp and misuse, yielded after a struggle and the sound of running water filled the room. A low background rumble told her that there must also be a river, and maybe waterfall nearby. All very Ruskin-esque, she thought, recalling the wild gardens at Brantwood, and the way Ruskin had hewn paths and intricate water courses from the rough fellside, and all very conducive to work on the new book.

Closing the window again, she crossed to the second one which over-looked the clearing screened by holly and twisted blackthorn, both draped with the bare threads of honeysuckle and traveller's joy, and beyond the purple-blue fells brooded. When this window was opened, the muted roar of the river was louder and briefly she worried about winter flooding, then shook her head rejecting the notion: the slope of the lane was such that this ground must be quite a bit higher than the river bed.

The cottage was tiny really. An exploratory tour revealed a small kitchen across from the sitting room, where a bottle of milk, four eggs, coffee and a handful of tea bags, half a loaf and a packet of butter had been left on the table. The unknown Finola, Jo thought picking up the coffee and unscrewing the lid to take an appreciative sniff before putting it down again. A third ground floor room had been converted into a bathroom. Thank God for that, she thought smiling to herself. At least a trip to the loo didn't mean stumbling her way through wet grass, briars and brambles to the bottom of the garden in the dark and in all weathers; nor did bath-night entail a tub in front of the fire.

A staircase which twisted and turned around the back of the chimney, treads worn at the centre and rail polished by centuries of hands, led to a couple of bedrooms. To her relief the larger of the two, which overlooked the garden, held her suitcase and bulging hold-all. The double bed boasted only pillows and a patchwork quilt, and she resolved to dig out sheets and blankets after making a cup of coffee. The smaller room, she decided, peering out of a miniscule window, would serve as storage for books and empty cases. Making her way downstairs to the kitchen, she turned on the supply to the calor gas stove as per Louise's instructions and filled the kettle.

But first, whilst waiting for it to boil, courtesy demanded that she thank her rescuers and let them know of her discharge from hospital. Expediency too she added to herself, making her way back to the sitting room; otherwise they might call round to check, and she wasn't ready to face visitors yet. On dialling the number Colin Gilmour had given her, a female voice – breathy and somehow conveying fussiness – answered.

Jo launched into a tactful explanation: "Oh, you must be Finola. Sorry, I don't know your surname. I'm Jo Cavanagh and I'm ringing to thank you both for being good Samaritans – and to let you know I've arrived safely at the cottage."

"Oh hi! Good – you're welcome. And I'm Finola Webb; but do call me Finola," the voice gushed, but Jo didn't miss the underlying wariness. "But how are you feeling? Colin said they kept you in overnight."

"Just a precaution. I'm perfectly alright now."

"Do you need a G.P., for medication or anything?"

"No, nothing like that."

"Well if there's anything . . . it must have been horrendous for you. Everything O.K. at the cottage?"

"Fine. Thanks ever so much for the coffee and things. "

"No problem. Colin has nipped down-valley to the village store to get you some proper provisions. Is there anything you need in the meantime?"

"No thanks. You're both being so good."

"Nonsense. Look, why don't you come on round and have a bit of lunch with us?"

Jo smiled to herself. *She wants to see what I'm like.* "That's really kind of you, but if you don't mind I'd rather push on here and get settled in. I'd love to come tomorrow, if that's convenient?"

"Absolutely. Around one?"

"Great. And thanks again, Finola. Oh, has Colin said anything about my car?"

"Sorry, can't really say. I only know it was taken to Faraday's garage."

Jo swallowed the spurt of panic that arose from feeling stranded. "Okay, no problem."

"Till tomorrow then." Finola Webb's voice died away.

As Jo put down the receiver, the silence in the cottage became an almost palpable thing. She shivered. It was cold too. Moving to the fireplace she picked up the poker from the hearth and stirred the pile of damped-down leaves and chippings that covered the smouldering logs. A tiny spurt of blue'ish flame escaped, then leapt higher and burned yellow. Immediately the room seemed more cheerful as air reached the logs and they got under way. This sense of isolation was only to be expected, she told herself, rubbing her forearm and glancing round. Okay, so she was a writer and therefore used to her own company, she told herself, but a remote cottage in the country was vastly different to a London pad. No problem; it would just take a little time to settle in. A cup of coffee first, she thought remembering the boiling kettle, and then unpacking was on the agenda, which was really about making the place feel her own. In the meantime, there were one or two short cuts to making the cottage more homely. Before making a drink she ran a fingernail along the sellotape sealing one of the boxes and took out her portable radio and cassette player. A further rummage around yielded a box of tapes. Armed with the means of breaking the awful silence, she headed more confidently for the kitchen.

She drank her coffee whilst listening to a Dire Strait's tape, but then replaced it with some vintage Dillon when the title song *Brothers in Arms* proved a little too atmospheric, the lyric of mist-covered mountains, poignant death and baptisms of fire somehow evoking, due no doubt to her recent experience, an ethos of knights, battles and medieval chivalry. She rinsed her mug at the sink and emptied two of the boxes of books and papers before going upstairs to start on her clothes. There she hung her one dress, two skirts and a coat in the wardrobe, and filled the drawers of the chest with sweaters, underwear, socks and a couple of pairs of jeans.

But then when she sat down again in the kitchen silence and solitude crowded in. Worries began to gnaw at her mind like a maggot. She had told Finola Webb that she was 'perfectly alright', but was it the truth? Her hand went tentatively to her forehead then dropped again. The strangeness was still inside her head. Occasional flashes of light – not unlike those prior to the migraine attacks of her teenage years – were a reminder; those and the sense of unreality that accompanied them, serving to remind her that the opening to the tunnel was also there. It's nothing, she told herself, staring out of the window at the stunted apple trees in the bleak wild garden. Nothing to make a fuss about: a touch of delayed shock that's all; it would pass. Listlessly she moved to her lap top and switched on, but unable to face a session of work, switched it off again.

Consequently, the knock at the front door later that afternoon came as a welcome break rather than an intrusion. Keeping busy had staved off loneliness, but now even the blood and thunder of Wagner from the cassette player couldn't diminish the essential silence of the cottage. An odd thought that, she reflected moving to open the front door. Given the sound of running water from the garden and the distant grumble of the river. But it was true: she had found herself feeling for it above the sound. And it was there, lurking behind the music. "Colin! Come on in," she invited, trying not to sound too delighted to see another human being.

EIGHT

~

Jo poured coffee and placed a cup in front of Colin Gilmour. He had carried in a carton of groceries from the boot of his car, and Jo duly expressed her gratitude and settled the bill.

"Are you the writer by any chance?" he had asked, handing back her 'Rescue' card which bore her full name.

She nodded, glad to have it out of the way, and relieved that he didn't seem unduly impressed.

"Clever," was his only comment; Jo had the feeling he would have like to have added 'bitch'.

"But you've both been wonderful!" she said now as he brushed aside further thanks.

"No problem. Glad you're Okay. It could have been nasty."

"Absolutely." She nodded and thought if only he knew the half of it, then swiftly shut off the nightmare image of the tunnel that arose. "The car? Was it bad?"

He blew on the scalding coffee and half closed his eyes as he risked a sip. "No." He took another sip and put down his mug. "A bit of adjustment to the suspension and tracking that's all. You should have it back tomorrow or the day after."

"Do I need to make myself known to them?"

"They'll ring when it's ready. I'll run you there if you like."

"Thanks. But I hate to be a nuisance."

"You're not."

There was a moment's silence as his gaze held hers a moment longer than it should. He was an attractive man, Jo acknowledged, albeit in a gruff macho sort of way, with his lean frame, taut muscles and those grey flinty eyes that seemed to look through her to the person within, but she had no intention of finding herself caught between him and Finola. Especially not whilst she was still licking her wounds over Blake. She resolved to use the taxi firm from Beckdale when the time came to collect her car. Costly, but no obligation.

"You must have thought me one crazy woman yesterday," she said in a bantering tone, feeling the need to puncture the bubble of intimacy. "But I really did think I saw someone on the road. I reckon my agent's to blame, at least in part."

"Oh, why's that?" He collected himself smoothly, and picking up his cup of coffee watched her over the rim as he drank.

Jo shrugged and pushing aside her empty cup, affected an air of nonchalance. "She made some comment about the area being haunted. Of course she was having me on?"

Colin shrugged. "There's some old wives' tale about a medieval knight. But I doubt it was him you saw," he said wryly.

"Tell me. Just out of curiosity," she added, feeling slightly foolish.

"Don't really know, except he's supposed to ride that road on stormy nights, or some such crap."

Jo smiled. "I take it you don't believe it then."

"Do you?" he said derisively, draining his coffee cup.

She shook her head, feeling the colour rush to her cheeks. "No of course not. But I guess Louise – my agent – sowed the seed in my mind and my subconscious supplied the rest," she said with a little laugh.

"More than likely." Colin Gilmour played with his coffee spoon. "Doesn't your husband or whatever mind you trekking off into the wilds for weeks on end?"

"There is no husband."

"And a 'whatever'?"

Jo, who had been getting prickly at this blatant questioning had to smile. She shook her head. "No 'whatever' either. I'm here to work," she added pointedly.

He laughed ruefully and pushed back his chair. "Okay, so I'll leave you to it. Tomorrow lunch then?"

"Thanks, yes I'll be there. I'll look forward to meeting Finola," she said stressing the point. As he shut the front door behind him, loneliness once more filled the cottage.

It was, she decided after putting away the groceries, time to explore her surroundings. According to the notes on the tourist map found in the bookcase, the nearby church dated back to the fifteenth century and the site itself to the first century A.D. There wasn't a lot of time to spare: the nights were drawing in and daylight would fade fast here in the hills. Donning a jacket over her sweater and jeans, she slipped a slimline torch into her pocket as a precaution, and locking the front door of the cottage behind her, set off down the track.

The muted murmuring became progressively louder as she left the rutted track and turned left into a lane flanked on either side by rowan, blackthorn and oak. The lane led directly down to the river, the church and graveyard being situated on an adjacent flat area surrounded by dark and sinister yews arranged like sentinels around the perimeter walls. She stood on the banks now, watching the powerful surge of the current and the murmurs had amplified into a roar. Immediately below the water was crystal clear, revealing a bed of green slate and trout-speckled granite, and gnarled alders clung to the banks and dipped their branches to the flow. The source of the tumult she now saw, lay a hundred yards or so downstream where white-water falls cascaded down the wooded slope of the fell and creamed the rocky basin beneath.

Jo walked closer for a better view and watched the water foaming and bouncing over boulders from which it had scoured the algae and moss. She remained there for several minutes, fascinated by the power; by the gleam and slide of sinuous green snakes that slid between each boulder and burst into shaving foam upon the next outcrop. After a spell of heavy rain it must be pretty spectacular, she thought, noting the smooth bowls and hollows carved out of the adjacent rock by the expanded force.

The church was a low building of granite and Westmorland slate. The squat gothic-shaped bell housing, glimpsed between the yews, stood stark against the greenish light in the western sky. She paused at the lych gate, struck by the rows of ancient headstones peeping over the wall overlooking the lane. Almost, she thought with a little *frisson*, as though their occupants were trying to escape. She smiled at her foolishness and pushing open the gate, walked down the path to the porch.

It was the tiniest church she had ever entered. Cool, dim and redolent with ancient wood, beeswax and flowers, the atmosphere was palpable and a little disturbing in its intensity. The air felt to be permanently damp from the spray outside, and the cold struck up at her from the stone slabs beneath her feet. A cruck truss, the massive timbers forming an 'A' shape, dominated the east end and a basket of flowers stood on the horizontal tie beam. Jo ran her hand along the polished rail of a box pew, then advanced down the aisle towards a simple alter with crucifix and candles. Oil lamps with glass funnels belonging to the last century lined the thick walls. A midnight carol service in here with lamps lit and candles flickering would be quite something, she found herself thinking. Especially if the wind howled and snowflakes were mottling the stained glass windows. She could almost hear the tolling of the bell echoing round the mountains. She sat for a while, reflecting on her life, on Blake's safety and the people of Bosnia, then dropped a donation into the box and went back outside.

Knowing that the oldest and therefore most interesting graves would be situated closest to the church building, she inspected those first. So engrossed did she become that daylight faded without her noticing. One slab marked *De peste mortui* set her wondering about its occupant. A man aged twenty nine years who died in 1565 according to the barely legible inscription. How had the plague reached a remote valley like this? Was he a traveller from a nearby town perhaps? And how had the spread of the pestilence been avoided? The deepening shadows cast by buttresses and trees at last made her aware that it was time to think of returning to the cottage. The prospect of stumbling in darkness down that rutted and overgrown track was anything but alluring. Still thinking about the unfortunate plague victim, she approached the corner of the church then stopped. Ridiculous, but she sensed someone was there. She hesitated, her nerves jangling. She looked up: the light in the west had almost died. The diamond panes of the gothic windows winked in the residual glow, watching her like sinister eyes. This was ridiculous. Bracing her spine she rounded the corner and stopped dead. Her involuntary cry was stifled.

NINE

~

Justin St. Clair's finger nails bit into his palms as he watched the entrance to the ancient temple. So engrossed were they in their fornicating that they had no suspicion of his presence. He shrank further back into the alders that lined the river bank as something moved in the shadows surrounding the ruins. The blood boiled in his veins as he watched his wife slip across the sward and disappear into the dusk. A moment later the drum of hooves on earth told him she was on her way home.

Faithless bitch! She thought he was away at a war council called by Edward to plan the invasion of Scotland, but he had deliberately misled her: it would not take place until the following week. His face darkened as he reflected upon the escalation of events. Balliol, Scotland's king, had refused to meet Edward at Berwick when summoned – some would say like a dog – and Edward had brutally sacked the town. A bloody revenge indeed – which took his thoughts back to his wife. He scowled; she would arrive at the castle hot and flushed from her pleasuring. And when had they arranged their next tryst? Soon he'd wager. Christ's blood, she was like one of his bitches on heat.

He indulged himself for a moment with the fantasy of surprising her in her chamber, and taking a raw hide whip to flay the skin from her white back in ribbons. he could almost hear her begging to be allowed to die. His tongue wetted his dry lips. But patience; his turn would come. He drew further back into the shadows as a second figure emerged from the ruins and melted into the dusk. And so will yours, Chase. The knowledge cooled his blood and turned the heat of his anger to ice.

Blake listened to the buzz and crackle in his ear then slammed down the receiver in frustration. Picking it up again he spoke curtly to the girl at the reception desk. "Check this number please," and he relayed the telephone number of Twilight Cottage, gleaned from Louise earlier that day; if anyone knew where Jo had gone, he reasoned, it was Louise. His hunch proved correct but wasn't doing him much good. He glanced at his wristwatch – the one Jo had bought him last Christmas – and sighed with annoyance. In twenty minutes or so he was due at a meeting followed by dinner with his boss. The telephone rang; he picked up the receiver again. "Okay. Thanks." He frowned as he replaced it. No fault on the line, the girl had said. The number was ringing out but no-one answering. One last time, then he must shower and change.

It was no use: just that buzzing along the line, and a loud crackling like the interference caused by storms or a high wind. Emptying his pockets of keys, wallet, loose change and American Express card he tossed them onto the bed and headed for the bathroom.

As he made his way to the lift and pushed the button for the ground floor, annoyance and frustration turned to worry. He didn't know why, what he was worrying about – just a feeling that all wasn't well with Jo. He shrugged. There wasn't much he could do about it, if she chose to go legging it off to some remote love-nest of Louise's. He half grinned to himself. Louise had tried to get him there once; thank God he had resisted. Jo and he were newly acquainted in those days, it hadn't got serious then. It was bad enough to have bedded her agent, but he could imagine Jo's reaction if the cottage had been the scene of seduction and Louise was bitch enough to tell her – which of course she was.

Come to think of it, what was Jo doing at Louise's place? Why visit a primitive cottage in the back of beyond? Was there some significance in the fact that it used to be an illicit *rendezvous*? Unpalatable thoughts whirled round his head as he stepped from the elevator into the almost deserted lobby. He recollected the explosive and immediate impact of their first date, saw Jo with full soft lips, the first bloom of desire on her cheeks and her pupils dilated and black, and the way they had drowned in each others gaze across the restaurant table, each unable to pull away. She didn't hold out too long against him he reminded himself, then felt guilty because it was something special between himself and Jo, a spark of magic that made them feel they went back a long way instead of having just met. "Jo, Jo," he whispered, as he relived the hunger and intensity of those early days and was swept along on a moonstruck tide of yearning and nostalgia.

Until a paralysing thought beached him with a jolt. Perhaps that's why she wasn't keen to settle down and get married. Maybe she missed the magic, the thrill of a new relationship, and was searching for excitement some place else. As he walked on, that possibility overwhelmed him with misery and blood-pumping jealousy, feelings made worse by the fact that he couldn't understand, because for him the magic was still there and always would be.

He started as something touched his cheek. He was preoccupied, not watching where he was going. Angrily he brushed aside the frond of the potted palm. The fickle bitch, if it was true. Okay, so he had slept with Louise once or twice in the early days, but that was then, and there had been nobody since he'd made the decision: that Jo was for him. She was his – and his alone.

He clenched his fists and felt the sweat bead his forehead. She was there with some guy. The guy he had seen her with maybe, the one driving the E-type. He stopped and frowned. No, that had been a dream. Confused, he stroked his forehead with a hand that shook slightly. Going into the lounge he sat down and brought from his pocket a slim gold cigarette case and lighter. Breaking his self-imposed rule of no smokes before evening dinner, he took out a Marlborough and tapped it on the case. The sound hammered in his brain. He lit up and inhaled deeply, then blew out a thin, angry stream of smoke. *Damn her.* He would *kill* her if she was there with a lover. He blinked and looked up, becoming aware that someone was speaking to him. "What was that?"

"I said good evening, Blake. A bit early for you isn't it?" The broad loose-limbed man with the American accent indicated the smouldering cigarette with its long trail of ash. "Everything okay?"

Blake blinked a couple of times. "Yeah, fine. Sorry Chad. I was miles away."

Chad Wallis grimaced. "Pretty soon, I guess you'll wish you were! Coming?"

"Yep – be along in a minute." Leaning forward Blake stubbed out his cigarette in the ashtray whilst wondering what the hell had got into him of late. Whatever it was seemed beyond his control or understanding. He wouldn't hurt a hair of Jo's head; for God's sake, he loved the woman.

He stood up and contemplated Chad's retreating back. Possesiveness and jealousy weren't normally his kick, he worried. At least, no more than his Italian descent dictated, he thought with a wry grin, recalling Jo's 'take off' of a fiery latin lover with a preposterous accent. It had to be down to Bosnia-nerves, that and the trauma of breaking off the relationship. It could also be said, he realised, that he had only been feeling this way since Jo arrived at that damned cottage. He shrugged and rammed his hands in his pockets as he walked to the door. It was ridiculous of course to assume any connection.

Five minutes later he followed Chad Wallis, services co-ordinator, out of the building and into autumnal twilight.

TEN

~

Jo took her hand from her mouth and gave a nervous little laugh. "I'm sorry. You startled me!" Her heart was still thumping uncomfortably in her chest, but it was alright. The man gaping at her looked like a 'local', a farmer probably, judging by his open-necked shirt, snagged pullover and stained green body warmer. He appeared reasonably mortal and substantial, she thought with humour born of relief, and also lacked fangs and voluminous black cloak. Apart from lurking in a graveyard at dusk and being struck dumb by her sudden appearance, he seemed normal enough. Until she looked into his eyes. Then she recoiled. There was something there: a shadow. Something she couldn't fathom but which struck some chord of recognition within herself. "Good evening," she said, seeking to infuse the situation with normality. "Sorry if I gave you a fright too."

He stared at her with those awful haunted eyes and still didn't speak, then backed off, his mud-caked boots slipping on the damp grass. Regaining his balance he stood knees bent in a half crouch, his gaze locked on her face. In the near-twilight Jo recognised fear staring out from his eyes. That, or some other strong emotion, emanated from his person and hung about him in a malignant aura. Jo shivered as she felt it touch her soul. Her hand went to her head; the bruise left by the accident was throbbing, and the 'lights' were bursting behind her eyelids as blood roared in her ears. Dark panic rose up to engulf her courage.

He took a step forward and it was Jo's turn to step back. "Who are you?" he whispered hoarsely, his eyes glazed with terror.

"I'm Jo Cavanagh, and I'm staying in the area," she said calmly, deliberately not telling him exactly where, and on her guard for any sign of sudden movement in her direction. Obviously the man was disturbed and this was a potentially threatening situation. "I've been exploring the church, but must have startled you," she added evenly. Which, she thought smothering a desire to laugh hysterically, must be the under-statement of the century.

The calmness in her voice seemed to convey itself to him. He stared a moment longer, then his shoulders sagged as though in profound relief. In fact the shadows around him appeared to visibly lighten. He touched his battered cap and grunted. "No matter miss," he mumbled and brushed past.

As he did so the stream of cold air caught her by surprise, that and the darkness that seemed to reach out and touch her as he passed. She shuddered at the near contact.

"What's your name?" she called on impulse.

He half turned at the corner. "Seth. Seth Rigby," he mumbled, then disappeared.

*   *   *

Jo stood for a moment, unsure of what to do next. The incident had shaken her and her legs felt like water. Which was ridiculous really, and she told herself sternly she was over-reacting, but then comforted herself with the knowledge that the crash and the train of events it triggered were enough to faze anyone. Not wanting to bump into the weirdo again, she decided not to retrace her steps to the main entrance, but instead made her way towards the postern gate visible at the end of the path. Albeit he seemed more afraid of her than she of him, she reflected; and to think she had accused herself of over-reaction. Bolstered by such thoughts she lengthened her stride and moved forward with greater confidence.

Yet that feeling was still with her, and growing stronger as she approached the mound on her left. Instinctively her hand went to the nape of her neck. That was all she needed: a freshly dug grave. The grim humour of her situation didn't pass her by. If only Blake could see her now. Bubbles of hysteria threatened to escape and burst. She cast an anxious look over her shoulder, caught her breath sharply then let it out again. In the deceptive twilight the stunted bush had appeared to move. There was no sign of the man who had called himself Seth Rigby.

An owl screeched from amidst the yews, and a jolt which started in her belly buzzed along every nerve in her body. A ghostly white shape glided overhead and she automatically ducked then almost laughed aloud. A barn owl setting out on its nightly hunt. Pull yourself together, Cavanagh. What a crazy situation: wandering alone in a graveyard at dusk, owls screeching, bats fluttering over the belfry and a full moon rising over the scene. All it lacked now was a figure cloaked in black, rising from behind a headstone and flashing Maclean-white fangs. Only none of this was funny. The sense of being trapped in a nightmare persisted.

Against her inclinations, she paused by the open grave. It was as though the feeling – the *energy* she felt buzzing around her – had led her there; like walking a ley line – at least, according to her sister Barbara who was sensitive to such things. Nobody else in the family shared it, or her affinity with herbs, crystals and natural healing. Perhaps it would be a good idea to give her a ring, see what she made of all this. The grumbling of the river was loudest here, that and the gush and splash of the falls. Jo stared down into the black pit. Water was seeping through, sucking and bubbling, black and evil-looking and scum collected like yellow pus in one corner. She shuddered but was unable to draw away her gaze. Fancy being lowered down there. If ever there was a case for cremation, this was surely it.

She wanted to move on, but felt as though she were rooted in earth that was red with iron ore, *red with blood*. Why did she think that? She put a hand to her temple and kneaded it with her fingertips. The water, black and shiny like ink, reflected the dying light in the western sky. But that wasn't the only source, the lights in her head were flashing again and the tunnel threatened. It would be easy to let go. She was dizzy, unstable – reeling through the darkness, the water drawing her, so that she teetered on the brink. Closer and closer she leaned, like an iron filing to the magnet and helpless against the pull. The screech of the barn owl jolted her out of a near-trance. She blinked several times, then with one last look of disgust hurried away from the grave and through the postern gate.

The greenish glow in the west had died by the time she reached the turning for Twilight Cottage. Purple shadows constantly shifted, and tendrils of mist snaked above the ditches and around the roots of trees so that they appeared to be floating on a ghostly sea. The track was even less inviting in the dark, Jo worried peering into the tunnel of trees. Her 'pencil' torch was already failing, the beam a sickly orangey yellow that penetrated the darkness for a mere couple of feet. Her foot twisted in a deep rut and she cried out with pain. *Stupid mistake:* both torch and shoes were inadequate she castigated herself, pausing to rub her ankle. This was country-side proper, not some make-believe 'village' with phoney duck pond and yuppy residents somewhere on the fringe of London. She pressed on angry with herself for not leaving the churchyard before dusk.

To make things worse, clouds billowed across the sky as a light wind arose. She peered into the shadow of tree, outcrop and hedge-row, starting nervously at each rustling or shifting of form. A shrew scuttled down the bank and across her path to the opposite side, the sudden movement causing her to start. Spiny blackthorn and hawthorn met overhead, their stunted arms and thorny fingers ready to pluck and clutch at her hair and clothes as she passed beneath. She ducked as a pair of bats fluttered around her head, their skinned-finger wings suggesting miniature pterodactyls.

She stifled a cry as a shadow slunk through the hedgerow, a low-slung body carried close to the ground. She caught a glimpse of bushy tail, bristling pelt and sniper-snout. A pair of yellow eyes glowed in the meagre torchlight. Fear touched the nape of her neck and trickled like icy water along her spine as for a second, only a second, her mind cried *Wolf!* and she froze with fear. A rancid dog odour reached her nostrils. And ridiculous though the notion was, here, if anywhere, any surviving wolf-species must slink. But common sense told her it was only a marauding fox. Jo lengthened her stride but reined-in her rioting imagination.

Yet no matter how hard she summoned common sense, the feeling that she was being followed persisted. It was, she thought with mounting hysteria, as though the shadow she had sensed around the man calling himself Seth Rigby had attached itself to her psyche. Which was fanciful rubbish that sprung directly from making too much of yesterday's incident. It was psyching her out and breeding fear. A twig snapped loudly behind her, the sound magnified by the silence. She spun round and cried out as a drooping branch scratched her cheek. There was nothing to be seen. The fox must still be around, be rustling through the undergrowth. She increased her pace again and cast frequent glances over her shoulder. Her feet faltered over the deep ruts and she stumbled over a tree root that sprawled across the path. Leaves rustled and twigs crackled – yet nothing revealed itself.

Then came a sense of presence so profound that it sent her spinning round again. This time there was no mistake: a shadow moved close to the bank, an upright human-type shadow. Terror like an electrical charge ran through her body. "Who's there!" she cried, peering through the gloom. Her torch was by now a dirty amber glow and worse than useless. Nothing stirred and the only sound was the wavering cry of an owl. Her heart thumped in her chest. "What do you want?" she cried succumbing to hysteria. Still no movement or response. The cottage – she had to get back to the cottage. Out here she was sitting duck. Her legs, previously paralysed by fear pumped into action.

Turning to look over her shoulder, she stumbled again over a rut. Scrambling to her feet she paused to rub her ankle. The twilight deceived her senses: hedges and tree-forms wavered in purple haze and nothing was as it seemed. She felt a scream welling up from the depths of her belly as unmistakable this time, the same shadowy figure slid between the trees. Seth Rigby was following her; she was sure of it now. Gasping from fear and exertion, Jo pressed forward, terrified that feet would pound in pursuit, hands grab her and drag her to the ground.

She burst into the clearing. An apricot moon, round and hazed with mystery loomed over the fell. Tendrils of mist trailed across its face but a diffused glow shimmered around the clearing, distorting form and warping reality. The pines at the rear of the cottage swayed and sighed in the wind whispering age-old secrets in a tongue no mortal could understand. Blood pounded in her ears, and a stitch cramped her groin as she sped across the glade. The breath caught in her throat; the wind was suddenly rising. The arms of the pines threshed the air, making a sound like rollers crashing over shingle and clouds whipped across the moon, obscuring its light and plunging the clearing once more into primordial darkness.

At last the front door. She fumbled in her pockets for the key, her hair streaming medusa-like about her head in wild tendrils. Within minutes the wind had risen to near gale force. It howled and shrieked round gable and chimney and threatened to haul her off her feet. Her fingers made contact with the key, but were so numbed with cold they wouldn't obey her brain. At last it was in her hand. With her left hand she felt in the darkness for the lock, and with the right struggled to insert the key and turn it. Her chest constricted with fear and premonition. She cast a frantic look over her shoulder and felt her heart miss a beat.

A shadow loomed at the edge of the clearing.

ELEVEN

~

Janice Rigby looked at her husband with consternation. His hair was untidy, his clothing dishevelled, his appearance in general unkempt. In their thirty-five years of marriage and farming together, she had never known him let himself go like this. And that haunted look is back in his eyes, she thought surreptitiously watching him as he picked up the newspaper, glanced at the headlines and listlessly threw it down again on the table. He wouldn't have said anything about this incident if she hadn't pressed, if she hadn't insisted he tell her what had upset him. He had come home looking bewildered as a lost dog.

"So did you go back in and apologise to the young lady then?" she demanded, drying her hands on her pinafore.

He shook his head and scowled. "She gave me a rare turn, coming round the corner sudden like that. " He shrugged and his mouth, perpetually unsmiling these days, turned further down at the corners. "Happen she'll understand."

"Aye, happen." But Janice gave him a wry look and appeared far from convinced. "Poor lass. What a welcome to the neighbourhood!"

"I didn't mean to get rattled."

"No." Janice's hand soothed and patted her apron, as though in some way to iron out the worry lines that scored her forehead. "Aye well, go and get cleaned up. I'll be putting tea on the table in a minute."

Thoughtfully, she massaged her throat as she watched him shuffle from the room.

She went over and listened for his footsteps on the stairs before closing the door. What was happening to her Seth? Folk would be talking about him, wandering round the graveyard like that in the dark. And she still hadn't got out of him what he was doing there, Maud's grave being finished and all. Admittedly, the girl had been doing the same, but that was the sort of thing visitors normally did, wasn't it? But not locals: not folk like her and Seth. What on earth would the lass think of him and who might she voice those thoughts to? Janice worried. Seth was Church warden, and they were both serving officers on the Parish Council. It wouldn't do to be conspicuous, to be thought 'odd' or in some way peculiar. They were 'pillars of the community' Vicar said.

Deriving comfort from this last thought, she smoothed her greying hair back from her forehead and patted it into place, but then her face crumpled in distress. What if folk knew about the way he carried on nights? The ranting and raving in his sleep until he woke himself up shouting. They would think he was going soft in the head, be wanting to send him away, and she couldn't have that. She stood for a moment listening to the footsteps overhead. Seth would be a while yet, the pipes were still clanging and making their friendly familiar noises as the hot water hissed through them to the bathroom. Moving decisively to where the telephone sat on the sideboard, she picked up the receiver and started to dial.

TWELVE

~

Jo's hand trembled as she struggled to turn the key in the rusty lock. She swore beneath her breath, cursing her freezing fingers. The sense of a presence, of being watched was now overwhelming so that she felt physically sick. The wind howled and tore at her coat, and the roar of the river throbbed in her ears heightening the drama. At last the lock yielded and the door swung open and was immediately buffeted by a gale-force gust. Jo cringed as it banged against the wall with alarming force. Not pausing to look behind, she stumbled inside and leaning with all her weight against the timbers, battled against the wind until the door slammed shut.

With hands that shook she shot the bolt and slumped with her back against it, absorbing the cessation of noise and naked aggression, the relief so intense it brought her to the edge of tears. But the danger wasn't yet over she reminded herself; Seth Rigby was still lurking outside, and knowing she was here alone, may even try to force an entrance. She edged her way into the sitting room and keeping to the wall, peered out of the window.

From here she had a view of the clearing, and the spot where she had seen the figure standing as the moon briefly illuminated the scene. There was nobody there now. No shadow watched from amongst the perimeter trees or skulked along the hedgerow. For several minutes she remained there in the dark, keeping vigil by the window. No shadow stirred, and no prowler edged a way round the trees towards the cottage. She breathed out deeply and noisily. Seth Rigby had gone. She drew the curtains across the window and switched on the light.

The shrilling of the telephone made her almost jump out of her skin. Perhaps Louise had told Blake she was here – the thought sent her moving swiftly to pick up the receiver. Hope died as a woman's voice with a local accent hesitantly spoke her name. "Yes, this is Jo Cavanagh," she confirmed, striving to keep the tremor from her voice. "Who is this?" She stiffened as the woman introduced herself as Seth Rigby's wife. "How did you know where to find me?" Jo was now finding it hard to breathe.

The woman's reply was reassuringly prosaic: "Had to be, Twilight Cottage was the only place roundabouts that was vacant."

Jo swallowed. "I see. But how did you know the number?" she persisted.

"We used to deliver milk and eggs. When the posh lady from London was there with her – friend," the pause being brief but significant and loaded with disapproval so that Jo had to fight an urge to exonerate herself from similar sins and protest she was there alone.

"So what can I do for you?" she said at last, marginally relaxing.

"My husband, he's a bit bothered like, thinks you might think him unsociable. It's just that you gave him a bit of a fright – not used to seeing anyone down there this time of day and in the dark," the woman explained, subtly placing the blame on Jo for being there in the first place and implying she had no right.

"He'd been finishing off old Maud's grave you see," she added as though by way of justifying his presence. "He asked me to ring and apologise, seeing as how he's in the bath right now."

Jo's knuckles were white as they clutched the flex. "You mean your husband is home with you?"

"Like I said, in the bath." The woman sounded puzzled by her question.

"No problem," Jo managed to say whilst compulsively twisting and untwisting the flex. "tell him I understand."

"I will. If there's anything we can do – you just moving in like –,"

"Thank you, very kind."

"If you need eggs and things, then stop by."

"I will, thanks."

There was a pause as though the woman wanted to say more, then a click and the line went dead.

Jo crossed to the window and eased aside the curtain a fraction. Nothing moved in wood or clearing. The wind had dropped as mysteriously as it had arisen, and no shadow stained the moonlight at the edge of the copse. If Seth Rigby was home, then he could not have been the man who had trailed her to the cottage. So who was? she worried. Her hand went to her head. Perhaps she had imagined it all, a result of delayed shock. She shivered and let the curtain fall back into place. So why did it feel as though the shadow had followed her into Twilight Cottage?

*   *   *

To cap it all the fire was almost out and there was no more wood in the basket. Jo felt like crying but didn't; instead she donned her jacket again, picked up the log basket, took a large hand torch down from the shelf and went out by the back door. Despite the drop in the wind the cold struck her forehead and felt raw in her nostrils; she could actually taste the frost in the air. She stood for a moment, scanning the edge of the pine wood and the shrubbery in the foreground but saw nothing suspicious. The moon was now clear of cloud and cast silvery light across her path and the overgrown flower beds close to the house. By contrast the shadows lurked purple-black and impenetrable. She raked them, poised for flight whilst watching for the slightest movement but caught nothing disturbing. Except – she shuddered and looked over her shoulder – a feeling of being watched. Well she couldn't stand here all night. Taking a deep breath she made her way to the stone outbuilding where Louise had told her she would find a supply of wood.

And here the feeling of presence was stronger. The door was unlocked and swung open when pushed. She stepped over the threshold and stopped dead. Frowning she directed the beam of the torch directly onto the ground. A pile of earth, red and damp like the iron-rich soil in the graveyard littered the floor, as though it had fallen from someone's boots. *Seth Rigby* – was her first thought. But no, he couldn't have been in two places at once.

She was about to turn and leave in a hurry, then remembered the reason for coming out. Her torch beam when flashed around revealed seasoned and split logs stacked at the back of the shed. With a glance over her shoulder she stepped forward, dropped her basket and filled it with fuel. As the piles were disturbed, the scent of resin and sawdust mingled with that of damp earth. Her shoulders felt heavy, as though a weight rested upon them.

She picked up her basket and paused. The sense of presence was growing stronger. It stifled her, made her chest heave for air. Breathing; she could hear someone breathing: a deep inhaling and exhaling of breath as though labouring under some deep emotion. Terror grabbed her by the throat choking the scream as it arose. Wildly she swung her torch, illuminating first the corners then behind the door. Nothing but cobwebs and the long rubbery tail of a disappearing rat. Could that have been the cause? She knew not, but wanted to believe it was the answer. Her nostrils twitched and her stomach heaved. The scent of wood had become overlaid with a powerful odour that reminded her of a butcher's shop, which was bad enough, but this was worse – the stench of bad blood and rotten flesh. She gagged and looked around her again. Perhaps some creature had come in here to die, a rat or cat maybe. With one last glance at the pile of earth on the floor, she turned to leave and her heart leapt into her throat. Fear rooted her, but seconds later she was racing for the house.

It was something to do with the quality and angle of moonlight, she thought, dropping her basket to slam the kitchen door shut and ram home the bolt. Her legs were shaking and she found herself wondering how she would get through the night. Her car would be returned in a day or two, she consoled herself, and if things were no better she could always drive back to London. But it was nothing. That shadow briefly barring the doorway had been a trick of the light.

The fire was rekindled, she had made and eaten some cheese on toast and drunk a fair-sized measure of brandy. Tomorrow she would attempt some work; tonight she was just too whacked. She sprawled in the armchair, her feet on the stool, watching flames devour the logs. Fatigue and reaction ached in her bones, but even so, the shrilling of the telephone was preferable to the loneliness of going upstairs to bed. Bestirring herself she reached for the receiver. "Louise – hi!" she said with enthusiasm, hiding her disappointment that it wasn't Blake. "What was that? Weather's changed – cold in London? Don't complain – it's *winter* here! Yes, no kidding. Yes, I got here – finally." Jo tucked her feet beneath her, preparing for a long chat. "What do I mean? Oh, I stupidly came off that bloody road, didn't I! That's right, that's the one," She deliberately made light of the accident, knowing Louise would feel in part responsible for sending her there.

Briefly she recounted her adventure, omitting the weird experience in the car. "No honestly, I'm perfectly alright. Just a precaution the doctor said. Who, Oh Colin? Yes, not bad. You never met him?"

Louise's laughter, deep and suggestive, echoed down the line. "There wasn't much time for socialising, darling!" she purred. "So what's he like, your sculptor?"

"Bolshy. Attractive I suppose – and spoken for." She smiled as she said it; it was good to relax into what Louise called 'girly talk' for a change.

"Look Jo, I don't know if I did right or not, but Blake dropped by – demanded to know where you were."

"You didn't tell him?" The colour rising to Jo's cheeks wasn't entirely due to the fire or the brandy.

"I thought you might sack me if I didn't!"

"Dead right!" Jo grinned and thought again that her agent knew her too well.

She swung one foot to the floor and adjusted the other beneath her thigh. "Yes, I've found everything," she said in response to Louise's query. "Just been outside for some wood. No, nothing." She paused and caught her lower lip in her teeth, then regaining control, carried on: "Louise, what's this about the place being haunted?"

There was a thread of worry running through Louise's voice. "Why, what's going on there, honey?"

"Just curious. There could be a book in it," Jo lied.

"No you're fazed. I know you well enough by now."

"Oh, there was this weird guy, down at the churchyard. Seth Rigby. He sort of loomed at me in the dark."

"He's Okay. He or his wife used to bring us eggs and things."

Jo nodded as though Louise could see her. "So she said. 'that posh London lady and her *friend,* was how she actually put it." She laughed at Louise's indignant expletive and immediately felt better: talking about it robbed it of that sinister quality. "No, I didn't meet her, she telephoned."

"Why should she do that?"

"That's just it – I don't know. Said something about her husband arriving home upset, thinking he had alarmed me. Which he did, Louise. He acted like a psycho."

There was a brief silence at the other end of the 'phone. "Doesn't sound like Seth. But he was the church warden and grave digger. Which would explain why he was there. But in the dark, you say?"

"Twilight actually, but there was a freshly dug grave." Jo shuddered despite the heat from the fire.

"There you are then!" Louise sounded triumphant.

"Where?" Jo countered.

"Look, chick, it was dark, you were in a graveyard next to an open grave, and you'd just come out of hospital after a bang on the head. Come on, Jo. You freaked out."

Jo twisted a coil of hair around her finger. "You really think so?"

"I do. Poor kid, you've had it real rough. You'll be okay tomorrow, you'll see. Look, if you're worried – about anything – call me. Now have a stiff drink and go to bed. And start some work – soon!"

"Thanks, I will. Wait! Louise? You didn't answer my question about being haunted." But Louise had rung off.

Jo had the feeling Louise knew more than she was admitting to.

After waiting in vain by the telephone in the hope that Blake might ring, she went to the bathroom. To her disgust the water ran rather less than luke warm. Being too weary anyway to do more, she had a 'cat-lick' of a wash as her mother would say, banked the fire and heated some milk. Carrying her mug and a book, she went upstairs to bed.

It was icy cold in the bedroom and the warm milk was a comfort. After putting down her book, she lay for a while on her back, gazing up at the ceiling beams and swirls of plaster between. Her breath rose in white clouds and the bedding still felt damp. *Christ. Where are you Blake? And what the hell am I doing here?* Switching off the light she huddled beneath the quilt. The beck bubbling past her window had a soporific effect. She must have left the window open a fraction for it to sound so loud. Well it could stay open, no way was she getting out of bed. The strain of the last two days began to catch up with her at last and her eyelids drooped. Strange how the grumbles and gurgles of the stream sounded like words. She found herself listening whilst half asleep. Beneath the watery sounds there lurked a voice: *love you, love you, kill. Kill you, love you.*

Jo groaned and her head moved to and fro on the pillow.

Forever. Love you, kill you, forever, forever, forever.

The voice followed her into uneasy sleep.

THIRTEEN

~

Seth tossed his head on the pillow and moaned. Moonlight streamed in through the mullioned window of the farmhouse and rippled across the bed. To either side of the silver tide, shadows breathed and shifted in purple dreams, and the wail of a barn owl quivered eerily beyond the window. A shudder ran through his body, then it lay rigid beneath the quilt. His eyes flew open, and he stared un-seeingly at the beamed ceiling. The shadow was with him again, pressed close against him, telling him things without words. Things he didn't understand yet which turned him mad with fury. The shadow shifted, suffocating him, creeping like evil black smoke into his eyes, ears, mouth and anus, seeping into his brain and smother-ing reason, urging him on to do what had to be done. Slowly he moved his head to the left. Beside him Janice was breathing with the regular breath of the sleeper.

Do it! Act now!

The paralysis left his limbs and he rolled over and placed his hands round Janice's throat.

"Seth?" she gasped, staring into her husband's face. "Seth, what are you doing?" Abortively she clutched at his fingers as they tight-ened around her neck. "No, Seth no!" she croaked, her breath rasp-ing in her throat. He watched fear flow over her flesh, drenching her in sweat. Her scream was cut off by the vice of his fingers as they clamped her windpipe. His thumbs pressed harder. Her eyes began to bulge and the pupils disappeared, showing only the whites as they rolled in her head. He could feel the strength ebbing from her like the life-blood from a slaughtered cow. Maybe, he thought dispassionately, it was like this for the beasts too: resigned to a fate they could not escape.

Paradoxically it was not his wife's struggles but their cessation that made him stop. He stared at her without recognition, then his eyes widened with horror at what he had done. "Janice! Janice?" he cried wildly, loosening his grip and removing his hands from her throat. *Mother of God! what had made him do it?* She opened her eyes and looked dazedly at him, then as though recollecting, raised a shaking hand to her throat. "Seth?" she croaked, fear still shadowing her face. She moaned and shrank from his outstretched hand.

"Christ, I'm sorry lass, I'm sorry." He rocked to and fro in his grief.

He saw the fear leave her eyes. She swallowed hard and he saw the disbelief, read the questions in her face. He stroked her hair clumsily. "God forgive me, I didn't mean –"

"I'm alright Seth."

She struggled into a sitting position and massaged her throat with a shaking hand. "What happened Seth? What got into you?"

He gave her a startled look, before realising there was no sinister meaning lurking behind her words. "A nightmare," he mumbled in fear and shame. "Aye, that's it," he added, recovering a little as he almost believed: "I was having a nightmare."

His wife bowed her head and pretended to smooth the hollows out of the quilt. "Don't you think you should have a word with Dr. Jordan?" she ventured.

"No," he barked, shrinking from her.

"Alright, Seth, alright." She shrank back again into her pillows.

He saw the fear return to her eyes and caught a hold of his temper. "Don't go fretting about me," he said in kindlier tone.

"But you – well, you're not yourself of late, Seth. I can't help but worry."

"Like I said, just a nightmare. I'll make you a warm drink, shall I? Aye," he said gruffly, turning to squeeze her arm as she didn't answer. "Aye, I'll do that, eh?" Leaning over, he switched on the bedside lamp and the shadows leapt into hiding. He could feel her gaze boring into his back as he walked to the door.

An hour or so later, Janice was fitfully sleeping. She made little whimpering noises and her head moved to and fro on the pillow. When she did that, he could see the thumb marks on her neck and he was too distressed for sleep. First his hand then his leg twitched and jumped beneath the coverlet. Inside his head still felt odd. *Was it a nightmare?* Occasionally a sigh escaped his sagging and partially open lips. He started in fear as beyond the window a shrill cry sounded, and a winged shadow was silhouetted briefly against the curtains.

FOURTEEN

~

He was unable to resist. Almost, he had given in to his better judgment and stayed away, but had given in to his need. Antony paced the clearing as he waited. The river, a tide of mercury in the moonlight, slid serenely past untouched by his turbulent mood. Edward the First of England, he reflected, was not a good man to cross. He saw in his mind's eye the tall athletic man known as 'Longshanks' (and handsome with it, despite that inherited drooping left eyelid), before whom he had made his vows. His love of chivalry was renowned, hence the Round Table revival. Edward had even gone so far as to open Arthur's alleged grave at the monastery in Glastonbury. More likely a ruse of the monks: a relic or two did wonders for donations.

Edward wouldn't think much of his favourite's exploits here in the woods of Cumberland, Antony thought wryly. He expected his knights to perform noble deeds and protect the Ladies of the Land, not tempt them into their beds. Soon Edward would command him to wed Eleanor de Guise who was a distant kinswoman of the king and handsome enough, but cold as the ladies adorning the tombs in Westminster Abbey. And I am in love with the lady Madeline, he thought in near desperation; he loved her now and always would.

A rustling came from the undergrowth. He paused in his pacing, his armour gleaming like pewter by the light of the hunter's moon. Surreptitiously his hand went to his sword hilt and he turned slowly on the spot, his keen eyes raking the shrubbery and the crumbling bat-infested ruin of the temple, but the deep purple shadows remained undisturbed. He relaxed, judging it to be a fox or badger in the undergrowth. An owl's wavering cry filled the night, and the only other sound was the low rumble of the river as it dashed over the stones. His hand moved from his sword and he stood on the river bank, watching the current carry silver moon-daggers on its back.

His senses were so aroused that the smell of damp earth, mossy stones and cold metallic water struck his nostrils and brought an ache to his forehead. There was a chill creeping down from the mountains. Soon it would be winter, and then where would they meet? But that wouldn't worry them tonight; not when they lay warm in each others arms; and unless he was mistaken, she was here.

He strode forward as she entered the clearing, her features partially hidden by the hood of her black cloak. A swift look over her shoulder, then she was running across the sward towards him. So urgent was his love, he dared not embrace her here in the open or he would take her where she stood. In silence he grasped her hand and led her into the ruins.

Later as they lay on his cloak in the warm shadow of lovemaking, he thoughtfully traced the line of her cheek and lips with his forefinger. Would she betray him even as she now betrayed her husband? The worm of jealousy writhed in his belly. He placed his hands at either side of her head as though he would crush it and any thought of infidelity it may contain. "I love you Madeline. Perhaps to the point of madness. But if you are lying with your sweet body –"

"Hush, Antony, how can you say such things?" she whispered, briefly placing her finger over his lips and he saw distress cloud her face. Moonlight filtered between the huge stone pillars so that her hair resembled frosted bracken in Autumn, and the skin at her temples was stretched, making her eyes appear more cat-like than ever. He grasped her wrist. "Don't fret, my sweet," he said lightly, then added with a smile whilst lacing his hands about her slender throat: "I would kill you – but love you forever."

She stared at him as though truly afraid for her life. Then the madness of jealousy passed and filled with remorse, he drew her into his arms.

Blake Durante lay on his bed in the penthouse suite of a secret hotel, arms raised and fingers laced behind his head. A glance at the travel clock on the bedside table told him it was nearly 2.30 am. He sighed and shifted position. He had snatched an hour or so, but then Jo had woken him up. Chance would be a fine thing. Rather, dreaming about Jo had done the damage. A dream in which Jo had taken on Louis's glitzy image: a *haute coutour* suit that clung like shiny film to her hips, breasts and buttocks; sheer black stockings with mega-high stiletto heels, a plummy mouth and anonymous mirror shades concealing her eyes. She had climbed into the latest turbo E-type driven away by some equally slick and anonymous guy. *Shit!* he ought to be able to get her out of his system. No other woman had held his interest for more than a couple of months let alone brought on the urge to propose. And Jo, damn her, had turned him down. O.K., so she was good at what she did. Pretty brilliant in fact, but to openly choose that career above their relationship? She could carry on writing from home, for God's sakes, and with all the help and encouragement he could give. But it was no use, he hadn't come even close to competing with the spectre of success that now beckoned. Well damn you, Jo Cavanagh!

He rolled from the bed and poured himself a stiff whisky from the bottle on the chest of drawers. Taking it to the window he looked out over the roof-tops of night-time London. Coloured signs and threads of street lamps blazed in a vast constellation of mock stars. On the street below taxi and limo, unimpeded by daylight snarl-ups, ferried revellers to and from restaurants, nightclubs and high class discos. On these same streets, he reflected sombrely, the homeless roamed. Nameless souls scoured refuse bins, queued for soup or dossed down in Cardboard City, seeking brief oblivion whenever they could in drugs or booze. And who could blame them? The 'have' and the 'have nots'. Christ, no wonder there are wars and social unrest all over the world.

That thought brought to mind the seemingly irreconcilable conflict behind his mission. He turned from the window, sighed and paced the room. Within hours he would be speeding to the airport to catch his flight out to Bosnia. He took a long pull at his drink and welcomed the fire when it reached his belly. She must care, he thought, rolling the glass thoughtfully between his hands as his thoughts wandered back to Jo. He had seen the worry leap to her eyes, and heard it in her voice at the very mention of his next assignment. He shrugged. There would be little risk attached to getting into the country. The UN still dominated the air space around Bosnia. Once involved in negotiations, well – he shrugged philosophically again – there was always the risk of a sniper's bullet, an assassin hired by those who didn't want the cease fire. But that was part of the job. When your card's up –, he left the thought unfinished, aware he was just on a downer over Jo.

He topped up his drink and carried it back to the bed. Scrunching up the pillow and stuffing it behind his back, he swallowed half the malt. Was her career the real reason behind Jo's refusal to marry and have kids? Or was there perhaps somebody else? The hand that was not holding the glass balled into a fist. She'd been away from home a lot in the past six months, he brooded, what with the lecture tour and book signing sessions. He pictured her undressing in some hotel bedroom, then in a fellow lecturer's room on campus at the University. Saw her naked with the guy in the dream, then with some intense, long-haired academic. The ugliness of his suspicions suddenly made him wince. Hell, what was he thinking here? This was Jo, remember? He ran a hand through his dark wavy hair, pushing it back from his forehead.

He had no reason to think that way about Jo. Filled with remorse, he stared at the telephone on the bedside table, then reached out, half inclined to call her, but decided he couldn't at this hour, and *wouldn't* because it could do no good. Maybe it was better to just let go and get on with life. He let his hand drop down again on the bed. He could live without her; had managed well enough before she came along, and could do so again. Gulping down the last of the whisky in the glass he poured another slug and immediately swallowed half. He swung his legs from the bed, hauled himself upright and paced the room again, coming to a halt before the wardrobe mirror. This part of the room lay beyond the halo shed by the lamp and the ghostly image stared back at him, the dishevelled hair, wild eyes and pallid face mocking his indignation.

Say, who was he kidding here? He could tell himself until the next millennium that Jo no longer meant anything to him, but it wouldn't alter the fact that her face haunted him across the conference table, imposing its image upon boss, colleague or foreign power; and stared reproachfully out at him from visual display or computer screen, and haunted him each and every night in his dreams. He glimpsed her in every corner, heard her voice and smelled the tantalising whiff of her perfume, and more devastating still the warm-earth female scent of her body fluids mingled with his after making love.

In short Jo Cavanagh, you are driving me out of my mind, he thought gulping the last of his whisky and somehow refraining from hurling the glass at the opposite wall. He punched his pillow and lay down, resolving to check her out before leaving in the morning. Crazy, but he couldn't help feeling he was picking up on something connected with Jo, that his thoughts were no longer his own. The sense that something, like the last potato left to ooze and stink in the bag, was turning bad.

FIFTEEN

~

Jo was awakened by the telephone. Not that it was ringing, more a sort of buzzing sound, like bare wires placed on a battery terminal. Disoriented she stared up at the ceiling, trying to focus on the shadowy outline of the beams in the silver-grey of dawn. Where was she, and what had woken her up? It was with a sinking feeling that she recalled the move from her cosy London pad to the austerity of Twilight Cottage. The buzzing and crackling penetrated her mental meanderings. The telephone that was it. Maybe it was Blake. Shaking off the remnants of sleep she reached for the receiver.

"Hello?" She strained to hear a voice behind the crackling and whining that distorted everything else. "Blake?" Frustration knotted her stomach. "Blake, is it you?" She glanced at the luminous dial of the clock and frowned at the earliness of the hour, then realised he could be trying to reach her before flying out to Bosnia. The thought that he might be at the other end of the line speaking to her but not getting through, was torture. "Blake?" She repeated his name speaking louder each time, but got no intelligible response. The more inaccessible he became, the greater her need to hear his voice. Almost crying with frustration she replaced the receiver.

It was freezing cold in the bedroom. She dressed hurriedly and went downstairs. To her disgust the water was stone cold and a quick splash had to suffice before – top priority – putting the kettle on for coffee. The scalding black liquid warmed and invigorated her sufficiently to tackle the fire which predictably had gone out. She sighed, pushed up the sleeves of her sweater and sank down on her knees. Country living wasn't all it was cracked up to be, and the knack of it evidently took a lifetime to acquire. Clouds of fine ash rose to irritate her nostrils and make her sneeze as she cleared the ashes.

Three old newspapers and half a box of matches later a feeble fire burned in the grate. By the time she had toasted a round of bread and poached a couple of eggs, it was blazing half way up the chimney. Pleased with her efforts she sat down to breakfast, but paused with her cup halfway to her mouth as an acrid smell that was different filled the room. *Now what?* Her nose wrinkled in distaste as the smell of scorching intensified.

"Oh my God!" She leapt from her seat and rushed towards the smouldering bundle on the floor as the newspaper blackened, curled and released a small greedy flame. She had left the debris from the fireplace there, intending to take it outside after breakfast. Although the cinders had looked grey and dead, they had obviously retained enough heat to singe the wrapping. Unlatching the window she thrust it wide and flung out the burning bundle, blowing on her fingers as she released it. Cinders scattered the garden path and a swarm of sparks rose like fireflies, then were swamped by a cloud of grey dust. Jo found herself choking whilst laughing at her ineptitude. Oops, sorry Louise, she thought, closing the window and kneeling to inspect the scorch mark on the carpet. After the sinister start at Twilight Cottage, it was almost a relief to have an everyday crisis she reflected, pushing aside the eggs on toast which were now leathery looking and cold.

So now to work. Making a start was the all important thing she told herself, booting up the computer. She stared at the screen impatient for the programme menu. Idly at first, then with growing awareness she watched the logos – little windows floating randomly towards her through space. The movement was fascinating, why had it never grabbed her before? One window above the rest claimed her attention. It was drawing her in, as though she could pass through it into – *what?* Her head was throbbing and the skin felt tight as though something was being drawn out and sought to escape. She put up a hand and stroked her forehead. Lights were flashing behind her eyelids and she felt herself leaving the room behind, travelling outwards towards the window, out of her body and into her mind.

So that was it. She was floating towards the tunnel; it was still there, waiting. All she had to do was let her consciousness travel through the window, through that fragile barrier to the unknown. *Go on, go on* the voice inside her head urged. The pulling sensation at the centre of her forehead increased. She was whirling towards the opening, closer and closer it loomed until the divisions between the panes disappeared and a single inky black square was left. Larger and larger it grew, and fear grabbed at her throat so that she could scarcely breathe. Faster and faster she sped, until with a rushing of wind and whistling of air she was through and on the other side.

The expected shatter and tinkle followed by lacerations from flying glass were absent. There was only a felt-like darkness, a softness enfolding her in concerntric folds that brushed her skin gently as she passed, a woolly deadening of sensation as though entombed in silence. Lights exploded inside her head and her mind spun. She was revolving through space like a lost star that was about to burn out. The blackness was swallowing her up, filling her eyes, ears and mouth so that she could almost taste it. Then, as despair fettered the will to live, a saucer of light appeared ahead. It steadily increased in size as she spun towards it. Her speed slackened, the pull eased and zero gravity buoyed her gently upwards towards the halo.

It was then, as she floated in slow motion, that the figure came into view. Silhouetted against the light, cloak billowing and the hawk sprawled livid across his chest. He was waiting for her, waiting at the end of the tunnel just as before. Fear and fatal fascination warred within. Closer, drifting ever closer so that she could sense the triumph in his stance. He was stretching out his hand to recieve her, the emerald in his ring sparking green fire. A strident sound, half forgotten half remembered, was pulling at her attention. Then her ears were ringing, her head hurting and her concentration broken by the shrilling. Her body jerked against the back of the seat as the ringing of the telephone shattered the silence.

She stared at it for several moments, unable to make sense of her surroundings. It went on ringing and ringing, until finally the meaning pierced her trance-like state. Somehow she made her way to it and lifted the receiver. "Hello? Barbara, how–?" She was puzzled at first, then recalled that she had written her sister and included the telephone number in case of emergency. Mum and Dad flew out to Europe a lot these days, and well, one never knew. "Yes, yes it's me, Jo. I, yes – I guess I must sound a bit odd." She rubbed her temple. "No, I'm alright, don't worry. But what is it? Is there something wrong?" Jo's stomach tightened as she braced herself for bad news. "No? Mum and Daddy alright then? Oh thank God! For a moment there-, What? Oh, I banged my head and I seem to be getting peculiar turns. No, I'm sure it's nothing to worry about. Okay, okay I'm about to tell you." Briefly she related her story again, only this time she did include a version of her tunnel experience, but omitting any mention of what had followed. "And I floated above myself, whirled along this dark tunnel towards the light, then suddenly woke up in the car," she concluded.

"And?" Barbara prompted.

"How did you know there was more?"

"This is big sister remember? You know I don't disturb you unnecessarily if you're on a writing binge. So why do you think I called?"

"I did wonder."

"I had a feeling something was wrong. So tell me."

"Okay, but be warned: you won't be believe it!" Haltingly, and feeling incredibly foolish, Jo told her about the man who had been waiting at the end of the tunnel.

As she finished there was a silence so that Jo, recalling the earlier travesty of a telephone call, anxiously asked: "Still there Babs?"

To Jo's relief Barbara answered immediately. "Do you remember anything about him? Any significant details?"

Jo paused. "He had a heavy emerald ring, and a hawk emblem on his chest. Which is pretty significant I would say," Jo added dryly, then laughed with embarrassment.

"You could say so! Hey sis, you haven't been drink-driving have you?"

"I did say you wouldn't believe me."

Barbara's voice lost the bantering tone. "I do kiddo, really. At least, I believe you did undergo this experience, but what we're not sure of here is exactly what it was, and why it happened. There could be a medical explanation: an hallucination brought on by the shock. You'd just hurtled off a mountain road For God's sake – and hit your head in the bargain."

"Dr. Cahill at the hospital said that," Jo admitted, refraining from worrying her sister further by confiding her latest 'delusion' from which Babs had unwittingly pulled her back. Babs could still be right, in that it would take time for the effects to totally disappear.

"And I was set up in a way," she added thoughtfully, half to herself.

"What do you mean?"

To Jo's relief, Barbara now sounded more intrigued than worried. "Oh, Louise made some silly remark about the area being haunted," she explained. "Throw in a freak storm, and the accident – not to mention splitting with Blake, and it's little wonder I imagined a shadowy figure on the road."

"Well look, if you're worried about anything, give me a buzz."

"I will. Might even ring you," Jo quipped with a laugh.

"Okay, okay I take the point! Go back to the doctor if these funny turns continue. Stay in touch – and take care Jo."

"Don't worry I will – and thanks."

Jo felt incredibly lonely when she heard the click of the receiver being replaced.

But she did feel ever so much better for having confided in Babs. Just talking it out had dispelled the sinister aura, and of course Barbara and Dr. Cahill were right in their assessment: there was a medical explanation for her experiences, and they would disappear once her nervous system settled down. The fact that the telephone had rung out this time but not earlier was a mystery, and a little disconcerting, but then the frown was smoothed away by the realisation that Blake had probably already flown out to Bosnia. That would explain his difficulty in getting through, especially if – God forbid – he was calling from anywhere near Sarajevo and communications had broken down along with the fragile cease fire.

Concerned for Blake but reassured about normality, she sat quietly for a moment, psyching herself up for work. Tentatively she approached the lap top and selected the software, clicking on 'Word'. So far so good. Now into the programme and the prepared document, the first for the new novel. Her confidence increased as nothing more macabre than writer's block occurred. Okay, title first: *Prisoner of Conscience:* And the qualifier: *A novel about the private life of John Ruskin.* Good. Now for the difficult bit: *Chapter One.* Next step, first sentence – once that was in place the rest would follow. *John Ruskin picked up the drawing of his wife Effie and deliberately tore it in half.* There, that would get her started. With an opener like that, the reader should be asking 'Why had he done such a thing?' Soon her fingers were moving across the keyboard. They did so with increasing speed and sureness as she became immersed in her subject. Before she knew it, it was time to wash and change for lunch at Throstle Garth, Colin Gilmour's cottage.

Before leaving, she selected a couple of bottles from the half dozen wines she had stuffed into one of the packing cases whilst still in London. A sensible precaution, she thought with a grin, given the nearest shop was on the next planet. One has to get the priorities right. She dropped the Bulgarian country wine into her canvas tote, but wrapped the South African Pinotard in a sheet of green tissue paper before placing that too in the bag.

With a last look round to check the fire was safe and the windows secure, she slipped on her jacket and left the cottage.

SIXTEEN

~

Throstle Garth was hardly a cottage but a one-time farmhouse that sprawled and rambled and was built of whitewashed stone. Standing just off the by-way close to the valley-road end of the lane, it was larger and altogether more accessible than Twilight Cottage, from which it was separated by a dense copse. And that wasn't the only difference, Jo thought as she waited. The walls were of rough-hewn granite that in the winter sunlight glowed with a warm pinkish tint. By contrast the whitewashed walls of Twilight Cottage usually sulked a moody grey, and even on a bright day like this reflected the cold cast of blue steel. Throstle Garth, she reflected, also had a benign air, as though it embraced the people within, a house built to be a home; whereas Twilight Cottage gave the impression of welcoming no-one, of somehow having mush-roomed out of the very earth to which it belonged.

Jo's uneasy train of thought ended as the door was opened by a woman of about twenty-seven or eight, with long fair hair, centre parted, and which she now looped back over her ears in what Jo guessed was an habitual gesture. She was wearing little make-up: a touch of mascara and eye-shadow accentuated the grey eyes which regarded Jo with a wide and almost childlike appraisal from behind trendy gold-rimmed glasses.

"Hi, you must be Jo." She pushed up the sleeves of her brown polo.

Earnest, idealist and not very street-wise, Jo appraised in turn. "Yes, and you must be Finola – what a lovely name."

"Gaelic." The woman pushed the gold rimmed spectacles further onto her nose and her gaze swiftly took in her visitor's glowing chestnut hair and slim figure. "Come in." She held the door wide, adding as Jo followed her down the hall into a spacious kitchen: "Make yourself at home, we don't stand on ceremony here."

"Thanks." Jo followed her inside.

The kitchen, Jo noted with approval, bore out Finola's words. Books were piled precariously on a shelf and spilled over onto the table, one or two lay open on chairs. Glazed pots and copper pans sat on every available shelf or hung from the beams of the ceiling; mugs littered the draining board, a rag rug covered much of the stone floor, and candles and dried flowers abounded. An ancient Aga exuded warmth and cheer and a kettle hissed and rattled as it came up to the boil. "What a lovely room," Jo said, earning a smile from Finola, who lifted the lid of a pan and gave the contents a stir releasing a herby fragrance. "We tend to live in here."

"I brought some plonk for with lunch." Jo put the Bulgarian wine on the farmhouse table, then held out the tissue-wrapped Pinotard. "This one is for you and Colin: a very inadequate 'thank you'.

"You shouldn't –, no need, but thanks awfully." Finola flushed and looked away as she took the gift, and Jo wondered how much they had rowed over Colin's 'destitute author'.

But perhaps it was grossly unfair of her to surmise that Finola had been dragged in rather than being a willing helper. Yet she couldn't rid herself of the feeling that Finola regarded her with suspicion, as some sort of threat. Maybe Colin had given her reason to mistrust any female newcomer? Or maybe she was habitually insecure. Jo watched as Finola busied herself with uncorking the wine. She placed it on the drainer adjacent the Aga and proceeded to pour wine from an already open bottle into three glasses. "Colin's out back; I'll give him a shout."

Finola disappeared, her long calico skirt swishing as she moved. Everything about her was intense, Jo found herself thinking. Her voice sharply calling Colin's name penetrated the kitchen. Poor Colin, Jo smiled and couldn't help sympathising if he was still work-ing. It was infuriating she knew, to be called away from creative work just to eat or be sociable. But then she felt guilty for siding with him, and mentally added that he could not be easy to live with, and that Finola must be in deep to put up with it. Even more guiltily she realised the implications for herself and Blake. He had probably put up with a lot from her over the past twelve months or so.

A wave of longing washed over her, intensified by the aura of cosiness and togetherness this kitchen evoked. Whatever Finola and Colin's problem, Jo thought wistfully, at least they were together. As she and Blake once were, and still could have been if only he'd recognised her need for space. But then maybe she should have understood his need to make a real home and start a family. And recognised his integrity. He had wanted the commitment of marriage when most of her friends took it for granted that their partners would simply move in with them – and out again when the relationship paled. Honourable or old-fashioned? Deep within she suspected Blake was the former.

"He's coming now – I hope!" Finola swept back into the kitchen looking exasperated. "He's dreadful when he's working."

"You shouldn't have bothered disturbing him yet; –" Jo started to say, but Finola butted in: "Oh of course, you're artistic too – and bound to indulge him."

"I was just going to suggest we two could have a chat and get to know one another," Jo said mildly.

"Sorry. More wine?" Finola abruptly turned away and as Jo shook her head, topped up her own glass adding: "I'd better not get squiffy before serving lunch."

"Personally, I find it helps," Jo quipped. That's better, she thought as Finola relaxed and laughed.

Within minutes Colin Gilmour entered the kitchen. "Hi." He gave Jo a curt nod. Jo, unoffended by his brevity, recognised the glazed far-away look that meant he was still coming down from a creative high.

Finola gave him an arch look. "I can't believe it! I wish you came in as quick every time, Col."

Jo cringed at the ill-concealed barb, the implication that Colin had only prised himself away from his work because of her presence at Throstle Garth. Colin however ignored the provocative remark and merely asked: "Lunch ready then, Fin?"

"Let me give you a hand," Jo offered, standing up.

Finola hesitated, then appeared to make up her mind. "O.k. thanks," she said taking four place mats off the dresser and holding them out.

As she took the mats, Josie was encouraged to think Finola might just be thawing.

"Thanks ever so. That was absolutely delicious!" Jo smiled at Finola and folded her napkin. The home-made soup and vegetable risotto, followed by a pudding packed with apples, pears and blackberries grown in the orchard at the rear of the house, had been cooked to perfection. They remained seated around the table, one and a half bottles of wine down and in talkative mood.

"Glad you enjoyed it." Finola briefly returned the smile then turned back to Colin with whom she had started a lively discussion that was bordering perilously close to argument. "But if Greenpeace doesn't take a stand now, who will?" she demanded.

Colin swirled the wine around his glass. "In the main I agree with you, but in this case I think they acted a mite reckless."

"Somebody has to do something instead of just talking."

Colin's face darkened. "I try to do my bit for the environment."

Finola looped back her hair then leaned forward, her elbows resting on the table. "A *safe* bit!"

Colin shifted in his chair, crossing his legs away from her and he answered with a terseness that betrayed his annoyance: "Safe – or *responsible?* Depends on your perspective."

"Somebody has to risk their lives for the planet," Finola protested. She turned and appealed to Jo. "Don't you think so?"

Jo thought: *I have to tread carefully here; I don't want to end up in the cross fire.* She had the feeling these disagreements on global issues were really battlegrounds for much deeper personal conflicts. "Sometimes," she said cautiously, but qualifying this with: "if putting lives at risk is the only way to make people aware of injustice."

Colin heaved a sigh. "*Theirs* yes, if they have the courage and choose to do so – but not the lives of others."

"But would the rest of us ever do anything?" Jo ventured. "I mean, don't we all suffer from complacency and apathy?"

"She's right Col!" Finola looked triumphant. "It's easy for you to sit there comfortably and condemn them."

Colin scowled and grabbing the bottle, splashed more wine into his glass. "At least I do something; I don't see you doing much else but talk."

"In what way do you help, Colin?" Jo asked with a warning look at Finola as the tension crackled. "No really – I'm interested," she added, noting the suspicion in his face as though he thought she was setting him up.

He shrugged. "My sculptures. I use driftwood, reclaimed timber and the like. And the subjects are designed to raise folk's awareness of natural life forms."

"He's good." Finola relented. "In fact," she turned and gave him a melting look, "he's brilliant."

Colin took Finola's hand and placed a brief kiss on the back.

"Very commendable," Jo commented, nodding approval, though whether with reference to Colin's work or his peace-moves she wasn't entirely sure.

"I think so." Colin sipped his wine then put down the glass and twirled it by the stem. "I could be earning mega-dough knocking out glitzy rubbish for fashionable London galleries. I did – before coming here."

"I'd like to see some of your work before I go," Jo said spontaneously, then instantly wondered if it was an unwise remark. One that would alienate Finola, and give unintentional signals to Colin.

But Finola, apparently mellowed by Colin's attentions, smiled and stood up.

"Show her your studio now, Col – whilst I make coffee."

Colin scowled. "Jo was just being polite, Finola."

"No; I wasn't." Jo reassured him, then followed as Colin gave in to pressure and led the way outside to the barn.

SEVENTEEN

~

Jo instantly recognised talent. "They're very good. You've got a rare gift."

"Thanks." Their voices bounced off the stone walls and echoed around the roof beams. Colin was busy switching on spot lamps arranged at intervals round the cavernous interior, and didn't turn round. She walked round a roe deer carved out of beech wood, admiring its lines from every angle. There was a paradoxical quality to his work: poised and delicate so that the whole suggested inner stillness, yet every line conveyed energy and movement. Other pieces were sculpted *au naturel* using shapes from nature. A stag woven from canes and vines with driftwood antlers; a badger emerging half-carved from a fallen section of tree trunk. She stroked the back of an otter sliding sinuously from a piece of satiny driftwood. "Beautiful. Who takes them?"

He left the bank of switches by the door to join her. "The Forestry Commission for forest glades; Visitor Centres for along nature trails; stately homes with grounds open to the public – that sort of thing."

Jo shivered involuntarily.

"You okay?"

She shrugged. "It's chilly in here." *And growing chillier by the minute.*

Whilst talking he had been moving closer. Jo felt suddenly uneasy as he looked into her eyes too often and for too long. A silence stretched between them, thick and viscous and muffling her senses. Unease mutated into a dull sort of fear that radiated from the pit of her stomach. A pass from Colin would be a nuisance, a minor embarrassment she could deal with and overlook. But something else lurked behind this. He looked odd; a different man to the one she knew. The air grew thicker, and a chill crept along her spine and through her veins, making her shudder. He watched her face still without speaking, his intensity accentuated by his stillness that was strangely reminiscent of his sculptures. Jo shook her head and her hand made a gesture of denial. "Colin –"

He closed the gap between them. Before she could recoil he had pulled her close and was kissing her hard on the mouth.

"No." She averted her head, speaking firmly but with calmness, not wishing to instigate a scene. He grasped her arms and pulled her to him. "I said *no!*" she repeated, holding his gaze. "Let go, Colin," she warned, frightened now for real as his grip tightened. Hiding her fear, she met the challenge of his gaze with glassy-eyed defiance. For a moment they were locked in a silent battle of wills, then suddenly he released his grip. She stepped back, appalled by the anger and bitterness in his face.

"Who's the guy?"

Jo pushed her hair back off her face. "Guy?" she repeated.

He smiled unpleasantly. "The one you're holding in reserve."

Jo flushed. "That's totally unfair!"

"I agree, poor bastard, but its true."

"You know what I mean."

Jo gave him a long hard look then walked to the door and turned. "Not only unfair but hypocritical. You know what they say about glass houses," she said pointedly. "What about Finola?"

His eyes sparked anger, then were hooded by an arrogance and flippancy that chilled her far more. "You're right. I forgot she was making coffee. We'd better go or it will be cold."

Jo made a sound of disgust. "I don't believe this!"

He smiled at her words, obviously unrepentant. Jo shivered. The temperature in the barn had dropped to what felt like sub-zero degrees. A feeling of unreality assailed her, the sense of being caught up in a bizarre nightmare.

There was a strange sort of buzz in the air that crept over her skin, minute electrical impulses that ruffled the surface of normality.

She had to put a stop to this right now, dispel his delusions. "His name is Blake Durante, he's a conflict resolution officer with the U.N. in Bosnia – *not* in reserve," she emphasised. An ambiguous statement which she hoped would encourage Colin Gilmour to assume she and Blake were still an item. "You were good to me and gave help when it was most needed, and for that I'm still grateful," she added, "But for the rest – from now on –" She paused, frowning at his expression. In fact his whole demeanour had changed. He rubbed his forehead in distraction and appeared to crumple. Anger and bitterness seemed to leave him in a rush, like air from a punctured balloon.

"You're right. I'm sorry." He moved his head slowly from side to side and took a tentative step forward. "Please," he pleaded as she recoiled. "I don't know what got into me. Can we forget this happened?"

Jo hesitated, raising a hand to stem his apology. Was this guy schizoid or something? He had changed in a second, had reverted to the Colin she knew. He rumpled his his hair, suddenly appearing weary and drained of energy. "Look, give me a break Jo."

She deliberated: this man was to be her neighbour, and the last thing she needed was a vendetta. A woman living alone in a place like this needed friends. A calculating approach maybe, but a necessary one given her isolation. She shrugged. "No big deal. I think we understand one another now."

"Sure. Thanks – let's start over, eh?" He moved forward, smiling. "Sorry I upset you; must have been working too hard lately."

"Something like that," Jo agreed ironically.

The smile faded and the blasé tone changed. "I really am sorry. I don't make a habit of this sort of thing. In my defence, you're one attractive lady. Felt drawn to you straight off. There's something about you." He raised one slender-fingered hand and briefly touched her cheek. "Charisma," he murmured as though trying to explain to himself as much as Jo, so she didn't recoil. "Only a wee bit on the dark side too. Know what I mean?" He let his hand fall to his side and looked at her in silent appeal.

"Like you said, let's just forget it Colin," Jo said, retreating a step. Someone had thrown the switch. The current was beginning to flow again, arcing from Colin to herself: a crackle of energy leaping between two terminals and beyond their control.

Colin coughed and picked up on her cue. "I just don't get it. But you're right, we'd best go and get that coffee." He opened the door and stood aside for her to pass.

In silence they left the barn and returned to the house. Feeling that a strained atmosphere must inevitably arouse suspicion, Jo struck up conversation about the sculptures. As they entered the kitchen, Colin was talking animatedly, and any awkwardness was buried beneath enthusiasm for his work. In fact he seemed his normal self again.

The remainder of the visit passed uneventfully enough. Over coffee Finola demanded to know about Jo's life as a writer, and Jo trotted out amusing anecdotes about absent-mindedness, missed deadlines and writers' block. They laughed at her account of putting the milk bottle in the wardrobe and her shoes in the fridge following a midnight writing binge.

"I hope you don't drive in that state," Colin commented wryly, grinning over his cup.

Jo laughed easily; Colin had behaved impeccably since returning to the house. "Blake used to hide my keys till I'd come down," she said without thinking, then her laughter died, choked by the tight pain of nostalgia in her chest. She fell silent and picked up her coffee cup to hide her confusion.

"Your 'ex'?" Finola prompted intuitively, huge eyes brimming with sympathy. But there was also, Jo saw, a flicker of anxiety behind her concern. Finola saw her as unattached and therefore a potential threat. "Not exactly," Jo lied, recalling what she had told Colin in the barn. "But he's on a mission in Bosnia." She placed her cup back on her saucer, wincing as the lip at the base jarred against the spoon and the contents almost spilled on the table. "I miss him," she stated baldly with a challenging look for Colin.

"Have you heard from him?" Finola pressed, as though sensing the loss beneath Jo's words.

"Not since I came here," Jo admitted. "It's difficult," she explained as Finola and Colin exchanged meaningful glances. "The war, you know," she added tartly, hating herself for feeling the need to justify and explain, when let's face it, these two should be worrying about their own bizarre relationship. Seldom had she seen anyone as insecure as Finola; and Colin, judging by his behaviour in the barn, had an outsize ego problem and the emotional age of an adolescent.

"Yeah, sure." Colin threw Finola a warning look as she seemed about to press the issue further. Jo turned away as he looked across at her and frowned slightly, as though puzzled by her reaction to the subject.

She realised her right leg was jiggling, her foot softly tapping the rug, a sure sign according to Freud that she wished herself some place else. And a symptom of too much research into Ruskin's psyche, she thought wryly. Glancing at the clock above the door, its face had been hand painted with bluebells and hearts ease, she judged they had spent a good hour over coffee, and that she could therefore leave without causing offence. Despite the apparent normality, she was still aware of an underlying tension. Some of which, she admitted, emanated from herself: a sort of urgency, a nagging feeling that something remained to be done, but what the something was remained unclear. Whatever – time to leave.

"Well, thank you both so much. That was really enjoyable," she said pushing back her chair and rising to her feet.

"Oh, must you?" Finola said, looking genuinely sorry.

I might be a threat, but I'm also a buffer for their relationship, Jo realised shrewdly as Colin added his protest. "Sorry, work to do," she excused herself, strangely driven to go even whilst reluctant to leave the warmth, light and cosiness of the farmhouse kitchen. The spectre of loneliness and a cheerless cottage beckoned, and it was then, as Finola took down Jo's jacket from the hook in the hall and Jo put it on, that it hit. The real difference. The contrast on entering Throstle Garth had pointed up the alien atmosphere of Twilight Cottage. It wasn't just the cold that made it unwelcoming. The cottage felt actively hostile.

"Come again soon," Finola was saying, backed up by Colin. "Do you have everything you need at the cottage?

"Yes thanks. Everything that is except hot water," Jo said ruefully.

Colin frowned and pursed his lips. "Have you got the damper out?"

Jo laughed and stared at him nonplussed. "Have I – *what?*"

"The damper," he repeated impatiently. "There'll be a back boiler. Slip the poker through the ring and pull; the fire will draw – then you'll get hot water."

"How quaint!" Jo said camping it up so that Finola smiled and Colin scowled. "I'll go check that out right now. " She felt slightly foolish, but all this talk about 'dampers' certainly put things back into perspective. Blessed normality, she thought whilst taking leave of her new friends. She turned at the gate. "By the way, has somebody from the valley died?"

Colin frowned. "Old Maud Bickley. But why do you ask?"

Jo shrugged, tried to appear unconcerned. "Oh, the newly dug grave. I was exploring the churchyard," she added by way of explanation.

"Funeral's tomorrow," Finola contributed.

Jo repressed an involuntary shudder. "I shan't be watching! See you folks," and with a last wave she turned down the lane towards Twilight Cottage.

EIGHTEEN

~

On reaching the track however, Jo walked on. The nagging feeling had clarified: inexplicably there arose an urge to return to the church. So she carried on down the lane whilst trying to make sense of the whole thing. There must be an idea simmering away on the back burner of her subconscious, she decided, her pace automatically quickening. Something to do with the Ruskin book. Experience had taught her that the feeling wouldn't go away until she did something about it. That was the way her writing life worked, she reflected, glancing up at a clamour of rooks wheeling above the ancient yews that encircled the church like dark sentinels.

The *ka-aar kaar kaa'ing* of the rooks filled the cold air, and the grumbling of the river grew louder with her approach. The lych gate groaned as she pushed it open, a slightly ominous sound that reminded her not to stay overlong. The western sky was streaked with green and red, and on her inexperienced reckoning there was less than an hour before sundown. Giving her subconscious its head, she followed her instincts and trod the path to Maud Bickley's open grave.

She found herself looking surreptitiously around for prowlers, but saw no sign of the man Seth: nothing moved in the deep and ominous shadows cast by the yews. She listened for a moment to the cawing of the rooks, and to the flute and trill of a robin – always the last songster of the day. The only other sound was the brawling of the river, and the distant rumble of the waterfall splashing and dashing over the rocks before plunging into its stony basin. She stood for a moment staring down into the grave, wait-

ing for some sort of revelation. Either her subconscious was nap-
ping, or it wasn't letting on, she thought wryly. As a writer, she had
to follow her hunches, but that didn't stop her feeling foolish for
the second time that day.

Patience. Her subconscious was usually good for a nudge in the
right direction. But why here? To her knowledge, Ruskin had no
connections with this place. She frowned and absently kicked a
stone with the toe of her boot and watched it rattle over the stony
ground, then drop over the edge and into the grave with a dull and
ominous thud. Jo shivered. Seth Rigby's wife had mentioned that
her husband had 'dug Maud's grave'. A small spurt of excitement
quickened in her belly. Maybe this hunch had nothing to do with
the book; maybe Seth Rigby was the catalyst. She recalled his face
and demeanour as she rounded the corner and they came face to
face. The man had been disturbed, frightened even. But by what?
And why this feeling that he was linked to her in some way? There
was no obvious common denominator, nothing to place them on
the same chessboard, let alone in the same game.

Interesting speculation, but leading nowhere, she decided admitting defeat: this time her subconscious had been way off beam. A
glance at the green and purple streaked sky told her it was time to
leave. The yews were already hazed with twilight, and the hills
draped in amethyst gauze. No point in risking a repeat of last
night's horror. As she turned to leave, her foot struck something
hard and she almost stumbled. Looking down she saw it was a
shard of broken masonry. She stooped to examine it: a piece off an
old headstone maybe? In common with many churches, this one
had probably been built on the site of an earlier place of worship.
The fragment was too small to yield any significant information,
so she cast about for another piece. Instead her attention was
caught by a dark object protruding from the red soil around the
grave. She bent to pick it up and her fingers closed around it.
Metal, it had to be made of metal: it felt icy cold to her touch.

Love you, kill you . . . forever, you . . . forever

Her head whipped round at the whispered threat and the breath
caught in her throat. The words had sounded in her ear – or had

they merely been inside her head? Resembling a pale stone angel guarding a nearby tomb, Jo stood motionless, ears straining for any sound, arm instinctively raised in a gesture of defence.

Silence beat back from wall and yew and throbbed in her ears. Even the rooks were still. So much for a writer's over-active imagination. Jo shrugged and began to scrape at the red earth and rust that encrusted the surface of the object in her hand. A coin? Her heart beat a little faster. Whatever, it was corroded and very old. The metal appeared to be embossed, but maybe it was an effect of the corrosion. Perhaps it ought to be handed in. But to whom? The vicar? She supposed there would be a vicarage somewhere in the valley, but why should he be any more knowledgeable than herself on such matters?

It didn't take an expert however to realise this could be a significant find, and that her handling of it could cause irreparable damage. The realisation filled her with guilt, but on the other hand it may be of no value – and then she would feel an absolute idiot. No, she would have a proper look at it back at the cottage before speaking with the vicar. Then, if it *was* of historical value, he could report it to the appropriate authorities. Conscience appeased, Jo slipped it into her pocket and made her way to the gate.

It took some getting used to, the way the temperature plummeted without warning after sundown. In the time it took to walk from the church to the track which led to Twilight Cottage, the ground was already beginning to harden. Her breath stained the air white as she hurried with care over the rutted earth. It was darker here than in the lane, the light scarcely penetrated the tangle of branches and evergreens. An owl screeched and bats fluttered about her head. From time to time she turned and looked nervously over her shoulder. No shadow seemed to be dogging her footsteps tonight. A sigh of relief escaped her as she entered the clearing, and the walls of Twilight Cottage gleamed palely in the gloom.

As she entered, the contrast with Throstle Garth immediately made an impression. The penetrating chill for a start. The fire must be out: on her approach there had been no smoke curling from the chimney. *But this is mega-cold.* And dark. In fact the darkness in the hall was so thick it was a tangible thing, muffling all sound and filling her nostrils and mouth so that she could scarcely breathe. She reached for the switch to turn the hall light on. Her fingers touched something cold, wet and slimy that moved beneath her hand.

NINETEEN

~

Her own scream compounded her fright. It fled up the stairs then hit the landing wall and ricocheted back, the echo surrounding her like the ripples of Munch's 'cry'. Her hand felt sticky. Retching with shock and disgust, she scrubbed it up and down on her jacket to rid it of slime whilst stumbling towards the sitting room. Once there she cautiously felt for the light switch. Like the pincers of some pale and nervous crab, Jo's fingers crept stealthily over the wall, the tips hovering, then brushing to test the surface before making contact and inching forward again. She held her breath, muscles of her arm tensed to withdraw at the slightest touch. Her fingers encountered the light switch and she heaved a sigh of relief. Light flooded the room and spilled into the hall. She turned slowly, afraid of what she might see.

An exclamation of disgust escaped her lips. Six or seven fat slugs, black and glistening, moved turgidly around the switch, their movements charted by streaks of silvery slime. She stared in disbelief, unable to make sense of the situation. Where had they come from? Wildly she looked about her, scanning doors, walls and ceilings for evidence of more invaders, but found none. She ran into the kitchen and turning on the tap, stuck her hand beneath the icy flow to sluice it clean. Throwing the towel onto a chair, she stood for a moment thinking, then hurried into the sitting room. Snatching up poker and shovel from the hearth she took a deep breath and returned to the hall. One by one she scraped the creatures off the wall and flung them outside. By the time she had finished her stomach was heaving. Her limbs were shaking with cold; it was even colder inside the cottage after working with the front door open. She banged it shut and rammed home the bolt. But the fire could wait, this came first. Jacket off and sleeves up and never mind the cold. After scrubbing the painted wall with Dettol and hot water from the kettle, she finally felt satisfied.

Now for the fire. The paper was damp – like everything in this bloody place she thought furiously, striking her fifth match. This one didn't splutter and die, but burned with a steady flame as she held it to the kindling which smouldered sullenly and gave off clouds of dense blue smoke, but at least it didn't go out. Then she remembered Colin's advice and scraped about on the fire back for the damper. The effect was immediate as flames were sucked by the back draught, and before long a cheerful blaze filled the hearth and the atmosphere in the room immediately improved. Thank God, she thought eying a basket bulging with logs, she had thought to fill it before going out. After this welcome, a trip to the shed in darkness would have been definitely out of the question.

Getting up from her knees she picked up a bottle of whisky from the top of the bureau and poured herself a generous measure. She swallowed and waited for the burn to hit, closing her eyes briefly as it fired her stomach. Hell but that was good. She took another sip and wandered into the kitchen glass in hand, trying to decide what to eat. The thought of cooking and eating a meal turned her stomach, which wasn't surprising. She buttered some bread and added a slice of cheese and a tomato. A shudder ran through her: the warmth hadn't yet penetrated the kitchen. She returned to the sitting room and huddled over the fire, sipping her whisky and trying to figure out why there should be slugs in the hall during winter, and how they had got there.

The bread and cheese marginally restored her vitality. It was time to do some more work, yet somehow the notion didn't appeal. Listlessly she shifted on her seat as guilt niggled. But then, she rationalised, the computer was best left till daylight – given the morning's strange occurrence. *But you don't wriggle out that easy, Cavanagh!* There was reading to be done, plenty of research on

Ruskin. She rose and moved towards the bookcase, then recalling the thing still waiting in her pocket, stopped short. The trauma of coming back to the cottage had driven it completely from her mind. Sorry Ruskin: no contest. Her jacket was still on the back of a chair in the kitchen. Her fingers fumbled in their haste, found the object and withdrew it into the light.

She sat at the table by the fire and placed it on a newspaper. With painstaking care, Jo scraped away the impacted earth to expose the underlying metal. It was badly corroded. Silently she worked on, oblivious to her surroundings and totally absorbed in her task. She gasped as the knife went through the centre, the point emerging the other side. At first this perplexed her, then trying to contain her impatience she turned the blade, fraction by fraction, thus widening the gap. Particles rained down on the paper. She exclaimed aloud as the centre plug of impacted earth hit the newspaper with a dull thud. Not a coin after all, but *a ring*. And given the size – a man's ring. She stopped work and picked up the plug, staring hard at it and gently turning it over on her palm. Was it really impacted earth? The soil encrusting the actual metal was the red iron-rich earth of the cemetery, but this was black and fibrous, jagged at the ends.

A worm of doubt began to stir and uncoil in her stomach. Was she looking at blackened and disintegrating bone? Experimentally she rolled the fragment between her index finger and thumb, then watched as it crumbled to dust. Had the ring still been on its owner's finger? It was possible. In digging Maud's grave, Seth Rigby could have unknowingly unearthed an earlier burial; maybe one so old that the exposed part would be unidentifiable. Had his spade smashed through the decaying bone of a hand? *Kill you, love you . . . love forever*. She screamed as a shadow fell across the table.

Heart pounding, she whirled around. A glimpse, then it was gone. A human form, a shadow – and the feeling of maleness rather than woman. An image came clearly to mind: a blackened hand stretching from the grave, fist clenched in a gesture of triumph over Death. The gleam of metal and a flash of green. She rubbed her eyes. The concept of the hand had been inside her own head, but not the figure. Fearfully she looked around the room, saw nothing unusual. But the temperature had dropped. A chill was creeping through it, despite the glow from the fireplace.

Jo shivered. There was a thickening of the atmosphere as though the space around her wasn't really empty, and a low-current electrical buzz that she was beginning to recognise. Then a flashback of memory, of whirling through the darkness once more. He was there just as before, waiting at the end of the tunnel. In slow motion he lifted his hand to beckon, and the emerald ring on his finger blazed green fire – then he was gone.

Her temples ached and her immediate surroundings were blurred as those viewed through a rain-washed window. Her hand went to her head, distractedly stroked her temple. Hesitantly she picked up the ring from the table. Do I really want to know? she asked herself. Despite her misgivings and hands that shook, she took the knife and using the tip, carried on scraping away the encrusted earth and rust. And there it was: a dull green glow that brightened as she gently rubbed with a soft cloth. The green of an emerald gemstone. More debris flaked away and the tip of her knife revealed a heavy claw setting. Jo held the ring between finger and thumb, turning it first this way, then that, so that it blazed briefly as the light struck a facet and was refracted. *The same green as his eyes.* That same lambent green that had flared with such anger. Battered and corroded it may be, but Jo knew beyond a shadow of doubt that she had seen this ring before.

Agitated she rose to her feet. I can't handle this, she thought: it's too heavy by half. So why not turn it in? It was obviously of value, not only because of the precious stone but also its antiquity. The find should be reported, all the evidence handed over for analysis. But then there would be repercussions: publicity and unwelcome fuss. So why not put it away somewhere and forget? Pretend this never happened. it wouldn't matter: no-one else knows about it. *Keep it. Put it away somewhere – it can do no harm.* An insistent voice argued inside her head. Gradually she became aware of subtly being dissuaded from parting with the ring.

She chewed at her bottom lip, then in a decisive movement scooped up the paper and tipped the fragments onto the fire. There, that settled the issue; she couldn't very well report her find now with the evidence wilfully destroyed. But she could replace the ring in the churchyard, drop it into old Maud Bickley's grave. That way nothing would have changed, she could pretend it had never happened. Impulsively deciding to carry through her decision, Jo snatched up the ring. She cried out as a sharp bit of metal, twisted and distorted by corrosion, pierced the fleshy mound at the base of her thumb. A dark bead of blood welled up, then another. Cursing beneath her breath she dropped the ring and blotted the puncture wounds with a tissue, then hurried to the bathroom. Rusty metal could be dodgy, she worried, holding her thumb beneath the running tap. Especially when it came from a graveyard. After dabbing on some Savlon, she stuck on a plaster and returned to the sitting room. Gingerly picking up the ring she dropped it into a drawer of the writing bureau. It could stay there for now; a trip to the graveyard in the dark was out of the question. The thought that her injury had been engineered with exactly this in mind did cross her mind, but was instantly dismissed as being insane. You're losing your marbles being here on your own, she mocked herself.

Nonetheless immediately the ring was out of sight her mood improved. But the atmosphere didn't. The chill and damp crept into her bones. And there was a strange air of expectancy, like on New Year's Eve for instance only not so pleasant. She frowned, her nostrils flaring slightly, then put back her head like a scenting dog and sniffed again. There was an odd smell in the room. She sniffed again experimentally. It wasn't her imagination. An odour of must and mildew which was perhaps only to be expected – but so strong. The furrows in her forehead deepened; and there was something else, something lurking just below the threshold of recognition. Then she had it: for some reason it brought to mind the night before Grandmother Cavanagh's funeral.

She had been close to Gran, Jo recalled, sitting down again at the fire. It had been her first experience of death at close quarters, so possibly the one which made the greatest impact. Eleven-year-olds are very impressionable and she had been an over-sensitive kid – signs of the writer to come perhaps. There had been a sense of fear yes, for the unknown, but also a horrible sort of excitement, the feeling that something momentous was about to happen, as though normality was suspended, and there was an increased sense of vulnerablilty. She remembered feeling like a snail or a tortoise without its shell. Something to do with our mortality, she supposed now, staring into the flames. Before that night, death was something that happened to someone else, in other folk's families and homes. Then suddenly the Spectre was standing on the stairs casting its dark shadow over their lives. It left with Gran, and nothing would ever be quite the same again.

Anyway, where was she? Oh yes, that was it: the thing that had stayed with her all her life was that strange and sickly odour as she stood by the open coffin the night before the funeral. To 'say goodbye to Gran' as her mother had put it. It flooded back, the odour of lilies, freshly-snuffed candles and Death. She had slipped from the room, bolted for the toilet and puked.

And the same sort of odour was present in this room. So what was going on here? Making a sudden decision she picked up the telephone and dialled Louise's number.

"Hi – Louise? It's me, Jo. Yes, fine," she lied, rubbing her forearm and glancing over her shoulder. "Well, actually, I wanted to ask you –," suddenly she was sick of pussyfooting around, this was now serious stuff. "The cottage, Louise. When you stayed here – were you happy with it?" she demanded. The silence told her, even before Louise began to speak.

"I was happy enough with Callum," came the cautious reply.

"That's not what I asked." There was an even longer silence, then:

"O.K. honey. I'll come clean. I have to say 'no' – I was never really at ease there."

"You should have said," Jo accused. "You know how important atmosphere is when I'm writing."

"I thought it was just me, Jo. You know, the guilt about his wife and kids, the usual stuff. And territory. I was out of my patch there; I'm a dedicated townie whilst Callum smelled of moors and mountains. To be honest darling, I was glad when Hank came on the scene and there was no longer any need to visit that godforsaken cottage."

Jo pushed back her hair. "Was there anything specific about the place?"

"Like I said: I just wasn't at ease. Why – what is it, Jo?"

"Oh, I guess the whole thing went wrong from day one, you know with the accident and everything. Anyway I came home in the dark this evening after lunching with Colin and Finola, and instead of the light switch found myself groping half a dozen or so fat black slugs," she quipped, playing it down.

Louise made an exclamation of disgust. *"Shit!* In the hall?"

Jo felt a perverse glow of satisfaction. "Precisely. Doesn't help one to warm to the place. Speaking as such, was it always so bloody cold in here?"

"Can't say I noticed, but then –"

Jo sighed with exasperation as Louise's throaty laughter came down the line. "I know – *Callum*," she said, grinning despite her worries.

"Yes, I was pretty wrapped up in him at the time! But *slugs*, Jo! On the wall? Where the hell did they come from?"

"You tell me."

"There was never anything like that. Just –" Louise hesitated before continuing: "well, a sort of atmosphere. Didn't feel quite right, if you know what I mean."

"I do," Jo commented dryly. "No funny smells?" she added, feeling faintly ridiculous.

Louise hesitated. "A bit musty after being shut up between visits. But par for the course I'd say, with such an old place."

"I'm sure you're right." Jo coiled a tendril of hair around her finger as doubts crept in again. Maybe she was making a big fuss about nothing.

"I take it you're coming back to London."

It was Jo's turn to be hesitant. "I'm not a quitter," she said at last.

"Look, you don't have to do this. There's no earthly reason why you should stay if you don't want. I won't be offended."

"No, but I haven't really given it a chance. And," Jo sighed, "after all this fuss, it would be a bit of an anti-climax. No, let's see how it goes."

"Okay Jo, your decision. I suppose now you're there –"

"Absolutely. And I have made a start on the book."

"Great! Keep it coming Jo."

"I will." Jo could tell that Louise was putting her twitchiness down to 'writer's temperament'.

"If you want me to cast an eye over – send the manuscript when you have the first hundred pages or so. But of course I'm happy for you to just bash on. Okay? Good. Must dash Jo; Hank will be waiting . . . Dame Kiri and Domingo in concert you know."

"Sure. Great. See you Louise."

Feeling Louise and her world were a million light years away, Jo replaced the receiver.

Before going upstairs to bed, she felt compelled to take a last look at the ring. It drew her like a magnet, yet at the same time repelled and filled her with anxiety. She stood for a moment looking down at it then closed the drawer. You don't know the half of it Louise, she thought grimly. Unconsciously she picked at the plaster at the base of her thumb with the nail of her index finger, then stopped as the movement of the dressing made the wound throb.

Twitching back the curtain she peered outside. The few remaining leaves on oak and rowan hung from the branches like shrivelled and dejected bats subdued by the onslaught of frost. The very air seemed to scintillate with brittle cold, the clearing to be cryogenically preserved in a wash of moonlight and mist reminiscent of nitrogen vapour. It was also breathtaking, she acknowledged. Crystal-fire sparked from branch and hedgerow, and blue rime traced the peaks of the mud furrows on the ground. In stark contrast shadows lurked beneath tree and hedgerow, and patches of ice gleamed like ominous pools of black and fathomless ink.

Writhing out of sight beneath the tunnel of blackthorn, holly and yew the track led into darkness, secrecy and enchantment, a path out of a child's fairy tale, and twice as sinister. Jo shivered. Letting the curtain fall back into place, she backed up the fire with logs and smothered the glow with chippings and damp tea-leaves. With a bit of luck it would smoulder beneath the mulchy mess until morning.

After heating some milk in the kitchen she paused on the threshold, mug in hand, mentally checking that the back door was bolted and window latched before turning off the light. It was then that she saw it: a dark shadow that moved in the second or so between the click of the switch and the room being plunged into darkness. A shot of adrenalin to the stomach made her gasp. Another click and the room was flooded once more with light. Heart thumping Jo scanned the kitchen. Nothing moved.

She was about to turn and go upstairs, but then frowned and crossed to the back door, dropping down on one knee. Small piles of reddish earth littered the stone flag. Her heart once more began to race. Freshly-turned soil, like that at the churchyard. Her breath caught in her throat and her tongue passed nervously over lips that were suddenly dry. But then she gave a little shake of her head in self-denial of her fear. It had probably lodged in a fold of her clothing and fallen out as she bolted the door earlier that evening. Easily enough done, and easily overlooked in the trauma of her homecoming. Yes, that had to be the answer. Resolutely she turned off the light.

It was on rounding the twist in the stairs that she sensed it again: the presence that had thickened the air of the sitting room. A stair behind her creaked with a report like a gun shot in the silence. Heart in mouth, she whipped round. The shadow again, glimpsed out of the corner of her eye – then gone. Something brushed by her side. Nothing tangible: more an icy blast of air that chilled her to the bone. She shuddered and rubbed her arm with a hand that shook, hovered there for a moment trying to compose herself by telling herself it was a bad attack of nerves. A draught from the front door, only to be expected in an old place like this. For God's sake, the whole of the cottage was draughty and damp. This masterly piece of rationalisation carried her up the stairs and into the bedroom.

So why couldn't she rid herself of the feeling that something had passed her on the stair?

Having drunk her milk and read several pages of an Iris Murdoch novel without taking in a single word, she lay down and tried to sleep. The place felt colder than ever tonight. Icy – and damp with it. She huddled beneath the quilt clutching a hot water bottle discovered in the bathroom, which let's face it, wasn't quite Louise's style. Why the hell had Louise needed it anyway – given Callum? The thought made her smile and for the moment things seemed more normal. Old fashioned or no, the bottle was a marvellous comforter. And she needed comfort, more than ever before in her life. The image of Louise snuggling up to Callum turned her thoughts inevitably to Blake, and sadness filled the space at her side in the bed. Where was he now, and what was he doing? *Oh God, keep him safe*, she prayed as the hot tears escaped her eyelids and scalded her icy cheeks. If he were to walk in now, it would take less than five seconds to throw herself into his arms. But the decision to leave had been his, and spilt milk and all that . . . With a sigh she tossed her copy of *The Sea, The Sea* down to the foot of the bed then turned on her side and tried to sleep.

In the crystal air the beck ran extra loud, despite the fact that the window was closed. Jo tried not to notice the voice beneath the tumble and spill of water over stone, it was too easy to put words to the muttering. Even the covers pulled up around her ears didn't completely shut out the sound. Gradually though her eyelids grew heavy and she slipped into uneasy sleep.

The wolf confronted her, eyes glowing green in the dark and yellowed fangs dripping saliva as, head back and mouth gaping, it loosed its howl on the night. She awoke with a start, lay staring up at the plaster between the ceiling beams, her mind still befogged by sleep. A nightmare? But sound had not drifted back into subconsciousness along with the visual dream. Her blood tingled along her veins as the wail rose again and haunted the night. Desperately she tried to order her scattered thoughts, make sense of the chaos. It was freezing in the bedroom; her body was shaking from cold and fear. No not dreaming. There it was again, a shriek that now she was fully awake brought to mind tales not so much of the wolf as the Irish Banshee: the Banshee Woman who wailed to warn families of the approach of Death. This is how it must have sounded, a pitiful but also angry wail of despair, muffled and echoing, a keening from another world.

Silence now. A silence that pressed against her eardrums and hurt her eyeballs because it contained expectancy of the next onslaught. Petrified and not daring to move she huddled beneath the quilt. Her limbs were aching with tension, so was her stomach but she daren't let go, could not afford to release the strain that was holding her screams under control. A movement out of the corner of her eye made her gasp in fear. Her head turned on the pillow, then her breath was exhaled on a near-sob of relief. It was the curtain, that was all, the curtains billowing in the wind.

And that was the explanation for everything, wasn't it? The wind howling and shrieking in the chimney. But what a wind, and so sudden in onset. It was roaring through the trees, creating the initial boom of a muffled depth-charge, then rising like columns of spume to the banshee-pitch that had dragged her consciousness into the waking nightmare. She cried out as a twig or some other object was hurled against the pane with sharp report. An icy draught whistled beneath the door, causing the mat to undulate as though shaken by an unseen hand. The curtains ballooned and flapped like living things, swiping a china figurine to the floor with a crash. Everything was noise and motion: a maelstrom of energy with the cottage at its centre. Only her body at the eye of the hurricane remained still.

A dreadful wail rose above the roaring, flapping and whistling. Despite the freezing cold, sweat beaded her upper lip and trickled down her armpit. It had to be the wind howling in the chimney and round the eaves. But never before had Nature made such a sound, and neither had Jo known such fear. The room was filled with it so that she tasted her own terror, and the air around her vibrated with dread. A rank odour of mustiness and decay made her want to vomit. She yearned to stretch out to the bedside lamp, flood the corner with comforting light but dare not move.

She lay like that for maybe a half hour or more, staring wildly into the darkness, her body rigid and unmoving, Gradually the movement and noise subsided and slowly but surely her aching muscles began to relax. Released from the panic-induced paralysis she switched on the light. Bathed in its comfort she began to breathe normally again and the room felt less cold. Even so, had the car been standing outside instead of in some remote garage awaiting parts, she would have been out of this hell hole and on her way back to London. But the car wasn't outside, so there was nothing for it but to shut off her mind, close her eyes and steel herself to wait for morning. After ten minutes or so she switched the lamp off again and lay back against the pillows. Maybe now sleep would come.

At first she put it down to an overworked imagination. That and the proximity of sleep: her mind was drifting, almost but not quite slumbering but enough to cause confusion. No, there it was again. The sound rasped through the night and sank through the various levels of consciousness to bring her fully awake. A scratching and scrabbling that set her nerves on edge. Mice. It had to be mice. Or given the volume – rats. She shuddered at the mental image of a thick-set body and long leathery tail. She sat up as the rasping became more frantic, terrified of seeing a pair of red eyes glinting from some corner.

Her hand groped for the light switch. That's better. She peered into corners, alert for any movement or glint of eye. No, nothing – just that horrible noise, and the thickening of the atmosphere she had felt downstairs. A horrible feeling, even with the light on, a tangible thing that touched her flesh with invisible fingers and crawled all over her body. The sensation as Seth Rigby passed her in the graveyard leapt to mind, and the feeling earlier that night on the stairs. Her eyes widened in terror: it felt as though there was somebody here in the room, a sense of presence so strong that it couldn't be put down to imagination. Yet the room appeared to be empty. Her gaze raked the shadow beside the wardrobe, then the dark corner between dressing table and recess but nothing moved. The noise continued, louder now and more frenzied as though something was trapped and fighting to escape. A bat maybe or some kind of bird. Yes, that had to be it. Her gaze went to the ceiling, yet it didn't seem to be coming from the loft but from downstairs. Swinging her legs out of bed she thrust her feet into her slippers and flung a dressing gown round her shoulders.

It was freezing on the stairs. Shivering uncontrollably she clicked on the landing light and crept stealthily down to the hall. The scrabbling continued, was definitely louder down here. The sound led her to the kitchen; some creature must have got itself trapped in there. A bird perhaps or even a stray cat. The possibility of opening the door to be confronted by a rat did briefly cross her mind, but was instantly dismissed. This was not the sound of teeth on wood and rats, she consoled herself, gnawed all the time; she remembered reading somewhere that it was necessary because their teeth grew so quick, and shuddered at the image this brought to mind.

She paused in creeping along the hall, aware of a sudden silence. Her stomach buzzed as though an electrified probe had been inserted. *It was as though someone was listening to her approach*. But there it goes again, slowly at first then gaining momentum. Something about it rattled her, wound her up, created an unbearable tension. Then she knew what: it was the sense of urgency the sound conjured up, evoking within herself a similar sense of panic. As she approached the kitchen the atmosphere thickened and the noise increased in volume. Her hand shook as it grasped the latch. Summoning all her courage she pushed the door wide and snapped on the light.

TWENTY

~

The clopping of hooves on stone penetrated Madeline's chamber. She laid down her hairbrush and sombrely studied her face in the mirror; it reflected her frustration and fear. She sighed and rising from her stool crossed the bed chamber and leaned from the casement to watch her husband's stallion canter into the courtyard below. With a snorting and flashing of burnished hooves it stopped in response to its master's knees and firm hands. He rode her like that, but with less care and consideration; a distinguished horseman and clumsy lover, Madeline thought with distaste, watching him dismount. Now that he was back from his meeting with the King there would be no slipping out to meet Antony, at least not tonight.

Thoughts of Antony brought a glow deep down inside. She imagined her hands stroking his taut and muscled body, felt the tenderness and strength of his arms around her, and the power of his youth and vigour as they made love beneath the stars. And those eyes. Green as the emerald he wore on his finger. Sometimes dancing with laughter like water in sunlight, at others dark with passion, the deep enigmatic green of the jade that Justin brought back from the Crusades.

Thoughts of her husband brought her attention back to the mud-spattered figure in the courtyard. As though sensing her scrutiny he turned and looked up at the casement. He stood motionless like that for a full minute, his face sombre, and with a darkness about him. Her lovely eyes clouded and her hand went to her throat. She had to force herself to remain, not to rush and hide from her husband's powerful presence.

Did he suspect? Holy Mother of God, surely not? The cold hand of fear released its hold on her throat. No, it was alright. Justin was waving, a thin smile on his upturned face, the best she was likely to get. She waved back, laughing in her relief. Sure once more of her power, she descended the stairs to meet him.

When Jo opened the kitchen door the sound had abruptly ceased. She stood for a while on the threshold, listening and waiting, then exhaled her fear and tension on a long sigh of relief as the silence settled, albeit as uneasily as a nun's veil on a whore's head. She almost decided on a another cup of hot milk, but the temptation to run back to bed and hide beneath the covers had proved too strong. On her return the bedroom felt cold but 'uninhabited'. Chilled, miserable and stressed she lay coiled in the bed in foetal position, having half made up her mind to return to London, by rail and coach if necessary. But then the wind had dropped, the chill had lessened and the silence inside the cottage was absolute. So was the loneliness. As the immediate threat faded, Jo found herself thinking of Blake. The atmosphere was somehow conducive to it: the very walls and ceiling beams seemed impregnated with yearning and a sense of loss. Desolation engulfed her, that and disbelief at the turn her life had taken. Her isolation, her alienation from any other living being seemed complete. The longing to feel Blake's arms about her became so intense it reduced her to tears. Eventually she had fallen asleep from sheer exhaustion.

However by mid morning of the following day she was feeling much better. For one thing the car was back. It stood outside the front door, good as new and a reassuring passport to freedom. Strange, but now that she could leave at any time, there wasn't the same compulsion to do. She looked up from her computer to watch the acrobatics of blue tits and tiny coal tits as they nibbled the pieces of cheese she had strung on a length of string. Also the sun was shining, latticing the newly thawed ground beyond the window with bare-branch shadow patterns. And she had managed a good morning's work on the book, she mentally added, aware that she was compiling arguments in favour of staying on at the cottage. She finished reading the last sheet of her print-out and put it to one side. Ruskin was coming alive through the words on the pages. Yes, things were definitely better.

Except for the cut on her hand. In fact it was giving her a fair bit of pain. She peeled off the plaster and frowning, studied her palm. The fleshy base of her thumb was red and swollen, and overnight the puncture mark had turned a nasty shade of blue. Taking herself off to the bathroom she bathed it in Savlon and hot water – at least the damper had worked and a bath was on for tonight – and applied a fresh dressing.

Thoughtfully she returned to the sitting room and took the ring from the bureau drawer. It nestled in her palm almost, she mused, as though it belonged there. The elaborate claws seemed to grip her memory. They were, she could see now, wrought in gold to resemble the claws of a bird of prey. An eagle *or a hawk*. Why did that also tug at her memory? Stronger than ever came the conviction that she could not hand this ring over to faceless officials, to be pored over, catalogued and displayed.

Picking up the soft cloth she had been using the previous night, she rubbed gently, dislodging still more impacted earth and rust then held the ring up to the light, moving it first this way then that. Suddenly the stone caught and blazed, momentarily dazzling her with its power. In that split second she saw him. There by the window, scarlet hawk emblazoned on chest, green eyes lambent with fire, and the emerald glowing on his outstretched hand. There, yet not there. A Turner water colour image: form shimmering and distorted, colours and edges vibrating and melting into light. At once yearning and excitement coursed through her, yet at the same time the hairs at the nape of her neck prickled with fear. A lethal concoction of love and deadly threat. She blinked; the image was gone.

Jo raised her hand and stroked her forehead. A trick of the imagination, she told herself, replacing the ring in the drawer. Something to do with the accident. Yes, that seemed likely. The image was already there, dated back to the bump on her head. A set of neural connections and firings that had somehow become fixed, an illusory image unable to fade and disintegrate as it normally would. She frowned and let her hand drop to her side. But what had triggered this latest delusion? Her mind switched to replay, scanning the last few moments of the scene. The ring, the emerald, the flash of green fire as she held it up to the window. An effect of sunshine dazzling through glass perhaps? Her face cleared as she recalled reading somewhere that sunlight flashing through foliage could trigger an epileptic-type fit in otherwise healthy cyclists or motorists. Maybe she should go back and have a word with Dr. Cahill about it, but the possibility of neural damage was scary stuff. Her chest felt constricted, her heartbeat disrupted. No, ignore it for now, and hope to God it doesn't recur.

Time for a walk. To get out of this claustrophobic tardis of a cottage and catch a breath of sanity. Going into the hall she pulled on boots and extra socks and shrugged into her thick woollen jacket. Wrapping a scarf around her neck and stuffing her hands into mittens, she opened the door and stepped outside.

The gorse bushes on the open fell behind the cottage made her give an involuntary gasp of pleasure. Spangled with droplets of moisture now that the frost had melted, they shimmered with an ethereal beauty. Each prickly branch hosted a million prisms that vibrated with colour as the sun glanced through. Such a land of contrasts. The ancient dry stone walls, mocking the transience of the moment, snaked over the fell, dark and solid and built to last for ever. Yet there was variety here too, she found removing her glove: lichens the colour of verdigris felt rough beneath her fingers, but then gave way to cushions of damp moss that soothed and cooled her burning palm.

She climbed higher onto an outcrop of rock then turned to look back. The valley spread below, a patchwork of green latticed with dry stone walls and flanked by banks of bracken, winter bronzed and copper dusted, the colour of dried blood. Here and there a whitewashed cottage or granite-built farmhouse intruded, and in the middle distance sat the village: a huddle of cottages, their upper storeys inclining towards one another as though enjoying a gossip.

And viewed from here the river – its roar muted by atmosphere and distance – was a ribbon of silver winding past a miniature pottery church. She looked away. The church was reminding her of things she would rather forget.

But then it began. The tolling of the bell, in sombre monotone, rising and echoing around the fells. Ancient recognition stirred as the bell summoned the living to come bury their dead. She had forgotten about the funeral. *Ask not for whom the bell tolls . . .* The sound struck a chord deep within, dredged up the immortal lines but with new and chilling significance that had little to do with old Maud Bickley's passing. The wound on her hand throbbed, and the sun was blotted out by dark clouds from the past. She picked her way back down the fell, the tolling of the bell growing louder with each step of her precipitous descent. She quickened her pace, having no desire to witness the unknown Maud's funeral.

But was not quite quick enough. As she reached the shelf of volcanic rock protruding above and behind Twilight Cottage, she stopped dead. From here there was an uninterrupted view over the trees to the lane below and beyond. Jo watched with morbid fascination, an unwilling but mesmerised observer. Never had she seen a funeral such as this. No shiny impersonal limousine ferried the deceased to the church. In a scene from a previous century, Maud was borne to her resting place on the shoulders of six solemn-faced men. If she *can* rest there, Jo found herself thinking. The foot-procession was a necessity, she now realised: any limo attempting passage would be in danger of getting stuck. Not to mention having its flanks scarred for life. Even so it was an eerie sight.

Who were they, these men who bore the weight of a coffin and life on their ancient shoulders? Past school friends maybe? Could be: each looked old and lined enough to occupy that indecently new pine box. A husband? Could the youngest of the men be a son? The age-old and fear-driven fascination of someone's else's death kept Jo riveted to the spot.

The mourners too were all on foot. The two leading ones – a man accompanied by a woman wearing a black overcoat and headscarf

– carried a wreath. Several of those walking behind carried simple posies or sprays. The bell tolled on, the sound thrown back by flanking walls of rock with an eerie 'ghosting' effect. There was no other sound. Even the bleating of sheep and lowing of cattle in the surrounding fields were stilled.

It was then that she saw him. The last in the file of mourners, and instantly recognisable despite the white shirt and dark suit donned for the occasion. *Seth Rigby*. The woman by his side must be his wife. Fascinated Jo watched, able now to put a face to the female voice that had spoken over the telephone. She noted the stout build, straight back and broad shoulders of the farmer's wife; the slightly swaying and long pace of a woman used to striding the fields to herd cattle and sheep. And then the man at her side stopped dead. Jo instinctively shrank back. Seth Rigby stared up at the fell as though alerted and drawn by her presence.

Jo shivered as though at indefinable contact. His stance suggested tension and something else: a complicity, a shared secret. The strangeness stretched between them, linking them by an invisible cord. He stood like that for several seconds, until his wife's head bobbed urgently forward and she whispered in his ear. He stared at her a moment longer, then carried on walking behind the coffin.

A thin cry keened overhead. Tearing her gaze from the retreating figure of Seth Rigby, Jo looked up. Above her a hawk circled, wings almost motionless as it glided in search of prey.

TWENTY-ONE

~

Jo poured another cup of coffee. The encounter with Seth Rigby had thrown her out of gear. What did he know? What had happened to him? The obvious solution would be to go and talk to him, but given his hostile attitude towards her he would be unlikely to respond. She finished her coffee; the caffeine hit and she rose to her feet as the idea struck: *but his wife might*. Time to wander down to the churchyard. She put on her boots and jacket again and glanced at the clock. The funeral service and committal should be over now, and if she timed it right, this may be the chance to get some answers.

As she entered the churchyard by way of the lych gate, she was met by the chop and grate of shovel striking earth. There was no-one in sight; the funeral party it seemed, had departed. Seth had dug Maud's grave, she recalled, and must now be about the business of filling it in. But she then remembered that he was a mourner and would hardly be working in his best suit. This was borne out she rounded the curve in the path. Two men wearing gum boots and navy overalls were engaged in piling earth into the newly-occupied grave. On hearing the rasp of her boots on the gravelled path, the older of the two men looked up, nodded curtly and carried on wielding his spade. "Good afternoon," Jo responded, averting her eyes out of respect. She had been about to turn and go, but here was an opportunity for research. The lights were on in the church, which probably meant the vicar was still within. It wouldn't be in very good taste to barge in there and start asking questions, given what had just taken place. But if she hung about, timed it right.

She hadn't much fancied getting in close, but writers had no business being squeamish, she reminded herself, effecting great interest in the floral tributes that were still arranged in a row on the grass.

"Knew old Maud, did you?" the man who had nodded asked, pausing to lean on his spade.

"No, actually I didn't. I was just going to have a look round the church. My neighbours did mention it – forgot the funeral was today."

"Oh aye. Neighbour eh?" The man drew a khaki coloured handkerchief from his overall pocket and wiped first his forehead then his mouth. "You moved in hereabouts then?" he asked, stuffing the handkerchief back into his pocket. His weathered face had brightened, Jo noticed, and his eyes, corners scored by lines and looking as though they often squinted into the sun, sharpened with interest. The younger man – his son possibly given the same broad nose and keen eyes – also looked up and subjected her to unabashed scrutiny but remained silent. Any newcomer must be a source of curiosity, she realised, glancing quickly at the church porch. *Come on Vicar, where are you?* "I'm over-wintering at Twilight Cottage," she explained.

The leathery face of the older man split in a grin. "You're the lass that got stuck on top of yon pass then?"

"Yes, that was me," she said ruefully, catching a movement out of the corner of her eye but pretending not to notice. Obviously news travelled fast on the valley drums. "Lucky for me, Colin Gilmour was passing at the time."

"Oh aye, sculptor feller?"

"That's right."

She pretended to be startled at the voice from behind: "But I believe he's not the only one with a claim to fame."

Jo turned to face the vicar.

He wasn't exactly what she had been expecting, she thought giving him a surreptitious look as he accompanied her to the lych gate. Instead of being white haired, portly and benign as any rural vicar had a right to be, this one was about thirty six or seven at a guess, with unruly black locks and a trendy beard. He had exchanged his funereal regalia for faded denims tucked into boots, a Guernsey sweater, leather flying jacket and simple clerical collar. An unconventional cleric, she thought with a smile, politely answering the spate of inevitable questions about her life as a writer. She still hadn't got used to 'being famous'. Still, like Colin Gilmour, he didn't seem over-impressed and to her relief soon dropped the subject.

He paused, half turned and gave her a look of challenge. "You could have come to the service, you know. Everyone's welcome."

"I didn't want to intrude."

"Old Maud wouldn't have minded," he said equably, holding the gate for her to pass through.

She smiled. "No, probably not."

He closed the gate. "Will we be seeing you in church?"

She gave him a direct look. "I doubt it, vicar."

"Shame. And it's John Penrose, but everyone calls me John, so feel free to do the same." He swung round to face her. "But as far as beliefs go, we're pretty liberal here, you know. Have to be."

"Oh, how's that?"

"Farming community, the old ways. Here The Great Mother rubs shoulders with the Father. Earth Mother, Sky Father – No problem. So whatever your thing, feel free to join us."

"Thanks. I just might."

Refreshing, this evidence of new style priesting and tolerance. Inner city experiments yes, but she hadn't expected to find it here. "But doesn't your bishop mind?" she asked mischievously.

"He doesn't have to fill a rural church and minister to a *real* flock," he shot back.

Jo grinned. "You farm too?"

"A bit on the Q.T. One somehow has to make ends meet. What is it?" he asked, obviously noting her quizzical expression.

"You don't come over as *rural,*" she said bluntly.

"That's because I'm not. My living was inner-city Liverpool before I came here three and a half years ago."

"That explains it. Don't you find this – well, a bit *cosy* by comparison? You know after all the poverty and deprivation?"

He nodded slowly as he stroked his beard. "Sometimes. But then inner cities don't have a monopoly on spiritual poverty. As you may know, farmers today are way up top of the suicide league. It's the isolation. Money problems, personal ones, all seem worse when you're shut away on some remote hill farm and maybe no partner to share them with." He paused to fasten his jacket, the heavy duty zip making a satisfying buzz and whine. "But then I feel closer to something here too." He turned and indicated the purple fells with a sweep of his arm. "I'm not quite sure what name to put to it, but it's a spiritually potent brew."

"Wordsworthian pantheism?" she taunted.

He didn't answer. New-style priesting indeed.

"Now tell me," he had been leading the way to where the church wall recessed and the lane widened, but swung round to face her with a direct look. "Why were you waiting to see me?"

Jo gave him a startled look. "But I –," she started to excuse herself, then something in those intense eyes told her it was no use. "I wanted to ask about an item of local history. But how did you know?"

"You saw me leave the church but pretended not to. And your feigned surprise wasn't very convincing," he added with a decidedly unclerical grin.

"Okay. I noticed an inscription back there – a victim of plague, and wondered how he came to be here, and how they stopped it spreading," Jo improvised, buying time before launching into her subject.

"He would have been a traveller. From the town," John Penrose supplied, though his sceptical expression told Jo he had sussed her tactics. "And you can see for yourself how locals dealt with it," he continued as she looked at him with polite interest, "by the worn stone trough outside Throstle Garth. The farm folk would leave out produce; travellers wanting provisions would help themselves, and drop their money in the trough. At the day's end the farmer would come down to the gate and fish out the coins – cleansed of disease and carrying no risk of the plague."

"Ingenious. Thank you. That's very interesting."

"Now what do you really want to know?" he asked shrewdly.

She flushed, but answered smoothly enough: "I hear there's a local legend. Something medieval. Might be good book material," she added to account for her interest.

"You must be meaning the St. Clairs."

"A local family?"

"That's right. Bit of a scandal. Justin St. Clair was supposed to have been cuckolded by his lovely young wife. She disappeared – and so did one of Edward 1's dashing young knights! Rumour had it they were seen together at Dover, were set to embark for France. After she'd gone, St. Clair forbad her name to be mentioned on pain of death. He had one of her kinsmen strung up for defying that edict."

"A pleasant type, Justin St. Clair."

As Jo softly repeated the name a chill wind blew down the lane. It ruffled the tide of dried leaves piled at the verge, setting them rustling and skittering until they rose in a spinning vortex, then just as suddenly dropped and lay still.

They continued walking, albeit slowly. "For a newcomer, you seem to know a fair bit about him," she ventured.

He shrugged. "Everyone knows that Barrowburn Castle was the St Clair's family seat."

Jo fought to contain her excitement. A name at last, and a family history. Progress – and more than she had ever dared hope. "I must go take a look."

"Years ago, I believe the place used to be quite a tourist attraction. It's unmanned these days, little more than a ruin. But of all the St Clair's – Justin seems to be the one who is remembered locally."

"Inevitable I suppose, given his wife ran off with the medieval equivalent to a toy boy," Jo said lightly to hide her growing obsession.

They had reached the end of the churchyard wall. As they

rounded the corner, Jo stared and her eyebrows rose. "*Very* trendy. Vintage?"

"50's. One has to get around somehow." He picked up the red and white crash helmet resting on the seat of the lovingly preserved Triumph Tiger 100 and fastened the strap beneath his chin. "Like a lift?"

Jo grinned. "Wouldn't that be seen as awfully fast?"

His eyes sparkled with fun. "Terribly but there's no-one to see."

Jo laughed. "Okay, thanks."

"Jump on."

The beast roared into life. Jo – pressed up against John Penrose's leather-clad back and her arms clutching his waist, wondered how life in the country could ever be thought of as dull.

He declined her offer of tea or coffee. "I think we'd be pushing it out a bit there," he said with a grin, sitting easily astride the machine as she stood at the door of Twilight Cottage.

"As you say – no-one to see," she teased.

"That's the problem." He gave her a wink, revved up the engine and pulled down his visor. "Actually I have a previous appointment," he added smiling,

"– lunch with a sticky infant and street-wise wife."

"Shame."

"I agree. I'll watch for you in church, mind."

"I'm sure you have no congregation problem."

"No. In fact I'm told there's a waiting list for the flower arranging and brass cleaning rota." He had spoken with perfect gravity, but his eyes held self-mocking laughter, thus robbing his words of arrogance or vanity. "Women's Institute has record attendance too." His gaze mocked her, challenged her to respond in this illicit and delightful game of oblique flirtation. "Wouldn't like to join would you?"

She laughed. "You're outrageous."

"I try."

"Well sorry John, I'm not about to join the eccliastical fan club!"

"Pity."

But he looks cheerful enough about it, Jo thought with amusement. John Penrose may enjoy flirting with members of his flock, but her guess was he never strayed too far from his wife. "What do the local kids make of you?" she asked, curious.

He nodded and gave the thumbs up sign. "Real cool. They dig!"

"I'll bet!"

He winked. "They go for the disco nights and barbecues – a bit more lively than the old style youth club!"

Suddenly he dropped the bantering tone. "Look, it's lonely out here. If ever you need anything – help or advice or just to hear another human voice –," He ratched about in his pocket and pulling out a grubby notepad scribbled something on it with a biro, tore off the sheet and handed it to Jo. "I'm just a phone call away."

"Thanks. I appreciate that."

"And my wife – wonderful woman really."

"I guessed as much," Jo said smiling.

"Great listener – if you're ever stuck for a female ear!"

He swung round the bike, raised one gauntleted hand and roared away, dipping and bouncing over the ruts in the manner of a professional trailer.

Jo sat by the fire, sipping coffee and feeling well pleased with her day. Her ego, still raw over Blake's defection, was temporarily soothed by her 'brief encounter' with the charismatic vicar. She smiled at the image of him with the sticky infant on his knee, and a street-wise (and probably very attractive) wife keeping a watchful eye on her handsome and eccentric husband. It might have been interesting, she mused, then laughed aloud. Unlike Louise, doomed love affairs were not her forte: so *wearing*.

Thoughts of which brought back to mind the disgraced lady St. Clair and her dishonoured knight. As yet it was hard to see how this fitted in with the ring – if indeed it did at all. But one thing was now beyond reasonable doubt: the identity of the knight who supposedly haunted the area. Obviously, due to his wife's tragic betrayal, Justin St. Clair's soul was unable to rest.

TWENTY-TWO

~

With a sense of annoyance Jo looked at the clock and realised it was now too late to go to Barrowburn Castle. Winter days were so short in the north, come four o'clock and that was virtually it. On a good day that is; overcast days – forget it after three. It was like living in permanent twilight, which made the cottage aptly named, she thought wryly. She curbed her impatience, and on impulse decided instead to telephone Colin and Finola and ask them over one night for a meal. Finola answered, and after the merest hesitation, accepted the invitation for Wednesday evening at seven thirty.

"Yes fine, thanks," she replied in response to Finola's queries about her health. "Look forward to seeing you Wednesday then," she concluded, seeing no point in mentioning the funeral and Seth Rigby's peculiar behaviour.

Jo realised that her walk on the fell had made her ravenous, and that lunchtime had come and gone without her noticing. After poaching two eggs, toasting some bread and brewing a pot of tea, she sat by the sitting room fire and ate whilst doing a crossword. I'll start clucking if I eat many more of these, she thought with a flash of humour, spearing a yolk so that it ran over the toast and congealed like cooling lava on her plate. Life had narrowed down since leaving London: the culinary delights to a pot of tea with beans or eggs on toast; a session at an exclusive health club to a simple hot bath and, she reflected ruefully, poking the embers and tossing a log onto the blaze, the epitome of luxury was now a fire that stayed in for more than an hour. A far cry from a sensual sauna, followed by champagne and a candlelit dinner for two at Luigi's, then a passionate night between the sheets with Blake.

Not that they'd made it past the sauna very often during the past six months. 'Passionate nights' had boiled down to a late-night telephone conversation from some anonymous hotel room or spartan on-campus resident block. The sense of opportunities lost was overwhelming, and pangs of regret gripped her chest momentarily restricting her breathing. But then to be honest she had enjoyed her success. And why not? She'd worked hard enough for it, hadn't she? No, no apologies on that score, and if at times the price seemed too high, well there was nothing to be gained from whining. And that was where the cure lay – in work. Her appetite no longer keen, she pushed aside her unfinished meal and went over to the computer.

Evening was spent in working on the book. At first, due to the throbbing of her thumb, she confined her efforts to reading and note taking, but then as ideas presented themselves was unable to resist a couple of paragraphs on the new chapter. Warily she switched on and watched the screen of her lap top shudder into life, looking away as the windows logo floated towards her. No problem. Soon she was tapping away, lost in Ruskin's lonely but artistically rich world. Flexing her fingers she rose, winced at the pain in her hand, and pouring herself a whisky went back to work. She had only taken one sip when it happened, or otherwise might have been tempted to blame what occurred next on the drink. In disbelief she stared at the screen. There, amongst the text relating Ruskin's final and dramatic confrontation with Effie before her elopement with Millais, were alien words, words she had not typed:
Love you, kill you, love . . . forever, forever . . .
Jo stared at the screen, a sick feeling growing in the pit of her stomach. What was happening here? Questions whirled around in her head as her abdomen churned. *Justin St. Clair.* The words rose unbidden in her mind. Somehow she had conjured him up again, perhaps because his identity had been revealed. Okay, crazy – but ancient cultures had believed something like that: in those days you never gave your name lightly, never willingly divulged it to an enemy or stranger, to do so was to surrender one's personal power.

So was her knowledge of his identity somehow attracting Justin St. Clair? A ridiculous thought of course, but the words screamed at her from the screen, and the atmosphere in the room had subtly changed. For one thing the temperature had dropped, and the fire smouldered sullenly in the grate as though starved of oxygen and smothered by dense emotions. A sense of hatred and anger was seeping into the room.

Fearfully she looked round. A cry was jerked from her throat as the central bulb fizzed and the light dipped to a dirty brown. She turned back to the computer. The screen shuddered, went blank then returned to normal text. Feverishly she scanned it for the dreaded words. They had gone; the text of her novel was uninterrupted. The light bulb crackled and appeared to function normally again. She massaged her forehead with a shaking hand. Could she have imagined it? Earlier thoughts of possible brain damage returned to haunt her, as desperately she searched for explanations. Anything, other than what was becoming obvious. She switched off the computer and almost jumped out of her skin as a door banged upstairs.

She sat for a moment, rigid with fear and ears straining for further sounds, her gaze fixed on the ceiling. The spare room was overhead. *The window.* That was it, she thought as nothing further disturbed the silence. The window had probably been left open a fraction and a gust of wind had blown the door shut. Relieved to have found a plausible explanation she rushed for the stairs.

A quick check showed her bedroom door to be open. No problem there. The door to the spare bedroom was shut. Heart thumping she listened outside; no sound came from within. Slowly she lifted the latch, then pushed hard so that the door banged against the wall. A flick of the switch and light flooded the room; it was empty. It was also freezing cold, but the window was shut. So much for her gust of wind theory. Her attention was drawn by a movement on the floor directly beneath the window. She took a step forward, then screamed and her hands flew to her mouth. A small pile of dry red earth was deposited on the carpet. Next to it writhed a heap of pale and undulating earthworms.

She had gingerly scooped up the spaghetti-like mass and thrown it outside, and was bolting the door when the telephone shrilled. She jumped like a startled rabbit and when answering fought to keep her voice steady. Her knees threatened to give way and she sank down on the chair. "Blake? Oh, Blake, I'm so glad. Where are you?" The line was crackly, his voice indistinct. A repetitious thudding sounded in the background.

"About fifteen kilometres outside Sarajevo."

No wonder the line was bad; she realised the thudding was artillery fire. "Are you alright, Blake? Not in any danger? Sorry – I didn't catch that." The line cleared.

"I said, I'm fine."

"You sound –," she struggled for the appropriate word and settled for "exhausted."

There was a brief pause. "It's tough going. The same old sticking points that have cocked things up for the fast four years: the Serbs insistence on access to the Adriatic and a northern corridor linking West Bosnia to Serbia proper. And as always, the future of Sarajevo. But we're working on it. In the meantime the war goes on."

Jo felt desolation wash over her. "I wish you weren't so far away."

"I'm missing you. We must talk when I get back. You're crying. What's wrong, Jo? Jo, are you Okay?"

"Yes. That is –," she tried to explain, but given relief at hearing his voice, and frustration at the appalling line, she was aware of not making much sense. "And just now," she concluded, "worms – in a heap on the carpet. I don't know what's going on."

"This is crazy, Jo. I mean, what are you doing out there anyway – alone, and in winter?"

She sighed. Blake's frustration was obvious too, yet his irritation, she knew of old, was a symptom of his concern. That, and to his way of thinking, having to worry about her at this isolated cottage had made his job that bit more difficult. Suddenly they seemed so far apart, separated by more than just geography.

His voice came over again, brittle with worry and tension.

"Look, I'm ringing because I'm worried about you, okay? It's seems I was right to be. What's going on, Jo?"

She tried again to explain, playing down the trauma of her arrival, but this of course was exactly the point he picked up on.

"What's this about the car? An *accident?*" He sounded frantic.

"I'm *alright,* Blake. That part's done with. I only told you so you'd understand how it all started."

"What all started?"

She heard the irritation in his voice and knew she wasn't getting through. "Justin St. Clair. And the things that keep going wrong here at the cottage."

She heard his sigh of frustration. To make things worse the crackling returned.

"Look, Jo – I'm sorry, but I've seen homes laid to waste, men who have been tortured, women raped and left for dead, and kids crying for their murdered parents. And you're asking me to take on board what happened to some guy over six hundred years ago, for chris'sakes!"

She knew it was his stress talking, but something within her rebelled. She was stressed-out too. At least he could identify the source of his problem, didn't have to doubt his own sanity. "No, I'm not, Blake. It's happening to *me* – and NOW!"

Her imagination supplied the muffled expletive, and she pictured him thrusting his fingers through his dark wavy hair.

"Jo?"

There was so much she wanted to say, but her tongue remained glued to the roof of her mouth. "Yes." It was all she could manage. The crackling was getting worse.

"I have to go. I'm sorry, Jo. We'll talk when I get back."

His last words were distorted by the crackling. It sounded like he said he still loved her – seconds before the line went dead.

Love you, forever, love you –

No, wait a minute it wasn't quite dead. She pressed the receiver back to her ear. It was now. Silence hummed along the wires, resonant with menace.

Weariness swept over her in a wave, and her thumb started to throb. On peeling off the dressing lines of concern creased her forehead. The wound was gathering: a yellow head had formed and the surrounding skin was angry and inflamed. For a moment panic flared. No point in worrying, do something about it, she told herself. A hot bath, with the addition of soothing essential oils given to her by Barbara, seemed the best option.

And appeared to do the trick. The abscess or whatever it was hadn't burst, but the hot water and oils had reduced the pain and swelling. As an added bonus, the scents of lavender and chamomile drifted through the cottage to soothe and comfort. Glowing, and cocooned in a fleecy dressing gown, she checked that windows were closed and doors bolted for the night before mounting the stairs. Half way up she remembered, stopped and felt a stab of unease: the mystery of the door slamming shut upstairs remained unsolved. Not to mention that disgusting mess on the floor. No point thinking about that now and frightening herself to go to bed, she decided, walking into a bedroom that felt like an ice-box.

TWENTY-THREE

~

The night passed without drama, the sole interruption to her slumbers being caused by the screech of a barn owl from somewhere in the garden, a sound to which Jo was now accustomed. The cold in the bedroom had prevented her from returning immediately to sleep, but eventually her eyelids had closed and on waking again and drawing back the curtains, she had seen that the world beyond the window was frosted with silver filigree. So the iciness of the room was only to be expected, and had no supernatural significance, she told herself with relief. A pale but welcome sun was now thawing out the garden, so that droplets of moisture sparked coloured fire from every twig and blade of grass. A winter wonderland of light that danced and glanced and lightened her heart as she made a pot of coffee and mulled over her plans for the day.

She was already half regretting inviting Colin and Finola round for a meal. At the best of times, she reflected whilst bullying the embers of the fire into a reluctant glow with a pair of bellows, her culinary skills were nothing to get excited about, but given her recent state of mind the outcome was rather more unpredictable than usual. It was just one more pressure she could do without, especially as Finola was such a good cook. Jo sighed and picked up a biro and notepad and began jotting down items on her shopping list.

She had a basic repertoire of two or three dishes that she should could do blindfolded and without thinking, so choice wasn't an issue. Pasta was the safest bet. Fashionable too, and Colin and Finola were the trendy sort who were probably into Italian cuisine.

Things could be worse, she decided with a shrug and self-mocking smile: they could be true locals who would expect roast potatoes and beef with three or four veg, and those elusively light Yorkshire puddings that her mother made to perfection, but which would sink like lead balloons should she attempt to make them.

Not that her lack of commitment in the kitchen had ever bothered her. There had never been any contest: from the start she had chosen career over domesticity. But now Jo found herself wondering if it pained Blake, how he coped with it, given his ancestry and the legendary dedication of Italian women to food and looking after their men. But even in Italy things were changing. A couple of years back she had spent some time there with Blake, combining a holiday with researching a book on Mary Shelley. They had stayed at a time-warped rural inn, where their host's ancient mother still dominated the cooking and domestic arrangements. Blake had translated as she sat by the kitchen range, wrinkled prune face etched with disapproval, complaining bitterly of young wives who haunted supermarket and delicatessen, instead of preparing by hand a multitude of dishes for feast days and family celebrations.

And good luck to them too, Jo thought now, remorse and regret forgotten as she reminded herself what marriage to Blake might mean: the 'barefoot and pregnant' syndrome, the rigid role casting that she was determined to avoid. Angry with herself as much as Blake for succumbing to nostalgia, it was in a mood of defensive defiance that she returned to her shopping list. Ten minutes later, good humour restored, she set off for the down-valley village stores.

Jo looked up from contemplating the contents of a surprisingly modern chiller cabinet as the previous customer left the shop with a cheery "see you now", and a jangling of the equally old-fashioned door bell.

"Sorry to keep you waiting," the man behind the counter apologised, replacing a rope of speckled Cumberland sausage the thickness of Jo's wrist. "Be with you in a sec," he added over his shoulder as he set about scrubbing his hands at a miniscule sink.

"No problem." Jo assured him as he turned back to his ablutions.

He had spoken in a soft southern voice and not, as expected, with the lilting flat-vowelled local dialect. The store was hardly your local corner shop either, with a whole section devoted to wines and video hire. She was surprised to find a good selection of cheeses including Parmesan and Mozzarella. Fortunately most of the items she needed were lurking on the laden shelves. The fresh basil on her list was probably over-ambitious, but ready-made pesto sauce would make an acceptable compromise she decided, noting the jars stacked next to packets of various types of pasta. If only she was preparing this meal for herself and Blake, she thought wistfully, and in spite of her earlier reservations.

The sound of water gurgling away down the plug hole interrupted her reverie. "So what can I get you?" The proprietor as Jo guessed him to be, turned with a smile and vigorously dried his hands on a Persil-white towel. His plump cheeked and heavy-jowled sallow face reminded Jo irresistibly of a waxed pear.

"The Mozzarella please, and some Parmesan," Jo said pointing.

"About how much?"

Jo watched in fascination as he dried each podgy white finger separately in the manner of a surgeon preparing to operate.

"Staying locally are you?" he asked five minutes or so later, counting out her change into her palm.

"Twilight Cottage."

"Ah, down by the church there."

The waxy flesh furrowed and dimpled as he frowned, irresistibly reminding Jo of cellulite thighs. "A bit out of the way – don't you get lonely?" he added.

She shook her head and with a polite smile, shut off and prepared to leave. Her experiences at the cottage were making her reticent, she realised with a jolt, as though she harboured some guilty secret.

He appeared not to notice but carried on folding the towel, smoothing each layer and pressing the crease with the heel of his hands until left with a neat rectangle. "You're a southerner like myself then?"

Jo nodded again, reluctant to let him invade her privacy.

He leaned over the counter and spoke in conspiratorial tones: "I'd recognise that civilised accent anywhere. Though doesn't do to say so in local company," he added with an exaggerated wink. "Nice to hear one of our own kind though."

The man irritated her. Why settle here in the first place if that was how he felt? "Yes, but when in Rome –," she rebuked him, making her escape before he could reply.

The sound of running water as he turned on the taps to wash yet again followed her from the shop. What was he trying to wash away? The culture of the North, or his own ingrained prejudice? she wondered with a half smile.

*   *   *

She drove back to the cottage in thoughtful mood. The flash of resentment she felt when that man had identified with her had been unexpected. A fierce raw sort of feeling, it seemed to have little to do with herself: after all, she practically despised the place – certainly the cottage and its immediate vicinity. Yet something in her had balked at being excluded, at being identified with the sophisticated push-button world of the South. No doubt it was simple distaste at being classed with that pasty individual with his proprietorial air and pedantic ways, she decided dismissing any hint of mystery. Yet as she placed the key in the door of Twilight Cottage, it was with a mixture of dread and *déjàs vu* that had something to do with coming home.

Making her way to the kitchen with the groceries, she paused at the door. It was pulled to but not fastened. A low-pitched sound came from within, a sort of *buzz*. Jo frowned, trying to place it. She hesitated a moment then pushed open the door. "Oh, my God!"

As the door swung back, a dozen or so fat bluebottles rose from around the frame and swarmed angrily around her head.

Dashing to the window she flung it open and turned to the

attack. Her arms flailed wildly until the swarm dispersed, then reformed in an angry undulating column. Her hands lashed out again, and a shudder ran through her each time they made contact with a fat black body and droning wings. When all but one or two renegades had buzzed through the gap, she slammed the window shut and slumped against the door. Slugs, worms, and now blue-bottles in winter. Where in God's name had they come from? A rapid search of surfaces, cooker and cupboards revealed no forgotten food left to go rancid and breed maggots. She gagged and made for the door. The odour of damp and decay in the kitchen was overwhelming. That and a stench like rotting meat.

That night she was awakened by the scratching and scrabbling sounds that had disturbed her sleep several night's back. Rats, she told herself: rats and mice in the loft. Except that it seemed to be coming from downstairs. For a split second the bluebottles buzzed angrily into the air and around her face, and she squeezed her eyes hard to shut out the memory of them. It was hard to say which had been worse, the flies or the stench. My God, she had never smelt anything like it. As before, a search of the kitchen had revealed no forgotten food or decaying animal that had become trapped, or wandered inside to die. Well scratching or no, there was no way she was going downstairs again tonight. God, but it was cold, and the smell of damp was all pervasive. She rubbed one icy foot against the other to increase the circulation, then lay perfectly still again, listening. Her face ached from cold and her nose felt numb. The scrabbling and scraping noises grew louder and more insistent. Determined to ignore them, she pulled the covers over her head.

Jo tipped the cooked pasta into a warmed dish, then filled the mill with fresh peppercorns and placed it on the table, mentally doing a check. Yes, it looked quite good considering the limitations: the candles were the same dark green as the napkins (paper for sure but up-market ones), set off by the sparkle of glasses which were not exactly lead crystal but at least matched, and there had been four matching plates in one of the cupboards. Except they would only need three.

A cloud dimmed her glow of satisfaction. And stop right there, she scolded herself; this isn't the time to go on a downer. And let's face it, rather than fretting over her, Blake would be getting on with his life. Besides – she thought tossing back her hair with a theatrical gesture and grinning at herself in the mirror above the sink – self pity is *so* unattractive. I do hope they're not late, she agonised, checking the pasta in case it was drying up or going cold. There could be nothing worse than serving luke warm stodge to a seasoned cook like Finola.

But her guests weren't late and the dinner went down remarkably well. "Thanks, that was great," Colin enthused, wiping his hands his hands on his napkin after demolishing the last piece of garlic bread.

"It certainly was," Finola agreed, helping herself to the last spoonful of tomato and onion salad. The expression in her large eyes softened as she looked across at Jo. "And yes 'thanks' Jo; it's so nice to be invited out like this. Usually it's just Col and me."

Colin assumed an aggrieved expression. "Gee thanks, Fin!"

"Oh, you know what I mean, idiot!" Finola leaned over and taking Col's hand planted a kiss on the back of it, so that watching, Jo felt a stab of pain. If only things were the way they used to be, with Blake seated at her side. But she had sent him away, and it was mean to envy Finola's evident enjoyment of the evening. "You're great company Col," Finola was continuing, "but we are out in the wilds here, and this is, well, *so civilised* darling," she said camping it up. The impish smile suited her better than well meaning over-intensity. In fact, she looks quite radiant tonight, Jo thought, noting how the vibrant blues of Finola's batik-dyed dress off-set the gold of her hair. "Please." Jo nodded at Colin as he let the wine bottle hover over her glass. Poor Fin, she thought as he topped it up: there must be times when she longs for some feminine company, and like tonight, a chance to dress up a bit. Tweeds and green wellies were all very well, but they didn't do much for a girl's ego.

"You've not brought it with you!"

Jo watched bemused as Colin scowled at Finola who was pulling something out of her tapestry tote. "You're bloody obsessional!" he added with an expression of mingled disgust and amusement.

"Hark at the cat calling the kettle black," Finola retorted serenely, unrolling a scrap of linen so that some skeins of silk dropped onto the table. "You're jealous because you can't bring chisels and a lump of wood," she added with a smirk.

"Nonsense," Colin growled.

"You do embroidery?" Jo asked indicating with a gesture that she would like to see.

"Keeps my hands out of mischief." Finola passed it to her and Colin groaned.

"Oh not tonight Fin! We're not holding a Women's Institute meeting here!"

"But this is exquisite." Jo ignored Colin's sarcasm and stroked the tiny stitches with the tip of a fingernail. Each was perfectly placed in the chaffinch and honeysuckle motif. "You're very gifted Finola," she said with genuine admiration.

"Oh, Colin's the real artist," Finola replied dismissively.

Jo felt bound to remonstrate with her, but then Colin began to speak. "Give us a song, Fin," then as Finola shook her head and looked faintly embarrassed: "Come on, sing for us pet."

"You sing as well?" Jo asked, seeing Finola in a new light. "As well as embroider I mean."

"Fin's of Irish descent," Colin supplied before Finola could desist. "Her great grandmother and gran both had the voice; and now her mammy's a celebrated performer of Irish folk music over there. They're all great at the sewing and singing, aren't they colleen?" he teased with a corny overdone accent.

"I'd love to hear you," Jo said persuasively.

Finola gave a little smile. "You don't have to be polite, Jo. Just ignore Col!"

"But I'm not –," Jo protested.

"O.K. you can stop playing the prima donna now."

"Get lost!" Finola dipped a finger in her wine and flicked it at him. She giggled at his exclamation of disgust as he wiped a drop of Burgundy from the end of his nose.

Colin sighed and leaned forward, allowing the front legs of his chair to touch ground. "Get on with it! Before you get too squiffy."

She stuffed the embroidery and silks back into her bag. "Okay," she mocked, sitting back after dropping the bag onto the floor. "Are we sitting comfortably? . . ."

"This song is about a young mother's joy at the birth of her first child." Finola leant back and closed her eyes. Colin and Jo lapsed into silence, aware that she was psyching herself into the mood. Jo glanced at Colin, suddenly aware that of some sort of transformation, of a magic that was taking place here. The candles on the table flickered, casting Finola's face into the dramatic patterns of light and shade reminiscent of a Caravaggio portrait. She looks incredibly lovely like that, Jo marvelled, as Finola's normally pale and nondescript features glowed, and candle-power meshed the web of her hair with gold thread, spun by some mythical and magical spider. As her eyes opened they held a faraway look, as though her spirit had travelled beyond their presence to an Ireland of long ago. Smiling faintly, Colin glanced back at Jo, who smiled to show that she understood. Finola began to sing, the notes flowing forth with the purity of a mountain spring, rising like larks giving thanks to heaven; falling soft as a roe deer's footfalls in a carpeted autumnal wood. Jo sat transfixed, allowing the magic of Finola's voice to flow over and into her heart and mind.

"Wonderful." As the last note died away, Jo briefly closed her eyes and slowly shook her head in disbelief. "Absolutely wonderful." And who would have thought it of 'Fussy Fin' as she had already secretly dubbed her.

Colin was nodding agreement, and despite his habitual air of exasperation, the look of pride on his face was unmistakable. Finola, no longer appearing embarrassed, and seemingly infused with a new confidence from her singing, smiled and accepted their admiration.

"More!" Colin demanded, banging the table with the heel of his hand. "Encore I say!" His face, Jo noted, was flushed, his voice slightly slurred. Suddenly she wasn't at ease with the situation. A strangeness had crept in, a sense of things about to spin out of control like a formula racing car slewing off a circuit. But perhaps it was just her oversensitivity at Colin becoming a little drunk. No prude, she nonetheless never felt comfortable once alcohol loosened inhibitions to the point where it threatened control. Not since, as a child, she had witnessed Uncle Frank punching a glass door panel in drunken temper. Finola merely smiled indulgently as he reached for the bottle of wine and divided what was left between the three glasses.

Mentally shrugging off her unease, Jo sipped her wine then touched Finola's arm, adding her entreaty: "Yes, please do."

Colin set aside the empty bottle. "Give us 'Londonderry Air, Fin."

Finola shook her head and gave a little laugh. "You must be getting tight, Col!"

Colin looked injured. "No I'm bloody not!"

Fin tucked her hair behind her ears. "It's the 'chucking out time' song!"

"Well I like it," Colin said defensively.

"Why do you say that, Fin?" Jo asked, puzzled.

"Well it's so sentimental. 'How do you follow that?' as they say. Nothing for it but to go on home!" Finola said laughing. "Mammy always saved it to the last at family parties – for when she was tired and wanting her bed!"

"Can't remember the words – it's ages since I heard it," Jo confessed.

"There you are then, Fin," Colin exclaimed. His face was still flushed, though with the effects of alcohol or triumph, Jo was hard put to tell.

"It's your moral duty to fill the gaps in this poor girl's cultural education!" Colin finished with a flourish of his empty glass.

Finola effected a mock Irish accent: "Oh go on wit' ye, idjit!" and bent down to pick up her embroidery bag.

Jo caught her forearm. "No, please sing it – for me," she

pleaded, wondering at the sense of urgency, the growing, and seemingly irrational desire to hear this particular song.

Fin shrugged. "Okay." She sat back and began to sing.

Jo listened entranced as the notes flowed through and around her, suffusing the room with a keening sadness. Captivated by the lilt and musicality of Fin's voice, the lyric only gradually invaded her consciousness.

> *But come ye back when summer's in the meadows*
> *Or when the valley's hushed and white with snow*

As she listened to the lover mourn her loss, it seemed to Jo that there was an inevitability about it; as though all that had taken place since leaving London had transpired to bring her here to this room, to hear Finola's voice in timeless lament. Notes and words washed over her, filling her mind so that nothing else was left, crowding her heart with unbearable love and sadness. Fin's voice, previously pure and gentle to the point of fragility, now seemed to gain a power and raw energy, all the more potent for being unaccompanied.

> *And when you come, and all the flowers are dying*
> *And I am dead, as dead I may well be*

Jo felt a prickling along her spine and a bristling of the hairs at the base of her neck. The flames of the candles, previously burning steadily, now wavered and dipped in response, it seemed, to the rise and fall of Finola's voice. Jo shivered and lacing her arms across her chest, clutched her upper arms for comfort. The air in the room was affected too, charged by the energy and power of the voice that filled it. It was becoming tactile, brushing Jo's skin with a light caress. But it grew more insistent by the second, crushing her chest like the stones on a witches' press.

> *You'll come and find the place where I am lying*
> *And you'll kneel and say an Ave there for me*

Tears stung her eyes and the all-consuming sadness clasped her chest until she could scarcely breathe. "Oh, my God," she breathed, covering her face.

Colin seemed unaware of her distress, and Finola carried on singing, the sadness and longing palpably building around her. Jo felt a sob rise in her throat as the strength of Finola's voice increased, and the beauty of it all became unbearable. At the same time she became dimly aware of another sound. The haunting sigh and moan of the wind as it whistled around the eaves and breathed down the chimney, provided a natural and eerie accompaniment to the words: echoes of an old song, played on lost souls with half-remembered emotions.

> *And I shall hear, though soft you tread above me*
> *And my grave will softer, warmer be.*

Hot tears ran down Jo's cheeks and the pain in her chest became excruciating. The build up of tension and emotion brought to mind a simmering volcano waiting to erupt. Still Finola sang on:

> *For you will bide, and you'll tell me that you love me*
> *And I shall sleep in peace*
> *Until you come to me.*

The last trembling and drawn-out note died. The sound of Jo's sobbing filled the room. Finola screamed and Colin leapt to his feet as the candle flames dipped and the wine bottle rolled off the table and smashed on the floor.

Finola glared at Colin over her shoulder as she placed an arm around Jo's heaving shoulders. "For God's sake, Col – you frightened me half to death!"

"I never touched it!" Colin protested, his voice steady, his mood no longer ebullient. Bending down, he picked up the shattered neck and pebbled bottom of the bottle, gingerly holding them one in each hand. He cleared his throat; the wind had dropped and all was still.

"Well I certainly didn't! Over there." Finola pointed at a plastic bin by the sink as he looked around, apparently at a loss. With an injured expression he crossed to it and dropped in the dripping shards. The *clunk-clunck* they made as they hit the bottom seemed an affront to the silence. The sound also seemed to reach Jo, for her shoulders stopped shaking as her sobbing subsided.

"Are you alright Jo?" Finola said, watching as Colin picked up the smaller shards and wrapped them in a couple of serviettes before dropping them into the bin.

Jo sniffed loudly and wiped her eyes on the piece of kitchen roll offered by Finola. "Yes. Thanks Fin," she attempted a self-effacing laugh but it came out thin and shaky. "So bloody stupid – don't know what came over me."

"An excess of wine and sentimentality," Colin supplied with a grin, wiping his hands on the side of his trousers. "I mean, I know Fin's pretty moving – but you were a bit over the top, Jo old girl!"

She blew her nose and laughed, trying to go along with his coping strategy, to lighten the mood which still patently oppressed them all. "Sorry folks – can't explain it."

"Was it Blake?" Finola asked with a sympathetic look at Jo.

"Yes, yes that was it." Not wanting to accept the strangeness of her behaviour, Jo leapt to the excuse like a starving fish to the bait. "Your singing brought it all back. Stupid, but memories, and all that."

"*All alone in the moonlight . . .*" Colin warbled, spreading his arms theatrically.

Finola looked embarrassed. "Pack it in, Col."

Col looked offended. "Didn't mean any –,"

"It's not funny; Jo's upset," Finola remonstrated.

"Sorry. Only trying to cheer her up."

"No, I'm fine now, really. Like I said – bloody silly." Jo sniffed and self-consciously blew her nose. "Look, be a good lad, Col and pour three 'revivers' – oh, but perhaps –," she faltered flushing, not liking to voice the suspicion that Colin had drunk enough.

"Not driving tonght," Colin reminded her. "Besides, sober as a preacher now – you saw to that!"

"I did nothing!" Jo laughed too loudly. "But in that case – don't stint the measures." She pointed to the bottle of cognac on the shelf below the spice rack. Colin wiped his hands on a piece of kitchen towel. There followed a welcome squeaking of cork being coaxed from bottle, then the satisfying *glug-glug-glug* of spirit being poured into glasses.

"Okay, before we go, let's lay our Danny boy to rest." Colin proposed, grinning at Finola's frown and Jo's patent look of unease. "To lovers past!" he cried flourishing his glass.

Finola shrugged then raised her drink. "May they rest in peace!"

"Amen." Jo said wryly, gulping down her brandy.

She ignored a ruffling of the air that chilled and caressed her face.

Later, when she had cleared the dishes and stacked them on the sink for morning, she lay in her bed and worried about her uncharacteristic response to a mawkish song. Simply over tired, and stressed-out because of Blake and the book, the voice of common sense reassured her. And this bloody cottage, she mentally added, shivering in the dampness that pervaded blankets and quilt. Stupid song. Why wouldn't it get out of her head? She tried to block Finola's voice as it echoed round and round the caverns of her mind.

And when you come, and all the flowers are dying
And I am dead, as dead I may well be

I don't even particularly like it, she told herself, mulling over the events of the night whilst the song richoted off the walls of her mind in its endless circuit. *And I shall hear, though soft you tread above me*

Nonetheless the words churned on, mingling with the voice of the brook, seeping into her consciousness like water trickling over stones in the blue-rimmed garden beyond her window.

TWENTY-FOUR

~

The hum and whine of the chain saw rose and fell on the cold windless air. Then silence, as Seth put down the machine and rolled away another section of trunk with a thrust of his booted foot. He'd been meaning to get around to this wind-blown ash for some months now. It had come down in the last march gales, roots clawing air and limbs sprawling the earth: a pale dinosaur felled by an irresistible force. That's what they reckoned had caused the big fellers' end, the latest theory about how the ice age began: a massive meteor hit the Earth, and dust clouds blocked the sun's light so that nothing could grow or thrive. He prided himself on keeping abreast of things out there in the world. The lads down at the Pheasant thought him a bit daft, he reflected, wiping a drip from his nose with the back of his frayed cuff. He would come out with things sometimes, as they downed real ale in the snug, snippets he'd heard on the radio or read in the Readers Digest. 'A mine of useless knowledge' they laughingly said – but they listened just the same. Anyway ash burns well and winter was coming on. He picked up the saw again intending to switch on, but paused as a clamour broke out overhead.

Seth lowered the saw and looked up sharply. No problem: just rooks cawing as they circled the treetops, no doubt annoyed with him for disturbing the peace. But them other things – they were a different bundle of rags. He glanced at the blackened grass of the field in which he was working, black that is, with crows. They stared back in silence and stillness, in a way that ratched along his nerves. Never known 'em settle like that, he worried, except perhaps at lambing in the hopes of picking at afterbirth, or a helpless ewe's eyes. Or even the odd sickly lamb, he thought darkly. Never known 'em so quiet either, usually their clatter was enough to drive him crazy.

He shrugged and dipped his broad shoulders. The weight was on him again, the shadow with him, darkening his mind. The largest of the crows, black and sinister as an undertaker's coat-tails, rose with a leisurely flapping of ragged wings and perched on a branch above his head. "G'orn!" he shouted, shaking a gnarled and white-knuckled fist at the bird. It made no move, but blinked its yellow eyes just once, then fixed him with unwinking stare. Seth scowled and looked uneasily about him. So quiet – with the sort of hush that filled the barn at a midnight calving, when hands were red and raw with cold and even winter held its breath in the seconds before the calf was dropped.

He clutched his stomach and absently rubbed it: the muscles of his gut were contracting and knotting in painful cramps. Sniffing as another drip threatened, he switched on the machine. The teeth vibrated and whirred as cold sunlight glinted on steel. His nostrils were filled with the acrid smell of sawdust and hot metal as the blade bit into the ash trunk. A hawk hovered overhead, feathering thermals with barely discernible movements of its wing-tips. It sailed in closer, so close that the movement distracted Seth as he worked. He could actually see the yellow and black of its eye, the deadly orb of retribution. The whining spinning blade jumped out of the groove with an angry shriek. Heart thumping at the near miss he steadied it again, and his arms shook from the effort of holding it stable. The whine grew in pitch and intensity. Sawdust flew. Hot metal and burning wood. Seth began to shudder and sweat beaded his forehead. His mind darkened; the shadow pressed at his back.

The ground, the trees, everything was spinning around him in slow motion. The hawk, the shadow, a sudden flash and a glimpse of an image, red hawk on white chest. Red for anger, the stranger's anger filling him, hurting his mind. Angry with poor Seth. *Kill, kill; kill, forever, forever . . .*

From its branch the lone crow emitted a harsh cry. As though at a signal the others rose as a single body from the stubble field. They darkened the sky, shutting out light, much as that dust cloud that killed the dinosaurs must have done, and filling it with their raucous cries. The hawk was still, hovering directly above him, suspended as though from an invisible string, yellow eye fixed, body tensed for the drop. The whine of the saw grew louder. Sawdust sprayed, the particles trapped in a sunbeam. The blade flashed in the light, briefly blinding Seth and making him squint. A cacophony of crows bludgeoned his ears, and ragged wings beat about his head. Directly above, talons hooked ready to gouge, the hawk was dropping like a stone. Hawk or emblem upon the stranger's chest? In his fevered mind the two images were confused. Seth's arm came up to protect his head. The blade flashed as it swung out of control and his scream rose above the din. Sky turned black and sawdust sprayed red. The saw clanged to the ground, teeth still abortively spinning. Seth also sank, amid screams, blood and minced pink flesh.

TWENTY-FIVE

~

Barrowburn Castle imposed its considerable presence upon the parish from the top of a hill at the dalehead. It resembled, Jo speculated as she approached along the valley road, some huge and ferocious beast crouched to spring. With its crenelated walls and towers bathed in the ruddy glow of a wintry sun, it was impressive, she admitted; as it was intended to be, of course, when Justin St. Clair ruled the roost in this corner of medieval England. Which he was welcome to do, so long as he kept out of her cottage, she thought with grim humour. Briefly the events of the previous evening troubled her thoughts, and Finola's voice once again haunted her mind. She suppressed a shudder. The castle gave the impression of being bathed in blood.

Jo made a conscious effort to relax as she followed the *tourist Information* sign. The Rover coupé was handling well, and apparently none the worse for the accident, climbed the road which wound up and around to the deserted car park at the rear of the castle. She parked up, smiling at her foolishness; it was now obvious that the intense redness of the edifice was an effect of sunlight on sandstone. She remained behind the wheel for a moment or two, flexing her left hand then relaxing it. An expression of concern spread over her face. Surely the puncture wound should have healed by now? Yet this morning it had looked as angry as ever, or was that her imagination too? She shrugged, put it out of mind and opened the door of the car.

At close range the castle was overpowering, despite the piles of fallen masonry, roofless chambers, and gaping lancet windows where stone lattices had long since crumbled from cusped heads. Feeling dwarfed by its bulk and towering structure, she followed the signs to the weed-infested stone slabs of the main entrance.

Sandstone steps, worn in the middle by countless feet, led her to a doubled-centred arch carried on massive carved corbels. She was about to pass beneath and enter what remained of the great hall when an inscription caught her eye and arrested her progress. Carved into the central sandstone block it dominated the entrance. Moving closer she deciphered the ornately-carved words:

> *When the sun turneth black*
> *And the blood-moon sails high*
> *And the pale horseman rides,*
> *Pray the Kings Stone lies beneath the throne*
> *And the hawk be last to rise.*

And the date: *1297*

Excitement gripped her. Enigmatic and sinister, it was almost certain that the lines held some cryptic significance. Taking a note-book and pen from her jacket pocket, Jo wrote down the lines to peruse later.

She wandered around the ruins for a half hour or so, constantly looking over her shoulder and peering into dark corners and turrets. Unconsciously she had been expecting some manifestation: a movement in the shadows perhaps, or at least a sense of presence. As with all historical sites there was an aura of history and antiquity about the place, but nothing more. The realisation that nothing unusual lurked here brought relief, but also a faint sense of disappointment. But it was worth a visit for the inscription, Jo consoled herself.

She allowed herself to relax and explore the ruins: the over-grown courtyard, the worn steps spanned by arches that led to turrets open to the sky and with breathtaking views over valley and fells; or down to underground vaults and crypts with dank walls and no windows, the darkness and musty dampness discouraging penetration to their murky depths. She tried to imagine it all as it must have once been: the cries of sentries and visiting vendors, the odour of roasting meat mixed with that of rotting refuse and ordure, and the sharp catch to the nostrils caused by vats of urine stored in the tannery. These stone ramparts would have bristled with sentries, the kitchens and courtyard be filled with a bustle of servants, administrators and traders. Then the domestic animals. The air would resound with the mewing of cats, lowing of cattle and bleating of sheep and goats, and of course the inevitable barking and baying of dogs kept for hunting, and guarding the castle from would-be invaders. She tried to picture Justin St. Clair in his armour arriving home from battle, or arrayed in ermine-trimmed robes and presiding over banquets in the Great Hall. *And watching his faithless wife?*

Ill at ease she remained for a time sunk in thought, testing the atmosphere and staring into dark corners, but apart from an odd rippling of the air, as though a stone had been tossed into the waters of Time, nothing untoward occurred. Yet the feeling persisted. Something wasn't gelling. She could not with her mind's eye see the shadowy figure with the hawk emblazoned on his chest. No, not here. But when summoned by her concentration, he appeared in a halo of light at the end of a tunnel, or some dark corner of Twilight Cottage. Despite all her efforts he declined to be envisaged *here*.

And there was something peculiar too in connection with that crest. If, as she believed, the hawk was the family emblem, then why that odd last line of the inscription? *And the hawk be last to rise.* On the surface this would seem a negative wish, as though he was cursing his own family. *First* to rise would surely be more appropriate? Unless of course her initial hunch was correct and there was some obscure and secret meaning attached to the words. Perhaps the answer would present itself later, when she could sit quietly and think it all through.

Maybe a visit to Barbara wouldn't go amiss. This sort of thing was more in her line; she was lecturing in mythology and anthropology at Lancaster University. A trip to the City Library first perhaps, to check out the factual bits such as the St. Clair family and its coat of arms, then on to Barbara's home. If nothing else, it would give her a break from the cottage and its stifling atmosphere. Not exactly the sort of research I had envisaged, Jo thought ironically as she looked around one last time before walking back to the car. This place was a far cry from the peace and elegance of Brantwood. But then, she thought driving down to join the coast road, Ruskin would wait. There was little point trying to work on the book until the mystery was solved, and her mind quiet again.

Whilst out, it made sense to drive around a bit and get an idea of her location, and also to buy in some food. With this in mind she struck out north along the coast road. Fifteen or so miles on she swung north-east along a single track sign-posted 'fell road' which traversed high and open country devoid of habitation. Snow capped the distant Wasdale and Ennerdale mountains, and a passing place afforded a moment's respite from driving and some wonderful views, with skyscapes every bit as spectacular as the land. Banks of cumulus and nimbus billowed over the summit-range, the cotton-wool white shot through with yellow ochre and apricot from the westering sun's rays. But their base Jo noted with a slight sense of apprehension, was tinged with a violety-brown that presaged the first snows. How soon before they sailed down from the high ground to release their burden over the valleys? Weeks? Or maybe only days? Being snowed-in at Twilight Cottage wasn't exactly an alluring prospect. Like it or not though, winter was moving in and there wasn't much to be done about it. Dropping down from the high moors she joined the main road which by-passed Cockermouth and took her eventually to the historic market town of Penrith, and the welcome sight of shops, cafes and the trappings of civilisation.

*   *   *

The winter day passed quickly, and night was falling as she drove along the valley road towards Twilight Cottage. Unaccountably her previously restored spirits began to flag. Taking her hand from the wheel she winced but managed to place an *Enya* tape in the cassette player. *The Celts.* – and very appropriate too! She hummed along to the music, imaging Celtic warriors crossing the high moors in the mist, their horses stepping in time to the insistent beat of the drum. Rousing stuff, she felt better already. Besides, it had been a good day. There was food, wine and a fresh bottle of whisky in the boot, and the prospect of visiting Barbara the following day.

The first stars were visible between the lattice of branches as the car lurched down the track to the cottage. She gasped as the nearside wheel stuck in a deep rut and spun abortively, then heaved a sigh of relief as it found a grip and pulled clear. At last the cottage appeared in the clearing, framed by the silhouette of giant pines. Safely back. And despite her expectations, her visit to the castle had been accomplished without being besieged by trauma, anger and fear.

They were waiting for her as she stepped from the car.

TWENTY-SIX

~

The slam of the car door sounded extra loud in the silence of the clearing. Jo's heart began to beat faster; she sensed a presence seconds before seeing the figure emerge from the trees. The man stood before her, his stance conveying menace as she peered through the darkness, trying to guess his identity. "Who is it? What do you want?" she demanded, hearing the quiver and fear as she spoke. *Seth Rigby?* The first name to come into her head. Danger prickled the nape of her neck. He was unbalanced, the last person she wanted to meet out here on a dark night, and there was no help within shouting distance. Desperately she fought down the rising panic. Her hand was trembling as she fumbled in her jacket pocket for her torch. "What do you want?" she repeated, pressing the torch's button and aiming the beam at the intruder.

She gasped aloud. Not Seth Rigby after all. "Colin!" Her voice now held a note of hysteria, and she felt giddy with relief, until the beam shone full on his face. She took a step back on seeing his expression. Fury had etched a stranger's lines on his once familiar features. "Colin?" she prompted nervously when he still didn't speak.

He stepped forward, half crouching in menace. "Where have you been?" he grated, his eyes glittering with fury in the torch light.

"I beg your pardon?" Despite her fear, Jo bridled at his tone.

"I've been waiting. You were out. I've been waiting hours in the dark."

She stared, unable to believe this was happening. "Go home Colin. I'll talk to you tomorrow," she said striving to keep her voice steady whilst edging her way to the front door.

"Stop!"

The command echoed around the glade, an undying echo of the past. Petrified, she halted and slowly turned.

His eyes now held a manic look. His right arm was raised, palm outward, in peremptory manner, reinforcing the spoken command. He slowly lowered it as she obeyed. Clouds bowled sluggishly southwards, revealing a moon that was close to the full. In the cold and eerie half-light he seemed more a stranger than ever; she had to keep reminding herself that this was Colin, the guy who had come to her rescue and driven her to hospital. Only it didn't *feel* like Colin. A slow-worm of panic began to stir and uncoil in the pit of her stomach. A ghostly shape gliding through the trees briefly distracted her, and she had to stifle the spontaneous cry that rose in her throat. The owl swooped and somewhere in the thicket a vole or other small creature shrieked. Silence settled over the glade and her attention swung back to Colin. Seemingly confident now he approached, his eyes holding hers with every step he took.

"Won't you come inside for a drink, Colin?" she asked, striving to keep her voice even, and thinking that if she could only reach the door she could maybe get inside and slam it shut in his face. But a crafty look was spreading across his features as though he guessed her intention. "Stay where you are." He closed the gap between them. "Now tell me where you've been," he said persuasively, his voice caressing her like a velvet glove, but Jo sensed the suppressed anger and menace beneath. She decided the wisest course was to humour him. "Barrowburn Castle."

Immediately the mask slipped and fury stared out from his eyes. "You're lying!"

"Why should I?"

"To cover up what you were really doing; your secret meetings."

"You're mad."

She gasped as he drew back his arm to strike. "Colin!" she screamed.

Indecision and confusion flitted across his face, were mirrored in his eyes. As his hand wavered she added: "Don't do this Colin," stressing his name. "I told you, I went to Barrowburn Castle."

"Lying bitch! You have not been home since you left this morning."

Jo stared at him, her face ashen. *Justin St. Clair.* The name scorched her mind.

As a cold sweat began to break out on her forehead and she felt about to faint, he lowered his arm to his side. He crumpled then, just as he had in the studio after making that clumsy pass; his behaviour had been bizarre on that occasion too, she recalled. He stumbled now like a blind man, hands pressed to his temples, his body shaking as though from shock. Jo took a couple of deep breaths. The intense cold hurt her forehead and revived her senses. For a moment she stood in silence, wondering what was to be done. He couldn't just be left here, and didn't look capable of getting himself home. She made up her mind. "Come on, Colin," she soothed, gingerly taking his arm. When he made no effort to pull away or attack, she led him towards the car and opened the passenger door. "Get in, I'll run you back to Throstle Garth."

Obediently he climbed in and sat down.

He looked at her dazed. "What happened?"

Jo, about to turn on the ignition, switched on the interior light and swivelled round to face him, scanning his drawn and pallid features through half closed eyes. "I don't know," she said at last, "you had some sort of funny turn." Despite the vacant expression there was no smell of alcohol on his breath, she noted. "How did you get here – on foot?"

He nodded, then sat in silence for a moment rubbing his forehead. "What did I say?"

"You got all uptight and demanded to know where I'd been. I told you Barrowburn Castle and at that you threw a wobbler."

He frowned and absently rubbed his forehead. "But why? Why on earth should I?"

Jo shrugged. "You accused me of being a liar. Said I had not been *home* all day." She watched his face closely for a response, but the fazed look remained.

"Why in God's name should I say that, Jo?" he looked genuinely distressed, and his voice was not quite steady. "It's your own business, if you want to go out for the day."

It was Jo's turn to frown. Had she misunderstood? Read too much into the remark? she wondered now, watching his face and feeling almost as confused as Colin Gilmour looked. She decided to test him out. "I think there's something very odd going on here at this cottage," she said evenly.

"Like what?" he asked wearily, resuming the rhythmical stroking of his forehead so that she felt she would scream. Impetuously she leaned forward and grasped his arm to make him desist. "Well don't you think it strange that twice now in our short acquaintance you admit to acting out of character?" she demanded releasing his arm. "In fact this time" she continued as he let it drop like a lifeless thing into his lap, "on your own admission, you don't even remember what you said."

"Oh, come on Jo, let's not get this out of proportion."

"Colin, you were about to hit me," she said quietly.

He stared at her, horror and incredulity warring in his expression.

"It's true," Jo insisted.

Tension vibrated between them, an elastic band stretched to snapping point. "Jo, I'm sorry. I don't know – that is, I have to take your word for it," he shook his head in a gesture of helplessness. "Look -I wouldn't hurt you for the world. I'm not a violent man."

"I know Colin, and it's alright. I had to tell you. If we're to beat this thing, we have to accept there's something going on here."

He shook his head again in bewilderment. "But why would I want to strike you?"

"I don't think *you* did," she said levelly.

"What are you getting at?"

"Well, that remark of yours – about Barrowburn," she insisted. He looked at her blankly. "So?"

"Don't you see, Colin? It's as though you were referring to the castle *as my home*."

He grimaced. "I suppose you could take it that way at a pinch. But why should I do that?"

"It was the home of Justin St. Clair – and *his wife*."

"Justin who –?" He snorted with disgust as realisation struck. "Christ – not that medieval knight again! Come on Jo, this is just a little O.T.T. don't you think?"

"Okay, so it's sounds crazy," she admitted stubbornly. But it fits, don't you see? It's not your emotion at all – you're just a vehicle for Justin St Clair's anger." She sighed on seeing his expression. "So how else do you account for it?"

"By way of one crazy woman! I was okay until you came, Jo. You've been a problem since I clapped eyes on you – one way or the other." He gave her an ironic smile, and a look which told her it was time to switch off the light, turn on the ignition and get him home to Finola.

She stopped outside Throstle Garth, knocked the car out of gear and let the engine idle. "By the way, why *did* you walk over to the cottage?" she asked out of curiosity, but also expediency as it dawned upon her that Finola might not be too thrilled with the situation.

He looked at her blankly, as though he had forgotten. "Oh, er, to ask you over for a drink. We thought you might be a bit pissed off with your own company."

Jo grinned. "I'm not. But thanks anyway."

"You might as well come in now you're here – there's nothing to rush back to."

"I want an early start in the morning."

"Going somewhere?"

"To visit my sister actually," she said coolly, her tone implying it was none of his business.

Before he could pursue the matter, the door to the farmhouse opened shedding a wedge of light into the darkness. Finola appeared and stood silhouetted against the glow, her anxiety apparent in her stance. "Is that you, Col?" she called, as they got out of the car.

"Yes – it's okay. Jo's here." He slammed the car door and waited for Jo at the gate. "A case of 'least said', I think," he said under his breath.

"Sure."

Jo followed him up the path.

Finola looped her hair over her ears for the third time since Jo had arrived. "I was getting worried," she complained, looking across at Colin who was sitting moodily by the log fire, glass in hand. "You'd been gone an age."

"I was out," Jo said quickly. "and Colin was – well, a bit concerned at the place being in darkness, so he waited. I've only just got back."

"Oh." Finola sipped her gin and tonic and tried to sound casual, but without much success. "I thought perhaps you'd asked him in for a drink before coming on here."

"No." Jo, becoming irritated by her obvious suspicion and the need to explain, made it clear there was nothing more to be said.

"It would have been alright of course, if you had," Finola persisted, thus making it even worse.

"Forget it, Fin." Colin glared at her over his glass, then held it out for a refill.

"I was only saying –," She peered at Colin over her gold-rimmed glasses and looked hurt.

"I could do with another drink, please Fin." Colin's hard-eyed look gave the lie to the softness of his voice.

Finola shrugged and took the glass from his outstretched hand. Not for the first time, Jo thought how wearing it must be for Colin to live with Finola's intensity. Was that the reason behind his outbursts of bizarre behaviour? The frustration and irritation of constantly feeling he was under the microscope? Comforting thought. Or did it make him susceptible to someone else's influences and moods? *Someone like Justin St. Clair?* came the unwelcome rider.

"Heard the crack then?" Colin asked rousing himself, then seeing her puzzled expression he added: "Local-speak! You know – news, gossip."

Jo smiled. "Oh, I see. No, what's that?"

"Seth Rigby. He's had a bit of a tussle with a chain saw."

Jo grimaced. "How awful. What happened?"

"He was sawing logs in the bottom field," Finola supplied, mellowing after two and a half gin and tonics coupled with an apologetic smile from Colin. "Apparently the blade slipped."

"Is he badly injured?" Jo inquired.

"His arm's stitched up," Colin answered. "Could have lost it. He was bloody lucky really: could have died out there from loss of blood. Fortunately his son-in-law called round, wanting to speak to him about leasing a field, and Seth's wife sent him out looking."

Finola leaned forward and said in a conspiratorial voice: "Seems folk are saying Seth's not been himself of late. You know, vague – and sort of preoccupied. His attention must have wandered."

"Easy done," Colin commented. "You have to watch what you're doing with chain saws. Bloody dangerous things."

Jo shuddered and said nothing; Colin, evidently picking up on her discomfort, swiftly changed tack. "Could be snow soon," he prophesied as Finola showed a marked disinclination to relinquish the subject of Seth.

Finola was on her fourth gin and tonic when she returned to it and disclosed: "Some-one has been putting it about that Seth is having some sort of breakdown."

"From what I can make out, he's no odder than many others around here," Colin said mildly.

Finola shook her head with vehemence and said in a hushed voice: "You don't understand. He thinks he's been *cursed*."

"Oh, come on Finola!" Colin exclaimed, looking irritated.

"It's true," Finola protested, her cheeks flushed.

Colin shook his head. "Village gossip. It's a wonder they're not still burning witches!"

"Colin – get your facts right," Finola said waspishly, "I didn't say he was cursed – only that he *thinks* he is. There is a subtle difference!"

"Gossip," Colin repeated with a dismissive wave of his hand.

"So why is his wife so distressed?" Finola demanded.

Unable to remain silent any longer, Jo intervened. "Finola's right."

"What?" glass in hand, Colin swivelled round on his chair.

"It's true," Jo insisted. "Something odd *has* happened to Seth." She looked round at the other two, aware of Finola's gratitude. "If you ask me he's totally flipped. And it's something to do with that old legend. It's my guess Seth disturbed something when he dug Maud's grave."

Love you, kill you

Jo froze. The words seemed to echo around the room. Fear spread in ripples, as from a pebble tossed into a pool. Or had it just been inside her head? No, because a curious silence had fallen. Odd, because as at Twilight Cottage, it persisted despite the clunk-ing of ancient pipes and the ticking of the clock. Finola looked at Colin then peered into the shadowed corners. Picking up a scrap of embroidery stretched on a miniature frame, she fiddled first with the needle then a skein of red silk. "Do you really believe that Jo?" she whispered, putting down the frame. "It's a bit far-fetched, but scary too. What do you think Colin?"

Colin scowled and massaged the nape of his neck. "Oh, change the subject, for God's sake."

Jo drew in breath sharply as a draught of cold air brushed her cheek.

She blinked as a voice penetrated her reverie.

"Jo?" Colin was prompting.

"Sorry," Jo started as he touched her hand, and looking across at him, forced herself to concentrate on what he was saying. But it was difficult, like trying to follow what's being said on T.V. when somebody is talking from close behind your chair. "What were you saying?"

"I asked if you cracked the hot water problem."

"Oh, that – yes. Yes, thanks." She half-turned her head as she spoke, feeling again the touch of cold air against her cheek.

"What's wrong with you?" he asked, frowning with irritation.

Forever, forever.

"Didn't you hear anything?" Jo asked, looking from one to the other of her companions.

"Like what?" Colin demanded, whilst Finola shrugged and shook her head.

"Oh, nothing." Jo played with her glass. They may not have heard it, but they certainly felt something, she thought resentfully. Colin was as jumpy as a racehorse at the gate. Obviously the subject was taboo, talking made it real. Jo rubbed her arms; the temperature had dramatically dropped. Thirty seconds later the electric light dipped and the bulb exploded with a *plop*. Jo exclaimed aloud, and Finola gave a little cry as the kitchen was plunged into darkness.

"Shit!" Colin swore softly. He could be heard moving around the room. "Okay, Colin?" Jo tried not to panic as she strained to see through the pitch blackness.

"Yep. Just stay where you are."

"Col? Oh, Col what's happening?"

Finola, Jo realised with a jolt, was just this side of hysteria and ready to freak out at any moment. "It's okay, Finola," she said, groping for the other woman's hand. She found it, and Finola's fingers curled round her own and clung on for dear life. There was the rasp of match on box. A flame flared and Colin's face, eerily lit from beneath, was visible as he held the match to one of the candles on the table. Then a second wick glowed and the flame waved gently and elongated, and Jo felt her panic abating.

"It's okay, folks," Colin said in his laid-back manner. "They're probably having some snow up north."

"No!"

Jo and Colin gaped at Finola.

"It's more than that. There's something going on here – and I don't like it," Finola added before either of them could speak.

Colin sighed with exasperation. "It's a power failure for God's sake – stop reading something else into it."

"I'm not!" Finola snapped with an unusual show of spirit. "There *is* something wrong, and it has something to do with Jo." She stared defiantly at Jo.

"Hey, steady on Fin," Colin remonstrated, glancing at Jo then away again with obvious discomfort.

"It's true! Things have not felt right since the day she arrived," Finola insisted, her mouth setting in stubborn lines. But there was fear in her eyes too, and she stared about her from time to time, peering into corners like an animal in a trap.

"I don't believe this! Have you been reading *The Witches of Pendle* again by any chance?" Colin sneered. "If I remember right, you had that temp. barmaid down as one, not to mention the midwife."

Finola flushed scarlet. "I only said they would have had charges laid against them had they lived in those times," she said hotly.

"Huh! You would be first to be burned, according to –,"

"No, you're right, Fin. There *is* something odd going on," Jo admitted, cutting in and raising a peremptory hand to halt Colin, who shrugged and looked away. "I take your point, but I could say my life was normal until I came to your valley," she countered. "And it isn't helpful to pretend it doesn't exist, but that's what people do when they're scared," she said with a challenging look for Colin.

"If that's directed at me it's bullshit! there's nothing to be scared *of*," Colin said scornfully. "Look, Fin's had a drink or two and it tends to make her over-sensitive," he explained, his tone and gestures conveying his distaste.

"And it certainly doesn't help to blame alcohol or Fin," Jo replied with asperity.

Colin rose abruptly. "I've had enough of this. I'll be in my studio."

"That's right – run away like you always do when I need your support," Finola accused. "It's a form of betrayal – know that?"

She screamed as the candle flames dipped and almost went out.

For a moment they sat in shocked silence, then the flames steadied and Jo could see the tears wet on Finola's cheeks. She frowned at Colin and indicated with a gesture that he should offer comfort.

"I'm scared. Really scared," Finola said before he could move. "Something dreadful is going to happen before this is over."

"What makes you say that?" Colin floundered out of his depth, managing to look worried and exasperated at the same time.

Finola's anger evaporated in the cold flame of fear. "I just know it," she whispered, looping her hair behind her ears with hands that shook. Silent sobs wracked her slight body. Jo could smell and taste the other woman's terror.

"Finola, please, try to calm down." Jo rose and moving around the table, tried to put an arm around her shoulders.

Finola shrank back and shook her off. "Leave me alone!" she cried. "It's all your fault. You've brought something here with you!"

Colin crossed to Finola and awkwardly put his arm around her shaking shoulders, then looked helplessly at Jo. "I think you'd better go. Sometimes, when she's had too much –,"

"Not this time, Colin," Jo said grimly, giving him a hard look. "This isn't down to drink. Wake up to what's happening here, will you?"

He smoothed the top of Finola's head with his hand and she became quieter. Gradually her trembling ceased and she sagged against Colin. "She's had too much gin," he insisted, his mouth setting in a familiar line of stubbornness.

Jo shrugged. "Okay. Have it your own way. But if you need any help –"

Colin's defensiveness fell away like a discarded coat. "Thanks, that's good of you. But she'll be alright now. Won't you love?"

Finola looked up at him, then across at Jo. She had stopped crying, and looked less distressed. Jo felt the tension drain from her shoulders, and noted with relief that the sense of menace had slunk back into the shadows.

"I'm sorry Jo. I don't know what got into me," Finola said haltingly, tears of remorse welling up and threatening to overspill again.

"It's okay, Finola." Crossing to her side, Jo lightly kissed Finola's cheek and was relieved when she didn't pull away. "Besides, I was to blame," she added, giving Finola's hand a squeeze before letting go and walking to the door.

Colin frowned. "How do you make that one out?"

Jo turned and shrugged. "I happen to think Finola's right: I brought something here with me tonight." She left before either of them could speak.

Weariness and trepidation assailed her as she parked the car and opened the front door of Twilight Cottage. Along with all else, her hand was aching and felt red hot. Warily, she shone her torch on the wall, examining it carefully before flicking down the switch. Good: no slugs, and any power failure seemed to be confined to Throstle Garth. She went through the rooms switching on lights, her gaze sweeping from corner to corner. Nothing out of the ordinary leapt to her attention; it seemed to have played itself out for the night. Except that this evening the cottage felt exceptionally cold and hostile.

Emptying the contents of her jacket pocket, she left the notebook on the table, resisting the urge to study the inscription. It may only instigate more phenomena, she decided, or its enigma keep her awake and she was desperate for sleep. Not bothering to wash, she went straight upstairs, dropped her clothes on the floor and climbed into bed. Once or twice she awoke to the sound of scratching, but pulling the covers over her head, resolutely ignored it and slept.

TWENTY-SEVEN

~

Shadows were beginning to lengthen on the sward. The air was growing chill, the dampness rising from the white chock stones lining the riverbank and there was little warmth left in the rays of winter-sun that struck low through the doorway of the ruins. Nonetheless, he wished they could stay there forever. Madeline stirred and tried to disentangle herself from the cocoon he had made of his thick woollen cloak. She sighed and lifted her head from his shoulder where it had been resting, and pain caught his chest as her eyes brimmed with sadness and longing. "I cannot stay long today, my love."

He held her close, refusing to release her from the confining swathes of material. "Come away with me, Madeline."

She looked at him in silence, her eyes holding fear now as well as love. He must persuade her, this way of life was becoming impossible for them both. "Come away with me, love," he urged again, his green eyes river-dark with passion.

Almost imperceptibly she shook her head. "We should be outcasts, Antony. Exiles without a country."

He frowned and held her tighter. "There can be no home anywhere without you."

Her eyes darkened with sadness. "He would never release me. We should never be safe; he would hunt us down like wild beasts."

He pulled her close again and stroked her chestnut hair. "Death is preferable to separation."

"Yes, always." And his heart leapt, but then she shook her head and sealed his lips with the tip of her index finger. "And William?" she whispered.

He sighed and closed his eyes in desperation. Her child – and Justin St. Clair's heir. As such St. Clair would never let them go. To put their own lives at risk was one thing, but to risk an innoncent child – that was another matter. He sighed as a black tide of frustration and hopelessness choked him. Unless perhaps –, if she were to leave the boy, St. Clair may be content to let them go. But how could he ask that of her?

It was still dark when Jo left the cottage to set off for Lancaster. The world shivered in the pre-dawn cold and a thick frost whitened the fields. It was to be hoped the high road over the moor wasn't iced, but the water in the butt wasn't frozen, she noticed on getting into the car, so maybe it would still be passable. Her heart sank as the engine coughed sluggishly and the battery objected to the intense cold. She had been meaning to put a new one in for the winter, but good intention had been overtaken by recent events. Exasperated she turned the key in the ignition and throttled-up again. A movement in the trees caught her eye and made her stomach lurch.

Leaning forward she peered through the patch cleared by her scraper on the frosted windscreen. She could have sworn there was somebody lurking amongst the shrubbery. Fear stabbed at her belly causing her to feel physically sick. It wasn't her imagination: the man, who had been partially hidden by the trees, ducked back into the shadows, but not before the moonlight had struck the knife-blade in his hand. Her breath rose in small white clouds as it quickened in terror. The engine coughed as she pumped the accelerator. Then came the tell-tale whine as the engine lacked sufficient juice to turn over.

She stared out of the window on the passenger side, heart thumping as the man's shadow moved darkly across the frosted glass. The crystals of ice blurred her vision, but not enough to obscure the flash of metal in his hand as he moved around to the back of the car. Feverishly she pumped the pedal and repeatedly turned the key as panic rose and choked the scream that rose in her throat. The engine gave a series of staccato coughs and whined intermittently, refusing to bite.

Automatically her gaze went to the mirror; the figure was standing at the rear of the car. She saw him clearly this time: the strong features beneath dark unruly hair, the white robe with the fiery splash of the emblem on his chest. He was standing quite still, yet a maelstrom raged around him. Pulsing, beating anger screamed inside her head, dazing her with its intensity, and at the same time a towering love consumed her, but a love that fuelled the hatred and fury, because it was doomed and bittersweet. Sobbing with fear and frustration she banged the steering wheel with her fist. Still the car refused to start. Filled with dread she looked again in the mirror; the figure had disappeared. Nothing moved on the road or beneath the trees at either side.

At the same time insight struck like lightning: *given the frosting, she should not have been able to see so clearly through the rear window.* The dark strips, growing wider by the minute, should have told her immediately but her mind had been numbed by panic. She checked, and with mingled relief and foolishness at her own stupidity, pressed the rocker switch that controlled the heated rear panel to the 'off' position. It had turned frosty on her journey home last night, and she must have left it on – which explained why the car was reluctant to start. With a bit of luck the plugs would fire now that the heater was switched off, or had it already seriously depleted the juice? She forced herself to wait a minute or two before trying again. Finally the urge to escape proved too insistent, and praying she had not flattened the battery further by continually trying, Jo took a deep breath and turned the key.

The banging on the window close to her right ear made her whip round, and at the same time her scream reverberated around the car. Shock waves ran through her like an electric current; a figure was peering in through the porthole cleared by her scraper, the distorted face bizarrely framed by thick whorls of white. Not Justin St. Clair as expected but Seth Rigby, and he was gesticulating and grimacing horribly as he scraped the glass in order to see her more clearly. In that brief second it registered that his left arm was in a sling and the triangle of white was stained red where blood was seeping through. His fist hammered again at the car window. Holding her breath she grasped the key in the ignition, held it there and stamped on the throttle. She almost wept with relief as the engine fired. The wheels whined as they spun on the frosty ground, finally bit and the car shot forward. She was left with an impression of Seth Rigby's contorted face as he fell back from the window.

By the time the car climbed the winding road out of the valley, dawn had broken and she was having doubts about what she had actually seen. Her mind was still reeling with shock, but with darkness gone and normality restored it became increasingly difficult to accept. As she drove over frosted moors stained red by a rising sun, she was ready to believe it had been a delusion. Fear, panic and expectations had coloured her preception. There had been no Justin St. Clair, only a paranoid farmer called Seth Rigby. The iced-up windows had distorted his form, and there had been no white robe with a red hawk crest, only a sling stained with blood. Sleepless nights and her own imagination had supplied the rest. It all sank back into true perspective as the space, beauty and isolation of the moor surrounded her and brought a rush of exhiliration.

But then as the fell road stretched on into loneliness and seeming infinity, the pain of her own bandaged hand claimed her attention, and doubts began to creep in again. Strange that Seth Rigby should pick her, a complete stranger, as the object of his paranoia, that he should also have connections with the newly dug grave, and also have suffered an injury. No, the theory voiced to Colin and Finola the night before could not be discounted, she decided, unnerved rather than exhilirated now by the expanse of high moor, with nothing but the odd wedge of bent and gnarled-backed trees to break the aching emptiness. It seemed that something more than coincidence linked her, however unwillingly, with Seth Rigby. A glance in the mirror made her automatically shrink lower down in the seat: a backdrop of high peaks brooded on the horizon and glowered over her departure. Almost as though they disapprove, she thought removing one hand from the steering wheel to rub the nape of her neck. She sighed with relief as a grey roof below signified the existence of a farmhouse, and the end of lunar isolation. And with Colin too, she mused, navigating the twisting descent past a white walled pub to the main road, whilst recalling his bizarre and terrifying behaviour. And whatever it was had something to do with the cottage, the ring and whatever lurked beneath Maud's grave.

Due to the earliness of the hour and consequent absence of heavy traffic, she made good time to the motorway and on to Lancaster and its library, where she sat at a table in the English History section. The odour of leather bindings, dust and ancient wood filled her with anticipation as she began to turn page after yellowed page. Within half an hour or so she had found a couple of references to Barrowburn Castle and the St. Clair's who, it seemed, were a prominent local family. Excitement gripped her. Now she had another name: that of Justin St. Clair's wife Madeline. The scandal of her disgrace, it seemed, accounted for much of the family's local notoriety and prominence in the annals of history. *Madeline St. Clair.* The name had brought to life a hitherto shadowy figure. These were real people, with complicated and tragic lives. Lives, she thought disturbed, which were somehow impinging on her own.

The library had not long since opened its doors and was therefore devoid of browsers. In fact Jo had the history section all to herself, which was just as well, given her startled exclamation as she turned the next page. Madeline St. Clair stared out at her, the intensity of her gaze bringing a buzz of shock. The reproduced portrait showed a woman of beauty with feline eyes and tumbling chestnut locks. Most disturbing of all was the sense of *déjà vu,* the feeling that this was not the face of a stranger.

Jo shivered and stared at the picture for several minutes, telling herself it didn't make sense; despite the obvious gulf of time – almost seven centuries – and the fact that until recently Madeline St. Clair had been totally unknown to her, there persisted an odd sense of recognition, even intimacy. The woman seemed to be pleading with her, to be reaching out for compassion and understanding.

A chill crept down from the surrounding shelves, and the musty smell of old books combined with the rankness she had once smelled in an abattoir whilst doing research for a paper – an odour that had prompted a vow to go vegetarian – the unmistakable stench of fear. Jo blinked, looked away, then back again at the picture. The aura of fear remained. The disturbing visual changes were still apparent: the sparkle and vitality had drained from the face leaving a haunted, terror-stricken look; the mute appeal still wrung Jo's heart. She rose to her feet, moved to the right then left of the table, then round the nearest shelf unit and back again. It made no difference. Wherever she stood those eyes followed and bored into her own. Jo gripped the edge of the table until her knuckles turned white. Fear and desperation washed over her in waves, filling her mind with dread and darkness. She was back in the bed-room at the cottage, lying there in the gloom, hearing again those terrible wails splitting the night. She shook her head in denial. It had only been the wind howling in the chimney.

She slammed the book shut and pushed it violently across the table, then looked guiltily over her shoulder. One of the librarians had entered the section, was in the process of putting a book from her trolley onto the shelf. She paused to give Jo a mildly disapproving glance over her glasses, but then looked away again and discreetly moved on to the next section. Jo sat very still, fighting off dizziness and a wave of nausea. The sense of being invaded, of an assault upon her psyche by violent emotions, persisted. Enough research for one day, she decided, making her way unsteadily to the door. Because her search had also disclosed one other vital piece of information. The St. Clair family crest was a boar's head. There had been no mention of the hawk.

She left the motorway and was soon driving through the village of Quernmore where Barbara shared a house with Oliver, her live-in boyfriend who was also a lecturer at Lancaster. However Jo didn't slow down but carried on along the main route to the University.

There had only been time for a brief telephone call to let Barbara know she was coming, and unfortunately she had lectures and seminars booked for most of the day. So it was to be a pub-lunch at one of the bars on campus, and Barbara, Jo thought glancing at the clock in the dash would be finishing her morning lecture about now.

The University sprawled across a gentle mound surrounded by aspen, mature broadleaf woodland, and with the blue-grey Pennines for backdrop, giving it a sense of being secluded from the outside world. There persisted a rarefied atmosphere, an air of being sheltered from the frenzy of business, family pressures and the mediocrity of everyday life. "Toy Town" as Barbara sometimes affectionately referred to it; a mini-cosmos of its own. As always on these visits, Jo was aware of the buzz in the air as she left the car and made her way to Cartmel College. Only today it excluded her. Which, she recognised, was probably because she felt alienated from the rational world. The realm in which she now seemed to move rested on delusion, intuition and shifting realities she thought wryly, pushing open the door to the Sociology Department.

Barbara swept the crumbs from her 'ploughman's' off the table with the edge of one hand, and into the palm of the other. "I can help you there I think," she said dropping the bits into a black pot ashtray bearing a harp logo and the legend *Guinness* in gilt letters. Jo turned from watching Karl Marx, the resident cat of Cartmel College Bar, skilfully cajoling a macho, long-haired student into offering the last morsel of ham from his sandwich. "The rhyme, you mean," Jo said, smiling as Marx twitched his black battle-notched ears in anticipation, then she leaned forward, elbows on table, and the smile faded. "I rather hoped you could. It's been, well –," she broke off and made an expressive gesture with her hands.

"I guessed. The strain is showing in your face, Jo." Barbara commented, giving her sister an anxious look. "And what's wrong with your hand?"

Jo shook her head. "I'm okay. No really," she maintained, sighing with irritation as Barbara insisted on seeing.

For a moment Barbara stared at her younger sister in horrified silence. Jo, also alarmed and striving to hide it, replaced the dressing over the suppurating wound and surrounding blueish-green flesh.

"Kiddo, you have to get that seen to – like fast," Barbara said, her face and voice grim.

"I'll get some antibiotics," Jo said shortly.

"I should. Like yesterday," Barbara caught her bottom lip in her front teeth, her pallor and shocked expression betraying her concern. "Otherwise, it might need –"

"I said I will," Jo interrupted, not wanting to hear her own fear confirmed by being spoken aloud. "So what do you have for me?" she demanded, picking up her glass of Jennings Best Bitter. "Shoot!"

Barbara frowned. "Okay, but make sure you get that hand seen to."

She gave Jo a long look then settled on her chair as though deciding there was little point in pursuing the issue further. "So, that peculiar rhyme. Well the symbols are pretty obvious," she began: "the reference to the sun turning black, the red moon and the 'pale horseman' are all from *Revelations*."

Jo grimaced and put down her glass. "Sorry? I missed the connection."

Barbara unwrapped a plastic dental hygiene stick and delicately picked at her teeth whilst tilting her head to one side in a speculative manner. "The Day of Judgment – no?" She screwed up the wrapper and dropping it in the ashtray alongside the crumbs, "When the dead are supposed to rise from the grave," she prompted.

The sudden stillness was palpable over the hum and bustle of the bar. Jo stared into her sister's candid grey eyes. "How could I have been so dumb?" she said at last.

"I did wonder." Barbara grinned as Jo looked indignant. "But then it is my line of work remember."

Jo fiddled with a beer mat. Her eyes when she looked up at her sister were dark with anxiety. "I'm not sure I can handle this."

Barbara's flippancy evaporated and she leaned across the table to briefly touch Jo's hand. "Hey, let's not get carried away here."

Jo dropped the beer mat and ran her fingers through her hair. "I just can't explain, Barbara. These things that are happening to me – I'm beginning to think I've flipped or something!"

"You've done nothing of the sort!" Barbara said in bracing tones. "There's probably a logical explanation."

Jo gave her a sceptical look. "Such as?"

Barbara shrugged. "I've been thinking. It's possible that an ancient energy pattern imprinted itself on the area, into the rocks maybe. Violent emotions of the past can have this effect."

"So why should it erupt now? And affect *me*?"

"We'd be looking for something that set it off, a trigger. Something that could have reactivated the energies concerned. Any ideas?"

Unwilling to voice her theory about the grave, Jo shook her head. "Not really."

"Never mind, it's just an idea, something to be working on."

Jo nodded. "I'll let you know if I come up with anything. But in the meantime, what else have you got on the inscription?"

Barbara shrugged again. "I think the date is a major clue to the King's Stone bit. In 1297 Edward 1 invaded Scotland and stole the Stone of Scone on which the Kings of Scotland were seated at their coronation. He had it built into Westminster Abbey."

"*Beneath the throne*," Jo quoted, tapping her forehead with the heel of her good thumb. "How could I be so thick!"

"I guess you had other things on your mind, Jo." Barbara finished her drink and put down her glass. "From what you've told me, it can't be much fun, alone in that isolated cottage. Anyway, my guess is the reference to the Stone is designed to spell out the St. Clair family's allegiance to Edward and England. He was at war with Scotland, remember. But you were going to tell me about your trip to the library."

Jo frowned and absently watched Carl Marx selecting his next victim. "But that's why this thing still doesn't gel. You see, the –" she paused and made a gesture of helplessness, "thing, person, whatever it is I'm aware of in my psyche," she struggled on, "well I told you remember, he was wearing a white surplice with a –,"

"Red hawk on his chest," Barbara finished for her, nodding.

Jo felt a *frisson* of presentiment. From experience, her sister's air of confidence meant only one thing. She chose a wooden toothpick from the container on the table. "You know something, don't you?" she accused.

Barbara looked smug. "After you first told me about your 'accident', I got to thinking and did a little research of my own. It wasn't difficult. We have a data base of references for myths, legends, folklore and sites of interest which is nationwide. I simply entered the Cumbria directory and there it was. A colleague in the Department did some work on this particular one a couple of years ago. She left at Easter," she added quickly as Jo leaned forward, eyes shining with anticipation.

"Damn!" Jo subsided again, her excitement deflated.

"Most of the stuff you already have anyway," Barbara soothed. "The affair, the elopement, the alleged haunting and sitings of a figure. The orthodox version."

Jo's fingers tightened on the toothpick; it splintered. "There's another?"

Barbara shrugged. "There could be."

"So tell." Jo waited, tapping the table with her finger whilst a silent communication went on between Barbara and the young man behind the bar. Barbara smiled and briefly raised her hand to indicate they didn't wish to order again. The man nodded acknowledgement and called out "Last orders, please" and Barbara turned her attention back to Jo. "There's something I should maybe tell you first."

"About the inscription?" Jo prodded, still tapping impatiently.

"About 'your knight'. One thing is sure: his name isn't Justin St. Clair."

Jo's mind did a somersault, a backward flip. From the start, from first hearing the legend, she had felt sure of his identity. Had taken it for granted. And that was just it, she realised looking back, she had automatically assumed the figure in her visions and Justin St. Clair were one and the same. She took a deep breath. "So who is he?" Time seemed to stand still as she waited.

* * *

Sir Antony Chase. Not Justin St. Clair after all. Jo's mind was in turmoil as she made her way back to Cumbria and Twilight Cottage. Her one thought now was to arrive home and sort out the muddle of facts that swirled around her head. Reaching for the switch she turned up the heat: the car was becoming icy cold.

Antony. Antony.

The whisper echoed around the car. She swerved and pulled out into the fast lane just in time to avoid running into the vehicle in front. She gripped the wheel hard, stared straight ahead and resolutely ignored the furious blares which accused her of cutting in. That was a close one. No need to panic. Auditory hallucination that's all, the voice had been inside her own head. Get it together, Cavanagh! she exhorted herself, checking her mirror before moving back into the middle lane.

It wouldn't leave her, was still tormenting her as she swung off the motorway onto the dual carriageway and up over the moorland road with its stark rocks and isolated skeleton trees scraping a sky of violet and green. And she was shivering despite having the heater turned to full power. But frost was sparkling on the fields, she thought, trying to convince herself that the chill inside the car was entirely accounted for by the weather.

Antony Antony

Whenever the name came to mind she was swamped by a terrible yearning, a love that made her ache with tenderness. Paradoxically it also brought an inexplicable fear, a sense of threat and menace, of impending and inevitable doom. "Antony, Oh, Antony who are you?" she found herself whispering into the gathering twilight.

Longing consumed her, and her thoughts turned to Blake. They seemed worlds apart, separated by miles and misunderstanding, yet love lingered on. The sense of loss and need became suddenly overwhelming, spilling over in tears which streamed down her face as she drove along the twisting road to the cottage.

It was dark by the time the car turned down the lane and into the narrow track. The wheels skidded and spinned abortively in the frozen furrows. She revved and swore, urging the car forward as the memory of the morning's horror returned. Every few minutes she peered anxiously over her shoulder, or into the shadows at either side of the track. At last the car slid to a halt and the cottage loomed white and ghostly in the gloom. Stupid, not to have left on the light. How, she wondered miserably, had her life ever got into this mess?

But it wasn't all her fault. Blake shouldn't have tried to force her hand, should have been patient. Instead he had gone chasing glory in Bosnia. It would appeal to him that: winning a victory where so many had tried and failed. An international hero. *A traitor guilty of betrayal.* Working to save all those lives, but betraying her love. Yet still he obsessed her. *Which one – Blake, or Antony?* Nothing was clear any more; a mist of uncertainty clouded reason, seducing her with whispered names, and faces that floated beyond reality. She passed a weary hand over her eyes and remained seated behind the wheel, submitting to the surge and flood of emotion in which she floundered. Unable to contain her feelings any longer, she dragged herself out of the car and stood with face upturned and arms outstretched to the star-strewn sky. Sobbing as though her heart would break, obeying a sudden compulsion she called Blake's name then: " Antony! Antony!"

As she endured the waves of anguish, the two became confused in her mind.

She was released from the tension as suddenly as a puppet whose strings are cut. She sagged, feeling the energy drain out of her and away. Looking around she became aware once more of her surroundings, and shook her head like a boxer coming round from a knockout punch. This was madness: Seth Rigby could be hanging about just waiting to pounce. She spun round, her heart pounding and gaze raking the perimeter of the clearing. Every shadow seemed darker than normal with menace, every clump of shrubbery a cover for lurking figures. Making a supreme effort to pull herself together, she ran for the front door, her feet sliding on the icy surface and almost letting her down. At last she was inside the cottage and shooting the bolt across the door.

The first thing she did was to go into the sitting room, then upstairs to the bedroom, to draw curtains across the windows. The thought of that mad farmer lurking outside and watching her movements made her flesh creep. The cottage was ice-cold, in the grate lurked a clump of dead grey cinders and ash. Dredging the will from somewhere deep down she reached for newspaper and kindling. Within a quarter hour or so a cheerful fire blazed, changing her mood. Things were not so bad: the research had paid off, the confusion about the mystery man's identity had been cleared and her feet were now on the right track.

Antony Antony

The whisper seemed to creep out from the corners and sibilate round the room. Resolutely closing her ears and mind to it she threw another log into the grate and dusted off her hands. She wouldn't think about that now; after making herself a snack she would sit down by the fire with a large whisky and, systematically and without emotion, sift through the information. She was on her way to the kitchen about to put her plan into action when the telephone rang.

Jo lifted the receiver, trying not to hope it was Blake. "Oh hi, Barbara. What is it?"

"Good, you're there." Barbara's voice conveyed relief. "Just wanted to know you'd got home o.k., what with the icy roads –,"

"I'm fine. At least I am now the fire is going again. It's bloody freezing out here."

"I'll bet. Not too bad down here. Er, Jo –,"

"Yes?"

"I've been thinking. About what we discussed today. It's only a thought, but have you considered consulting well, a medium?"

Jo plucked at the telephone wire then wrapped the coils around her finger, then uncoiled them again.

"Jo? Are you still there?"

"A medium?" Jo laughed nervously, and with not a little embarrassment.

"Yes, you know, a clairvoyant. Just to see if he or she picks up on anything. Vibes, that sort of thing, or a name perhaps. Who knows? It might be confirmation that something strange has been going on around you."

Jo chewed her bottom lip. "Do you believe in these things, Barbara?"

"No. But I don't disbelieve them either. Anyway, just an idea. Give it some thought. Goodnight Jo."

"Goodnight, Babs – and thanks for ringing."

Jo shook her head in perplexity as she replaced the receiver. What a bloody odd suggestion, especially from her own sister.

Still thinking about it, and smiling at the absurdity, she pushed open the kitchen door and walked inside. God it was freezing in here. And the stench! It hit her immediately and made her retch. At the same time the angry buzzing of bluebottles rose around her head. *Not again, please God, not again.* Without pausing to put on the light, she made her way to the window with the intention of throwing it wide, but stopped short and cried out as her foot trod on something soft and spongy. It was slippery too, so that she almost fell. She threw out her arms to steady herself, regained her balance and stood absolutely still. The chill of horror began to creep up her spine. What was she treading on here? Nameless fear threatened to bubble over into hysteria.

Slowly she began to back up to the door. By the light of the hall lamp behind her, she could make out several bulky shapes on the floor. Without taking her eyes off them she felt for the switch, but with infinite care, her fingers creeping over the wall, her fingers barely touching the surface lest something slimy waited there. At last the switch was beneath her hand.

The sigh of relief turned into a cry of horror as light flooded the kitchen.

TWENTY-EIGHT

~

Seth Rigby shook his head and appeared to be arguing with himself under his breath. He winced as he brought his good arm down to slice another of the pleachers in the laid hedge he was making. Janice hadn't wanted him to come out and do the job, but a couple of days of sitting around the house were more than enough. Anyway the job was almost done, and there was another half hour to sundown. He cast a wary eye on the rooks and crows that circled the green and purple-streaked sky, and muttered angrily beneath his breath, then paused to scowl at a huge black crow hunched on a nearby outcrop. "Piss off!" he shouted, stooping to pick up a stone and lob it at the bird. Uttering a guttural cry of indignation, it flapped its blue-black wings and rose in slow motion, appearing to hover before making lift-off.

The pain that nagged at Seth's left arm reminded him of that other crow-and-disaster-ridden day, and he blinked hard to shut out the memory of whirring teeth and the sudden splash of red. Instead he looked up again at the circling crows. Bloody things. Everyone knew they were about death, magic and dark deeds. He picked up his slasher again and carried on working. "You can bloody piss off too!" he shouted suddenly, hitting out at the empty air. "No! No! Piss off I said!" A weary rambler complete with red woollen hat and scarlet leggings, paused in walking along the adjacent bridleway, and his mouth dropped open as he gaped. Catching sight of him Seth paused and scowled, bill hook raised; the walker put down his head and lengthened his stride. "Bloody crag-rats," Seth muttered under his breath. Why they should spend time and energy going up mountains just to walk down them again was beyond him. He applied himself again to the job at hand.

This out-lying field tended to be left till the last. But if he didn't get this hedge in shape now, it would have a gappy bottom come spring, and a gappy hedge was useless for keeping in stock. He paused in mid-stroke. "No, no – NO!" he said emphatically, shaking his head and glancing sideways and to the rear. "I keep telling you, don't I?" He gave a vicious nudge of his elbow as though pushing someone or something out of the way. "Get 'way – and let me get on wi' me work." The razor edged slasher glinted in the light of a wintry low-slung sun. Down it came again, all but severing the strong upright, except for the vital strip of bark at the base. He nodded with satisfaction. And that was the trick: it would allow the sap to still rise and new shoots to spurt in spring. Then he'd have a good bushy hedge that the bolshiest 'yow' wouldn't scramble through. Canny buggers, sheep. He shook his head as he worked. Dying art, these living fences, youngsters mostly didn't want to know. At least his own sons and son-in-law were carrying on the tradition at their own farms. Learned by his example they had, and he was right proud of that.

But not of these other thoughts, the ones stained with horror, the anger-red pictures that kept appearing behind his eyes. It wasn't his fault mind. It was the whisperer. Kept saying things, urging him on to unspeakable acts. "No way," he muttered, taking a swipe at empty space with the bill hook.

He panted as he struggled to bend the pleacher over into its new prone position. T'waren't easy with one hand all but out of action. But he wasn't doing badly. Only two more to chop then he could rest a moment and enjoy a cuppa from his flask before hammering in the stabilising stakes. He reckoned he'd just about manage that before twilight. *If this moidering bugger will let me be.* He wriggled his shoulders in discomfort; the shadow was with him again. Ignore it, carry on with the job before the light fades. The next stage – a heathering of hazel shoots plaited between the pleachers to hold them, could wait until Jed was free to give him a hand.

He half-turned and made an impatient gesture as though to brush someone aside.

Slice.

The day of Maud's funeral filled his mind. And an image of her, the girl, standing on the rock above the cottage. "The lass ain't done *me* no harm."

Slice.

Another sapling was splayed at the base.

He screamed as her blood splashed hot on his face.

"No! No!" he screamed, staring down at the blood-soaked earth. First his shoulders, then his arms and legs began to shake. She was sprawled on the ground amidst the hedge, her legs almost severed below the knee. He could see the white splinters of bone sticking up from sliced muscle and flesh. There was blood everywhere. It gushed in spurts from her terrible wounds, sprayed his hands and face. Her eyes were staring at him, bulging with shocked horror and disbelief; and her mouth gaped as she screamed. The stumps that had been her legs began to twitch and jump of their own accord. A 'nerve' thing, wasn't it? he found himself thinking dispassionately: like a chicken running around the farmyard after its head had been cut off. Strange how he seemed split into two these days, one side of him shocked by what he was doing, the other completely numb. Like a mangol split with a single blow of a machete – *or a girl cut down like a pleached hedge.* Her screams were hurting him, filling his head. He had to stop them. He raised his good arm again; the screaming stopped.

Oh, Christ, what had he done?

He dropped the bill hook, covered his face with his hands and sank to his knees.

He looked up and squinted into the haze of the dying sun and blinked. The figure wavered before him like a mirage. Advanced and receded, then advanced again, like that scene in Lawrence of Arabia, the one with Peter O'Toole in the desert with the music. The one everyone remembers. "What do you want of me?" Seth whined, cringing. Despite the intense cold, sweat beaded his forehead and upper lip; the lower one trembled like that of a blubbering child. The figure was moving towards him, the features set in anger, the green eyes glittering with malice. Then it was upon him, engulfing him completely, surrounding him with pulsating light. He felt the warmth and wetness inside his trousers as fear relieved itself.

But to his surprise, the light which consumed him felt good. A low voltage buzz of electric recharging all his cells. He closed his eyes, moaning with pleasure as it grew and spread, becoming erotic, like coming – only better. But now it was paralysing in it's intensity. A pleasure so keen it bordered on pain. No, too much. "Stop! Stop!" His genitals were on fire, consumed by intimate flames. His whole body now felt as though it were burning. White hot pain gripped his bowels, shrivelled his liver and melted his brain. His mouth gaped and his screams rang out across the frost-bound field. His breath was tortured, his windpipe blocked by a malignant ball of hatred and fury. He was about to die, and knew it.

"Alright – I'll do it!" he screamed.

The light went out and the pain stopped.

He stirred then looked across at the hedge, rigid with terror. The girl had disappeared. So had the halo of light. All that remained of his tormentor was that intense cloud of hatred, so thick you could almost taste it. Seth lay on the ground, whimpering with shock, then inch by inch crawled across the furrowed earth to the gate. He knelt there, leaning against it for a time, marshalling the strength and will to pull himself upright. He stretched out his arms and grasped the middle bar then paused to stare at his hands which he could see by the purplish twilight were livid as boiled lobsters. Hauling himself upright he tugged at his jacket and pullover with his one good hand, then at his shirt, pulling and stretching until two of the buttons flew off. He looked down at his chest: angry red weals followed the line of his ribs.

He leaned against the gate, his breath staining the frosty air with short sharp bursts of white vapour, and his eyes glazed with terror. His mind, numbed by weeks of fear and lack of sleep, fumbled with the problem, and stumbled over the truth.

It wouldn't stop, he knew that now. Not until he did what the shadow wanted.

TWENTY-NINE

~

Jo stared in disbelief at the toadstools, pale and evil-looking, that had poked through the gaps between the stone flags. Oozing, black and grey things, exuding slime and that obnoxious odour, filling the room with the stench of death and decay. The clump she had stepped upon was mashed into pulp, and as she watched a stream of pus-like fluid oozed from the stinking mass. The rising odour made her gag. Out of their normal context they looked bizarre and surreal; like the painting she had once seen of a fur-lined cup and saucer that had induced an involuntary shudder, simply because normality was turned on its head and so seemed sinister. The monstrous things swelled and split as she watched, spilling evil-smelling mucus over the flags. The gills were black as death, the scales and caps grey as a cadaver's flesh.

Clamping a hand to her mouth, she ran for the bathroom and was promptly sick.

٭ ٭ ٭

She huddled by the fire, hugging a large whisky and shivering with shock. That, and the cold. The place was freezing after having the door and every window open to get rid of the stench whilst cleaning up. She had laboured with a shovel, decapitating the disgusting eruptions before tossing them outside and well away from the back door. Then she had taken scrubbing brush and Dettol diluted in hot water to the slimy corrupted stones. Too late she recalled that the use of disinfectants was taboo in the country. To hell with the septic tank, this was an emergency. Only the fear that Seth Rigby might be lurking had made her finally close and bolt the door.

Oh God – was it ever going to end? Was this why her hand was infected, she wondered in sudden fear. Slugs, worms, fungi – was there something fundamentally unhealthy about the cottage? She gulped the whisky down taking comfort from its fire. Surely not: Louise had never complained of anything like this. Where are you Blake? Where are you now that I need you? she thought, a tear sliding down her cheek. Trapped in a situation that was abhorrent to her, yet unable to tear herself away. Chained by lethargy, and something else that was best left undefined, she lacked the energy and will to leave.

A bowl of soup and hunk of bread were all she could manage for her evening meal. Even then she found herself minutely inspecting the bread. Were toadstool spores air-bound? Could damp and mould and fungi get at her food? Galloping paranoia, but it was hard to check. Don't think about it – just eat she told herself, forcing down the food.

A half hour or so later she looked at the clock on the mantel and groaned: only six-thirty, but it felt like midnight. The trauma on top of the journey had drained her, but if she went to bed now she wouldn't sleep, and sifting through her research and Barbara's data would be decidedly dicey. Asking for trouble in fact, given the horror that had awaited her in the kitchen. *Were* they connected, or was she taking things for granted again, jumping to false conclusions? Maybe this was just a musty old house which had nothing to do with the legend, but now wasn't the time to go into that question.

Okay, work then. It took a supreme effort to switch on and boot up the computer, especially as waves of nausea swept over her from time to time. This general feeling of being unwell, she knew, stemmed from the infection that throbbed in her hand. The memory of Barbara's face as she looked at the wound brought a stab of unease, but there was nothing to be done right now, time enough to visit the hospital tomorrow. Having reached a decision she settled down at the computer and allowed work to take over.

Okay, so where to now? Ah yes, Ruskin came to Brantwood, the elegant house overlooking Coniston Water, in let's see – 1871. So when did he add the famous turret room? Her fingers began to move slowly at first, then ever more quickly over the keys as words and ideas flowed.

Before she knew it an hour had passed. Precisely because of the altered state of consciousness that always accompanied a heavy bout of writing, she didn't at first see it. When she did, her hand flew to her mouth and she leapt to her feet as though stung. "Oh my God!" *Not again.* Deliberately she looked away, then back again at the screen. The words were still there.

Love you . . . hate you . . . love you forever.

And then stretching the width of the screen:

Antony . . . Antony . . . Antony . . .

Jo acted swiftly. Her mind was reeling, her hand shaking, but she managed to set up the print menu and press the command button. The printer whirred into action and seconds later the printed page rested in the tray. In a fever, she snatched it up and scanned the text. *Nothing.* Only her own in-put on the novel. She looked again, this time examining the page in greater detail, then let it fall from her fingers onto the table. The monitor screen was now blank, having self-activated its power-saving device. With a tap of the 'suspend' key Jo reversed the function. The screen lit up, shuddered and settled. A quick scan of the text showed nothing abnormal. She paced the room, distractedly pushing her hair back from her face.

Subconsciously she touched the now completely healed cut on her forehead. Maybe she was suffering from a brain disorder, a result of that bump on the head. Had any one else noticed anything odd? Or was she also deluded about Seth Rigby, and Colin's bizarre behaviour the other night? That possibility loomed like a spectre in a nightmare.

Don't panic, she exhorted herself as memory and common sense came to her rescue. According to Finola, village gossip had it that Seth was undergoing some sort of mental breakdown. Yet Colin had commented, after she disclosed her first frightening encounter with the farmer, that 'Seth was okay', and so had Louise, so there was no history of instability. Seth Rigby's affliction coincided with her own arrival and strange experience, which was a mite too much for coincidence. No, something strange was happening around here, and she wasn't the only one affected.

Well that had put pay to work for tonight. But as she had already broken her self-imposed restriction by delving into the mystery, it made sense to take out her notes and make a proper job of it. Switching off the computer and tidying her books into a pile, she sat down by the fire and mulled over the facts. Barbara had to be right. The presence which seemed to be dogging her was not that of Justin St. Clair, who was a northern lord and husband to Lady Madeline, and whose crest was a wild boar. It could not be, because according to the in-depth research of Barbara's ex-colleague, Madeline's lover was a favoured knight by the name of Antony Chase, whose coat of arms bore a red hawk.

Okay: Jo sipped her whisky and put the glass down again, so much for the historical bit, but what about the present situation? Well for starters, she had mentioned the hawk to both Louise and Barbara *before* she could possibly have known it to be the Chase family emblem. This confirmed she was not 'making it fit' after discovering her mistake about his identity. Given all this, the presence, image or whatever had been waiting at the end of that dark tunnel had to be Madeline's lover Sir Antony Chase. But he wasn't the only one on the scene was he? Given Colin's bizarre behaviour, Justin St. Clair was also making himself felt. But why? Why should any of this be happening?

Thoughtfully Jo finished her whisky. Maybe Barbara's theory was right about violent emotions becoming imprinted on a place, and there was some psychic phenomena being played out here. And at times it would seem that Colin was being used as a channel by Justin St. Clair in order to manifest in the physical world. Which went a long way to explaining Col's mood and personality changes. But there was still the mystery of Antony Chase's apparent obsession with herself, and the intense hatred that always seemed to accompany his presence.

Jo picked up her glass and walking into the kitchen put it down smartly on the drainer and returned to the sitting room. Her movements were now brisk and assured, and she shook back her hair as if ridding herself of doubt and indecision. If she were to believe that something of the sort were possible – and given her experiences, what other option was there? – then she needed to know what had really happened between St. Clair, Madeline, and Antony Chase. So how was that possible, given that it all happened nearly eight hundred years ago, and her research seemed to have come to a dead end? She sat down again, clasping her knees and staring into the fire, sunk in thought. Then she nodded to herself and made a derogatory sound in her throat. *Okay Barbara, that leaves your option.*

She uttered an involuntary cry and when the knock sounded at the front door. She glanced at the clock, fear catching at her throat, then relaxed: it was still only seven forty five. If Seth Rigby was up to his tricks, he would hardly be knocking at her door in the early evening.

"Who is it?" she demanded from the hall.

"It's only me – Finola."

Relief flooded Jo as she drew back the bolts and opened the door. "Hi – you shouldn't say that you know," she added, inviting her visitor in with a welcoming gesture. Finola, muffled against the cold with trousers tucked into lumber boots, hung her duffle coat on a hook and added her fur-lined hood. She turned to Jo, a look of puzzlement on her pinched face. "Sorry?"

"It's *only* me," Jo explained with a smile. "You're putting yourself down every time you say it."

"Oh, I see." A tentative smile flickered across the other woman's features then disappeared like the light from a snuffed candle.

"Is anything wrong?" Jo asked, ushering her into the sitting room.

"No." She glanced round the room, avoiding Jo's gaze. "Colin's working out in the studio." She paused and shrugged. "I just popped round – it gets a bit grim sometimes – winter anyway. You know, a bit of female company."

"Great. You look half-starved, let's have a drink," Jo invited, sensing Finola's embarrassment.

Finola dug deep into the pocket of her Arran knit and drew out a small envelope. "Actually, I came to give you this," she said, holding it out.

Jo paused on her way to the whisky bottle and glasses. "For me?" she said taking it with a look of surprise. She drew out a miniature of an illuminated letter 'J' on an oval parchment mount. "Why it's beautiful," she exclaimed, taking it to the lamp to examine the intricate needlework and jewel-bright colours.

"The letter is from the Book of Kells."

"And these?" Jo touched with the tip of her nail the tiny blue flowers with thread-of-gold centres.

"Mysotis."

"I'm no gardener, I'm afraid!"

"Forget-me-nots," Finola supplied, still not meeting Jo's gaze.

How appropriate. Jo immediately quashed the dangerous thought.

Antony Antony

The whisper came from the furthest corner of the room. Jo stiffened and watched Finola's face intently, but Finola seemed not to have heard.

"How lovely," Jo enthused, adding casually: "Any particular reason?"

Finola's fair skin, already rosy with cold, flushed a deeper pink. "No. I just knew . . . Actually Jo, I saw it in a dream!"

"I often work from dreams myself," Jo said quickly, sensing the other woman's discomfiture. "Jot the content down as soon as I wake."

Forever Forever

"Great for creative ideas," she added in desperation, striving to pretend the breathy whisper hadn't happened.

So, Antony Chase is also working through Fin to get at me, she thought with sudden insight, and an accompanying flash of anger.

She cried out as the light dipped and the wiring buzzed and crackled ominously. *I'll fight you back, you bastard*! she silently vowed. Yet there was also a flash of excitement that was almost sexual. Is that why she didn't just get out and shoot back to London? Was there a morbid fascination binding her to this place? she worried.

"It's alright, it often does this in winter," Finola comforted her, evidently thinking her friend was disturbed by an apparent electrical short-fall.

Are you truly unaware – or just turning a blind eye to this thing? Jo wondered, watching her. "Anyway," she struggled on, "it's a lovely gift and one I'll always treasure. But why, Finola? I'm a little overwhelmed."

Finola's eyes hazed over with unshed tears. "A gesture I guess. I've been so hateful at times, and crass. I know you wouldn't do anything –. Well, I just have this stupid jealousy thing about Col. 'Guess I love him more than he loves me."

"Then he's a fool," Jo said softly, stepping forward to kiss her lightly on the cheek. "Now, let's have a drink," she said decisively, making for the whisky bottle.

They settled before the fire nursing their glasses. "Your work really is exquisite," Jo complimented, admiring the miniature afresh before putting it down on the coffee table. "Do you exhibit, take commissions and that sort of thing?"

"Yes, but somehow Colin's work –' Finola paused and shrugged dismissively.

"Seems to take over," Jo finished for her. "Perhaps I shouldn't say this," she pushed on, "but Colin is a very strong sort of guy. I can't help thinking –"

"I know, that I'm in his shadow."

"Corr-ect!"

"You're right of course." Finola sighed and sipped her drink then cupped the glass in her delicate hands. "But if I try and push things, well you know – he gets so moody and somehow it doesn't seem worth it."

"Line of least resistence!" Jo accused.

Finola picked at a loose thread on her sweater. "I suppose."

"We're all guilty of that one," Jo said wryly. "So what went wrong tonight?"

Finola shrugged again. "The usual."

Inhibitions melting in the fire of a good malt, Finola unburdened herself to Jo. It appeared Colin had been working all day in his studio, then returned there immediately after dinner without uttering more than a couple of words. "I went out there and we ended up having the most awful row. Now he's locked himself in and refuses to talk things over."

"Then he's being a selfish bastard," Jo said unequivocally, taking Fin's glass for a refill.

"I guess." But Finola still looked sunk in misery.

"But he's given us the perfect excuse to get better acquainted – and more than a little squiffy!" Jo said solemnly, pushing the refurbished glass into Finola's hand.

"Oh but I ought to –"

"Drink up!" Jo ordered sitting down again and stretching her legs to the fire. Finola, she noted with satisfaction, was grinning and lifting her glass.

"Blake does just that," Jo said reflectively a short time later.

"Does what?" Finola, face glowing from the heat of the fire and the inner warmth from the whisky, sat with one leg hooked over the arm of the chair in relaxed fashion.

"Shuts himself off to avoid talking about his feelings. 'Least, he used to," Jo added, shrugging. "Now he's walked out."

"You still love him?"

Jo grimaced, took a sip from her drink and thought before answering. "I guess. Leastways, it still bloody hurts, if that's anything to go by."

"I'd say so!" From her place across the hearth, Finola's empathy flowed across, soothing Jo's open wounds.

"You've obviously been there yourself."

Finola unhooked her leg from the arm and leant forward to briefly touch her hand. "Too true. Want to talk about it?"

Jo, encouraged by her third drink of the evening, Finola's confidences and ready sympathy, talked about Blake and her own dilemma. By the time the bottle had been passed again, the bond was cemented.

So much so that Jo felt able to confide the apparently taboo subject of the recent bizarre happenings, and her visit to Barbara. "Anyway, just a suggestion, but as a last resort, it might be an idea to go see a medium," she concluded, twirling her glass between her hands.

Finola's eyes were huge behind her gold-rimmed glasses. "Do you think it wise? I mean, why mess about with this thing?"

At least she's quit pretending it doesn't exist, Jo thought with relief. "Because, my dear, I have the awful feeling it won't just go away," she said camping it up, and therefore playing the seriousness down. A timid soul, Finola. No point in scaring her off before they even got started. "And maybe trying to understand what's happening here is the only way forward. So what do you say?"

Finola shifted on her chair and folded her arms across her chest. "About what?"

"About giving me some moral support."

"You mean, go *with you*?"

"Absolutely."

"Well I don't –"

"Good. That's sorted then," Jo said ruthlessly. "I'll 'let my fingers do the walking' and fix something up tomorrow."

Finola's whisky-languor suddenly evaporated. "Look, I'll come with you – but I'm not actually sitting in, okay?"

Jo nodded. "I'll settle for that."

They both jumped and looked startled as the telephone rang. Jo picked up the receiver; she listened for a second or so then winked conspiratorially at Finola. "Yes, yes she's here, Colin." She held up a hand to halt Finola who was about to rush forward and take the receiver. "A bit careless with her aren't you? What do I mean? Well, for starters it is a freezing night, and gone eleven-thirty," Jo remonstrated whilst resolutely ignoring Finola's agonised gestures. "I should think you *were* worried. You mean you've only just realised she's gone?" Jo looked across at Finola, then raised her eyes to the ceiling in a gesture of exasperation. "I'm not sure; hang on, I'll have to ask. She had decided to spend the night here," she added recklessly, fortified by the alcohol she had consumed. She gave Finola another exaggerated wink. "Just bear with me, I'll see what she says." Placing her hand over the receiver she said sternly: "Have some self-respect girl, and he'll have some for you."

Finola seemed about to protest, but then shrugged and nodded. *Good* Jo mouthed, then removed her hand from the 'phone. "Yes, alright Colin, she's prepared to come home – if you come and fetch her. But she says to make sure you're suitably attired." She placed her hand over the receiver and gave Finola, who was becoming agitated again, a warning glare. "Why, sack cloth and ashes of course." Jo choked back the laughter as Finola gestured wildly for her to stop. "Ten minutes then," she concluded and replaced the receiver.

Finola, prey to conflicting emotions, struggled between laughter and dismay. "Was he mad?"

"As fire!" Jo said laughing. "Believe me, Finola – tonight will do Colin Gilmour a world of good."

"I hope you're right," Finola breathed, anxiously glancing from clock to door as though expecting her irate partner to burst in at any moment.

"I am, trust me. And you should do it more often. Now – one for the road." Jo stood up and took Finola's glass in a manner that defied challenge.

As it happened, Colin had mellowed considerably by the time he arrived. Either that, or he had decided it was tactically unwise to take on *two* bolshy females, both of which were 'well-oiled', Jo thought smiling to herself later. Finola had tackled his ill-concealed annoyance with admirable spirit, saying that as he was so fond of his own company, it had seemed better to take herself off without disturbing his solitude. From the look on Col's face, the notion that Finola could have ended up with some-one less suitable than her new neighbour, had not escaped him. She had thanked Finola again for the present, and watched them drive away beneath spangled frost-laden branches. As she closed the door, a wave of incredible loneliness swept over Jo.

THIRTY

~

The following morning she drove to the Cumberland Cottage Hospital and asked to see Dr. Cahill. The answer from the nurse at reception was 'not without an appointment' until Jo peeled away the dressing, wincing as she did so, and displayed the festering wound. The nurse's expression immediately changed and she directed Jo to a seat; within a quarter of an hour she was sitting in a cubicle opposite Dr. Cahill.

"This is quite nasty." The doctor's face also registered concern. "On a rusty piece of metal you say. Been feeling unwell at all?"

Jo nodded. "Nausea – some dizziness."

"Right. Your temperature is raised. So when did you last have a tetanus jab?"

"Last year."

"Okay. Fine," Dr. Cahill flicked off the electronic thermometer and put it back on the trolley. But you should have come sooner than this," she admonished. "I don't want to alarm you, Miss Cavanagh, but this peripheral tissue is all but necrotic."

Jo looked up in alarm. "What will happen?"

"Hopefully, we will get it in time. I'm going to give you some antibiotics to take, some cream to apply locally, and an injection now to hit it quick. Roll up your sleeve, please."

Jo did as she was bid. Minutes later Dr. Cahill discarded the syringe and applied a small plaster over the puncture. "Now – I want to see you in a week's time. But if there is any change – if you begin to feel ill, or the wound shows no sign of healing, then you come back immediately, is that understood?"

"Yes, Doctor."

Jo rose from the treatment chair and was almost at the door when Dr. Cahill spoke again.

"You seem to be rather accident prone. Is it an occupational hazard?"

Jo paused and thought quickly. "Well, writers are notoriously vague and preoccupied at times, I guess – which doesn't help," she hedged, smiling.

Dr. Cahill looked politely amused, but quickly became serious again. "No. But you've only been here a week or so and I've treated you twice already. And for two different accidents. In fact, I'm rather curious to know what's happening down your end."

"Oh, why's that?"

"Well I was doing a stint of emergency cover over at the General Hospital A&E the other day. A chap from your village – Seth, let me think, yes Rigby – was brought in." She paused and frowned as Jo noisily caught her breath. "Nasty chain saw wound," she carried on smoothly whilst watching Jo closely. "In the five years I've been at this hospital I've not treated anyone from your area – then all of a sudden – bingo! a hat trick."

"Coincidence?"

"Probability is against it."

Jo frowned. "You're seriously interested?"

"I'm writing a paper on the incidence of endemic accidents."

"I see. Sorry – can't help you," Jo said firmly, opening the door.

Dr. Cahill finished writing in Jo's notes and threw down her pen, then leaned back on her chair and regarded her with a thoughtful expression. "Tell me, is he the local 'character', this Seth Rigby? Most villages have one," she smiled.

"I don't quite know what you're driving at doctor," Jo said warily.

"Well – has he always been a bit odd? You know, not a full twenty shillings to the pound, as the locals would say."

"As you know, I've only just moved into the area; I really couldn't say."

"Of course." But Dr. Cahill didn't look convinced.

"Should you be asking me these things doctor?" Jo challenged, giving her a direct look.

"Not if I go by the book – no. But around here we tend to go more for what works. This isn't London Miss Cavanagh. Here, people count."

"And each looks out for the rest. Yes, I know – sorry, I didn't mean to criticise," Jo apologised.

Dr. Cahill made a dismissive gesture with her hand. "No problem." She leaned forward, frowning. "I was concerned about this guy; he was very disturbed. Kept saying he was 'cursed.' In a fair old state really – seems his life is falling apart. I thought you might be able to fill me in as to whether this was his usual state, or something recent."

Jo hesitated, then made up her mind. "From what I hear he was perfectly normal until a week or so ago. He's certainly weird now. In fact, he's been pestering me out at the cottage. Nothing overt – yet," she added quickly, seeing the other woman's swift frown. "More like hanging around in the dark, spooking me out, that sort of thing. Just weird," Jo repeated, then feeling the need to escape, opened the door wider. "Thank you, doctor," she said formally.

"But –," Dr. Cahill was tapping the desk with a pencil, seemed about to say more, but then threw the pencil down. "Okay, back in a week, remember."

Jo closed the door after her and walked briskly down the corridor to the exit. It was, she decided, as well to let somebody in authority know that she was being pestered by Seth Rigby. *Just in case –*

She left the disturbing thought unfinished.

THIRTY-ONE

~

Antony continued to brood over the problem of Madeline and William. Arrangements could be made for himself and Madeline to flee in secret and start a new life in France, but when he dared to broach the subject again, she had wept as though her heart would break, saying she could not bear the thought of leaving her son. Yet if they took him with them, St. Clair would never be content to merely cast her off; he would relentlessly hound them, and they would be forever looking over their shoulder. They had to escape, yet there seemed no solution to the dilemma.

The next time they met by the river, the answer struck him like a blow to the head from behind with a mace. He drew her closer as the idea grew and flourished: a flower bursting forth from the bud, petals unfurling and spreading to bask in the warm sweet light of hope. So intense was his excitement that she must hear his heart hammering inside his chest. What if she were to have another child? His child. The breath caught in his throat at the simplicity yet magnitude of it. He had no right; he could not give her up. Conflict raged in his breast.

They could not have everything, he saw that now. He must give up position, power and Edward's favour; Madeline would have to relinquish her husband's child. If they didn't they would lose everything, including their lives. Time was running out, a wonder they had got away with it thus far. This was a way of forcing Madeline's hand.

He loved her then. Laying her down on his cloak he entered swiftly not giving himself time to waver, plunging and delving until she wept and cried out, and clung to him like a drowning woman tossed on a stormy sea. He loved her as never before, his

*ardour fired by mingled hope and desperation. She cried out as he
wound ropes of her chestnut hair around his hands, imprisoning
her and at the same time binding himself to her service. His body
went rigid as the tension in his loins became unbearable. Blood
beat in his neck, at his temples and in his groin. He shuddered
from head to toe and called her name aloud as his seed burst forth.
This time it was not to be wasted, not to be spilled on the ground.*

*At last he sank down upon her, his pain and frustration spent.
Now they were bound for ever. She looked up at him, and he saw
that her eyes were moist with tears.*

He realised she was aware of what he had done.

Having made an appointment with a certain 'Katrina – Genuine
Clairvoyant' practising in Lancaster and sifted from Yellow Pages,
Jo and Finola decided to make an outing of it. The unknown
Katrina had been unable to see them until the evening, (probably
serves in the local supermarket during the day, as Jo cynically
observed), but as the morning dawned bright and with a frost
glittering over fields and hedgerow promising a cold but fine day, a
browse round the Lancaster shops followed by a cream tea was on
the agenda.

"Mind you, it's supposed to change by evening," Finola warned
as they set off in Jo's car for the motorway and civilisation. "There's
snow forecast," she added anxiously, peering wide-eyed at Jo through
her glasses.

"Just 'wintry showers' – nothing much," Jo reassured her, giving
her a quick smile. Finola, she knew, was torn between elation at
the prospect of a 'girlie' day out – in her own words 'a rare treat'
since moving out here – and trepidation at agreeing to consult a
clairvoyant, which was something 'other people did', secret and
therefore shameful. "Now sit back, relax, and let's have fun!" she
ordered, pushing her foot down on the accelerator as they reached
the 'A' road that led to the dual carriageway, and eventually to the
M6.

They chatted and giggled their way through a selection of second-
hand shops, trying on feather boas and hats, and holding against

themselves fringed and beaded dresses from the twenties whilst posturing in front of a full-length mirror. From there they moved on to Next, where Jo bought trousers and a sweater, and Finola a fitted woollen skirt that accentuated her slimness and femininity. They then wandered in and out of a plethora of shoe shops. Jo, clutching a newly-purchased pair of green wellies, reflected wryly on how much her life had changed as she watched Finola trying on a pair of stylish boots. Then came a browse through antique book-shops, Jo relishing the odour of dust and old leather whilst doing her best to steer clear of the local history section. No point in tempt-ing fate, she thought glancing at Finola who was engrossed amongst the poetry shelves and exuding enjoyment. Consolation was on offer via the wealth of material on Ruskin, and from one volume in particular which focused on his private life and was therefore directly relevant to the book she was writing. When she saw the price, it also brought that particular thrill that came from having spotted a bargain.

"Come on, let's go find some tea," she said, stuffing the book into her bag as they emerged from the book shop. She cast a swift and anxious glance at the sky but then smiled sunnily at Finola, taking her arm and jollying her along the precinct. However she knew that Finola had not missed the dimming of the day, and the banks of cloud, violety-brown and ominous, lumbering in from the east like a convoy of tanks across a desert.

The tea shop had a cosy atmosphere, and was redolent with comforting bakery smells and the fragrance of coffee being perked. They chatted about inconsequential things: clothes, the weather, London life whilst studiously avoiding any mention of the even-ing's appointment. As the surrounding tables began to empty, and waitresses, no doubt impatient to be home, discreetly hovered, Jo felt the muscles of her stomach begin to contract with tension. Glancing at the window, she saw that night was pressing its nose to the glass and creeping stealthily along streets and alleys. "I guess we'd better make a move Fin," she said pushing aside her second scone; the crumbs began to stick as her mouth and throat felt sud-denly dry.

Finola's cup rattled a little too loudly as she replaced it on her saucer. "Yes, of course." She dabbed nervously at the corners of her mouth with her serviette. "Do you think –," she started to say, but Jo saw the anxiety in her eyes and interrupted: "No problem Fin. It'll probably turn out to be a complete waste of time."

A spark of hope flared in Finola's eyes. "Do you think so?"

"Come on, it's time we went." Jo laughed at her and gestured to one of the waitresses who hurried forward with the bill.

The locality in which they found themselves didn't augur well, or do much to alleviate Finola's fears: the streets were narrow, the properties sad and run down. "Next left," Finola instructed in a subdued voice. Jo guessed as she made the turn that Fin was ardently wishing herself some place else. The terrace of dingy houses shrank into the shadows, watching with windows that winked from behind lace curtains, or brooded from empty squares of darkened glass. Jo peered anxiously through the windscreen as snowflakes eddied, stuck to the glass then rapidly melted. There was the sound of a page being turned, then Fin's voice saying: "Number forty-five. It's on the right, the even numbers are on my side."

"I hope this doesn't get any worse," Jo said, cruising close to the kerb and leaning forward to peer up at the sky. Ballerina flakes danced briefly in the halo shed by a street lamp, then disappeared behind a curtain of darkness. Cold: so cold. She realised suddenly how chilled her body had become, despite the stream of warm air from the car's heater. Unconsciously her hand moved to the ring which after much thought she had hung from a chain around her neck.

If it were possible for any object to give off 'vibes', then this certainly should; the question now was whether the mysterious 'Katrina' would pick them up. If the way it felt was anything to go by, she'd stand a pretty good chance: the ring was burning her like a nugget of ice.

"Here we are." Jo pulled the edge of her coat over the ring to conceal it as they drew to a halt outside a dingy terraced house.

"Won't you come inside, Fin? You'll be freezing out here," she pressed.

Finola shook her head, then as Jo opened the car door and a blast of cold air swept in, she looped her hair behind her ears and opened the passenger door. "I'll come in then – but to watch. I don't want to be 'read'."

"Fine. But whatever happens, don't give anything away," Jo warned.

The front door was shabby, its chipped and battle-scarred paint resulting no doubt from years of bikes, prams and a scuffle of children.

"Not very promising is it?" Finola said giving her a sideways look.

Jo made an expressive face and rang the bell.

The door was eventually opened by a man with a beatific smile and a lager belly hanging over the waistband of his denims. "Come in love, go straight through," he invited before they could speak. He stood aside for them to enter a vestibule with a bare light bulb, faded wallpaper and yellowed paint. "Through there, ducks."

He pointed to a door on their right and shuffled off into an adjacent room.

They knocked and entered at the bidding of a female voice. Jo's first impression was one of oppressive heat, overpowering perfume, and mellow lighting after the glare of the naked bulb in the vestibule. The heat came from a hissing gas fire, the lighting from a cluster of candles ranged on the mantel above. The cloying scent of jasmine and sandlewood was dispensed by a couple of smoking incense sticks.

"'Ello love, come in and sit down." The woman was seated at a round table that dominated the centre of the room, and on it a squat red candle burned in a glass globe. Her hand, the long nails painted a vivid crimson, reached out for an ash tray on which a cigarette smouldered, and pulled it within easy reach. "And your friend," she added, nodding at Finola.

"Thanks." Jo moved forward, noting as she did so the crimson velvet curtains and the clash of scarlet cushions forming a rash along the back of a black vinyl settee. She tasted acrid fumes as the woman pulled on her cigarette and exhaled.

"Both want a readin' do you?" Smoke curled from the woman's lips and rose in lazy coils to the yellowed anaglypta ceiling.

Jo sat down. "I do. My friend has just come for moral support."

'Katrina' looked dubious. "I don't normally allow it."

Jo prepared to rise. "I don't normally visit a clairvoyant – perhaps I made a mistake?"

"No, no that'll be okay," Katrina said hurriedly, giving Jo a shrewd look as she reached for one of several packs of Tarot. "You sit down there then," she said with a hard-done-by sigh, waving Finola to a chair at the back of the room. The red nails gleamed in the light of the candles as she shuffled the cards.

Jo took advantage of this activity to observe the woman. 'Katrina' she guessed was in her early thirties. Her eye make-up was flamboyant, with heavy shadow that extended in wings beyond the lids, and a thick line of Kohl top and bottom for emphasis. The gold jewellery and low cut clingy cocktail dress seemed incongruous with both the setting and the woman's untidy hair.

"Did he mention?" Katrina said, looking up to jerk her head in the direction of the door. "Ten quid for the cards. An extra three quid with palms and tea-leaves." A tendril of hair escaped from her top-knot; she brushed it back from her cheek.

Cost conscious spirits? Jo almost laughed aloud. "The cards will be fine."

Katrina shrugged her plump white shoulders. "Just as you like, love."

Jo frowned. The woman was staring at her, or to be more precise, looking beyond her as though someone or something hovered behind her chair. Instinctively Jo looked round, but saw nothing. Katrina however was rubbing her forearms and Jo noted the skin was raised in gooseflesh. Instinctively Jo touched the ring that dangled between her breasts.

"Cut the deck, duckie." Jo complied and Katrina balanced her cigarette on the rim of the ash tray in order to deal the cards. "Ah, yes, the Empress, a very good card for your luck, my love. And the ace of pentacles – a good money card," she intoned, flicking the cards over as she worked down the row. "Especially if you're in business – know what I mean?" she fished, and her gaze ran over Jo's expensive jacket and hand knitted arran. But then she frowned, rubbed her arms again and rose from her chair. Bending down she turned the gas fire up until it hissed even louder, then returned to her seat. "And in the position of relationships here we have the two of cups," she continued as though there had been no break, "A partnership is about to be forged. Know what I mean, my love?" she droned on, with a quick glance at Jo's left hand. She took a drag from her cigarette and replaced it in the ash tray. "A marriage I shouldn't wonder. In the New Year perhaps?" she added, dribbling smoke from the corner of her mouth.

Jo and Finola exchanged looks. *My own prediction was more to the point,* Jo thought smiling to herself: this was a complete waste of time. Cliches drivelled from this woman's mouth along with the smoke.

Ten minutes or so passed in this fashion and Jo became aware of Finola fidgeting. The aura of menace had receded, as though neutralised by the triviality of the proceedings. The gas fire belched its heat into the room, and after the cold outside the effect was soporific.

"And December will be a lucky month for you . . ."

Jo stifled a yawn. Then her attention was jerked back to the woman's voice, or rather to its absence: it had ceased in mid sentence. Jo frowned. Why was this Katrina woman staring at her breasts? She glanced down and saw that her coat was gaping. The ring gleamed dully in the candlelight and she raised a hand to pull her jacket over it. The movement caused the emerald to spark green fire. The woman seemed mesmerised but at last looked up. Jo could have sworn there was naked fear in Katrina's eyes.

"And your main card, the overall view if you like," she continued smoothly as though nothing had disturbed her, "Is this."

Katrina had placed her hand over the card, but then removed it with a dramatic flourish. Jo heard Finola's gasp as the image was exposed; there was a look on the woman's face that Jo couldn't fathom.

"*The Devil*. You must be on your guard," Katrina said in an urgent undervoice.

"What does it mean?" Jo pressed.

"Enslavement. Someone seeks to enslave you. Not a good situation – know what I mean?"

In her agitation, Jo had allowed her coat to open again. The woman's gaze went once more the ring. One hand went to her throat, and the lacquered nails reminded Jo of droplets of blood. The woman stared at a point above and behind Jo's left shoulder. Jo's head whipped round. A slight movement claimed her attention, a dark shadow caught by the corner of her eye, then gone. "What is it?" She asked sharply.

Katrina had risen to her feet. "Why did you come here?" She pointed her cigarette at Jo as she spoke. Her hand shook and the smoke kinked crazily as it rose in a thin stream. With a vicious movement she ground out the butt in the ash tray. "What do you want?" she spat. "Look, I'm as honest as the next in this game. But you, you're something else. Are you into something black?"

Jo stared at her perplexed. "I don't know –"

"Yes you do! What have you brought here with you? Whatever it is, I don't like it, I can tell you that!" She moved from the table, paced up and down before the fireplace and returned, placing the table between herself and Jo. "You don't need me. You're far stronger. So far out I can't even reach you!"

Jo frowned and held up a hand to ward off the tirade. "Really – I don't know what you are saying."

Finola rose to her feet, her face white and scared looking. "I think we should go."

"Yes. Go! Go on, get out of here – and don't come back!" The woman Katrina was now beside herself.

"Okay, okay we're going," Jo said angrily, counting out ten one pound coins from her pocket. There had been no time to make use of a cash dispenser, even had she known where to find one. "Sorry I haven't a note —" she started to say, but the other woman was shaking her head. She put her hands behind her back. "I don't want your money. Just go!"

The room changed. The temperature was rapidly dropping. In seconds the room had turned icy, the atmosphere thick with hostility. Something seemed to be crawling over Jo's skin and her scalp prickled as though charged with minute electrical charges.

"*Please* Jo!" Finola moved to the door and stood with her hand on the knob. Her face was now drained of all colour, and her eyes behind the gold rimmed glasses were huge with apprehension. Jo paid no heed. She was watching the woman Katrina, who had fallen silent. Her eyes rolled to the ceiling and became opaque, her mouth went slack and saliva dribbled onto her chin. To Jo's horror the woman's shoulders and arms began to twitch. Soon her body too jerked in spasm. Katrina's voice when she spoke was curiously flat. "Who is Antony?"

Jo gasped. The pound coins dropped from her grasp and rolled across the carpet, winking wickedly in the candlelight.

The candles on the mantelpiece spluttered, the flames bending and curving as though standing in a wind. A cry escaped Finola as first one then another was extinguished until only one remained burning, that and the red candle in the jar.

Love you. Kill you. Love you forever – forever – forever

The whisper echoed around the room.

Antony.

Jo started and whipped round. The breathy whisper had sounded in her ear. "What do you know about him? Tell me more," she demanded.

Katrina appeared not to see her, but looked beyond with eyes that were clouded like those of a person with cataracts. The pupils had almost disappeared, had rolled back into her head. She made strange wavelike gestures with her hands. "He is from a long, long way back," she intoned, answering her own question. Again the fluid motion with her hands. "A long way. But the feelings still bind. He will never let go. He preys on you." Her fingers spread like wings. "Bird of prey. Hawk. Hovering. Hovering over you. He is the one. The Devil card. He seeks to enslave you."

"But why?" Jo urged.

Katrina seemed unaware of Jo's presence, and even of her own surroundings. Her face contorted as though with pain. Despite the intense cold in the room, sweat beaded her forehead and upper lip. "Such power. He is so strong." She became increasingly agitated, plucking first at the strands of her necklace, then at her red satin dress. When she spoke again the flat monotone chant was replaced by an almost manic urgency: "Go away from that place! Have nothing to do with him. He means to destroy you. *You must go right away.*"

"But why?" Jo persisted. "It doesn't make sense. Tell me," she urged, reaching out to grasp her arm.

The woman shuddered and closed her eyes. When she opened them again they appeared normal but she frowned and seemed disoriented. Taking out a handkerchief she wiped the sweat from her forehead and saliva from the corners of her mouth. Her limbs and body no longer twitched and Jo heard Finola's sigh of relief.

"Come on, Jo. Let's get out of here," Finola hissed from the doorway.

"Yes go on, get out!" Katrina flung at them, as though nothing untoward had occurred. Her voice sounded normal and, Jo guessed, the woman had no recollection of what had just taken place.

"And take your money. No – don't leave it!" she urged, and backed away from the coins that littered the floor. "I want nothing of you left here," she added, pointing belligerently at Jo who was about to protest.

Leaving the money where it was, Jo followed Finola through the door.

THIRTY-TWO

~

Katrina lit another cigarette then poured herself a large Bells and took a gulp without adding her usual mixer. Stan had gone down to the Brown Cow for a couple of pints, but reluctantly; he hadn't wanted to leave her, saying she looked like 'one of them dead 'uns you reckon to talk to'. Stan wasn't a believer, but a good guy and he thought the world of her. In all honesty, she hadn't been one herself up until tonight, but it didn't do to go around saying so. She shivered involuntarily and took another swallow of whisky. He'd gone in the end, with a bit of persuasion: she hadn't felt up to facing company, had needed some time alone to think things through. Or not. Better forgotten, not dwelt upon. Still you couldn't help it could you? When something like that happened, it was bound to prey on your mind. *Prey – bird of prey?* Now why had that popped into her mind? She frowned as memory stirred, flared then died like the tail of a shooting star. No, it was gone. She shook her head. Rum carry on tonight. Look at that. She held out her free hand and grimaced at the tremor.

She sniffed and sat down, kicking off her stiletto heeled shoes. Ironic really. All these years of putting on a class act – and wham! just like that, the real bloody thing! He had definitely been there. Oh yes, standing large as life behind the girl. Only he wasn't alive was he? He was dead. Long dead. But she had seen him alright. Knocking back the last of her whisky she rose and crossing to the sideboard, poured another double before returning to the settee.

And to think she had waited all her life for a moment like this. But there was no flush of triumph here, no comforting warmth from the realisation that there really was another life after this. *Or the same one going on and on and on . . .?* Why was he stuck here, and what did he want from the girl? It wasn't that he was missing his oats: he wasn't after stealing in and sliding up her nightie whilst she slept. Some did, she reflected nodding to herself, or so she'd been told. Read about it too, about young girls writhing in ecstacy in their sleep, deflowered then enslaved by their invisible lover. Not that there was anything virginal about her, the one that was here tonight. A cute bitch that one, canny as they come, and she smirked at the unintentional pun. Load of rubbish in her opinion, but that was what they reckoned – missed the carnal pleasures of the earthly life they did. Katrina speculated idly on what it might be like. Would it feel cold and hard, like being stabbed with an icicle? And would there be anything there when he come? She giggled girlishly and wriggled on the settee, pressing her thighs tightly together. She and Stan didn't get round to doing it much these days, but maybe if he wasn't late back and hadn't had more than three pints –, she wriggled some more and sighed with anticipated pleasure.

Only it hadn't felt funny or sexy in there, had it? She pursed her lips and shook her head as the memory returned. Definitely not. And not much of the lover about that one. Whatever the link with the girl, he wasn't after sneaking into her bed of a night, she thought with a lewd grin – not given the hatred and anger he was spewing out. A rustling in the corner made her nervously start and look over her shoulder. Nothing moving in the shadows, but still the sense of unease persisted. Her hand went to the back of her neck, her fingers massaging the tightening knot of tension. Almost as though he was listening in to her thoughts, she mused uncomfortably, and was affronted. Not one to cross from what she could make out, but it had only been glimpses, a shadow that had fixed itself to the girl. The only thing she remembered clearly was those green eyes. Green like a cat's. *Green like the emerald in that ring the girl had been wearing around her neck.* She shuddered and swallowed another large mouthful of whisky.

If only it was possible to recall what happened later. Something did, given all that sweat and mucus, and the blinding headache on 'coming to'. But it was like a temporary blackout. Or an epileptic fit like that poor kid at school used to have, sometimes in the class-room or playground, once in the hall at assembly. She'd never for-gotten that. Reaching for her lighter she took out a cigarette and lit it, taking a long draw and closing her eyes tight against the smoke whilst forcing her mind to spew up its hidden contents. No, it was no good – it had gone. Amnesia, they called it, didn't they? What the hell did that woman bring in here? She shivered and moved closer to the gas fire. And was the cocky bitch really so innocent? Most unlikely. You couldn't carry that sort of karma around with-out knowing.

She took another pull at her cigarette, feeling the nicotine hit as she inhaled. Her head turned sharply and her body stiffened, then relaxed again. The noise, whatever it was, had stopped. There was a growing sense of something in here though, and it reminded her of how it had been back there, earlier on. The air was icy too yet the gas fire was on full blast. She cast another look over her shoul-der, then glanced at the clock. Stan wouldn't be back for at least another half hour. Suddenly she missed him, his down-to-earth no nonsense attitude and comforting physical bulk. There it was again, a sort of tapping noise. Low key, but loud enough to penetrate her whisky and nicotine buzz. She gave a little sigh of impatience that was really disguised relief. What the hell was Stan up to now? He was always larking around, an overgrown kid, she thought with affection. The tapping grew louder. Heaving herself reluc-tantly off the soffa she made her way to the door. It sounded like he was rapping at the kitchen window.

She saw nothing at first. Just heard the repetitive tapping sound. And smelled the stench. An odour so thick it was palpable, wrapping itself around her in cold sweaty folds as she entered the darkened kitchen. The sudden stink when a rotten egg is cracked open, or she thought in sudden terror, that of rotting flesh on a decaying carcase. She jumped and gave a strangled cry as the tapping started up again, sudden and staccato like a hail of machine gun bullets. *Christ! Whatever it was would break the glass as this rate.* "Stan? That you Stan?" The pick-pick-picking got louder. Her eyes widened as something fluttered against the glass. She stared at the window.

Not Stan, not by any stretch of the imagination. Get out of here fast, snatch up a coat from the hall and run down the pub and he would be there.

Turning she made for the door, stopped in her tracks, watched it swing to and click shut. Ice-water trickled down her spine and premonition darkened her mind, swishing silently into place like a crematorium curtain. Her limbs at first refused to move, her mind not really wanting the confirmation. The repeated tap-tap-tapping at her back released them and she shot forward. Bloody door, it was always awkward. How many times had she asked Stan to take a drop of oil to the catch? Doggedly she refused to accept it was anything more than a spot of rust that was making it resist all her frenzied fumblings. She began to shiver as the chill reached out from the walls to touch her spine with clammy fingers. And the smell was making her choke. It rose up in a visible miasma, a sickly yellowish fug that clogged her nostrils and mouth and contaminated her lungs. Her fists pummelled the panels of the door until her knuckles split and oozed blood. Then she stopped and gagging, scrubbed them against her dress, oblivious to the pain. In the pale half-light from the window, the panels of the door were beaded with disgusting greasy moisture.

Desperate now and fighting down rising panic, she turned to look over her shoulder as a fresh hail of whatever it was hit the window. Stupid this. Nothing psychic about it, so get a bloody grip of yourself and stop acting like an idiot, she told herself severely. You're the street-wise one, a smooth operator ripping off punters stupid enough to believe all that life-ever-after crap. The stink and the dark closed in and next minute she was screaming. The screams bubbled up from her gut like bile, and sickened, she fell silent. Of course she could get out of here. Okay, so the door had *accidentally* jammed but there was still the window. *And whatever it was waiting outside.* As though in response to that thought there was another spasm of movement and something pale and brown fluttered against the glass.

THIRTY-THREE

~

The first part of the journey was conducted in silence, punctuated now and then by the 'we should never have come' brand of comments from Finola.

"It's okay, Fin, it's okay," Jo reassured, trying to batten down her growing irritation. It was hard enough trying to find her way through driving sleet and an unfamiliar network of one way streets, without the distraction of Finola's snivelling. Besides her tone implied blame and that, Jo thought shrugging off the blare as an irate driver hit the horn, was making her feel defensive.

"That woman –" Finola began hesitantly, "do you think there was any truth in what she said?"

"No," Jo replied laconically, telling herself that this was an inappropriate moment to discuss it, but in truth not trusting herself to do so.

"I'm scared just the same. This Antony guy . . ."

"Shit! I've missed the exit." Swearing beneath her breath, Jo circled the roundabout for the second time.

"Sorry."

An injured Finola lapsed into a silence that condemned Jo louder than any words.

It had been Jo's intention to stop off at the Brown Cow for a much needed drink, but Finola's expression, her white-knuckled hands and the rigidity of her back as she stared straight ahead through the snow-flecked windscreen, made it abundantly clear that she wished only to be away from Lancaster and its associations. Jo sighed and drove past the lights and people surrounding the inn and followed the signs for the motorway. A maelstrom of thoughts and emotions whirled like snowflakes inside her head and it was a struggle to keep her mind on the route. The castle, crouching ominously on its hill and silhouetted like a black paper cut-out against the sky, was now behind them, and soon they were on the dual carriageway and clear of the town.

The motorway, dual carriageway and lights of civilisation were all left behind; narrow roads now snaked between black and forbidding fells. The muscles of Jo's stomach constricted with tension. Here no street lamps shed their friendly glow and the darkness was thick enough to taste. Sleet still dappled the windscreen and slanted across the headlight beams, but at a sharper angle now that the wind funnelled through glacial valleys, and raked a countryside bare of sheltering buildings. Anxiety rippled through her stomach. This scenario evoked that first night, when Colin had come to her rescue and driven her through similar lanes to the cottage hospital. Her hands gripped the wheel a little too tightly as she leaned forward to peer obsessively through the windscreen because the memory of the crash was making her nervous. That had been the beginning, the reason behind their crazy mission tonight.

With each mile, she became aware of a conflict raging within: a reluctance to continue clocking up the miles between herself and civilisation, and a compulsion to return to Twilight Cottage. *Antony Antony* Despite her phoney image, that Katrina woman had picked up on something after all.

"Okay Fin?" she asked, suddenly remorseful of her earlier harsh manner and ashamed of her self-indulgence. Finola too had her fears, and had been pitched into all this without any say in the matter.

Finola turned, her face a pale oval, her features indistinguishable in the gloom. "Fine. How about you – want me to take a turn driving?" she offered, but the lack of conviction in her voice told Jo she was hoping her obligatory offer would be refused.

"It's okay. Helps keep my mind off things. But thanks anyway, Fin," she said with a brief look at her companion before turning back almost immediately to the road and its treacherous bends. Empathy restored, they sped through narrow lanes and white-slashed darkness into the wildness of Langdale.

When they reached the welcome lights of the Three Shires Inn perched high at the old county division, Jo made a spot decision and pulled in. "You need a stiff drink," she said, noting Finola's pinched features as she turned and gave her a questioning look. "And so do I," she added grimly before Finola could object, "before tackling Wrynose and Hardknott." Her stomach lurched at the prospect of facing these two notorious mountain passes with their hairpin bends and three in one gradients that were bad enough in daylight, but twice as daunting at night and in wind-driven sleet. But time to worry about that later, with a couple of stiff drinks under her belt. Half-closing her eyes, she bent her head against the icy blast driving down from the fells and moved round to open the passenger door. "Out you get," she commanded, as Finola seemed frozen and incapable of making her own decisions.

As Finola climbed out of the car, Jo turned up her coat collar against the hail of icy needles and surveyed the black silhouettes of broad flanks and angular summits streaked with the first traces of white. "We'd better make it a quickie," she cautioned, "in case it sets in for real," but saw with relief that the road remained an inky black ribbon: no snow had settled at this level, and given the rainy texture of the sleet, was unlikely to do so tonight.

"I ought to 'phone Colin," Finola murmured, looping her hair behind her ears and shaking off the snowflakes with a quick nervous flick of her head.

"What – and let him spoil your fun?"

"He'll be worried," Finola said uncertainly.

"Sod Colin for once," Jo said with asperity, taking Finola's arm and propelling her towards the lights, laughter and strains of music that issued from the inn.

They were met by a warm fug, and the reassuring sight, smells and sounds of normal people doing ordinary things, like chatting or eating food out of baskets, or stamping their feet to the raw earthy music of a folk group. They threaded their way through a throng who, given the 'uniform' sweaters, thick socks and body warmers and in some cases knee breeches, were obviously walkers staying at the inn. Others, wearing jeans or cord trousers and jackets in subdued hues of brown or olive green, were more likely to be the residents of the nearby hamlet, Jo decided, recalling photographs in a guide book of a church amongst a huddle of houses built of local slate. "Right, what are you going to have?" Jo asked as soon as she had settled Finola as close to the fire as it was possible to get.

"What did you say?" Finola cupped a hand over her ear.

Jo raised her voice in order to be heard over the group enthusiastically playing in the corner. "I'm going to get the drinks in."

"Just a *small* G & T for me then." Finola emphasised the point by holding her thumb and index finger close together.

Jo made a dismissive gesture and made her way to the bar.

"Two large brandies please – on their own, no ice," she demanded of the girl behind the pumps.

"Oh but," Finola began to protest as Jo returned and placed the drinks on the table; Jo silenced her with a look saying: "Get it down – it's what you need," in a tone that discouraged argument. She watched with satisfaction as Finola sipped the brandy and the colour gradually returned to her cheeks and lips.

"Better?" Jo asked, touching her hand.

Finola nodded. "Much. Thanks Jo."

"Sorry if I seem to be playing the bully," Jo apologised with a rueful smile, "but you were freaking out back there."

"That's okay. Hell but I was scared."

"I'll let you into a secret – I was too." And she had to admit, Jo reflected sombrely, that it was true and not just said to make Finola feel better.

Finola mouthed something to her; Jo frowned and shook her head to indicate that she hadn't heard. The lead singer – a muscular bearded man with laughing dark eyes – was taking a break whilst accordion, flute and traditional drums struck up a stirring gaelic number that bounced off the walls.

"What are you going to do?" Finola repeated louder.

Jo, aware of the interested gaze of the couple nearest them, frowned. "About what?"

Following Jo's look Finola moved her seat closer and leaned across the table. "Well she – Katrina or whatever she called herself – warned you away from the cottage, claimed you were in danger."

"You don't believe all that crap?" Jo, noting the fear had returned to Finola's eyes, deliberately allowed a touch of scorn to enter her voice.

Finola's eyes widened behind her glasses. "Don't you?"

Jo gazed up at the beamed ceiling. "Come on Fin – most of what that woman said was absolute bull-shit! Fairground stuff that's passed on to every punter!" She fiddled with her glass then took a large sip of brandy.

"But *the name* – how could she know it?" Finola persisted, becoming agitated again.

"A fluke," Jo said shortly, wondering now at the wisdom of having disclosed to Finola the outcome of the visit to Barbara. "It's a common enough name," she added with a shrug, "first letter of the alphabet – a natural choice. If we hadn't reacted she would no doubt have gone on to try us with others." She stood up to hide her scepticism at her own words. "Now look," she leaned forward, hands on table, "I'm going to get you another drink, and a basket meal for us both, and we're going to forget all this and just enjoy ourselves awhile, okay?" she said dropping her voice as the music ended, and the adjacent couple resumed their interest in the conversation.

"Well . . ." Finola gazed longingly at the logs blazing in the hearth, then around the room at faces flushed with enjoyment, and Jo knew she was reluctant to leave the reassuring warmth and normality. "Okay Jo," she said simply at last, shrugging as though to dislodge the burden of her timidity from her shoulders.

"Good. Don't go away," Jo said with a grin.

Despite her protestations, Finola ate with obvious relish, and downed her supper with a half of real ale. She sat now, rosy cheeked and feet tapping in time with the music whilst sipping her second brandy. "Thanks, I feel much better," she confessed, impulsively touching Jo's hand.

"You certainly look it. In fact –" Jo turned from watching the lead singer and leaned across to Finola, "the big guy over there – the one with the tawny beard and hunky shoulders – fancies you like hell."

Finola's cheeks immediately flushed pink. "Don't be silly!"

"See, he just winked at you again."

The man smiled at Finola and gestured for her to clap in time with the music; Finola laughed and began to beat time on the edge of the table with her fingers. Jo smiled to see the sparkle in her eyes, and the way she allowed her hair to swing forward across one cheek instead of pushing it behind her ear. Bloody hell, the girl is beautiful, why doesn't Colin spoil her a little and appreciate what he's got? Jo thought in sudden anger. "You know, Fin, you should get out and enjoy yourself more often," she said seriously.

Finola ceased tapping the table and gave her a thoughtful look. "So should you, Jo. You never know – you might meet someone."

Jo stared at her for a moment, then turned abruptly to look at the window by her shoulder. The dark square was mottled with flecks which melted on contact and slid in silver streaks like tears down the pane. She turned back to Finola. "We should be going now."

"You're too young and attractive to be alone," Finola persisted, in a loud whisper now that the band had finished and were packing up.

It was Jo's turn to flush, but with anger rather than embarrassment. How could Finola possibly advise on relationships when she couldn't sort out her own? "To bury myself in the country you mean?" Her mind went back to the London scene and her busy varied life with Blake. *Past life you mean.* The thought hurt, and pain made her brittle. "Or is it Colin you're worried about?" she snapped, then regretted the words the instant they were out, and even before she saw the hurt in Finola's face. "Oh *shit!* I'm sorry. What a prize bitch I am! – but I didn't mean it, Fin."

"It's okay. We're both stressed out tonight, that's all," Finola said generously.

Jo shrugged. "Absolutely, but it's no excuse." She fiddled with a beer mat, pushing it round and round on the table top. "Guess I resented your suggestion I should find someone else," she admitted at last. Finola's insight had taken her by surprise. She had seen herself as the one in control and Finola as the wimp, but she *was* stressed out, and all the more so for not being able to admit it, at least not without scaring Finola further. "You caught me on the raw, and that's the truth of it," she confessed.

Finola gave her a direct look. "Blake?"

Jo pushed her hair back from her forehead, allowing the curls to slip through her fingers. "I'm missing him more than usual I guess. That shock back there, and not being able to tell him, to share it. Then with you and Col – well it just brings it home."

Finola's eyes brimmed with sympathy. "You okay?"

Jo nodded, then attempted a smile. "just wallowing in self-pity."

Finola shook her head emphatically so that her hair bounced and shone in the firelight. "No, no you're not. It's an awful feeling; I know, I've been there."

"Men!" Jo sighed, "are they worth it?"

Finola shrugged. "Nope! But that don't make any difference; we'll go on agonising over them. Isn't there any chance of you and Blake getting back together?"

Jo shook her head. "I rather think I screwed that one up."

"Couldn't you tell him so?" Finola said gently.

"You don't know Blake. Besides, it wouldn't solve the underlying problem. I don't want kids yet – he does. Stalemate."

Jo emptied her glass of bitter and stood up. "Right, those bloody passes are waiting – and I'm just about fired up and ready to take my chance."

Finola pulled her coat around her. "I wish we were safely home."

"Just roads, Fin. Don't let the bastards get you down!" Laughing, Jo led the way to the door.

Finola rose to her feet and followed. "I do sometimes worry

about Col," she confided, "you know, about how maybe he fancies you."

Jo paused and turned to meet her gaze. "No problem, Fin."

"I know," she said looking down at the floor in embarrassment. "It's just that you're so attractive and feisty and a famous writer – and well, I'm such an awful wimp. You know what I'm saying – the glamorous image and all that."

"And that's all it is, a fantasy; even if he did give me a passing thought in that way, which I don't believe he does." Jo paused, wondering whether to spell out the probable truth: that it was not Colin who was interested in her, but something coming through him, and not in her as such, but in Madeline St. Clair. No, she thought deciding against it, Fin's had enough of a fright for one night. "It's you he's in love with, Fin," she said instead, squeezing the other girl's arm, "and your gentleness and sensitivity. He couldn't put up with my 'feistiness' for more than a week! And I promise, you've nothing to fear from me."

"I know." Finola gave her a grateful look and followed her through the door.

They turned simultaneously as a deep voice sounded from within:

"Hey, you girls need a lift? If so hang around five minutes."

They turned to find the bearded folk singer standing in the doorway of the room they had just left.

"No thanks," Finola said quickly, adding: "she's got a car."

"And she's got a man!" Jo shot back with a grin, jerking her thumb in Finola's direction before hustling her, giggling, to the door.

"What about yourself?" the man called good-humouredly.

Jo grinned and looked over her shoulder. "Who needs 'em!"

The big man's laughter followed her outside and was lost in the sleet and darkness.

"He's got nerve, I'll give him that." Finola was still laughing as they stumbled to the car aided only by the wedge of light cast by the porch lamps. She felt her way round to the passenger door, "Men," she said whilst waiting for the 'click' that would tell her Jo had unlocked it, "have such bloody big egos."

Jo laughed as she felt for the lock. "At least you were first choice!"

"Reckon I'll stick with Col after all," Finola said laughing. "Better the devil . . . and all that!"

"Dead right! Now come on, he's waiting for you," Jo chivvied, stifling an immediate pang at the prospect of entering Twilight Cottage alone.

"It was stupid to get so wound up about that pathetic woman," Finola said as they left the lights of the inn and Chapel Stile behind and headed for the wilderness of Wrynose Pass.

"Yep! I have to admit, it wasn't one of Barbara's best. Never mind, now we can forget it ever happened," Jo consoled.

As she peered through the darkness and psyched herself up for the hairpin bends ahead, she felt a buzz of premonition prickle the base of her neck.

THIRTY-FOUR

~

Katrina stared at the spread-eagled shape that briefly filled the window pane. Then it was gone, leaving her with an impression of yellow eyes beneath beetling brow. Yellow like the fug that still poisoned the air of the kitchen, clogging her nostrils and throat and bringing a wave of nausea and panic. And the stench: it was like a charnel house on a hot July day. Except that it was freezing in here. Gooseflesh rose on her bare arms as the temperature continued to drop.

Turning back to the door she abortively rattled its handle, then let go with an exclamation of disgust as the greasy film that covered it clung to her hand. She scrubbed the palm up and down her side, sweating despite the cold and irrelevantly thinking that her best cocktail dress now looked like it had been used in one of those jungle ads for antiperspirants. A machine gun hail of sound hit the window like bullets. Despite the fact that there was nobody to hear she began shouting and kicking the lower door panels, "Help – let me out. Please Stan, *someone* – let me out!" The pleading and terror in her voice made her cringe with shame, until the death rattle rapping at her back galvanised her into a fresh paroxysm of shouting. Her terror bounced back from the walls, winding itself around her in a tornado of negative energy. A saffron tornado as it combined with the miasma, the same colour as the rice Stan sometimes brought back from the takeaway next to the pub. *Oh Stan, Stan where are you?* Tighter and faster it whirled until the air crackled and split beneath the energy-onslaught. The tapping at the window increased in volume and the fluttering became more frantic. Katrina began to back off, recalling in time the greasy ooze that coated the door and stopping just short of it. Bile burned the back of her throat: the very thought of that slime sticking to her bare shoulders made her want to puke. Now chill out girl, there's got to be a way out of this little lot. The light dipped, rose and dipped again so that shadows loomed and retreated into corners, entities with a life of their own stealing her last glimmer of hope.

With the dulling of the electric light she became aware of the fug's phosphorescence. It glowed a dull sulphurous yellow, the yellow of thunderclouds, of sickness and bruised unhealthy flesh. She clenched and unclenched her fists, her finger joints stiff and aching in the accompanying stream of unnatural cold. This wasn't for real. Tricks, that's what they were, the tricks that every 'medium' learned along with the jargon. But who was pressing buttons and pulling strings? She cowered and whimpered aloud as the tornado raged and a high pitched whine filled her ears. Her legs were sagging, the muscles turning to jelly. Only the knowledge of yellow grease beneath her feet kept her upright on them. The light bulb crackled and spit like water drops in boiling fat. This couldn't be happening. She screwed her eyes tight shut, then opened them again. No, it wasn't her imagination. It was ink-black outside and the glass threw back multi-reflections, but beyond the reflected pots, pans and kitchen units he was clearly visible as a faint glow surrounded his form. She shook her head and blinked again. He was still there. The one she had seen lurking behind the girl's chair. She had been mistaken about the hawk, it wasn't real but some sort of emblem. Bright red, it spread like a bloodstain across his chest. Trapped in some terrible nightmare, she brushed a hand over her eyes. It was then that she began to pick up on his feelings. Confused at first, then with frightening clarity: a fury that seared her with white hot heat. In a flash she remembered her words: *Stay away from him . . . have nothing to do with him . . . get right away from that place.*

Then she knew. He was furious at her intervention.

She screamed as wings beat the air and the hawk rose from his chest. The figure disappeared, melting into the darkness, gradually fading like washed-out watercolours. Nothing now but the bird filling her vision, pinions and talons outstretched. A muted high-pitched shrieking reached her ears through the glass. The hawk hovered for an infinity, watching her with its jaundiced eye. She screamed as it hurtled straight at the window, head held back and talons outstretched. The window imploded: glass rose and fell in a slow-motion crystal cascade, a shower of solid raindrops twinkling in the electric light. She screamed and screamed as though unable to stop. The world had exploded into beating wings, rasping claws and vengeful eyes. She automatically ducked as the light bulb flashed and exploded into a myriad fragments, plunging the room into darkness. But not for long; the phosphorescence grew in intensity, assuming the sickly glow of a clapped-out star intent on destruction. All around her chaos raged, sound and movement combining in confusion. In that split second the famous *Psycho* shower scene came to mind. When it first came out, that film scared her half to death. Staccato screeches pierced her ears as pinions beat the air into submission. "Oh Stan, Stan, please come home!" she whimpered, and didn't quite manage to stifle the afterthought: *before it's too late.*

She automatically ducked as the bird's wings beat close to her face. The phosphorescence surrounded its form, seemed to draw energy from it until walls, floor and furniture glowed with the same unhealthy light. Her hands instinctively flew to cover her face. The sense of menace grew stronger. It was the same as back there in the seance room, a sense of hatred so thick you could cut it with a knife. But this was for real, not the usual harmless pretence to make a modest living. No, something vile was happening here. Something an honest-to-goodness clairvoyant could do without.

She opened her eyes, parting her fingers to risk a peep, and reeled as it launched the attack. A different shrieking hurt her ears: her own voice screaming into the night. Blood splattered the wall behind her as the beak punctured her eye. At the same time the talons ripped at the bodice of her dress and the shiny material peeled away and hung in tatters. Frantically fighting for her life, she struggled to dislodge the bird as its talons fastened on her plump white breasts.

233

The high-pitched squeals mingled with her own screams. The shrieking rose higher as feathers floated from her grasp. She writhed on the floor, floundering and helpless against the frenzy of fluttering, beating and clawing. One last dive, a maelstrom of fury and revenge.

Then blackness and silence.

THIRTY-FIVE

~

Finola brought the newspaper round to the cottage the following evening. "Here, you look as though you need a drink." Jo handed her a glass containing a generous amount of brandy, whilst with difficulty hiding her own sense of shock after reading the front page report in the Lancashire Post.

"Dead, Jo. That woman's *dead*." As she raised the glass to her lips, Finola's hand was trembling, her face drained of colour. "I didn't take to the woman – I mean, she was pretty awful, wasn't she? But this –," she shook her head before continuing: "and in such a God-awful way."

Jo struggled to keep her voice steady. "I can't believe it. Such a coincidence."

She stood by the window staring absently out over the clearing. A bloody sun was slung low in the sky so that the trees cast long shadows, their symmetry broken by the ruts and undulations of the uneven ground. *Dead. Ripped to pieces.* And according to forensic reports, it had happened not long after she and Finola had left. *Oh Christ!* was she responsible? Maybe it wouldn't have happened if she hadn't gone there in the first place. Bile burned her throat.

You can't possibly know that, Cavanagh. She struggled to hold down a rising tide of panic.

"But was it?"

Finola's voice cut in on her nightmare thoughts.

Frowning, Jo turned. "Was it what, Fin?"

"A coincidence," Fin whispered, chewing her bottom lip in anxiety.

"Yes." Jo moved from the window and poured herself a drink. "A terrible one, I grant you – but a coincidence," she stated firmly, whilst desperately fighting for control over her emotions.

"I don't think I believe it." Finola stared at her, her thin face taut with anxiety and her eyes begging for reassurance.

She was, Jo thought with a rush of compassion, truly frightened. "Of course you do!" she said in bracing tones. "What does Colin think about it? Come to think of it – where is he anyway?" *Always missing whenever Finola needs him,* she thought contemptuously. *Just like Blake.* The rider came before she could stop it.

Finola shrugged her slight shoulders. "Like you, he thinks it's just an unfortunate coincidence."

Jo spread her hands in a theatrical gesture. "There you are then: 'two against one' as we used to say at school!"

Finola nodded and gave a watery smile. As Jo gestured for her to drink up, she took a gulp of brandy and coughed as it went down. "He had to go up to Carlisle," she continued, then paused to clear her throat. "An exhibitors' meeting at the gallery."

Jo put down her glass and tended the fire, taking a couple of logs from the basket in the hearth. She straightened up and wiped her hands on the sides of her jeans. "Will he know where to find you?"

Finola nodded. "I left a note."

Jo frowned; Finola she saw, was looking anxious again. "Stop worrying, Fin. It's not our problem," she said, ruthlessly forcing from mind the thought of Katrina's savaged corpse.

"But it said in the paper there was no apparent motive – nothing missing, no sexual attack," Finola persisted.

"So? Jo retorted, forcing herself to look Finola in the eye. She deliberately made her voice callous. "What has that to do with us?"

Finola frowned and gave her a look of disapproval. "The only weird thing that happened was that incident before we left – when she came over all peculiar."

"Finola – you can't possibly say that! We have no idea what happened after we left. Whether she had any enemies for instance. Or a lover! A jealous husband perhaps – anything." *Now give it a rest,* she felt like adding, because her own nerves were being shredded.

Finola it seemed was not so easily put off. "They said 'a frenzied attack.' Horrific injuries that could have been caused by a large bird of prey."

"Or an ice pick – as in the best who-dunnits," Jo said brutally. She blinked hard to dispel the image of Katrina's bloody and sightless sockets. The tabloid had pulled no punches.

Apparently unconvinced, Finola shook her head and reached suddenly for the paper. "Look, look it says here," she insisted, brandishing the newspaper at Jo. It crackled loudly in the silence that stretched like a tangible barrier between them until Finola began to read: "*The only similar case in recent history was in 1976: a man with compatible injuries found on Dartmoor.*" No listen," Finola continued as Jo began to protest: "*Feathers were found clutched in the dead man's hand,*" she quoted, "*After exhaustive and abortive investigation, the death was finally attributed to an unprecedented attack by a raptor, possibly a buzzard or hawk. The preceding heat wave and subsequent draught conditions were blamed. Animals under stress display aberrant behaviour, an eminent zoologist stated.*" She flung down the paper, "And that says it all for me," she said bluntly.

"Hey come on Fin – there hasn't exactly been a heat wave," Jo argued desperately, pointing to the whorls of frost already forming on the windows.

Finola tossed the paper down on the chair and rounded on Jo: "No – but that woman said something about *the hawk,* remember?" she challenged.

Jo sighed with impatience. Give credence to this one and they'd all be stark raving loonies. "As I said – coincidence, so don't let it faze you," she said coolly.

"And the 'Antony' bit? You told me about him – and the St. Clair guy – before we even went," Finola said, her voice rising in pitch and volume as she worked herself up into a panic. "Are you trying to say that was coincidence too?"

Suddenly she crumpled, and covering her face with her hands began to weep.

"Come on, Finola, chill out," Jo said bracingly, but then drew the weeping girl into her arms. "It's going to be okay," she soothed, stroking Finola's long fair hair. As she did so, Jo glanced around her furtively. The room was growing cold, the air of hostility creeping back in. It seemed any display of violent emotion was sufficient to trigger the phenomenon, she realised, recalling earlier instances. "Now come on," she said pushing Finola down onto a chair by the fire, "Have another drink and you'll feel better."

I sincerely hope so anyway, Jo prayed, swooshing brandy into Finola's glass.

Colin arrived about fifteen minutes later, when the atmosphere in the cottage appeared to have settled and Finola was much recovered. Which is bloody typical, Jo thought handing him a whisky as he sat on the opposite seat to Finola by the fire, but preferable to a full-blown scene, she secretly admitted as Colin briefly commiserated with Finola then markedly tried to change the subject. He's doing what I'm doing, she thought with insight: he knows it's dangerous to bring the possibilities into the open.

"I was saying perhaps we ought to go to the police," Finola was saying, looking anxious. "But Jo says not."

"And I agree!" Colin said forcefully, demolishing half his whisky at a gulp. "It has nothing whatsoever to do with you two!"

"That's what I said," Jo chipped in.

"Quite right. You'll get yourselves caught up in police interrogations, and all the publicity – and for what? You can shed no light at all on that unfortunate woman's death."

Ignoring Finola's intake of breath Jo, stricken with guilt, lowered her head and bent over the hearth. Picking up the poker she prodded a burning log until it gave off a cascade of golden sparks. "What are the chances of them finding out we were there?" she asked straightening up.

Colin took another gulp of his whisky and stared into the fire. "Did you give your names? Either to her, or the guy who let you in?"

Jo shook her head emphatically. "No. Nor did we refer to one another by name throughout. That was the plan – give her nothing to play on."

"Some bloody plan!" Colin said gloomily, scowling at her in disapproval. Draining his glass he banged it down on the table. "I mean, what in God's name made you go there in the first place?" he demanded, glaring first at Jo then at Finola, who looked aggrieved but remained silent.

"It's done now, Col," Jo said quietly, meeting his gaze.

He looked about to argue, but then shrugged as though thinking better of it. "Right, so no-one knows who you are. Was the car parked directly outside the woman's house?"

"No, a few doors away."

"Beneath a street lamp? And were there other cars parked or just yours?"

"No to the first, and yes to the second," Jo shot back.

"Then we take a chance on it," he said decisively. "It's unlikely anyone noted the number, and if they did, the police wouldn't trace you to here. Agreed?"

Jo nodded, and after a moment's hesitation, Finola followed suit.

"Good! Now for Chris's sake, Jo, pour me another drink," Colin demanded, thrusting out his empty glass.

"Anyway, what I suggest is a day out. Something normal, to take our minds off all this," he said a few minutes later. "I was going to mention it the other night, only the time wasn't quite right," he added, with a rueful glance at Finola. "So," he said quickly before she could take him up on the controversial topic of their row, "ever been to Wastwater Jo?"

She shook her head. "Leastways, I don't think so."

He grinned. "You'd know if you had. You can't come to the Lakes and not see Wastwater and the screes. I propose an expedition tomorrow," he added, warming to his theme, "A quick lunch first at the pub, then a trot across the screes and back along the other side of the lake. Are you game?" he asked, turning to Jo.

"Okay. But what's so special about this place?" Jo demanded, folding the newspaper and handing it back to Colin.

"England's deepest lake, her highest mountain for backdrop – and the screes, well, I'll let you judge for yourself!" he said grinning.

"The weather's a bit 'iffy' for it, Colin," Finola ventured. "It could be icy."

"No problem if we're off before nightfall."

"Aren't you keen, Finola?" Jo asked, noting the other woman's anxious expression.

"I just don't like the place," she confessed, looking shamefaced. "It's the Valley Time Forgot!"

"Sounds intriguing!"

"That's settled then," Colin said, ignoring Fin's protests. "Right Jo, be at our place about ten thirty in the morning," he added.

Jo looked at Finola and shrugged. They had it seemed, been presented with a *fait accompli*.

After they had gone, Jo decided on a bath and early night. For one thing, immersing herself in warm scented water would soothe the shock of that terrible newspaper report, for another, her hand was throbbing again and the essential oils might be of benefit. Wincing, she carefully peeled off the dressing and frowned over the wound. Yesterday there had been a marked reduction in redness and swelling, in fact it had all but healed. Tonight the skin was shiny, and painfully drawn over an inflamed swelling with a festering yellow head. Moaning softly she applied the antibiotic cream and a fresh dressing. Perhaps she had forgotten to take the antibiotic capsules at lunchtime? she tried consoling herself, but knowing it wasn't true.

Tying her dressing gown as she went, Jo made her way back to the sitting room and opened the bureau drawer in which the ring was kept. The talon-like claws of the setting conjured horrific images: Katrina with her sightless sockets and savaged breasts – *and you brought it upon her.* As she stared mesmerised, the emerald glowed ominously in the subdued light. *Like his eyes,* she couldn't help thinking. She hastily closed the drawer, and a frown creased her forehead as a fresh thought struck. Was it just coincidence, or had her hand dramatically improved whilst the ring was about her neck? And had the wound rapidly deteriorated once she had removed it and replaced it in the bureau? Was it possible?

A ridiculous notion. Flagrant superstition, she castigated herself whilst heating milk to take up to bed. Colin was right: she needed a change of scene and a bit of fun. Yet an outing at this time seemed trivial, in the light of what had happened, she worried, pouring milk into a mug. *Don't think about that.* Colin was right: it was coincidence, and nothing to do with herself or Finola. Hurriedly she glanced round the room. Having convinced herself that no worms, slugs or toadstools lurked, she switched off the light and selecting an Anne Rice novel to read in bed, climbed the stairs.

Which puts vampires, betrayal, and vengeance firmly in place between the front and back cover of a fictional story, she reflected closing her book after about twenty minutes or so of reading. Or at least, of attempted reading, because her mind kept returning to a dingy terraced house in Lancaster, and a kitchen splattered with blood. *It was nothing to do with you. Coincidence, remember? Fact being stranger than fiction and all that.*

She switched off the light and lay on her back, watching the movement of leaf patterns and moon-shadows on the uneven plaster between the ceiling beams. With a sense of anticipated pleasure her thoughts turned to the proposed walking trip. It would be good to do something ordinary, simply for enjoyment, and escape from the cottage and its environs for a time.

Antony Antony

She tried her best to ignore the sibilant whisper. Less easy to shake off was the feeling of intense pain and longing. Tenderness flooded her, so poignant, so desperate that her cheeks were wet with tears.

"Antony. Antony!"

Her body stiffened as she strained to listen.

Then she realised the words had come from her own lips.

THIRTY-SIX

~

*Had he been less preoccupied, he may well have heard the horses
snicker a warning. But he wouldn't have heard Madeline: she
uttered not one word, not a solitary cry. He came out from the
ruins, curious at not hearing the sound of retreating hoofbeats as
she left. The he saw her. She was standing rigidly on the sward, her
hands straight by her sides, knuckles white, fists clenched. All colour
had drained from her face, her eyes looked dead. "Madeline!"*

*Her eyelids flickered and her body swayed forward slightly as
though she must run to him, but then she was still.*

"Madeline!"

*She made no answer but stood in that unnatural stance, head
ever so slightly tilted as though listening.*

*St. Clair's men had formed a semicircle around him. They began
to close in.*

Colin slowed the car almost to a halt as a turn in the road brought
Wastwater into view. Jo stared at the pewter-coloured lake and its
glowering backdrop with undisguised horror. The screes soared
some twelve to fourteen hundred feet above the sinister surface,
and as Colin had pointed out during their approach, plunged some
eight hundred feet beneath the water.

"Walk *around* the lake?" she echoed, taking in the near-vertical
plane of the screes as Colin finished outlining their plan.

"There is a path," he assured her, removing one hand from the
steering wheel to point across the brooding lake to the far side.

"You are joking of course?"

Colin shook his head. "Look again."

Jo's heart sank as she eventually made out a thin scar running just above the water line on the sheer escarpment. Her eye then travelled upwards to the summit: whisps of cloud coiled and snaked around wicked looking gullies, and icicles clung like giant stalactites to the deeply etched crevices in the rock face. "I see what you mean by the Valley Time Forgot," she commented, turning to Finola.

Finola nodded. "I actually wouldn't be surprised to spot Tyrannosaurus Rex lumbering across the top," she confessed with a grin.

"Come on wimps!" Colin teased, pressing his foot down on the accelerator.

"But it's positively *miles* – even down this side," Jo exclaimed after they had travelled some way along the narrow and winding lakeside road.

Colin grinned at her in the mirror. "So?"

"It's going to take hours and hours to walk all the way round."

"Towny!" he taunted, laughing.

Which made Jo determined to complete the walk at all cost.

They alighted from the car at the Wasdale Head Inn in hazy sunshine. Jo took a deep breath, then gasped as the cold struck the top of her nose and a pain shot between her eyes. "Now that's what I call fresh air!" Stretching her legs, she stared at the barren snow-capped mountains which dominated the dalehead.

"Scafell, Lingmell, Great Gable and Kirk Fell," Finola supplied, pointing out each one.

"You say that as though they are old friends," Jo commented.

Finola smiled. "They are."

So you're not such a wimp after all, Jo thought regarding Finola with new respect. The uncomfortable feeling of being the only rookie in the group wasn't doing much for her self esteem, and the prospect of disgracing herself in front of these two obviously experienced fell walkers became a distinct possibility.

"And that's where we start out," Colin said, indicating a track that led to the far side of the lake and the start of the screes. "But first, a bite to eat and a swift half."

Jo grimaced. "A couple of stiff brandies would be more appropriate!"

"Don't worry; you'll be okay," Finola whispered.

Jo squeezed her arm and followed them into the pub.

Fortified by food and a modest amount of real ale, they kitted-up in boots and anoraks, left their vehicle in the car park and set off in single file along the grassy track. Colin had slung onto his shoulders a rucksack containing torches, compass and a coiled rope, which they likely would not need but should nonetheless carry, as he jauntily told them. The track took them across stubby farm-land, and eventually alongside the lake itself. *This doesn't look too bad,* Jo thought as they trod a well-marked path traversing a modest slope which ran down to the water's edge. Maybe the screes had just looked intimidating from across the lake, a trick of perspective. Reassured, she strode out with confidence and pre-pared to enjoy the walk.

She was jolted into reality as they hit the screes proper. Nothing now but water, barren mountain and more water. There was too an overpowering impression of greyness. Grey rock, grey water, grey sky. She saw anxiety flit across Colin's face as he glanced up at steely clouds drifting in from the north to obscure the hazy sun. There was a dampness now to the chill, and their breath stained the air white as the temperature dropped still further. The path, becoming less and less distinct over the past mile or so was now virtually non-existent, a mere broken scar traced across an impos-sibly steep mountain flank. Jo began to seriously wish she hadn't come; despite thick gloves her hands felt raw as her fingers sought for handholds in the rock. They were all but crawling across the face now, pulling themselves around massive boulders, flattening their bodies against them so as not to lean too far out and risk overbalancing. Jo shuddered. To their left rose the near vertical escarpment, to the right a vertiginous drop staight into the water. Scree rolled beneath her boots like so many marbles, and pain shot through her ankles due to the unaccustomed but necessary angle of her feet. Adrenalin surged through her system whenever loose stones gathered larger rocks with their momentum, and splashed into the water some thirty feet below.

The sound they made filled her with foreboding. That water down there was seriously deep: something like eight hundred feet, and nothing between herself and its icy embrace. Not only the deepest lake in England but also the coldest, she didn't mind betting. "I bet it's freezing down there," she commented, scrambling more quickly over the rocks to lessen the gap between herself and Colin.

"You wouldn't survive long in there – especially in winter," Colin replied as he picked his way expertly over a shifting bed of marbles. She tried not to think about it, or of what may be lurking in these primordial waters.

The distance between them lengthened as Colin's experience and greater physical strength began to tell. "Okay, girls?" he called over his shoulder.

"I think so." *As long as I don't look down,* Jo thought, scrambling over the huge white boulders that barred the way forward. They were roughly at the centre-lake point; there was no going back now. Despite the cold she was sweating profusely and the inside of her anorak felt unpleasantly moist.

"Fine." Finola was effortlessly bringing up the rear, and obviously holding back so as not to pressure Jo.

A few minutes later Colin paused and pointed to the far side of the lake. "That's were they found that doctor's wife, you know – the one from Cheshire."

"What's that?" Jo called, catching up slightly as he waited.

"He did her in, then drove up here in the early hours and dumped her in the water. The media went to town on it – you must remember?"

"I'd rather not," Jo said with a grimace thinking, *I shouldn't have come.* In front and behind her the lake stretched into the distance, and at her back a solid wall of rock towered. *No escape.* But she must stop thinking this way.

"They'd never have found her if her body hadn't lodged on an underwater shelf," Finola commented.

"I'd have made a better job of it. So just watch your step Fin!" Colin said, pulling a horrible face. "If you're ever tempted to two-time me, just think again."

Finola laughed. "I'd come back and haunt you forever."

Forever . . . forever . . .

Jo shivered; the words seemed to echo along the chambers of rock overhead. Instinctively she swung round and almost lost her footing.

"Take care!" Colin admonished. It was obvious he had heard nothing, and neither had Finola, Jo deduced, looking back and noting her untroubled face. No doubt it had been a perfectly innocent remark. Yet from that moment on, she knew she had been foolish in agreeing to come to this place.

THIRTY-SEVEN

~

Jo was never quite sure when the suspicion that she being followed became a certainty.

Antony Antony

She glanced over her shoulder. Perhaps it was then – when the whisper first drifted in and out of the teeth and crevices along the jagged rim of the escarpment.

Antony Antony

There it was again, like a breath from hell it hissed with menace and venom. Or maybe it was down to the change in weather: a mist was rising across the implacable sheet of water. Within a very short time she could no longer see the lake, could only hear its incessant sucking and lapping at the rock face below.

"Colin!" she shouted in sudden panic as he disappeared from view and she was crawling alone in a prehistoric world with vapour curling around her feet.

"It's okay, I'm here," came the answering shout from ahead.

"Fin – are you okay?" Jo's voice, thin and scared, was instantly swallowed up by the freezing fog.

Finola's voice reached her from immediately behind: "We'll be alright, Jo. Just keep going."

"Get this bit done and we're over the worst," Colin shouted, pausing briefly to allow the gap between them to dwindle. Jo sucked in her breath, wishing she could go with his prediction.

Behind Finola, a figure was moving in and out of the mist.

Immediately Seth Rigby came to mind. The image of his face pressed against the window, the contortions of hatred and madness. *And the gleam of metal in his hand.* "Fin, behind –," she started to warn desperately, but Finola interrupted: "It's alright – stay cool, Jo."

That wasn't hard – she was bloody freezing. Jo called again, this time to Colin but her voice was wrapped in damp cotton wool and there was no answering shout. She stumbled and her heart pounded in her ears as stones fell with a dull *plash* into the water below. Instinctively her arm was flung out and her hands clutched for handholds in the rock. *I won't make it.* Darkness and shadows crowded her psyche. This was like trying to find her way out of a maze whilst wearing a dense veil over her eyes.

"Keep up Jo!"

Colin's voice penetrated the silence and mist, driving her on. She was even able to convince herself that the fleeting shadow had been an illusion, a trick of the half-light and shifting vapour.

Doggedly she pressed on. This was the worst bit all right. Her ears strained for the reassuring thud and scrape of Colin's boots out front and Finola's at the rear. She had to stretch now, and her muscles screamed at the unaccustomed effort. Her toes ached as they searched and groped for holds, her feet testing the boulders that over time, had plunged down from the summit. They rested precariously now, balanced at various heights on the almost vertical slope. In some cases, a mere touch would send them plummeting into the water. An awesome and over-powering landscape.

Spoil-piles mined by ice, gales and centuries of wind-driven rain.

Finola was now closing in at the rear, calling out the occasional encouragement as she went. Turning to acknowledge her, Jo felt a thrill of shock run through her body. The shadow had returned – and it wasn't Seth Rigby. Almost she wished it was, because Colin could deal with a half-crazed farmer. But there was no dark figure trailing Finola along the ridge. Yet there should have been, Jo thought panic-stricken. Because something invisible was casting a shadow on the mist that shrouded the lake's surface It moved slowly and purposefully, keeping pace with Finola who seemed blissfully unaware of its presence A stench like the one that had plagued the cottage rose to her nostrils.

Love you . . . kill you . . . forever, forever, forever.

The whisper hurtled around the jagged black rim above her head. As Finola advanced, the shadow moved closer.

"Oh, my God! Finola – *move!* Get out of the way." Jo stumbled on as fast as she dare. *Faster, faster*, she urged herself, despising her cowardice but unable to control it. A scream was wrenched from her as a rock shot away from underfoot. The ground rolled away and the water loomed closer. Digging in her heels and grasping at a boulder, she managed to halt the slide.

"What's going on?" Colin's voice came from somewhere out front. "What is it?" Eerily his figure materialised out of the mist.

"Finola – there's something-," instead of attempting to explain, Jo pointed with a hand that shook.

"I don't know what you're talking about," he snapped, anxiety making him irritable.

"*There!*" Jo screamed, "there's something behind her!"

As Finola deftly picked her way forward the shadow surged forward, silent with menace.

Antony Antony

Jo sensed that she was the target, but to get at her the shadow would have to pass Finola. "Finola, look out!" she screamed.

As the shadow below Finola's feet drew level, a dark cloud seemed to drape itself over her body. The mist swirled around her as she opened her mouth to speak and her cry was choked. Suddenly she staggered, flung out her arms and swayed wildly on the narrow ledge. For an interminable moment she seemed to hang suspended, as though frozen in some grotesque dance.

Then she toppled and fell.

Jo's scream coincided with the sound of a dull splash.

Within a couple of seconds this was followed by another as Colin dived. Numbed by fear, Jo watched for their heads to break the surface. Nothing. Just aching loneliness, and the ominous lapping of water on stone. Beneath her breath she prayed for them to appear. The sound of splashing, of feet treading water brought tears of gratitude and relief. "Colin? Finola?" She peered through the shredded curtain of mist that partially veiled the surface. *There – there he is.* But where's Finola? she agonised as his head broke clear of the water. Cold dread gripped her insides. "Col!"

She screamed as his head disappeared again beneath the surface.

She buckled, weak with relief as he reappeared, one hand supporting Finola's chin to keep her head clear of the water.

"My rucksack," he shouted, spitting and choking. "The *rope*."

Jo, her mind frozen with shock, tried to force her brain to connect with his words. She could hear his teeth chattering from where she crouched on the hair-line path.

"For Chris'sakes move! Get the bloody rope!"

The urgency in his voice galvanised her into action. Scrambling forward on all fours, she crept to where Colin had dropped the ruck sack. The rope, must find the rope. *Yes, here it is.* Her numbed fingers fumbled with the clips that held it in place . . . *wouldn't last long in there, especially in winter.* Colin's words returned to fill her with terror and make her fingers even more clumsy.

"Quick Jo!"

At Colin's desperate cry, she leapt up, rope in hand.

"Run it around a rock and throw me the end," he instructed, his words scarcely discernible due to the shudders that wracked his body.

Jo secured the rope and tossed the other end out to where Colin's head and shoulders bobbed above water. The movement caused her to lose balance; she stumbled and the rope fell short. Cursing beneath her breath she hauled it in and struck again. It hit the water with an audible smack. *Almost, but a little wide.* No tears now, only icy determination. This time she swung it to and fro, gauging her aim. The rope snaked out over the surface. Colin's arm shot out and the rope jerked convulsively. "Yes!" Jo exulted. She had him. It was then that she saw the shadow moving silently across the water towards him. Colin threshed about at the end of the rope, inch by laborious inch hauling himself and Finola clear of the water.

"Quick Col, quick!" Then Jo's breath was stopped by fear as the shadow glided closer.

THIRTY-EIGHT

~

Jo dug her heels into the scree and tugged on the rope. "Hurry, Col! Hurry!" she yelled. They were into the side now and Colin gave a shout of encouragement. He seemed unaware of the advancing shadow and from his stance, Jo guessed his feet had touched the rock face below. This was borne out when the rope suddenly tautened, as he braced himself and strained backwards, momentarily throwing Jo off-balance. She shouted again for him to hurry as the dark shape surged forward and the air became a sulphurous yellow and thick with menace. She watched in horror as the shadow crept over Finola's white face, laying upon it a stain of hopelessness and extinguishing her light.

But there was no time to indulge dark fancies. The rope jerked and Colin dropped back into the water, taking Finola with him and showering Jo with icy droplets. Jo cried out in despair; just here the water was something like eight hundred feet deep. Both of them would be lost if she didn't get them out soon. Laboriously Col hauled himself up again whilst supporting Finola with one arm.

"Pull me into the side Jo!" he shouted, treading water.

Jo hauled on the rope and braced herself as he inched fly-like up the submerged section of the escarpment, fighting the suck and drag to place each foot a little higher. At last he was sufficiently high in the water to enable him to slip the rope beneath Finola's armpits. Jo watched with white-knuckle tension as he struggled to secure the knot with fingers which had to be numb with cold. How long before both he and Finola succumbed to hypothermia or cramp? she fretted.

"Pull Jo! Pull like hell!" he yelled, though teeth that were uncontrollably chattering.

The sudden increase in weight as Finola came clear of the water sent a knife shooting along Jo's spine. Gasping with shock, she braced herself and fed the slack around the back of her waist. She gritted her teeth and hauled harder on the rope. Every muscle screamed, and sinews felt about to snap with the strain like overstretched elastic bands as Colin trod water and shouted encouragement. *A dead weight. For God's sake, don't think that way.* Inch by painful inch Finola moved closer to safety. At last Jo hauled her, dripping and spluttering, onto the narrow ledge.

"It's alright, Finola, you're going to be alright," she soothed as she reached for the rope. Her own hands were blue with cold and shaking with trauma. She swore beneath her breath and forced her fingers to move faster. At last the knot gave. Standing up she saw Colin directly below and treading water. "The rope's coming – be ready Col!" she shouted. It snaked out and with a sigh of relief she watched him deftly catch the end.

Finola coughed and vomited a small amount of water. "Thank God!" Colin breathed. His hair was plastered to his head and water dripped from his clothes. He was shaking with cold. Turning Finola over, he made her sit up with her back against a huge boulder. She remained where he placed her, a limp rag doll wracked at intervals by tremors. "Finola! Finola!" he said urgently. Her eyes flew open but she stared at him seemingly without recognition.

"Quick, Jo – strip off those clothes."

Jo hesitated. "All of them?"

"Yes dammit – but top half first," he growled, crawling to where the rucksack lay. After fumbling with the straps, he dragged out three spare sweaters, hats, scarves, thick hiking socks.

"Raise your arms Fin," Jo ordered, then shouted in desperation as Finola stared straight in front: "Do it Fin!" Finola obeyed without a word, moving slowly and jerkily like an automaton. "Hurry Col – she'll catch her death!" Jo urged as the mist swirled around them, touching them with damp chilly fingers. Finola's thin torso was shaking like a leaf in a storm; her small breasts were pinched and blue.

"Don't panic, and grab these." Colin held out the spare clothing but retained a thick woollen scarf. Kneeling down by Finola he gathered and twisted her sodden hair into a rope and squeezed out the excess water. He then rubbed her head with brisk circular movements, using the scarf. Next he scrubbed at her bare shoulders and breasts, using a second, dry scarf. Finola whimpered as the coarse wool scoured her fair skin but Colin didn't desist. "Roll her over," he commanded, and as Jo did so he scrubbed at Finola's back, working swiftly and with economy of effort. "Sweater," he commanded, and as Jo handed one to him: "help me get her into it."

"Herdwick wool," he commented as they pulled the heavy-knit down below Finola's waist. "Our native sheep – they date back to the Vikings. The natural oils make it wind and waterproof." His tone was conversational, his words unhurried, thereby injecting a note of normality into the trauma. Jo was grateful; he must have guessed she was close to freaking out.

"That feel better Fin?" he asked, giving Finola an anxious look but without pausing in his work. Finola stared at him and did not answer. Her eyes were sunken in their sockets, but her colour had marginally returned.

Colin frowned. "Must be shock – or hypothermia. She hadn't much water in her lungs."

"Is she going to be alright?" The image of that dark shape devouring Finola returned to fill Jo with dread.

"If we act quickly enough," Colin replied grimly.

"This is the plan," he began taking a second, larger sweater from Jo and pulling it over Finola's head and down over the first one. "We've got the worst part of the screes behind us. Which is good for Finola – but not you, I'm afraid Jo. Because you have to go back."

"Alone?" Jo chewed her lip as he paused to unclip his car keys from his belt and hand them to her.

"It's the only way. With a bit of luck I can get Finola off the screes, but she would never make it all the way round the lake to the car." He jammed a woollen hat over Finola's hair. "Two thirds of body heat are lost from the top of the head," he commented, pulling it down to cover Finola's ears; she was shaking less noticeably now. "So you must get to the car and drive it back to the foot of the lake. You'll be waiting for us there. Got it?" he rapped, whilst winding a scarf round Finola's neck.

"I'll try," Jo whispered, not daring to think of the journey back across the screes alone.

"No – you'll *do it*," he said remorselessly, expertly stripping off Finola's boots and socks. "Because if you don't, he added in an undervoice, "Finola will die of exposure."

"Are you feeling warmer now, Finola?" he asked, pulling onto her feet a second pair of dry socks after scrubbing at her feet with a spare scarf. He then added forcefully when she failed to reply: "I'm talking to you Finola – answer me please!"

She stared at him as though without understanding, but at length admitted "Warmer," in a voice devoid of expression.

"Good girl." He chafed her hands and pulled on a pair of woollen mittens. "Can you stand up for me now?" he cajoled.

She looked at him with a vacant expression, but then as he repeated the words, with help struggled to her feet.

"Okay. Well done. Now in a minute you're going to walk." Finola stared through him and he added as she didn't respond: "it will warm you up, alright?"

Jo marvelled at this show of uncharacteristic patience. Obviously he was aware of having almost lost Finola.

"Yes. Walk."

Still that dullness of tone and expression, but at least she was communicating, Jo thought, watching Colin unwrap a mint cake and place a piece in Finola's mouth.

"There's a couple of torches in the rucksack – take one," Colin instructed, turning to Jo. "And take a mint cake too. Your own sugar levels must be dropping by now."

Jo realised she was feeling weak with exhaustion. "Thank God you were so well prepared, Colin," she said with feeling, helping herself from the rucksack.

"Nearly came unstuck once – taught me a valuable lesson," he said tersely. "Now off you go. Fast as you *safely* can."

"I'll be okay, Colin," she said, realising that he was feeling bad at having to send her back alone. Impulsively she squeezed Finola's arm. "Just keep going, Finola. Colin will get you to safety."

Finola stared at her with huge eyes. Jo saw and recognised the struggle behind them; the struggle to make sense of the nightmare. "It's okay, Finola, we'll make it, remember?" she said gently.

She set off then, and looked back. "I'll be there," she promised them both as they watched her moving away. "I'll be waiting for you."

She looked back again after crawling several yards along the ledge. Colin and Finola had already been swallowed up by the mist.

THIRTY-NINE

~

For a second or two Colin allowed the panic he had bolted down to break free and surface. It wouldn't have done to let Jo – or Finola if she was capable of understanding, which he doubted – know how desperate was their plight. What if Jo funked out and didn't make it to the car? Or worse, slipped on the screes and fell into the lake; or broke a leg? And then there was Finola. It would be a Herculean task to get her off here, given her mental condition and physical exhaustion. He shuddered at the probable outcome for them all. He looked at Finola, wide-eyed, arms straight at her sides, and looking like a lost child on a Sunday school outing. He shrugged the straps of the back pack into a more comfortable position on his shoulders, and at the same time fought to pull himself together. He was wrong in thinking it all rested on Jo. They were a team, and success depended on each of them playing their part. In fact, he castigated himself, he was being irresponsible: by neglecting himself he was increasing his chances of succumbing to hypothermia, and that would put all of them in jeopardy. At last his resolve and courage were more or less back in place.

"Right," he said to Finola, dragging off his wet sweater and shirt and trying to stop the chattering of his teeth sufficiently to speak again; his lips were so numbed that he had difficulty forming the words. "My turn." Finola made a small sound then stood listlessly without speaking as he scrubbed vigorously at his chest and arms. Colin frowned as he scrutinised her face. "Okay, my girl, off we go. The sooner we walk the warmer we'll be!" He made his voice hearty and kept up a running monologue, knowing the importance of holding onto her awareness. He wound a scarf twice around her wrist then gave her the end to hold fast. "That's it, hold onto your end," he encouraged, taking up the other and leading her slowly along the pencil-thin ledge above the water that sucked and slapped inches below their feet.

They pressed on, Finola stumbling behind with agonising slowness, and Colin fighting the urge to lengthen his stride and drag her bodily off this hellscape. The mist swirled and eddied, at times thinning and at others muffling them in a damp grey blanket. "Fish and chips at Ambleside if you hurry!" he said with false cheerfulness, watching heart in mouth as Finola staggered and almost fell. "Okay, lass? Good, good – just keep right on moving," he intoned as though talking a sick ewe back to the fold. A low grumbling sound above their heads made him glance up in alarm. "And a carton of curry sauce if you're really good!" he continued desperately, aware that fear sharpened his laughter to the edge of hysteria. "Remember how it used to warm us up after coming down from Helvellyn or Blencathra in winter? Basic stuff – but it makes the juices run thinking about it, doesn't it?"

He pulled the scarf taut in an unconscious effort to make her move faster.

"Tired, Col. Tired," Finola muttered.

Christ, she was sinking down on the ground where she stood. "Get up Fin! Get up!" he shouted brutally, then added with remorse as he saw her weary shoulders sag and her head droop: "For me, Fin. Do it for me!"

He looked around him and shivered with new intensity. There was something wrong. An atmosphere that made him feel like a hare with the scent of fox in its nostrils. The rumbling noise echoed along the ridge again. As he looked up a smattering of stones rolled and bounced down the scree and around their feet, pitting the surface of the water below. "We have to hurry Fin," he urged, grabbing her arms and hauling her to her feet. Her pallor, he noted, had increased. Finola moaned and sagged against him so that they both almost lost their balance. One more dip in there would be our last, Colin thought grimly, feeling a sudden and humiliating urge to relieve himself as he looked down at the heaving grey stretch of ominous water. "Stand still a moment – don't move, Fin," he said, not taking his eyes off her as he fumbled with the zip then urinated. "Right, off we go again," he said with more confidence than he felt.

Instinctively he glanced at intervals over his shoulder. This fear he felt was not the simple survival-type fear of a tricky situation in the fells. That he was used to; that he could handle. No, there was something ominous here. An atmosphere of hostility, a power and presence he did not understand. Finola cried out as she stumbled again. He leapt forward, catching her just in time as one foot lost its grip on stone marbles, and for one heart-stopping moment her leg dangled over the edge.

Suddenly Finola began to struggle and scream. "No! No!" she cried, her eyes starting in terror as she looked wildly over her shoulder. She plucked at her clothes with compulsive jerky movements, her voice rising to the pitch of a wounded animal. Her screams, blanketed and confined by the mist, echoed around his head. *For God's sake Finola, shut up!* For one red, blazing, crazy moment he felt the anger steal in and take over, the compulsion to push her back into the water to still the shrilling of her voice. He stood perfectly still, not daring to even touch her until the sensation passed.

It was then that he saw it. A shadow looming behind her. For a split second he clearly saw the man: the broad shoulders, the white of a tunic-style robe with a splash of scarlet on the chest. He became aware of the gleam of metal, and felt a shock of fear on realising the man had a knife. Briefly he saw the square determined chin, high cheekbones, the sweep of dark brows – and was afraid. But the thing that made fear grab him by the throat and choke his breath was the man's eyes: green and lambent, they seemed lit from within by a fanatical and malignant will.

Jo threw a nervous glance over her shoulder, then stumbled on over the rocks and forced herself not to look down at the heaving water. The constant *lap-suck-lap* was driving her crazy. It seemed like the lake was biding its time, patiently waiting for her to make a fatal error, as though it was inevitable that sooner or later her hand or foot would slip, and she would take the place of Colin and Finola in those icy depths. *To complete the sacrifice that was only partially made.* Oh God, she must be going mad to think such things.

But then who wouldn't succumb to madness, she thought, easing her way slowly and laboriously around a gigantic boulder that barred her path; given the freezing fog that transformed this place into a primordial ice-scape peopled with shifting shadows. Because that's all it is, she told herself firmly, that drifting form half-glimpsed and half imagined. Fear lodged like a rock in her stomach, and Jo glanced over her shoulder for the umpteenth time since leaving Col and Finola. It was simply the mist spiralling and drifting into forms that could almost be human – nothing more sinister than that. Without warning a wave of misery swamped her being. Hopelessness made the physical pain the keener: her hands were cut and bleeding, and the unaccustomed boots were rubbing fierce blisters in her heels. A cry was forced from her as her foot slipped and a pain shot through her ankle. Sobs welled up in her throat and caught at her chest but she suppressed them, despising her weakness. Her heart banged against her ribs as she almost fell again. The torch was dimming; the mist was closing in. *Blake, Blake where are you?* she silently cried.

Lost love and loneliness overspilled, drowning her in self pity.

Love you . . . kill you . . . Love you forever, forever . . .

She froze: one foot on the next rock, one arm about to reach out for a handhold.

Love you . . . kill you . . .

The whisper bombarded her through the mist, echoing round the rocks and gullies above her head. She glanced up and shivered. Mist wreathed like phantoms amongst the jutting heads and haunted the ice-bound gullies.

Love you . . . kill you . . .

She turned, saw the flick of a cloak, the whiteness of his face and greenness of his eyes, and the dull gleam of metal in his hand.

Crying uncontrollably and with the breath rasping in her throat she struggled on. He was shadowing her, she could feel the pressure at her back as his malignancy hit her like a stream of ice-chilled air. Pushed beyond endurance she sensed despair settling over her shoulders, a black cloak that weighed her down and robbed her of hope. She forced the image of Blake to the forefront of her mind, held him there, drew on his strength, and the love they had once shared. *Help me, Blake; for God's sake, help me now.*

Over and over she said the words, in her head at first, then aloud: softly, beneath her breath, and in time with each tortuous movement. It was then that she felt a change, subtle at first but growing in intensity. The waves of hatred at her back were tempered with sadness, love and longing. Not unlike her own desolate feelings over Blake – only a hundred times more potent. Confusion, conflict, pain and rejection, all of these feelings raged around and within her, the whole combined with longing and helplessness. *His or mine?* she found herself thinking, aware that it was no longer Blake who claimed her thoughts.

Antony. She had murmured the name without thinking. Tears overspilled, wetting her already damp cheeks as she slithered over gravel and fragmented rock. *Or Blake?* No answers. She knew only that the ground was now grassy beneath her feet, the path broader and more distinct, and her tears were now ones of relief.

She was off the screes.

The trek to the car seemed endless. Her own safety assured, she worried now for Colin and Finola. Had they also made it off those murderous screes? Would Finola hold out, or succumb to hypothermia? But this wouldn't do; nothing was to be gained from indulging in gloom, doom and panic. She had to believe they would make it, anything else was unthinkable. But it was hard to ignore the fading light, the knowledge that time was running out; if Col didn't haul Fin off the screes before dark, there could be little hope of her survival. Jo stifled a moan; the stitch in her side was excruciating. She limped on, then encouraged, broke into a trot as she hit the walkers' trail that led to the single track road. And there it was – never had she been so glad to see a car.

She turned the key in the ignition and held her breath, half believing the malignant power could reach her here and do impossible things. But the engine coughed into life and she gave a huge sigh of relief. Nonetheless, just to be sure she leaned across and locked the passenger door, then pushed down the button on her own side. Illogical, she told herself with a grim smile, given the nature of her pursuer, but it did make her feel more secure.

The drive along the narrow winding road that flanked the lake was a nightmare, but a lesser one and one she could just about manage. Leaning forward on her seat she peered through the windscreen, searching for the edge of the road in the twilight and shifting mist. In the absence of any kind of barrier between car and water, there was no margin for error. For comfort she groped about for a cassette and finding one, slipped it into the slot without taking her eyes from the road. *Clannad*. The tape Colin had played the night he took her to the hospital. How much, she reflected, moving her head in a gesture of disbelief, had taken place since then. A minute later she pushed the eject button; it was too distracting. Not only that, she acknowledged, the setting and silence somehow prohibited the playing of music. It seemed irreverent, like whistling in church.

At last the shallows loomed through the mist by the diffused light of the headlamps, and minutes later the car left the lake behind. This should be far enough: the end of the screes could just be seen rising through the gloom and fog. She pulled in at the side of the road and switched off the engine.

Now for the big one: where were Colin and Finola?

The freezing fog was less dense and seemed to be settling at ground level. Even so, it wreathed and distorted reality, and confused Jo's sense of orientation as she stood uncertainly by the car. It muffled the sound of the beck that fed the lake, so that she was unsure of the general direction. Trees and shrubs floated eerily on a drifting sea of white. The screes end at the foot of the lake, she reminded herself, forestalling rising panic and a growing sense of isolation. And Colin and Finola were out there – and alive. *They had to be.*

The chances were they had heard the approach of the car and would take heart. But an extra hazard was now presenting itself: night was falling, and the temperature along with it – at a guess, to a couple of degrees below zero. Pulling up her collar she clenched her teeth to stop them chattering; the sound was unnerving in the silence. Time was running out for Finola, unless that is she had already succumbed to hypothermia. Jo set off on foot, making for the grim dark ridge etched against the skyline.

She pushed forward, moving as fast as she dared through mist and gathering darkness, and eventually stumbled into the beck. The crack of ice shattering as her boot went through sounded like several pistol shots being fired. The visible flow, she saw now as the mist wreathed and shifted along the surface, was reduced to a sluggish ooze at the centre where the ice was thin and honey-combed with holes, which explained why there had been no sound of running water to alert her on her approach. With a muttered expletive she pulled her foot out of the water and did her best to ignore the creeping chill inside her boot. At least, given that this must be one of the becks which fed the lake, the path leading off the screes must now be close at hand.

Nonetheless anxiety flooded in, as cold and pervasive as the water inside her boot. Surely they would come. They had to – *but what if they didn't?* She faltered, wondering whether it would be better to search for a farmhouse in the hope of being able to telephone for help. But there may be nothing for miles, and in these conditions she could be walking around in circles. No, better keep faith and stick to the original plan. Indecision was a killer.

Cupping her hands over her mouth she shouted: "Colin! Finola!" several times and as loud as she could. She paused to listen, head to one side, ears straining for the slightest sound; if there was to be any hope of rescue, they had to be close enough to hear. As there was no response she carried on stumbling through the wood. There must be a bridge here somewhere. Plunging into the icy stream, she decided, had little to recommend it.

The sturdy stone bridge loomed reassuringly out of the mist, ice already forming miniature stalactites on the parapet. When half way across, Jo paused to listen and take some deep breaths. The panic inside her was growing along with the sense of isolation. It seemed there was nobody else alive in the world. No comfort, no hope, only this futile searching through an uninhabited void.

As the minutes passed so did the sense of being alone. Nausea hit her stomach along with the surge of adrenalin. *He* was back. Lurking somewhere in the gloom. Hostility and menace swirled around her and touched her with cold clammy fingers. Every few steps now she glanced over her shoulder, starting at shadows and staring panic-stricken at shifting forms created by aimless drifts of vapour.

Antony

The whisper could have been the breath of imprisoned water rasping on ice.

She stood for a moment as though frozen herself, then whirled round in terror. A sound she could not place beat against the chill mist-laden air then was still. It came again, a muffled beating and whirring as though something had passed close. Something else stirred, inside her head this time: a childhood memory of a plastic windmill bought by her mother during a day trip to the seaside. The sails of bright blue and yellow had started to turn and make a soft purring noise as they spun in the breeze brisking off the sea, developing a harder more insistent whirr as they gained momentum. At five years old that sound and gathering speed had made her laugh aloud with excitement; this sound made her heart beat faster with trepidation. She stood for a while listening, head slightly to one side, spine rigid with tension, but nothing now disturbed the hush of the forest. She stamped her feet then sniffed loudly, blaming the cold yet aware of making these small human sounds in a bid to thwart the oppressive silence. Encouraged, she cupped her hands to her mouth and shouted Colin's name, then listened in deepening despair to the echo bouncing off rock. Fatigue and cold were taking their toll, robbing her of hope and resilience. She stumbled forward, legs feeling like lead and every muscle screaming. "Colin! Finola! For God's sake, can you hear me!" she screamed at last in frustration.

At first she thought it an illusion, a product of wishful thinking. Her body stiffened, her diaphragm going into spasm and briefly preventing her lungs from rising and filling with air. No, there it was again. Her heart leapt at the answering cry and she gave a choking sigh as air entered her lungs with a rush. She staggered forward then paused to listen.

"Jo-o-o-o!"

The cry, thinned by mist and cold, trailed through winter-trees and undergrowth to cocoon her in blessed relief.

"Here, Jo! Over here!"

Jo lengthened her stride. Brittle twigs snapped beneath her boots and branches whipped angrily back as she pushed them aside and crashed through the gaps, sweat dampening her forehead despite the cold. "I'm coming! I'm coming!" she yelled, knowing Colin's relief would be as great as her own. She didn't dare think about Finola. About whether she would still be alive. Jo paused and stared straight ahead. How dreadful if only one desperate figure appeared. She peered into the gloom, afraid to trust her eyes, then grasped the end of the bridge, weak-kneed at the suddenness of the reprieve. Two weary figures, one half-carried by the other, were stumbling towards her out of the mist.

Colin suffered her ecstatic embrace, then watched as Jo enfolded Finola in a bear hug which left Finola clinging to Jo for support.

"Okay – the car!" he said tersely as Jo released Finola, who sagged against him, eyes closed and cheeks deathly pale.

Jo glanced nervously around. "You sense it too?"

"Just move it, Jo," Colin muttered, as though reluctant to admit to the hostility pressing in on them from all sides.

"How is she?" Jo mouthed, slipping her shoulder beneath Finola's armpit and supporting her other side.

"She'll do. Exhausted, of course. But it's not that –," he paused in speaking, then shook his head leaving the sentence unfinished.

"Are you okay, Finola?" Jo asked. Finola fixed her with a vacant stare and didn't answer. Jo frowned. Finola had survived the threat of hypothermia, but something was dreadfully wrong. The lights were on but Finola wasn't at home.

They had squeezed, three abreast, across the narrow bridge and the bulky outline of the car was now visible in the mist. "Thank God," Jo breathed, for the past five minutes having doubted her sense of direction. "Hang in there Finola," she encouraged, hitching her up again as Finola slid towards the ground.

"I'll carry you to the car," Colin offered, stopping and preparing to take her into his arms. Instantly Finola's eyes flew open and with an amazing surge of energy she fought him off. "No! No, leave me alone!" Her limbs were shaking and her eyes wide with fear.

"Come on now, don't be silly –," Colin started to say, but she cringed and backed away.

"It's only another hundred yards or so, Colin," Jo soothed, noting Colin's pallor and the strain of exhaustion in his face. "She can make it, can't you Finola?"

Love you . . . hate you . . .

Jo's head snapped up; Finola screamed. Jo whipped round then turned to confront Colin. "Did you hear anything?" she demanded.

He glared at her and snapped irritably: "No. Why?"

Forever . . . forever . . .

Finola screamed again. And again. Jo watched, immobilised by horror as Colin's face changed before her eyes: the lines became deeper etched and his expression hardened into naked malice. "No!" Jo shouted, reaching up to grab his arm as he raised it to strike Finola. Finola cowered and slid whimpering to the ground. He loomed over her, his face contorting with anger, and something else that made Jo's stomach muscles contract in fear.

"Bitch!" he spat.

Jo shivered. It was more of a snarl than a human voice, crackling with hatred and bitterness. *Justin St. Clair*. She didn't hesitate. Her hand shot out and the slap reverberated throughout the silence. Relief surged through her as the old familiar Colin put his palm to his cheek and gave her a stunned look.

"Quick! Help me get her to the car," Jo commanded, dragging at Finola's arm. Without a word he stooped and followed her instructions.

It was then that the nightmare began. Jo didn't immediately connect the sudden onslaught of sound with the whirring she had heard previously. She and Colin automatically ducked as something beat and flashed about their heads then receded. *Then* she remembered. And something else nudged at her numbed and terrified mind: a woman with sightless sockets for eyes. She tried to warn Colin but fear strangled the cry in her throat.

Yet something of her terror must have communicated itself to him. "The car. Run for it Jo!" he shouted, picking up Finola despite her protests. He lunged forward, staggering beneath the weight of his burden. At the same instant the beating and whirring returned to disturb the air and uneasy silence. Jo's feet pounded the frozen earth as she slithered past Colin, intent on having the car door open before he reached it. She stopped in her tracks and skewed round, instinctively dropping into a half-crouch. The beating of wings was now overlaid by a hideous screeching. A dark shadow stained the mist, looming closer to Colin's head, a powerful downbeat of wings driving it closer by the second.

"Colin, look out!" Jo screamed.

He ducked and held onto Finola as the thing swooped and attacked, its cries shredding the night and the mists of time. He cried out when Finola slid almost to the floor as he lifted one arm to ward off the blows. Jo broke free of the stupor which seemed to be claiming mind and limbs and lunged for the car. Her numbed fingers were clumsy with cold, and the screeching tore at her nerves as she struggled to open the door. *Come on, damn you, come on.* She swore beneath her breath as her hand yanked up the handle and a fingernail tore. The pain shooting through her finger was intensified by the coldness of her flesh. But the door was open. She swung it wide and turned to Colin. A flash of Intuition make her suddenly shout: "Colin, put Finola down!"

She rushed forward, slipped and almost fell. "For Christ's sake, *put her down*," she repeated urgently, tugging at Finola as Colin wavered. The ferocious shadow wheeled in the mist for another strike. "Don't you see, that's what's making it attack! It's mistaken Fin for me!"

Again that ominous whirring of wings as with the speed of lightning it turned in mid-air and dived. Colin cried out, and blood trickled down his forehead. The air was thick with the screams of the bird; Colin stood in a daze, Finola still in his arms.

"For God's sake, get away from her!" Jo prised open Colin's fingers and dragged Finola clear. Colin beat at the air with his arms; the hawk screamed its fury and wheeled for another attack. Jo bundled Finola into the car then turned back for Colin but stopped dead. Confusion boiled about his head: a beating of wings, flashing of beak and tearing of talons that filled the air with dread. Irrelevantly she noticed how the sleeve of his jacket gaped at the shoulder seam, the lining stark in its whiteness. Jo stepped forward, shaking with fear and rage. "Leave him alone you bastard! I'm here!" she screamed, her own voice vying in pitch and volume with that of the hawk. "Try *me*, you bastard! Come on, try for me!" she challenged, carried along on a rage that blinded her to both fear and reason.

The sudden silence was cataclysmic. The hawk hovered, feathering the air noiselessly with minute movements of its wing tips. The screeching had ceased and the yellow eye fixed her with unwinking stare. For one endless moment it held her gaze. Jo opened her mouth to scream but her voice was stifled by emotion. The form of the hawk disintegrated at the edges, then blurred, shifted and reformed like a computer graphic in the making. Subsided, became stylised and fixed, then settled. On his white surplice.

She saw him clearly then. Emotion ripped through her, laying bare her soul. "Antony, Antony!" she cried without making a sound. But he heard. The green eyes sought hers and held. She stretched out a hand; the flowing sleeve of her red velvet over-dress trailed a bloodstain through the snow. The jewelled point that touched the base of her middle finger emphasised the ring. His ring. The ring he had given her as token of his love. The emerald blazed, caught in the reflected light of moonlight on frosted trees. The pain of love seared her with ice-cold fire.

"Antony," she whispered, and stretched out her arms.

His eyes blazed with the emerald's fire. His handsome features, the features she had so loved, contorted in pain. His lips mouthed the word: *Why?* Sobbing in her anguish she opened her mouth to explain, but the figure melted into the snow.

Why, Madeline? Why?

The words hung in the air after he was gone. Hung from the trees like thin wisps of mist, or the shade of Judas's body as it swung from a skeletal branch.

With a stifled sob, Jo turned back to the car.

FORTY

~

"*Madeline!*"

She stood as if turned to stone. Like the ancient stones of the temple ruins from which she had watched him, unsuspecting, emerge. As Antony called out, she didn't dare breathe let alone move or speak – but her heart and mind screamed. They had tacitly admitted the possibility of this day, yet had never really expected it to happen. As though acknowledgement in itself were some sort of charm to keep reality at bay.

Her gaze was fixed on Antony. His arms were pinioned behind his back and he had been forced to his knees. Nobody now moved or made a sound. Death and silence hung on the air; Life itself held its breath. For one terrible mad moment she contemplated defying her husband, despite the unspeakable consequence. Yet it would not save Antony's life. Nothing could do that now. They were both doomed, this she had already accepted. But if she were to rush to his side and perish with him, he would not die thinking she had betrayed him.

But herein lay the cream of St. Clair's revenge.

"Remember, I shall be watching your every move my dear," he whispered malevolently, leaving her side to approach her lover.

As though to emphasise the whispered threat, from within the shrubbery at her back a child whimpered. Her child, and Justin St. Clair's heir. But so crazed, so intent was he on revenge, that she knew he would carry out his threat should she disobey. She had no choice. William could not be sacrificed to their illicit love.

Yet how was she to go through with it? God alone knew how she was to keep herself from screaming, crying and crawling across the red earth to Antony's side.

"Madeline!"

His cry pierced her heart as surely as any sword. She stood perfectly still; her nails dug into her palms until they were warm and sticky with blood. The grumble and roar of river and falls cursed her name. Those terrible, beautiful green eyes accused her of betrayal. My love, dearest sweetest love, you must know I could never do this of my own free will. Desperately she willed her thoughts towards him, releasing them like captive birds from a cage.

Antony Chase stared back at her with loathing and contempt

The journey out of Nether Wasdale was fraught with dissent. Colin had managed to crawl into the car and had been sitting in the back comforting Finola, however he had taken one look at Jo's face and jumped down after ordering her to take his place.

"You're not fit to drive," he said tersely as she protested.

"I'm fine," Jo insisted, thinking that being forced to concentrate on the road would push other things out of her mind.

"I'm better with driving than distraught women. You'll be of far more use holding Finola's hand."

Unable to deny the sense of this argument Jo capitulated and Colin slid into the driving seat. Blood dripped onto the upholstery from the wounds on his forehead and arm. Jo held her breath as he turned the key in the ignition, then slowly exhaled as the engine sluggishly kicked into life. Ten minutes later Colin let out a sigh, whilst wiping away a trickle from his eyebrow with a handkerchief, and his white-knuckle grip on the steering wheel marginally relaxed. The fog was lifting at last; in fact it had all but disappeared now that they had left the primitive track for the road, and a watery moon shed a diffuse pearly light over the scene. "I still say we ought to take you to hospital to be checked-out Fin," he was saying over his shoulder.

Jo heard him speak, but was struggling to make sense of the words as the final moments of the hawk's attack were replayed over and over in her mind.

"I'm alright now. I want to go home," Finola was protesting, but in a strange thin voice, and from a distance, down a long echoey tunnel.

There followed five minutes or so of blessed silence, during which Jo fought the fog of unreality that cloaked her rational mind. Finola's hand moved restlessly beneath her own. Jo glanced down and froze as the unfamiliar pointed cuff and the folds of the sleeve sewn with thousands of seed pearls filled her vision.

Finola's voice pierced the veil of illusion. "But *you* need medical attention Col."

He grunted but didn't turn his head. "I'm okay. Nothing that hot water and Dettol can't sort out."

"But that bird was demented. It could be diseased," Finola protested.

At least she's sounding as though she's with us, Jo thought; maybe in worrying about Colin Fin was able to put aside her own trauma. *But what about me*, Jo worried. Awash with sadness, love and longing – but for who or what? Were those emotions hers – or someone else's? Had that really happened back there – or was it simply a delusion brought about by unendurable stress?

"What do you think, Jo?"

How irritating: Finola's voice reaching her from that echoey tunnel again. Another moment of silence, then: "*Jo?*"

Jo strove to fight off the torpor that weighed down her mind; a deadly chill was creeping through her body, numbing her senses. "I think we should," she managed at last, aware that she was not really making sense.

Colin eased the pressure of his foot on the accelerator and as the vheicle slowed, turned his head to give her a hard look. "Are you alright?" he asked with a frown.

Jo nodded.

"Sure? You look – well, bloody odd."

"I'll be fine."

"But you don't –,"

Jo sighed. "Leave it, Col."

"Okay. No problem."

He shrugged, revved up again and switched his attention back to the road.

Finola was half-dozing and Jo shifted position, biting her lip as pins and needles stung her blood-starved arm. Listlessly she flexed her fingers then craned forward to peer through the windscreen. The mist had now completely disappeared. Hoar frost on branch and rock sparkled when swept by the beam from the headlamps, and the whole landscape had an unearthly bluish cast. Jo slumped back again on her seat, overcome with fatigue now that the danger was past. She closed her eyes, but immediately opened them again. He was still there, on the screen at the back of her mind. He was taking over, dulling her grasp of the present whilst painting the past in vivid colours. Something somewhere inside her was aware of what had taken place. Whatever it was that had touched Finola in errror had now passed into herself. But she would fight it. Fight *him*. There was one small problem. A part of her had no wish to do so.

Jo sat alone in the waiting area, counting sprays of rose and peony in the wallpaper pattern on the opposite wall. Anything, rather than think. The staccato sound of footsteps along the corridor grew louder then stopped. Dr. Cahill pushed open the swing doors and leaned against the back of a chair, twirling the end of her stethoscope. "This," she said wryly, "is becoming a bit of an embarrassment, isn't it?"

Jo nodded and grimaced. "Something like that."

"So what's the script this time, Jo?" Dr. Cahill raised her eyebrows. "You don't mind me calling you that? Only I feel I know you well enough by now."

"Okay. Okay." Jo held up one hand and forced a smile. Dr. Cahill's features, like her voice, were strangely distorted, and her own voice sounded odd in her ears as though it was coming down a chimney or long tunnel. But she was winning the fight, she told herself grimly. The screen was blank; she had banished his image from her mind. At least for the present.

"How are Finola and Colin?" she asked, concentrating on each word as she uttered it, instead of the words that remorselessly circled her brain: *love you, hate you, kill you.* The problem now was that she was beginning to understand how he felt.

"Better than they ought to be!"

"Nothing serious then?"

"No, but they've been damned lucky. Finola's core temperature is now practically up to normal, and I've given Colin a couple of shots just in case of infection. They'll live! Though they are both exhausted."

"Thanks, doctor."

"And so are you; you look all in. As you're here, let's see how that hand is doing."

Dr. Cahill let go of Jo's hand. "That's vastly improved," she said nodding, about to move away. "What's that?" she asked pausing, pointing to the ring. The emerald winked in the overhead fluorescent light.

"Oh, a sort of family heirloom." Jo pulled away her hand and stuck it deep into her pocket. It was true enough, if not of her own family. It was also the truth that her hand was practically healed, she thought surveying the pink and healthy new skin. Which seemed to bear out her illogical and improbable theory about the ring having something to do with the state of the wound. As short a time ago as this morning the flesh had been festering. Now after wearing the ring for only a day the improvement was dramatic.

"Thanks again, doctor," she said preparing to rise, but Dr. Cahill was standing directly in front of her and was making no effort to back off.

"Okay, so are you ready to tell me what's really going on in your neck of the woods?" she asked with a direct look.

Jo looked up at her startled, then quickly away muttering: "I don't know what you mean."

Dr. Cahill sighed and ran her fingers through her short dark hair. "Now come on. See it from my angle will you? Three people turn up out of the blue: one on the verge of hypothermia, one suffering lacerations via an attack by a *bird* for God's sake! – and all three patently suffering trauma and exhaustion."

"It's hardly my fault!" Jo protested, roused from lingering torpor by indignation.

"No?" Dr. Cahill was eying her speculatively. "Okay, let me put it this way. Before you came to the area, nobody presented from that particular valley. Now the inhabitants account for fifty per cent of my patient population! Okay, so that's a slight exaggeration, but you take my point?"

Jo nodded. "I can see how it looks. But it's coincidence."

"No," Dr. Cahill said firmly. "It lies outside probability."

Jo shrugged. "What do you want me to say?"

As though aware that she was over-stepping her duties, Dr. Cahill retreated to the door. "Come back if there's any cause for concern," she said abruptly and left.

Jo thoughtfully watched the door as it swung to and fro and was then still.

Minutes later Colin appeared, the jagged line on his forehead neatly stitched.

"Christ Col, you were lucky," Jo exclaimed, noting the way the tiny beads of blackened and encrusted blood ended just above his eye socket.

"I'm okay." He continued pacing, then strode to the window and stared out at the frosted gardens sparkling with ice-fire beneath the floodlights.

Jo picked up on his reluctance to acknowledge what had happened. "Colin, we have to talk about this."

For a moment he ignored her, then turned from the window. "That bloody bird," he muttered, shaking his head, then wincing at the movement.

"We must have looked a pretty rum trio," Jo commented lightly, noting his torn jacket and flap of escaping lining. "God knows what the nurses thought when we staggered in!"

He half-smiled at this and ceased pacing. "Okay," he said crossing the room to sit on the adjacent chair. "So what do you reckon is going on?"

Jo frowned. "I've been thinking it through. You know, trying to make sense of it, given what we know about the tragedy in the past. I take it Finola told you about my research into Madeline St. Clair and Sir Antony Chase?" She paused, then continued as he nodded: "It came to me back there at the car, when the hawk began to attack you –"

"What is that bloody thing? Where does it come from?"

"I've thought about that too. The hawk was Sir Antony Chase's family crest. At first, when all this started up, I though there was only the one," she paused, choosing her next words carefully, "*source of disturbance*: Sir Antony himself. Now I think Justin St. Clair is also involved. And the Lady Madeline too. That's what struck me back at Wastwater. You were attacked *because St. Clair was coming through you!* As for the hawk – I think this is a manifestation of Antony Chase's fury and lust for revenge. It's very power means it must have some outlet, some physical means of expression." Jo watched his face carefully, waiting for signs of ridicule. Thankfully none came. Instead irritation flickered across his features and he rose from his seat.

"You're asking me to believe in ghosts here," he snapped.

"And you're letting yourself be beguiled by language," she sidestepped, drawing on Wittgenstein and her research at the time of writing the novel. "Instead of 'ghosts' substitute 'energies'. Think of Einstein," she suggested skilfully, "of the concept that energy once created never dies – only *changes*. Think of these energies as being trapped in some way, perhaps by their very power due to the tragedy, and triggered by circumstance."

This appeared to mollify Colin and soothe his sensibilities. At least he wasn't flinging back immediate denial.

"As I said," Jo concluded, "I think you are being used as a vehicle for Justin St. Clair's energy to express itself. We're all affected in some way by the backlash, but for some reason, Antony Chase has identified me with Madeline St. Clair."

"Okay," he walked a couple of paces whilst staring at the floor, then returned to the same spot. "I might just be able to go along with that. But why *now?*" Why have these 'energies' as you call them only erupted since you came to Twilight Cottage?"

Jo stared at him: neatly caught, stumped and LBW'd all in one.

She looked away before replying. "I don't know," she confessed, twisting the fringe of her scarf in nervous fingers. "I guess it dates back to that first day and the crash. The strange experience I had. He – *it*," she amended quickly, "made contact then. Mistook me, perhaps for the soul of Madeline who, it seems, must have betrayed this Antony Chase in some way. I think he must have died in terrible conflict, torn between love and hatred for Madeline."

Colin scowled and moved back to the window. "Count me out. I can't handle this talk about *souls*," he said abruptly, still with his back to her.

Jo cursed her clumsiness in letting the word slip out. "But you go along with the energies bit?" she ventured.

He shrugged. "So far."

"That will do." Jo felt a surge of relief. At least now she wasn't totally alone and bearing a guilty secret. She was able to smile when Finola came through the doors, still wrapped in a foil-coated blanket but with cheeks that were now a healthy shade of pink.

They parted at Twilight Cottage. Finola was insistent that Jo come with them to Throstle Garth for a bite to eat, but Jo had declined, being too exhausted to face the inevitable post mortem of the day's events. Besides, Colin had enough to digest for one day, she realised, noting his lack of enthusiasm for Finola's suggestion. To overburden him now with more in-depth ideas about what might be happening, was to risk losing even his minimal acceptance. So with a plan in place to meet the following day, Jo watched their car crawl drunkenly away. And it did look comical. Watching its unsteady progress as it dipped and lurched in and out of the frozen ruts, Jo even managed a smile.

Twilight Cottage skulked in total darkness. Cautiously she switched on the hall light and peered around. Nothing unusual. Letting out a prolonged sigh of relief she closed the front door and momentarily slumped against it. Now for a scalding coffee laced with cognac, she thought with relish whilst moving towards the kitchen door. Then some beans and a poached egg on toast, she mentally added, realising that she was utterly starving. Her fingers found the light switch and snapped it on.

Her scream ricocheted off ceiling and walls.

FORTY-ONE

~

As she pushed the door wider the stench hit Jo's nostrils and an aggressive droning assaulted her ears. The source of the odour wasn't immediately apparent, but the angry buzzing came from a swarm of bluebottles that hovered at the centre of the kitchen like a miniature black tornado. As Jo advanced, fighting down panic and nausea, she saw that they gyrated in a constantly forming and reforming column above a heaving mass of maggots on the stone flagged floor.

"Oh God!"

Jo's hand went to her mouth as she retched. *The stench. The puke-making stench.* As though a butchers' shop and its contents that had been sealed for a year before being opened up again. And the toadstools were back. Pale, deathly and oozing slime they pushed through every available crack in the flags. A fear of things that grew in the dark and appeared overnight, rose from the grave of childhood and haunted her anew. Inky pools of mucus spread beneath decaying caps and disintegrating gills. The stench arising from them vied with the dead dog smell of whatever lurked beneath the squirm of maggots.

She looked about in despair. How had they got there? A modern-day kitchen had changed in the space of hours into something little better than a sewer or neglected charnel house. Walking on the balls of her feet, desperately trying to avoid treading on maggots and rotting fungi, she crossed the floor and after struggling with the catch, pushed the window wide. She gulped the clean fresh air before turning back to face the nightmare of cleaning up. It was then that she saw it. The little piles of moist red earth by the door. She gave an exclamation of disgust as an earthworm slowly emerged from the nearest heap and wriggled on the cold stone slab.

When, she thought wearily scooping up the last of the squirming white maggots on her shovel, was it going to end. Opening the back door she flung the creatures outside and set to work on the toadstools. Even the sea-grass mat had not escaped, flat plate-like grey fungus sprouted through gaps in the weaving. This type grew in closely packed layers through which blobs of congealed mucus bulged: an evil parody of a vanilla slice, a puff pastry delicacy from hell. She shuddered as her shovel slid beneath the striations and yellow slime oozed from the decomposing flesh, then threw out the glutinous mess and slammed the door.

She leaned against the table. As though the trauma on the screes had not been enough. Against her will the tears rose and threatened to overspill. It was too much, the proverbial camel's back was broken and she needed help. Leaving the kitchen she picked up the phone, then realised with dismay that the dialling tone was absent. Still hoping, she dialled Colin and Finola's number. The line crackled and buzzed and wasn't ringing out, so the wires must be down. Suddenly the sounds ceased. But there was something odd here, a sort of expectancy that prevented her from replacing the receiver, a feeling that something was about to happen *As though someone was about to speak.*

The hairs at the base of her neck began to prickle. Convinced now that somebody was listening at the other end, she said sharply: "Colin? Finola? Can you hear me?" Nothing, just that sibilant silence that wasn't really devoid of sound. The crackling and hissing started again. Jo shivered and realised that the cottage was freezing cold. Granted the fire was long dead and the window open to rid the place of odour, but this cold that was creeping through her was something else. Death-cold. The chill of the grave and dampness of newly-turned earth. The electric light bulb flickered and dipped, then sparked into life again but with a sickly yellowish cast. She almost dropped the telephone as the whisper sounded in her ear.

Love you. Hate you

She slammed down the receiver.

Suddenly she was aware of the ring on her finger. It felt heavy, the weight tugging at her consciousness, and the emerald glittered like a malevolent eye. Tearing it off she crossed to the bureau and dropped it into the drawer. Sinking onto the nearest chair she slumped with her head in her hands. *I can't handle this*, she thought, rocking to and fro in her misery. *You'd better; nobody else will,* a voice said dispassionately from within. Minutes ticked by, then Jo sighed and rubbed her face with a tissue before making her way wearily back to the kitchen. It was true of course, nobody else would scour the disgusting residue from fibre matting and flags. Closing her mind to all but the practicalities, she reached for disinfectant and scrubbing brush.

Later that night as she lay in bed the scratching started. She huddled beneath the quilt, ignoring the scrabbling from below stairs, and concentrating instead on the wind as it moaned in the chimney and sighed beneath the eaves. The wind – or the whisperer? For most of the night Jo lay sleepless, reluctant to admit the dreadful suspicion that was forming in her mind.

FORTY-TWO

~

Seth hummed beneath his breath as he worked on the shears in the barn. Sparks flew satisfyingly from the blades and were immediately extinguished in the frosty air. The grating of steel on stone rang in his ears, and the smell of hot metal singed his nostrils. Lucky this grinder had a foot pedal: his left arm still hadn't healed and throbbed in protest when asked to work. Dusty sunlight streamed in through slits in the four feet thick walls and laid bars of gold on the stone floor. Another fine day coming up, but bloody cold. Seth whistled softly as he worked, his breath wreathing the air with opaque vapour. The feet of the pony in the yard outside struck and rang against the cobbles, and the cawing of rooks carried clearly into the barn.

A slight movement above his head made him withdraw the blade of the shears a fraction whilst he listened. The grinding wheel hissed and slowed as his foot paused in pumping the pedal. He nodded and smiled. Old Barney was back in his roost, the scratching of talon on stone confirmed it. It was good to know he was there. Terrible, should the white beauties die out for lack of a roost. It had been on the radio only the other day, that any new barns erected had to include an opening for the owls, which was only right. His foot found its rhythm again and the wheel hummed. Sparks flew from the second blade as he started honing its edge.

The rasping sound which had earlier brought him pleasure was now persistent and getting on his nerves. He looked up. Barney, a silent white wraith, was perched on a rafter above his head. One yellow eye watched him, the other was shut. Seth turned back to the blade. There, the shears were done. He stopped the wheel and placed them on a handy trestle, then stiffened and cocked his head to one side. That wasn't a sound made by owls. His flesh crept at the high pitched squeal above his head. He looked up and staggered back with a disbelieving grunt. White plumage had turned brown, the curled beak to a longer hook. He took another step back, his mouth slack and eyes starting in terror. The hawk screeched and fixed him with bilious eye.

Saliva dribbled from Seth's trembling lip and down onto his chin as he lost control. He covered his head with his hands, but the attack didn't come. Slowly, ever so slowly, he slid his fingers away from his eyes and dared to look. The hawk's yellow eye bored into his mind.

Hate. Kill. Forever. Forever.

The whisper rustled through the hay bales like a breeze through a stubble field.

It brought pictures inside his head and he rubbed his forehead in agitation. The barn was slowly revolving. Revolving like the wheel should be doing. The wheel shouldn't be still. His eyes went to the pruning knife on the trestle. He shook his head and backed off. *No peace, remember, until you do as it wants.* One thing for sure, if he didn't, this hell-bird would never leave him alone. The screech from the beam above him set his limbs trembling again. Seth reached for the pruning knife and started up the wheel. Sparks flew and the air hummed with the pungent smell of hot metal. Sunlight winked wickedly on the blade as he honed it to a razor's edge.

FORTY-THREE

~

Blake Durante looked from one face to another and tried to concentrate on the argument between Keradzic and Milosevic.

"It is essential . . . Bosnia must have access to the Adriatic . . ."

"But this northern corridor you speak of –"

"Yes, yes. It is vital to link West Bosnia and Serbia."

"Ah but that would cut across –"

And so it went on. Crucial stuff, yet all he could think of was Jo. Her face floated between him and the other men seated around the table, and drifted in and out of the blue tobacco fug that hung over them like all like the threat of a nuclear exposion. Christ, he thought in desperation, she's going to *have to* damned well marry me – if my career is to remain intact. Not the best possible reason for getting hitched, he acknowledged silently, and with a wry half-smile that caused Chad Wallis to frown and throw him a look of suspicion. He'd better watch out, keep his mind on the job. Fooling apart, the truth was that he loved her – and missed her like hell. But Milosevic was speaking again . . .

Blake sighed. Evening, and the protagonists had slunk from the table, leaving behind the ghosts of disillusionment and resentment. The day's talks had again resulted in stalemate and Chad Wallis was looking as pissed off as he himself felt. The two of them sat in silence, sipping whisky and each man lost in his own thoughts. Suddenly Chad heaved his large frame out of the chair. "I have to make a phone call," he said abruptly, as though a momentous decision had been reached after heavy deliberation. "A high level one," he added, "I'll be a few minutes – be here."

"Okay. No problem."

Blake reached for the whisky bottle and poured a generous measure into his tumbler then topped up Chad's for when he came back. He fidgeted and crossed to the window, glass in hand. For the second day now no guns pounded Sarajevo, but if anything the silence was unnerving. So was the total darkness. Night lay undisturbed over the beleaguered town, no flares, no spurts of flame from artillery fire, and no skyline-glow of burning buildings. Which had to be good, he told himself as the whisky went down and glowed in his gut, but there was a feeling of transience, of the fragility of this ceasefire. It felt like Sarajevo and the whole of former Yugoslavia was holding its breath.

He delved too into his own problems whilst Chad was making his call. No amount of rationalisation could dispel the feeling that all was not well at Twilight Cottage. *Christ!* I mean, what the hell had she gone there for anyway? There had to be something going on, somebody else in the background. Unconsciously his fingers tightened their grip on the tumbler. And all this talk of worms and slugs for God's sake. What was happening to the girl? Had she flipped?

This, he thought taking a gulp of his whisky, must be how boyfriends and husbands felt during World War Two when thinking about their women back in England, and knowing the Yanks were 'over-paid, over-sexed and over there'. Bloody impotent and frustrated, that's how. He picked up a half-full cigarette packet and crushed it until the carton split in his hand, but then forced the anger and resentment from his face as footsteps sounded along the corridor. Instead he looked faintly bored and pushed back his chair so that it balanced on two back legs. Wouldn't do to have Chad thinking he'd lost it, was freaking out. Cool was the name of the game.

Chad entered and picking up the drink Blake had poured, took a long pull. Blake waited, knowing Chad would speak when he was ready.

"Okay," Chad said at last, wincing as half the contents of the glass went down. "We have permission to adjourn proceedings – but with a five day deadline. That gives everyone time to chill out and consider the angles." Chad swallowed the rest of his drink and put the glass smartly down on the table. "But when they come back in here – they've got just twenty-four hours to reach agreement."

"Or what?" Blake sat up straight, letting the front legs of his chair drop back onto the floor.

"Plan 'B'. It was already in place if needed. U.N. intervention – like heavy. Immediate enforcement of 'safe zones' for a kick-off. And air strikes if the Serbs don't withdraw heavy artillery from Sarajevo."

Blake nodded. "A rocket up the arse. Will it work? End the pussyfooting around?"

Chad reached for the whisky bottle. "It'd better," he said grimly, pausing in pouring to look at Blake. "Or the proverbial shit hits the fan." Moving round to his chair he leaned forward, hands on table before sitting down. "And it's *your* deadline too, Blake," he stated giving him a searching look. "Go get yourself sorted out – whatever it is. And come back in here with your mind on the job."

"Sure. And thanks." A tough bastard Chad, but a fair one, Blake thought as he nodded and finished his drink.

Whatever it is. And that, did Chad but know it, was precisely the problem. Blake had no answer; he only knew that since Jo went to stay at the cottage, he had been thinking like a crazy guy. As though something bad was reaching out across land and sea to touch his soul with evil.

FORTY-FOUR

~

St. Clair spat full in her lover's face. "You took my wife, Chase. In return I shall take your life and your honour," *he snarled, pacing slowly around his prey before returning to confront him once more.* "Of course the King must be told of my doubts concerning your loyalty. When his men search your castle, certain 'evidence' will be found. How grieved Edward will be to learn of his favourite knight's defection to Scotland."

The gloating smile seemed to jerk Antony out of his impassive silence. "Lying bastard! It's true I love your wife – but you are the traitor, not I!"

Madeline managed to smother her cries as a back-handed blow brought the blood running from her lover's mouth. Do it now, he's suffered enough, *she willed her husband, her gaze boring into his chain-mailed back.* If only William would give a lusty cry – then Antony would know her betrayal was a lie. *As though aware himself of this possibilty, and of thus over-playing his hand, St. Clair drew his sword.* "My wife has repented and led me to you, and for that I shall spare her life."

Madeline's eyes sought the anguished face of the man at her husband's feet: No, Antony, no! My own sweet love I could never betray you. *For answer he spat on the ground. His eyes as they met hers blazed with malevolence.* Betray me, Madeline, and I shall kill you – but I shall love you forever. *The memory of his words chilled her now.* No matter: I welcome such a penance, Antony. For such a love as we had between us would surely survive beyond death. *That belief alone could sustain her through what was to follow.*

St. Clair's arm drew back. William. I must think of William. *She managed to hold back her screams of grief as her husband plunged in his blade almost to the hilt. The sword was withdrawn and her lover's blood spurted onto the frost-scorched grass. He clutched his stomach and coughed his life-blood into thirsty red earth.*

The green eyes accused her as he fell. She screamed then, as though she would never stop. In death, his eyes still watched her as she turned and fled.

Despite fatigue and aching muscles from the unaccustomed exertion on the screes, sleep was a long time coming. It was still dark outside when she awoke, but Jo found herself unable to drift off again. A glance at the alarm clock showed her it was 6 a.m. Shivering, she went downstairs and after lighting the fire and making coffee, attempted work.

It was no use; her mind refused to concentrate on Ruskin at Brantwood, and dwelt instead on Antony Chase. What scene had been played out between himself and Madeline and Justin St. Clair, and why did his unquiet spirit seem hell bent on revenge? Until there were answers to these questions, her mind would not be still and there was little point in attempting to write, she decided closing down the computer.

Whilst gazing into the fire nursing her mug of coffee, the next step presented itself and she reached for the telephone. The sound of the dialling tone brought a surge of relief as she dialled: the line was in working order.

Her fingers fidgeted with the coils of flex as the tone rang out. "Barbara! Hi. Didn't wake you did I? Oh that's okay then, yes I thought you'd probably be having breakfast."

Reaching for her spiral bound notepad Jo flicked it open and clicked down the point of her ballpen.

Armed with the name of the ex-colleague who, before leaving Lancaster University, had been involved in researching the legend, Jo drove down the lane to Throstle Garth. Also from Barbara she had learned that Deirdre Spencer was now a lecturer at Durham University. A second telephone call had yielded the information that Ms Spencer would be in the Sociology Department for most of the day. A good bit of detective work, Jo congratulated herself, leaving the car and knocking at the door of Throstle Garth. Whilst waiting she glanced anxiously up at a sky that was ominously brown and laden.

The door opened and Colin's face appeared in the wedge between door and frame. The scowl at being disturbed disappeared. "Hi, come on in."

"How's things?" Jo enquired following him down the hall.

"Not bad. Fin's just come downstairs."

"Sorry if I'm a bit early," Jo aplogised. The wound on his head was livid but clean she noted with relief. "But can't stay – I have to go over to Durham and what to be back before dark."

The scowl reappeared. "What the devil for – there's snow forecast."

"Tell you later. Hi Finola, how are you?" Jo said, sitting down near Finola who was wrapped in her dressing gown and ensconsed in a chair by the fire. Her fingers moved deftly as she embroidered a garland of tiny blue flowers on a scrap of canvas.

"More forget-me-nots?" Jo asked frowning.

Finola nodded and carried on stitching.

"But why–? Oh, never mind," Jo said, about to question her preoccupation with the flower, but abandoning this line as Finola looked up with an anxious expression. "My God, you look better than yesterday!" she said instead.

"I feel it. Though I still feel a bit odd. Know what I mean?" Finola gave her a direct look.

Jo nodded. "We have to try and get to the bottom of this thing."

"Oh, and how do you propose to do that?" Colin demanded, stirring the coffee in the pot with unneccesary force.

"You're pretending last night never happened." Jo said flatly, watching him.

Colin tossed down the spoon and shrugged as he turned to face her. "I didn't go for it last night. Not really." He scowled as the spoon bounced off the work surface onto the floor. "The mist,

Finola falling in the water – we were all fazed. Oh, what the hell," he broke off, bending to retrieve the spoon and drop it into the sink, an action which saved him from having to meet Jo's gaze. "I don't know!" He straightened up and ran his fingers distractedly through his hair leaving it standing up in spikes on the crown.

"Okay. Let's not argue about it. I agree we were all stressed out of our minds. But there's something you should perhaps know."

Jo took a folded piece of paper from her pocket. "I found this inscription at Barrowburn Castle, the seat of the St. Clair family." She read it aloud:

> *When the sun turneth black*
> *And the blood-moon sails high*
> *And the pale horseman rides,*
> *Pray the Kings Stone lies beneath the throne*
> *And the hawk be last to rise.*

"So?" Colin said dismissively as he offered her a steaming mug of coffee.

Jo folded the paper and put it back in her pocket before accepting the drink. "It's that last line."

"What about it?" Finola chipped in, looking as puzzled as Colin.

"Well, the first part of the motto contains symbols from the Book of Revelations and refers to the Day of Judgement when the dead are supposed to rise. But this is a contemporary inscription dated 1297 and its reasonable to suppose therefore that it was commissioned by Justin St. Clair himself. A hawk, as we now know, was Sir Antony Chase's family crest. So I think 'hawk' here is a symbol, a covert reference to Sir Antony Chase. A sort of curse consigning him to the grave – or hell if you like – for ever. Now if Sir Antony really *had* eloped with Justin's wife Madeline – don't you think that a trifle odd?"

Colin blew on his coffee and gave her a sceptical look. "I'm beginning to think it's *you* who's a little odd!"

But Finola held up a hand and gave him a look of disapproval. "Let her finish, Col. She's obviously gone into this much deeper than we have."

Jo gave Finola a smile of gratitude. "Don't you see?" she challenged Colin. "If Justin St. Clair genuinely believed Sir Antony to be alive and living somewhere in France with Madeline, then that line doesn't make sense. By 'cursing' him to remain in the grave as it were, St. Clair is implying," she rushed on without waiting for Colin to comment, "that Antony Chase *was already dead.*"

"What are you suggesting, Jo?" Finola's expression was sombre as she looked at Jo, intimating that she had already guessed.

"That Justin St. Clair *murdered* Sir Antony," Jo said quietly.

Finola's eyes were huge behind her glasses. She nodded. "I think you could be right."

Colin got up from his seat and banged his cup down on the table. "And I think you've both flipped!" he said scathingly. "Now if you'll excuse me, I've got work to do."

"It provides a reason for all the hate and anger we've experienced lately," Jo threw after him as he stalked to the door. "And a motive for revenge."

"Take no notice of him." Finola turned to Jo as Colin ignored her and went outside.

"He's running-scared."

"I don't blame him, Fin!" Jo said with grim humour, watching Colin slouch past the window on the way to his studio. "It's pretty scary stuff." She rose from her chair by the fire. "Now I must be off."

"More research?"

"I'll let you know if I find anything."

"But Jo, if you're right – then what happened to Madeline St. Clair?"

"Don't get up Fin, I'll see myself out."

Jo walked to the door and abruptly left.

The weather held out during the drive to Durham. She set off on the Cockermouth route then headed on to Penrith and was in Durham by lunchtime. After stopping at a cafe for a sandwich and cup of tea, she made her way to the University.

Jo looked the departmental secretary in the eye. "Tell her my name is Jo Cavanagh and I'm hoping she will be good enough to assist me with some research." She managed to say it without blushing, but felt her toes curl inside her shoes at trading upon her reputation. But desperate situations require drastic measures, she consoled herself. And it worked. The secretary – obviously miffed at being over-ridden – put down the internal phone, gave her a smile that would make a lemon seem sweet and escorted her out of the office and along the main corridor.

Deirdre Spencer had a tic at the corner of her left eye which periodically twitched. A woman in her early forties, she wore trendy gold rimmed spectacles from behind which watery blue eyes regarded her as she held out her hand in greeting; Jo noted the limpness of her clasp and the fine tremor. "So pleased – the Wittgenstein novel was remarkable," Ms Spencer gushed.

This woman has a drink problem, Josie was thinking. "Thank you. It's very kind of you to see me without an appointment."

Deirdre Spencer indicated the chair placed at an angle to her desk and Jo sat down.

"So how can I help you? I presume you are researching another novel?"

"That's right." Which wasn't a complete untruth, Jo thought guiltily, given the Ruskin novel.

"I'd be delighted to help if I possibly can. And you're staying in the Lakes, you said."

She's seeing her name and department cited in the 'acknowledgements', Jo thought suppressing a grin. "That's right. I'm using a local legend as a resource."

"I see."

Jo didn't miss the wariness that had crept into the woman's voice and expression. Perhaps she had already guessed. *Okay, fasten your seat belt Ms. Spencer, I have the feeling this is going to be a bumpy ride.* "Yes, the St. Clair family – and Sir Antony Chase. I believe you collated some of the material during your research at Lancaster University."

Whilst Deirdre Spencer may have suspected the reason for Jo's visit, the effect of those two names being spoken aloud was immediate and unmistakable. The tic began to work overtime. As the discreetly manicured hands aimlessly shuffled the papers on the desk, the tremor became more pronounced. "I'm afraid I can't help you there," she said abruptly.

"Oh, but I'm sure you can," Jo soothed. "I'll tell you what I already know of the story, then if you have anything at all to add . . ."

Ignoring the woman's obvious reluctance to continue with the interview, Jo launched into a summary of her research.

"And that's about all I've uncovered to date," she concluded, inviting the other woman's comments by adding: "I'm sure you have much to add."

Tiny beads of sweat glistened on Deirdre Spencer's forehead. She mopped them with a handkerchief then rose and murmured: "excuse me a moment please." before disappearing into a book-lined recess behind the desk. Jo heard the sound of a metal filing drawer gliding on its runners, followed by the muted clink of bottle on glass. A minute or so later Deirdre Spencer returned and sat down. Her round previously pink face was ashen. "I really don't think I can help," she reiterated, looking down at the papers on her desk.

As she spoke, Jo caught the astringent but slightly perfumed aroma of gin. Whatever the poor woman had encountered, it had obviously left her very frightened. "Look," Jo said leaning forward in a confiding manner, "I believe we must have certain –" she paused then continued with the euphemism: "*experiences* in common. I'm not here to pry into those; please, just tell me what you know of the historical facts – then I'll go away and not trouble you again. I have no wish to cause you further distress."

For about a minute Deirdre Spencer eyed her in silence The muscle at the corner of her eye twitched convulsively as she made up her mind. "You are right, I believe, about the 'Kings Stone'," she began reluctantly. "I'm certain this is a reference to the Stone of Scone. Edward 1 stole it in 1297 – the same year as the date on the inscription. As you probably know, it was the stone upon which the Kings of Scotland were crowned. Edward had it placed beneath the coronation throne in Westminster Abbey, thus symbolising that future monarchs of England were also being crowned king or queen of Scotland. As you can imagine, this didn't go down too well with the Scots," she said with a fleeting smile and rare flash of humour. "Edward invaded Scotland and was obsessed by the campaign for the rest of his life. Even to the extent that after his death, in accordance with his wishes, his body was carried around Scotland with the army."

Jo grimaced. "A smelly business," she commented.

Again that brief smile, so that Jo began to glimpse the woman Dierdre Spencer may once have been before her traumatic encounter with Antony Chase. "The corpse was specially treated," she was explaining: "It was wrapped in a bitumen-coated shroud before being placed in a lead-lined coffin. But whilst I agree with your conclusion about the reference to the Stone of Scone," she continued, "I cannot agree with your *interpretation* of its significance."

Jo frowned. "No? I thought it fairly obvious. Surely it has to be a statement of allegiance made by St. Clair."

Deirdre Spencer shook her head. "On the surface certainly; and that was how it was meant to appear. But my research threw up a Scottish ancestry that went back as far as the written records, and as far afield as the Shetlands! Once war with Scotland broke out, there must have been at least a whiff of healthy suspicion with regard to St. Clair's loyalties. No, it's my belief that he was boxing clever; we have a play on words here: 'Pray the stone *lie* beneath the throne, for my money at any rate, refers not to its position, but rather to its *lack of veracity*. In other words, that the English claim to the Scottish crown prove to be *a lie*."

Jo regarded Deirdre Spencer with a new respect. "That's clever. Quite brilliant in fact."

"And that's not all. There is no evidence of charges during his lifetime, but historians now suspect St. Clair money was behind the Bruce rebellion."

Jo let out her breath slowly with a slight whistling sound. "So how does all this tie in with the popular legend?" she asked after a thoughtful silence.

Deirdre Spencer shuffled the papers on her desk and rearranged several pencils and a biro. "My research into Sir Antony Chase," she paused and swallowed with difficulty after pronouncing the name, "revealed that he was doubly disgraced. Firstly on account of supposedly running off with Madeline St. Clair –"

"And?" Jo prompted, leaning forward on her chair in anticipation.

"By being labelled 'traitor'. A document, outlining a proposed agreement between himself and the leaders of the Clans, was allegedly found in his castle."

A bright light, a flare against the night sky, exploded in Jo's brain, illuminating previously dark areas of mystery. She regarded the other woman gravely. "Which would account for his terrible anger and need for revenge."

Deirdre Spencer dropped her gaze. "I'm afraid I don't follow –," she started to say, her tic spasmodically working.

"I think you do," Jo interrupted. She rose to her feet and walked to the door. "But as I said before, I won't pry. And thank you – it's been a tremendous help."

"This wasn't ever about a book." It was said flatly; a statement rather than a question.

Jo hesitated in the doorway: "It might be."

She departed then, leaving Deirdre Spencer to her memories and her secret store of gin.

Snow started to fall as she crossed the border between Northumbria and Cumbria. At first no more than widely-spaced flakes blowing dizzily in the wind, by the time she reached Penrith the verges were white but the road still clear. At Cockermouth shops and houses were thatched with snow, and pedestrians left trails of footprints and scored muffled pavements with shopping trolley and pram lines. As for the road, cars and buses soon churned the pristine carpet into a brown slush that peaked in ruffles, as though someone had piped the surface with coffee cream. As she cut across the moors to the coast road, stands of conifers were transformed into Christmas-card trees which, like the fells behind them, glowed eerily in the half-light. With a bit of luck she would be home before dark. It was, she thought peering through the windscreen into the whirling mass, going to be a sticker.

The thought didn't trouble her overmuch, her mind being preoccupied with what Deirdre Spencer had divulged, or to be more precise, with making sense of it within the framework of her own experience. There seemed now to be just one missing piece from the jigsaw: what had happened to Madeline St. Clair? And why did the brunt of Antony's hate and anger seem directed at her instead of her husband? The dreadful suspicion of the previous night returned, chilling her like the creak of a stair in an empty house, or a footprint in the dust of a derelict room. Fortunately there was little time to indulge it; the road to the valley was still open, but the lane which led to the river was little used and the snow was drifting in the wind. Negotiating it safely required all her concentration, and immediate practical needs pushed aside morbid speculation. As it was, the car crept along at snail's pace between rounded forms smoothed by falling flakes, and sculpted and dimpled by the elements into natural Henry Moore shapes. Night was drawing in fast: the first star, intermittently visible between drifts and flurries, had risen above the mountain ridge and was soon joined by more. On reaching the track to Twilight Cottage Jo's heart sank.

Here comes Mission Impossible. Snow clogged the ruts and lay in deep drifts piled at either side, narrowing the passage. Laden branches bent beneath the weight, creating an even greater impression of a tunnel. There was nothing for it but to have a go. The turning was successfully accomplished, but then the car lurched as the front nearside wheel sank into a deep snow-packed rut. "*Shit!*" Jo muttered as the wheels whined and spun but the car went nowhere. After trying for several minutes she acknowledged defeat and climbed out. Hence the folly of not being 'country-wise', she thought wryly, and the wisdom at winter's onset of carrying a shovel and bucket of grit in the boot.

She looked around her and shivered, not so much from the cold as the sense of isolation and deathly hush. Snow muffled valley and hills making the silence palpable. Never had she been so aware of her loneliness and vulnerability. An unearthly glow emmanated from fields, walls and felltops, suggesting a polar wasteland or moon-scape. By contrast the way ahead was steeped in forbidding shadow. Steeling herself for the walk down this lonely track, Jo gave the car one last look and set off on foot. Soon snowflakes clung to her hair, eyelashes, and jacket but at least her body felt warm as blood surged in response to the exertion. Suddenly she lurched and slipped as her feet disappeared in a drift. A trivial thing really, yet it brought a nasty sensation: a buzz of shock along her nerves and renewed sense of vulnerability. Picking herself up, she dusted the snow from her front, hitched her bag onto her shoulder and pressed on.

The car was still in sight when she first felt the need to turn and look back. She paused, straining to see through the silently-falling flakes. Was that a shadow by the car? The whole thing had a feeling of unreality about it, as though she were looking at a scene in the glass 'snow-dome' that took pride of place each Christmas on the window ledge of childhood. Anxiety, she reminded herself, did strange things to perception. Nonetheless stress was tightening the muscles at her shoulders and nape of neck, causing her heart to beat faster. She stumbled on, lurching like a drunkard as her feet found ruts and hollows.

Something was pressing at her back and this time the feeling was unmistakable. Swiftly she turned and a strangled cry escaped her as a shadow dodged behind trees lining the track. She hurried on, every few yards turning to cast a look over her shoulder. The shadow flitted from tree to tree. She paused and waited and as she remained still, so did the shadow. Fierce anger vied with fear. How long must she tolerate this reign of terror? She wanted to stand and confront her pursuer, shout: "Who are you? And what the hell do you want?" But given her circumstances it was hardly the wisest course to take, and in the end survival instinct took over. She crept closer to the hedgerow and bending down, picked up a heavy branch and continued walking.

With every step the silence and loneliness became more oppressive. Despite the stout stick in her hand, terror laid icy fingers around her heart. For a start, how did she know it would do any good? Was it Seth Rigby back there – or something else? Something against which a stick or indeed any weapon would be useless. The thought that her pursuer may not be leaving footprints in the snow fuelled the rising panic. She turned again. Pinpoints of light and form mingled and shimmered like a Monet winter landscape. It was hard to be sure of anything. But there it was; the shadow was closing in. Through the whorls of snowflakes she caught the gleam of a knife blade. *"Oh God in heaven help me!"* Her legs threatened to give way, then a crackling sound restored her sanity. Do ghosts make a noise? she thought smiling grimly as another branch snapped behind her. She rather thought not, this had to be Seth Rigby.

Anger surged through her swamping fear. With the abating of panic her mind magically cleared. If it was Seth Rigby then he was flesh and blood and could be dealt with, but the unwelcome thought also struck that she was leading him back to the cottage. She wouldn't dare go to bed. He might find a way in, be lurking inside without her knowing. No good relying on telephoning for help either, the line could be down again, in fact it was more than likely this weather. No, she thought plunging on, her only hope was to stop him here and now. Once in the clearing, she would be exposed and vulnerable.

Thank God for Blake and his survival training; he had to face some tricky situations in his line of work, and had passed on some hints. That the element of surprise could level uneven odds was just one of them. Her gaze darted from side to side, seeking a likely spot. She turned and the shadow slipped behind a gnarled trunk only yards away. Her hand flew to her mouth to stifle a cry. Making up her mind she plunged off the track and into the cover of the trees. Branches snapped behind her, and snow fell to the earth with a soft *plopping* sound. Obviously her would-be attacker was in pursuit. Her breath was tearing now at her throat but she didn't dare slacken her pace. She fell full-length in the snow and lay for a second winded and rigid with fright, waiting for the pounce, and when it didn't happen struggled to her feet and hurtled on through the undergrowth. It was terrifying, not knowing if the ground would hold beneath her feet or fall away into a ditch. She paused on spying a suitable target. The girth of the ancient stunted oak would lend her cover and conceal her direction.

Time for another of Blake's tips. Pretending to stumble, she groped about for a large stone then twisting at an angle shot off at a tangent. Once beneath the oak she lobbed the rock into the trees ahead and, heart pounding, flattened herself against the massive trunk. The sound effects were impressive: a battery of rustlings and snapping of twigs followed by a cannonade of soft thuds from falling snow. She held her breath and waited. The soft padding of feet on snow brought her heart into her mouth. She froze, the stick poised in her hand. The footsteps thudded on then paused by the oak as silence fell on the wood. She inched her shoulder across the rough bark and risked a peep. He was standing with his back to her, and in his hand he carried a knife. He began to move in the direction in which she had tossed the stone. *I can't do it.* Her feet felt rooted to the freezing ground, her mind numb. The shadow slipped behind a tree only yards away. *It's him or you,* a voice whispered inside her head. The surrounding whiteness reflected from the blade of the knife, which had the clean yet wicked look of one freshly sharpened. *Yes, to slit your throat.* Still she hesitated. A few seconds more and the moment would have passed for ever, and she would be at his mercy. *Do it, do it now!* the voice insisted. Jo took a deep breath and didn't allow herself to think, rushing up behind him she raised her arm and struck.

A throaty cry came from Seth Rigby's mouth. He turned and stared at her, his eyes manic and showing the whites. "Bitch! Bloody bitch!" Blood began to trickle down the side of his face. He started to raise his arm. The knife-blade gleamed in the light of moon and stars refracted by the snow. Jo didn't wait for him to strike but hit him again. Hard. Seth Rigby slumped to the ground and blood seeped into the snow around his head.

Terrified and sickened now that immediate danger had passed,

Jo retched into the undergrowth. As adrenalin ebbed her limbs began to uncontrollably shake. Forcing herself to keep a grip on reality, she backed away, not daring to touch him to see if he was dead. For five panicky minutes or so she lumbered about the copse in search of the track. Tears streamed down her cheeks and twice she fell. At last her feet were on the path that led to Twilight Cottage.

Even now, she looked over her shoulder in fear whilst struggling to turn the key in the lock with fingers that were stiff with cold. Of course he had not followed. Because he was dead, she told herself all but falling through the front door as it opened. *You've killed a man, Jo Cavanagh.* But she felt nothing. Only relief that he was no longer lumbering after her through that darkened snow-muffled wood. Horror and guilt would come later no doubt, but for now there was nothing but blessed relief.

She switched on the light and stared fearfully around. Nothing but stillness and quiet, and her breath escaped in a long drawn-out sigh. No obnoxious odours to greet her on this occasion, but the kitchen was the danger zone. A quick check showed her nothing was out of place there either. Making her way unsteadily into the sitting room she poured herself a large brandy, drank it a gulp, then poured another which she carried with her to the telephone. Must call the police. But the line, predictably, was dead. Nothing but that low humming along the wire and the hushed 'listening' silence.

Hurriedly she replaced the receiver and tried to think what to do next. A trip back down the lane to Colin and Finola was absolutely out of the question. She shuddered at the thought. No, all she could do was sit tight until morning, make sure every window and door was locked and open up to no-one. And there could be no going outside for fuel. There were a couple of logs and some kindling left in the basket, enough to warm the place through for an hour and that would have to suffice. But next on the agenda – a hot sweet cup of tea for the shock. Feeling better with even this rudimentary plan in place, Jo set about putting it into action.

Soon the newly-kindled fire took heart as logs caught, spat and crackled sending flames shooting up the chimney and sap spurting in a hiss of steam. Sitting there by the hearth, Jo also felt heartened as the first shock faded and a sense of reality returned. The brandy warmed her from within, and gradually the chill thawed from her limbs and they ceased their trembling, and her body succumbed to the glow in the grate. Things, she told herself with determined optimism, could be a whole lot worse. So she may have killed a man; but it could have been *her* body lying out there cold as the winter-earth, and *her* blood staining the snow red as a rose on a lily-white shroud. Because he would have killed you, have no illusions about that, the voice within urged. Guilt and remorse were all well and good, but they wouldn't help her survive, nor would they bring Seth back. No she could do nothing about it, and at least she was safe for the night.

The thought sustained her, helped her face the prospect of reporting the incident to the police the following day. There arose the unwelcome image of herself attempting to convince a po-faced bobby that a respected local had turned psychotic and murderous, and her spirit quailed. *If only Blake were here, he would know what to do, would get her out of this mess.* Well he wasn't, so no point in wishful thinking. She held out her hands to the blaze and rubbed the palms briskly together, then hugged herself as though to counter the chill of loneliness.

I'm alive and I'm warm and I'm safe for the night, she reminded herself, rising and walking across to the cassette player. What this place needed was a little lively music to break the God-awful silence. Selecting a *Queen* tape, an old standby for such occasions, she leaned forward to slip it into the machine. Something, the awareness perhaps of being observed, made her glance up. She screamed and the tape slipped from her fingers. Snowflakes obscured the features of the face at the window, but it was obviously male. Her second scream reverberated around the walls; the white blur pressed against the glass disappeared.

FORTY-FIVE

~

The snow had a determination about it now. Instead of that first wind-driven dash, it fell steadily and with the dogged purpose of a long distance runner who knows the end is in reach. Colin paused at the sitting room window to glower at shrouded shrubs, thick-pile lawn and trees that looked as though a giant hand had frothed their branches with cream from one of those 'ready whipped' cans. Where the devil was Jo? He had been pacing this bloody carpet for over an hour, and should have seen and heard her car pass by now. The reflected light bleached his face of colour emphasising his expression of concern. Hooking his thumbs into the pockets of his jeans, he glumly watched a robin land on a magnolia shoot re-leasing a flurry of white as it bobbed up and down on its perch. Spying him at the window, the bird flew closer and fluttered close to the pane. Crossing to the coffee table by the fire, Colin picked up a half-eaten biscuit and crumbled it in his palm then opened the window and tossed out the crumbs.

"Stupid woman. No right to have gone knowing snow was forecast," he muttered, shutting the window and watching as the robin pecked and left tracks in the snow-shallows beneath the lilac bush. In fact it was bloody inconsiderate of her, he realised; she must be aware of causing him grave concern. Yet it seemed to be of little account, given the way she had driven off the other day without a word of explanation. One indignant thought seemed to spawn another. A white worm began to uncoil in his gut, stirring up anger and distrust, converting concern to wrath. Who had she gone to meet? Who was she with right now and what were they doing? *Good God, stop it man! what do you think you're at? Is* this how Dr. Jeckyl felt? he wondered, catching a glimpse of his own Mr. Hyde in the distorted image reflected by the window. He tapped the heel of his hand firmly against his forehead as though to dislodge the maggot that gnawed within.

No problem, he told himself moving away from the window. Perfectly natural: simple concern about a neighbour, that's all. And a particularly vulnerable neighbour too, given she was a woman living alone at that poxy cottage. He paced the hearth rug, starting as a log spat and sap escaped in a hiss of steam. He shivered and pulled down his sweater to cover his buttocks. It was growing cold in here. Uneasily he looked over his shoulder. Shadows seemed to be drawing in from corners, and the hissing and crackling from the fire could almost be whispered words and cackles of unpleasant laughter. Still the thoughts uncoiled in his brain: why so secretive? What did she have to hide? God's blood, he of all people should be admitted to her confidence.

Why? Why should he be?

Odd too, how his thoughts gave voice to unfamiliar phrases. He sank down on an easy chair by the fire and kneaded his temples with fingers that slightly shook. At the same time he grimaced as though in pain. Not good to be alone. He needed some company, a voice that came from somebody else rather than inside his head. He rose and lifted the telephone receiver; as expected the line was dead. So what more natural than to go and look for Jo. Pausing only to place the wrought iron guard round the fire, he strode into the hall, rammed his feet into wellingtons and took his Barbour down from its hook.

His feet sank into soft powdery snow leaving satisfying tracks on the hitherto unblemished surface. He hoped to God Jo was back, otherwise her chances of not getting stuck somewhere were practically zero. He started and whipped round at a sudden noise from behind. "Bloody heron!" he muttered, as the grey pteradactyl-like shape rose and flapped its way with funereal pace through the snow-speckled air and across the field. Colin pulled up his collar and trudged on towards the spot where the track leading to Twilight

Cottage intersected the lane. On finding Jo's car half covered and listing in a drift, he felt a surge of relief. She must have arrived back safely and walked to the cottage from here. For a moment he agonised over whether to go and check it out, but finally decided against. Not wise to see her whilst in this mood. Hyde was lurking beneath the surface, he could tell by the waves of anger that were beginning to rise at Jo's lack of propriety and modesty. Why think that, when he had meant her lack of common sense? Time to go home, he told himself moving away from the half-buried car. Jo was safe enough and none of his concern. Where was Fin? Poring over her embroidery frame no doubt, like some latter day Lady of Shalott. Stitching more of those cursed forget-me-nots.

FORTY-SIX

~

Not dead after all. And now Seth Rigby would be doubly crazed.
Leaping up Jo reached for the remaining log in the basket and her
fingers closed around it. Someone was knocking at the back door.
She crept across the room and into the hall. The pounding at the
kitchen door grew louder and more insistent. She chewed the
knuckles of her free hand. More knocking and shouting, then a
crash as the door was flung back against the wall. Not waiting for
more, Jo raced to the front door.

Frantic, she ran blindly into the snow. Her laboured breath
changed to sobs as muffled footfalls pounded closer. He was catching up; her legs and lungs had gone and there was no escape.
Sobbing aloud she stumbled on then sinking into a drift, sprawled
full length in the snow. "Help me, Oh dear God help me," she
muttered between her sobs.

The footsteps were coming closer. She tried to rise but hadn't
the strength. A pain shot through her ankle. He was almost upon
her now. The heavy log had left her hand almost as soon as she
started to run, leaving her helpless and without means of protec-
tion. As she rolled onto her back his shadow darkened her face. A
scream ripped free from her constricted throat as his hand shot
out. She opened her mouth to scream again.

"Jo!" a voice cried urgently.

She stared blankly at the face, took in the details, as for endless
seconds Time and Reality were suspended in limbo. The dark
wings of the eyebrows, one slightly above the other, giving the face
a permanently quizzical look: the high cheekbones, damp with

melting snow, the full sensual lips and eyes that were almost black in their intensity. She half reached out to touch the hair, blue-black against a dusting of snowflakes, the crisp curl that fell over the broad forehead as the man leaned over her. Now she knew for sure this was some sort of incredible dream. The hand shook her by the shoulder.

"Jo!" The familiar voice repeated her name. "It's me!"

"Blake?" She rolled her head slowly from side to side in disbelief.

Grasping her upper arms he hauled her upright, picked her up and carried her into the cottage.

He set her down on the armchair by the embers of the burnt out fire. She wept quietly then, for all the pain, longing and fear she had endured throughout his absence but hadn't dared to express. From within the dream she heard the clink of bottle against tumbler, then felt the brandy-burn as he held the glass to her lips. The spirit braced her and gradually she stopped crying. Reaching out she touched his face with an expression of wonder. "It really is you."

He kissed her on the lips then murmured "Hi, Jo," against her ear.

"But what about Bosnia?"

"A few days leave. I flew to Carlisle then hired a car."

He kissed her again and stood up, then looked down at her and frowned. "So now do you mind telling me what in God's name is going on around here," he said quietly.

"Look Jo – how can I put this? –," he paused, speaking minutes after Jo finished her story, and ran his fingers through his hair. "These new friends of yours – I mean, you've not been sampling anything weird have you?"

"You mean drugs?" Jo's lips compressed and it was her turn to frown. "Come on Blake!" For answer she rose and went to the bureau. Opening the drawer she took out the ring. Still in silence she held it out for him to inspect.

"Where did you get this?" he demanded, holding it up to the light.

"The churchyard. At the grave Seth Rigby dug."

"I don't understand."

Wordlessly she peeled back the dressing at the base of her thumb.

"You need to see a doctor with this," he said frowning as he inspected the tight red skin and yellowish head.

"I already have. It starts to heal when I wear that." Jo held out her hand for the ring. Blake didn't respond. Instead his fingers closed over it. "May I have it, please."

He seemed reluctant to return it, and she recoiled at the look in his eyes, the change in his demeanour. "Blake!" she said sharply.

He blinked, then opened his fingers, looked down at the ring, and after a moment's hesitation handed it back. With a sigh of relief she dropped it into the drawer.

"Okay," he said rising and walking to the door, "so something odd has been going on here. But it's all pretty fantastic. You can't blame me for thinking you'd been tripping-out. Come on, Jo," he held the door open and beckoned. "Let's check out the kitchen."

She found herself holding her breath as he pushed open the kitchen door and felt for the light switch. She let it out with a rush as nothing unusual was revealed, then followed him into the room.

"No toadstools." He walked around as he spoke: "No red earth," he turned to face her with that darkly quizzical look, "in fact – no earth at all, red or otherwise."

"It doesn't happen every night," Jo defended herself, sensing his disbelief.

"No." He stood before her, put his hands on her shoulders and gave her a searching look.

Tears of frustration blurred her vision. "You have to believe me."

He drew her head down so that it rested against his chest. "I do. I do," he soothed stroking her hair.

Jo sighed, breathed in the familiar smell of Blake and damp wool, and wished she didn't have to doubt his words.

"But now," he pushed her gently away, held her at arm's length.

"We have to get down to practicalities. This Seth Rigby – he's still out there, I presume."

She nodded, suppressing a shudder. "As far as I know."

He released her then and started to walk to the door.

"Don't leave me Blake!" she almost screamed, fighting the urge to run to him, to cling and weep as a child waking from a nightmare begs its mother to stay.

He turned from examining the lock which he had burst open. "I have to," he said shortly. "Think it through, Jo," he insisted as she began to protest. "From experience and what you've told me, my guess is you only stunned him, but if we leave him out there he'll be dead of exposure by morning. You could be charged with manslaughter – or worse."

"I'll come with you," she said wildly, starting towards him.

He held up a hand in refusal. "No. He's obviously off his rocker and dangerous. You stay in here where it's safe and open the door to no-one. Now fetch me a screwdriver whilst I make this lock secure."

He pulled her to him before he left. "I love you Jo. I'll be back, and we'll work something out."

She nodded dumbly, terrified at the thought of him leaving her even for a moment. "Take care, Blake. He has a knife remember."

He kissed her on the forehead. "Don't worry. I said I'd be back."

As he left, the cottage felt lonelier than ever before.

FORTY-SEVEN

~

It wasn't his fault that he failed. He had tried, hadn't he? Seth muttered to himself as his body lurched from tree to tree for support and dislodged snow-flurries as it thudded against each trunk. "Not Seth's fault, not poor Seth's fault," he mumbled over and over, looking up fearfully as the whirring of wings sounded overhead and scattered loose snow from top-most branches. Bastard-bird. He knew it was there, hovering out of sight.

He turned to look behind. Every few steps, the snow was defiled by crimson drops of blood that stained the crisp surface, reminding him of sealing wax on parchment. Like that film *Treasure Island* he was taken to see at Whitehaven as a boy. For some reason that seal had stuck in his mind, had seemed ominous to his young mind. In fact he had started to cry and his mother had marched him out of the cinema and off to the bus stop.

But he was rambling. The cold was getting to him, that and the throbbing ache in his head. Bitch of a girl. He didn't feel sorry for her any more. He should have stuck her when he had the chance. The trouble was he couldn't remember why. He paused and rubbed his forehead. What had she done? And what was he doing here in the wood? By now, he thought wistfully, Janice would have cooked his tea. Home: he had to get home, that was the place to be. But again that whirring sound overhead, and more powdered snow drifted down onto his head and shoulders. He shivered in the biting northerly wind that whined around rock and sighed through branches.

Love. Hate. Betrayal.

The wind-voice hissed in his ear and played havoc inside his head.

Now he knew: she had played false, and that was why he was here in this wood. It had all started with Old Maud's grave, and that's where he ought to go. Something was wrong there; it wasn't a fit place for Maud to lie. He had to dig her up, place her in a better spot. He lumbered on then sank to his knees in a drift. He'd have to be quick though, his arm as well as his head was aching with the cold. He clambered out and staggered forward a couple of paces. The whirring of wings overhead brought his head up with a jerk, and he cried aloud as the shadow stained the moonlit snow. He clutched at his head with hands that were turning blue. Something was digging at his brain with a white-hot poker. *Not the grave, no. Go back to the cottage. Back to the girl,* the voice in his head urged. He lumbered to a halt, half turned then shook his head and turned back again in an agony of indecision. No, he wasn't going back there, he was going to sort poor Maud out. Then he was going home. Still silently arguing with himself he stumbled on.

The flurry of snow on the branch above his head caused him to cry out again. The bird blinked. Green eyes watched him, bore through his skull and into his soul. To hell with this he was going home. Images of a blazing log fire, the kettle bubbling on the Aga and most of all, Janice's broad, familar and safe figure sustained him, drove him on when weakness threatened. Yes, going home. His head felt lighter on his shoulders now that he had a sense of direction.

FORTY-EIGHT

~

"After her! But remember – alive!"

Justin St. Clair led his men out of the clearing in pursuit of his wife. He smiled grimly to himself and slackened his pace, allowing his men to pound on ahead. A blackbird trilled in the trees ahead. A paean for Madeline. The thought pleased him. There was no hurry; she could not escape. A woman's clothes were not designed for running through the forest, but more than that, she would not of her own volition go far. Any moment now blind panic would be stemmed by maternal love.

His heavy features contorted with rage and pain. Love? She didn't know the meaning of the word.

Had she shown one bit of remorse back there, he may yet have been prepared to spare her life. But no, her love for that bastard had been in her eyes. Even as she watched her lover die she had worn her sin with pride, he thought mortally affronted. He paused as a scream pierced the evening calm of the woods. The blackbird ceased its song and rose with a clatter of wings and scolding cry. Justin St. Clair smiled and walked on with brisker pace.

And now my lady, it is your turn.

Blake moved stealthily through the wood and occasionally glanced back at the cottage. The backdrop of giant pines reared dark and ominous against the snow-clad fell and moonlit sky. He walked on, his gaze sweeping ground and branches for signs of passage. *God what a mess!* And Jo was alone back there. He had been less happy at leaving than he had let her know, but this was a no-option situation. It required a damage-limitation exercise of epic proportions. But he couldn't allow himself to dwell upon Jo. He was fighting his own battle too, struggling to block the suspicion and irrational thoughts that plagued him against his will. Someone nearby was into psycho-power games, but he wasn't playing. His mind, like the ice forming on the wire fence became cold and clear, trained to focus upon the job at hand.

The spinning flakes were becoming sparser and smaller, scattered by an icy wind. The danger was, he thought raising his head to test the air like an animal, that this lot would freeze tonight and the roads become impassable, making it impossible for emergency services to get through. The car he had hired had not even made the lane, and he had been forced to leave it at the road end. So let's hope, he thought grimly, that he found this Seth guy before too long – if he wasn't already dead. Not that he was in sympathy. Anyone who threatened Jo with a knife had better not make too many plans for the future. But it could be awkward for Jo. So far as he could make out, the guy hadn't actually launched an attack. Without doubt he had plagued her and meant her harm, but it would be difficult to prove it in the absence of any witness. He groaned aloud as he pictured himself explaining to some dour local constable that a respected farmer had gone beserk and stalked Jo with a knife. He could almost see the 'neurotic towny woman' accusation in the imaginary policeman's eye. He hadn't been exaggerating back there; Jo really could find herself on a manslaughter charge – or worse. He made his way to the spot described by Jo and picked up the faint trail of bloodstains.

Eventually the trail went cold with no more blood staining the snow. He paused to get his bearings and decide on a course of action. At least the bastard hadn't been killed outright by Jo's blows, and there was every chance he was still alive. He sighed: that meant he had to press on and find him instead of making his way back to Jo, otherwise hypothermia might claim a victim. He might have been tempted to let nature run its course, but there would be awkward questions asked about the dead man's head wounds. So where to now? According to Jo, the Rigby farmhouse was past

Throstle Garth, and about a mile along the valley road. Ten to one Seth Rigby was trying to make his way home.

He looked up and started at a sudden whirring sound above his head, then gave a nervous laugh. A glimpse of a yellow eye and hook of a beak – just an owl. If he didn't get his head together he'd be believing in Jo's phantom hawk. Not that he thought she was deliberately making it up, but he'd seen too much psychological warfare to be taken in by a trick. Someone here was fooling around with hypnotism or something of the sort. He didn't know why, but sure as hell he was going to find out.

But then he thought of the ring. That was real, not the result of some hypnotic suggestion. And there could be no doubt about its antiquity, or that festering wound of Jo's. He frowned at the memory, at the feel of the ring in his hand and his undeniable reluctance to give it back. He shrugged, ignoring the promptings of doubt. He'd probably just been caught up in Jo's drama; she had made it all sound so real and plausible. He felt the urge for a cigarette but pride made him ignore it; smoking was a 'work' activity and no part of his life with Jo. Turning up his coat collar he trudged on through the snow.

The white mound of Jo's car was where she said it would be. So now a right turn into the lane should bring him out on the valley road. He was about to take this route when a series of shrill shrieks brought him to a standstill. He raised his head testing the air, they came from down-wind in the opposite direction to which he was going. He recalled Jo saying the river lay that way, and the muted roar could just be heard. Blake hesitated. It was probably a screech owl. No there it was again, too sharp and staccato for a barn owl.

Indecisive, he switched on the torch he had pocketed once clear of the trees, and directed the beam down the lane towards the church. The narrow beam revealed dry stone walls iced with white and an overhang of trees, and the lane unravelling like a bandage between. A dark line of erratic footsteps stained the otherwise untrammelled snow. Someone had lurched from side to side and stumbled as they went. But what could Seth Rigby possibly want down by the river? A stain on the snow caught his attention. Fresh blood, he confirmed after going down on one knee to investigate. Jo was all alone at the cottage, but he had to check this out. Bosnia, he reflected as he set off down the lane, was restful compared with English country life.

FORTY-NINE

~

Seth knelt in the snow by Maud's grave and began to feverishly scrape at the freshly-piled earth with his bare hands. "No, not a fit place for Maud," he murmured. Unevenly spaced clouds of vapour rose as his breathing became laboured. His hands began to bleed but he didn't notice; the pain inside his head was by now too great to allow any distraction. But this was too slow, he had to get some speed on before his blood froze along with the earth. That bastard-bird was still about too. On his approach it's squawking had sounded from somewhere within the yew, but muted as though simply letting him know it was there.

He stood up and looked about. No sign of the killer bird and all was hushed beneath the blanket of snow. The yews ringed him, dark and ominous, swaying and dipping to the north wind which cut through his jacket like a butcher's knife through fillet steak. He listened, head to one side as it sighed and whispered secrets in the dense dark foliage of the yews.

Love, hate, forever forever

He had to hurry. A spade: that was it, must get a spade – one was usually kept in the porch of the church.

The door yielded as he twisted the massive iron ring. Lucky for him the new vicar didn't believe in keeping it locked. He was a rum sort with his motor bike and leathers, but doing good work all the same. Likeable too, never too busy to stop for word. But he was losing track, Seth worried, pausing to knead his temples because the throbbing there made it difficult to think straight. Now what had he come for? He turned on the spot then stood immobile, as though the stilling of body and limbs might activate his addled brain. *Ah yes.* He nodded vigorously then cringed as shooting stars of pain exploded behind his eyes. Reaching behind the monk's bench he drew out the shovel and sighed with satisfaction. Now he could fettle poor Maud. Leaving the door to the church gaping, he hurried back, following the trail of his own erratic footprints.

He worked with demonic energy. Somewhere inside his fevered brain had sprouted the twisted green shoot of an idea. This thing had started with the digging of Maud's grave. He had disturbed something, he thought, throwing aside a shovelful of red earth. Something evil. They had no right to put Maud in a corrupt grave; move her, his addled brain reasoned, and things would return to normal. There was comfort in finding a reason for his hitherto blind and instinctive actions. His spade cut deep again and he heaved the soil to one side. He had to hurry; the earth was crisp to the shovel's blade, soon it would freeze in the bitter wind and digging would become impossible. Not that he felt the cold, his exertions saw to that. He grunted as he worked and wiped his forehead with the back of one grimy hand.

Love Hate

The wind soughed and whistled in the yews as he worked. The spoil pile of red earth loomed large against the whiteness of the snow.

The moon had risen beyond the line of the yews, but at last his spade struck wood. "Coming, Maud lass. We'll soon have you out of there," he muttered between grunts and the rasp of his breath. Fresh blood from his arm and his head stained the snow, but he felt nothing. His arms moved like pistons, his rhythm as paced and sure as a robot's.

Then he stopped dead. He couldn't lift the coffin out by himself. He stood still for a moment and pondered then he spat on his hands and struck the earth with renewed vigour. *No problem, our Maud.* He could manage her all right. Better to do without a coffin than lie any longer in that dank and corrupted earth. He gave a louder grunt of safisfaction as the shovel rang against the coffin lid.

Dispassionately he looked down at the corpse of Maud Bickley. A part of his mind wanted to scream; the other dominant part accepted the ravages of death and the rightness of what he was doing. The cheek bones, already jutting through rotting grey flesh, gleamed stark in the bleached light of moon on snow. As he watched a worm appeared at the corner of her mouth and wriggled down her chin. The part of him that was repulsed rose to dominance and he retched, turned away and vomited in the snow.

It was then that he heard it again. Only loud this time and meaning business. That terrible shrieking from within the yews, followed by the whirring of wings. He straightened his back and peered across the rows of sentinel gravestones. It winged towards him straight as an arrow and twice as deadly. *Maud.* He had to rescue Maud before it came with its beak and tearing talons. Kneeling, he reached into the coffin. No good, he would have to climb into the pit. Fearfully he looked over his shoulder and saw the hawk winging closer.

His head was on fire, burning with a terrible searing pain. The shrieks of that bastard-bird were to blame, they tore at his brain like white-hot pincers. He lay on the ground, shaking his head from side to side, slow and ponderous like some cumbersome spear-stuck bull. He reached up to touch his scalp and instantly recoiled. His fingers sunk into his skull as if it were one of Janice's home-made sponge cakes. He pulled them out, stared bulbous-eyed at the sticky glutinous mess. He opened his mouth to scream but putrid and foul-tasting fluid bubbled up instead. *Dear God, he was rotting away from inside.* The hawk hovered overhead, feathering the wind with its wing-tips and shrieking with demonic laughter.

Seth rolled on his back and struggled to rise. The yews closed in, beetle-black and filling his vision, blocking out light and hope. His damaged mind still tried to make sense of the nightmare. He was being slowly eaten away from within, he reasoned with the awful logic and clarity of the insane. And he knew now what had happened: one of those maggots from the grave, the ones that had wriggled into the mushrooms, had somehow crawled into his head.

It was there inside his skull, eating him away, he decided with morbid satisfaction.

Pluck it out! His fingers, nails black-rimmed with soil, clawed at his face and eyes. Pluck out the maggots – that was the only hope. He fell writhing to the floor, mouth gaping soundlessly like a beached fish. It felt like he was drowning in slime: it was clogging his lungs, filling his mouth and nostrils to stifle his breath. His arms and legs jerked convulsively taking him closer to the edge, until with one last contortion he slid into the open grave and lay still.

A tiny flurry of snowflakes sprinkled his body. Silently, the hawk circled the scene below before winging its way back to the yews.

FIFTY

~

Blake heard the scream as he approached the churchyard. He quickened his pace, boots crunching over snow that was freezing with every minute that passed. He felt something too, felt it even before he reached the graveyard: a full stop in the passage of Time, an ominous pause in reality. At the same instant he became aware of a heaviness, as though a dark cloud had draped itself round his head and shoulders, eclipsing hope and dulling his faculties. The lych gate groaned on its hinges as he pushed it open, a sound magnified by the fact that cotton-wool pleats draped the countryside in whiteness and silence, providing a startling foil for the barricade of dense yews. They gave him the creeps, seemed almost human, like a row of sentries who challenged the living and honoured the dead.

The trail of footprints led him along the path then at an angle between rows of headstones that glistened with crystals of ice. The feeling was growing in intensity, and there was something else too, that turned his spine to jelly. A sort of *familiarity* was the only way to describe it. As though at any moment he would come face to face with himself. A crazy thought yet one he could not dismiss.

Antony Antony

The name went round and round his brain, so familiar it seemed like his own. And then there were the feelings: he felt cheated, angry, ready to hit out at someone but without knowing why or whom. But it had something to do with Jo, of that much he was sure. What was she doing back there at the cottage? And how could he be sure she would not betray him and send him to his death? Unreasonable anger and jealousy poisoned his heart, and he was overwhelmed by a sudden desire to return to Twilight Cottage. Yet his saner self, the part of his mind untouched by the cloud of darkness, told him it was both crazy and reprehensible to think such things of Jo. Shaking his head from side to side as if to dislodge the evil thoughts, Blake doggedly pushed forward.

The sight which met him as he rounded the north eastern corner of the church drove speculation about Jo from his mind. He frowned as he approached, noting the piled up earth and blood-stained snow. Chilled by premonition he moved closer to the brink. Bile rose to his throat as he peered down into the grave.

Seth Rigby was draped over an open coffin embracing a corpse.

Blake stepped back in a hurry, slipping on the freezing snow in his haste.

Hate Love Forever

The words flashed into his mind as Maud Bickley grinned up at him from her grave.

FIFTY-ONE

~

Roz Cahill placed her medical bag in the car and climbed into the driving seat. It was sad: old Mrs. Grizebeck was frail and probably wouldn't last through the winter. It had been coming for some time, Roz told herself, driving slowly away from the cottage and down to the cross roads in the village, and Eliza was a grand old lady of eighty nine years. She persisted in this line of thought until professional detachment was more or less in place. She still found it difficult, but then Ros had been visiting Eliza Grizebeck – originally her mother's oldest friend and 'adopted' by Ros after her mother's death – for years. And now Eliza's time, bless her, was drawing near.

Roz peered through the windscreen and dithered at the crossroads. The sky looked to be heavily pregnant with snow. And it had been forecast, she recalled. On the other hand, she was only five miles at the most from where Jo Cavanagh was staying. *Was that why she had chosen to visit Eliza tonight?* She shrugged: who knows? But she did know that the mystery surrounding the visiting novelist was driving her crazy. It wouldn't do any harm to call and enquire about her hand, she reasoned, being in the neighbourhood as it were. Roz grinned at the crassness of her justification. *What the hell – you're just plain nosy Dr. Cahill.* Her title was new enough to still give her a buzz, but old enough for her to know when something was not quite right. And that was certainly the case here, she thought grimly, reviewing in her mind the events of the past weeks, since Jo Cavanagh arrived to be precise. Besides, she could leave before the fall started in earnest. Her mind made up, she put the engine into first gear and moved off.

Unfortunately it didn't work out that way, because big fat flakes began drifting down long before she even left the main road. By the time she reached the valley road the car was already at a crawl. Every now and then it skewed to left or right and she eased it out of a skid with a feathering of the brake pedal and white-knuckle grip of the steering wheel. *Oh great!* Reduced to crawling along an unfamiliar road at nightfall, and with every chance of getting stuck. The window wipers whirred and groaned as they laboured beneath their burden of piled up snow. And she had crossed the Rubicon, to turn back now would be absolute folly. "I hope you have a spare bed Jo Cavanagh," she said with a rueful grin.

And that was it, the car would go no further. The icy wind that swept down the valley was driving the snow into chest-high drifts. Not a pleasant thought, getting out into that whirling kaleidoscope of flakes in the middle of what looked liked an arctic waste. At least the car had brought her within a few yards of the predetermined goal: the turn off that according to the map, led eventually to the river. But with a bit of luck, first to habitation and a bed for the night. Grabbing her medical bag from the back seat, she locked the car and began the trudge down the lane.

A sigh of relief escaped her and her step lightened as the glow of a lighted window came into view through the trees ahead. By now her lips, nose and cheeks felt numb, and the loneliness was pressing in. So far as she was aware the inhabitants were unknown to her, but it was shelter and would therefore do. At least being a doctor usually guaranteed entrance, and in this case, she hoped, also a bed for the night. Pushing open the gate she walked along a path that someone had recently cleared and knocked at the farmhouse door.

"Hi there, I'm sorry to –," Roz paused and blinked in the sudden light then gave the man who had opened the door a closer scrutiny. "Hey, I know you, don't I?" she said, her face breaking into a smile.

"You do?"

"Roz Cahill. Dr. Cahill that is – Cottage Hospital."

"Oh – *right!*" The man gave an answering smile of recognition.

"Now let me –, Yes! Wastwater Screes. You're the sculptor guy. Colin, Colin . . ."

"Gilmour. The nerk who fell in then had an argument with a bird!" He grinned and held the door wide. "Come on in and get warm."

"Thanks. My turn to be the nerk. I'm stuck down the end of the lane."

"That makes us even," Colin led the way into the living room.

He entered the room and motioned to his uninvited guest to follow. "Look who the snow brought in Fin!"

"It's beautiful!" Roz exclaimed spontaneously, looking round the softly lit room in open admiration. The flames from the log fire warmed the yellow pine dresser to amber, and copper gleamed on mantel and hearth and hung from overhead beams. "Hi. Sorry to barge in on you like this," she said recollecting herself, and speaking to Finola who had looked up from her embroidery to regard her with mild surprise. "My, you look better than when I last saw you!"

"I certainly feel it, thanks to you doctor," Finola responded with a shy smile. "What exquisite work," Roz exclaimed, peering over her shoulder at the swags of blue flowers.

"Thanks for treating us," Finola said, shuddering at the memory and ignoring the comment about her needlework.

Roz pursed her lips and shrugged expressively. "You were damned lucky!" she commented then turned to Colin, "And what about you being attacked by –"

"It's history," Colin said tersely.

"Dr. Cahill is stuck down at the road," he explained with a lightning change of topic. Picking up a bottle from the antique dresser he brandished it in Roz's direction. "Whisky?"

"Wonderful. You're very kind."

"Nonsense. We get social withdrawal symptoms in winter, don't we Fin?"

"Yes it's great to see a fresh face," Finola said with a smile.

"Dump your bag on that table and sit by the fire," Colin instructed. "Ginger? Soda? Given the weather I won't offer ice," he joked, holding up the whisky tumbler.

Roz gave a mock shudder. "I take mine straight, thanks."

"Glad to hear it!" Colin handed her the glass.

"Is anyone waiting for you back home?" Finola asked looking concerned. "Anyone you should contact?"

"I live alone, but my boyfriend was coming round."

"He may be worried that your weren't there. The 'phone's on the table in the hall, doctor." Finola offered, rolling up her embroidery and putting it away in a wicker basket.

"Thanks. And I'm off duty. It's Roz."

"Okay Roz, make yourself at home," Colin said, pouring a whisky each for himself and Finola.

A minute or so later Roz returned to the sitting room. "The 'phone's out of order."

"Par for the course this weather," Colin commented.

"It was crackling earlier and making weird noises. Try again later, it may come back on again," advised Finola.

Roz sat down, nursing her drink. "Thanks, I will."

"What brought you to the last outpost of civilisation then?" Colin asked with customary directness.

"I was visiting an elderly friend of the family."

"Oh, who would that be, anyone we know?" Finola asked.

"Eliza Grizebeck."

Finola frowned. "Can't bring her to mind. Does she live in the valley?"

Roz hesitated. This could be tricky; "Not exactly," she said rolling her glass between her palms. "but close enough for me to decide on a second call."

"Who this time?" Colin pressed unabashed by Finola's look of admonition.

"Your writer friend actually – Jo Cavanagh."

"Jo?" Finola exclaimed. "She's not ill?"

"No. Just thought I'd check out that hand of hers whilst I was in the area," Roz answered smoothly.

"Well you almost made it," Colin said wryly. "Jo's staying at Twilight Cottage further down the lane. Is she expecting you?" he added, " I could walk over there and let her know."

Roz remained silent. It would look odd, were she to admit that she had come out here on a whim to visit a patient, and one she had seen on only a couple of occasions. It could be awkward too if Jo revealed that she was an uninvited guest. Why *had* she come? Roz glossed over that one, knowing the answer lay with intuition rather than logic, and would thus cause her professional discomfort.

"It's no trouble," Colin added, obviously misreading the reason for her delay in answering.

"I'm sure she'll put it down to the weather," Roz compromised, thus neither denying nor affirming his assumption.

"But won't she worry? Imagine you're maybe stuck somewhere *en route*?" Finola said frowning.

"Leave it for now Finn. We'll see how Roz feels about it later," Colin intervened, giving Roz a speculative look. "I could walk you over there, but if you'd rather, the spare room is at your disposal."

"I won't drag you out in this," Roz said quickly, already regretting her earlier impulse to visit Twilight Cottage. "I'd love to stay, if you're sure it's okay. I could call on Jo in the morning before I leave for home." *Maybe. Maybe not.*

"We'd love to have you," Finola said warmly.

"You're very kind."

"Nonsense – country hospitality," Colin said brusquely. "Now that's settled – time for a top-up. You'll not be driving anywhere tonight," he said taking Roz's glass. "Soup, bread and cheese do you think Fin?" he said turning to Finola.

Roz gestured with her hand. "No please, don't go to any –"

"No problem." Finola rose and began to ladle soup aromatic with sage and thyme from a large pan on the Aga, whilst Colin took garlic bread from the fridge and placed it on a baking tray before popping it into the oven.

Things, Roz thought as the saliva of anticipation filled her mouth, could very definitely be worse.

FIFTY-TWO

~

Jo had felt the change in the atmosphere as soon as Blake re-entered Twilight Cottage. It was as though something had been waiting and was now feeding off his presence. He poured them both a stiff drink before haltingly relating his story, his face white and features tense.

"You didn't kill him, Jo," he said earnestly, leaning forward to take her hand and give it a reassuring squeeze. "He *walked* to that grave yard, and something attacked him there. His face was," he looked at her apologetically as though wondering whether to continue, then evidently decided he must: "it was a mess, Jo. Do you understand – something attacked him, he didn't die from a blow to the head."

She struggled with mingled relief and horror. "It was the hawk, wasn't it?" then when he failed to answer she raised her voice: "Tell me the truth Blake!"

"I saw a bird, I suppose it could have been a hawk," he admitted with obvious reluctance. "But I didn't see it attack anyone," he added seeing her satisfaction. He had attempted to telephone the police then, but the line had crackled to such an extent that nothing, let alone a human voice, could be distinguished.

The horror of Seth and old Maud had numbed her, but the nightmare was bearable because Blake was here. She sat opposite him now by the fire he had kindled; watched as he leaned forward, grasped a log from the full basket and tossed it onto the back of the fire. The flames licked greedily at it and warmth began to creep into her bones, and the atmosphere she had noted earlier began to recede. Greedily she absorbed Blake's presence, breathed in his maleness and feasted her eyes on his solid muscular frame, luxuriating in the sense of safety after weeks of vulnerability, of battling on alone.

"Here, babe." He held out her replenished glass and gave her a warm look of reassurance as she accepted the drink.

"I missed you Blake." Tears threatened to spill again as she made the admission, because it was a reminder that nothing had basically changed. "I don't know how we're going to get around this one. I don't think I can change."

"Not now, Jo. Not now. Let's just be together." He rose and stroked her hair for several moments, then straightened up. "Look, we have a log fire, a decent malt and we have each other. All we need now is a little music to lighten things up a bit."

Jo pointed to the cassette player and stack of tapes. "Be my guest."

"I intend to." He gave her an intimate smile then left her side, their hands lingering each with the other until only fingertips touched, then reluctantly slid apart. He sifted through the cassettes then gave an exclamation: "You still have that celtic harp tape we bought in Dublin."

She smiled. "It's one of my favourites too, remember."

He gave her a long knowing look. "I remember last time we played it," so that she had to look away finally in case he discerned the depth of feeling the memory evoked. Minutes later the purity of harp and fiddle filled the room and also her heart. As she half-listened half-dreamed, one melody ran into another until one in particular caught her attention. Jo frowned, then it clicked into place: *Londonderry Air.* Unbidden, words began to form in her mind:

And when you come, and all the flowers are dying
And I am dead, as dead I may well be

and it was the echo of Fin's voice that gave them life.

Jo tried to forget that other night, when Finola had put words to this same tune and wrought emotional chaos. Concentrating on notes rather than silent lyric, she sipped her drink then leaned her head back, watching shadows dance on the ceiling in tune to the flames from the hearth.

But the words began to intrude, register along with the change in atmosphere. She sat upright on the edge of her seat, and a frown creased her forehead as she cast furtive glances round the room.

"What is it?" Blake asked, giving her a quizzical look.

She shrugged, tried to look casual. "Nothing."

You'll come and find the place where I am lying

The fire glowed red at the heart, yet the room felt cold. A north easterly wind moaned and sighed in the chimney. *Antony Antony*

The name lurked in each corner, was scrawled upon every shadow.

Jo moaned softly in her throat. Such poignancy, pain and longing as the whisper ricocheted around the room.

But come ye back when summer's in the meadow
Or when the valley's hushed and white with snow.

As it is now came the thought. She turned her head; the shadow glimpsed from the corner of her eye melted into the gloom. She had a sense of femaleness, and a faint almost 'violety' smell of cedarwood and musk. *Exotic scents such as a knight might bring back from the crusades,* but it was folly to speculate in that vein. She shivered and rising abruptly turned off the machine.

"Hey, what the –?" Blake grabbed her hand as she passed.

"Too sentimental," she said brusquely, fear of the thing that stalked them making her brutal. She winced at the pain visible in his eyes, but pulled her hand free of his and turned back to the fire.

Blake was silent for a moment, then masking his embarrassment spoke as though nothing had disturbed their rapport. "Okay, fine." He leaned forward. "I wonder, what in God's name made that guy dig up the coffin?"

The sudden change of subject jarred Jo's nerves so that her answer was unguarded. "Perhaps he figured he'd disturbed something when digging Maud's grave."

"You really believe all that don't you?"

She couldn't decide whether the note in his voice was one of scorn or concern; maybe he was paying her back for pulling away. Whatever, it placed her on the defensive. "What other option is there?" she replied, her voice sharpening in response to his implied incredulity.

"I don't know yet," he confessed, swirling the brandy round his glass. "But that doesn't mean there isn't another explanation."

Jo felt a stab of annoyance. "You haven't been here living it Blake. You don't know the half."

"No. I don't, do I?"

He gave her a piercing look that was almost an accusation.

He looks, Jo thought disturbed, as though he would like to ask who *had* been here in his absence. But they were both on edge, awkward with each other following the weeks of separation, and the night's horrific events. Which wasn't a good thing, she decided, feeling the atmosphere deepen, and suddenly becoming aware that their antagonism seemed to be triggering hostility in the cottage. "What are we going to do?" she ventured in mellower tones.

He rose then and his features softened as he responded instantly to her change of mood. "Right now, we're going to bed! Seth Rigby is dead, the phone isn't working, there's nothing we can do about him – or the coffin – until tomorrow." Taking her hands he hauled her gently out of the chair. "We'll hold a council of war in the morning, okay?" he said, smiling as he brushed a stray strand of hair back from her forehead with his finger.

She did her best to respond with a smile. "Okay."

Suddenly he pulled her into his arms. "I've missed you Jo! It's been hell without you," he whispered into her hair.

Love you, kill you

She stiffened in his arms, recoiled from his kiss and her gaze swept the room.

"What's wrong?" He was frowning down at her, appeared not to have heard the whisper.

She scanned his face. "Nothing. I thought I heard something."

"Your nerves are shot to pieces – and no bloody wonder. Poor Jo." He kissed her again full on the lips. Jo sighed as the old passion quickened and stirred, and the flame of longing flickered and licked in her loins. She leant against him. "It's a miracle – you coming here."

He kissed her again, deeper and with growing passion, crushing her to him as though he would never let her go. But he did, to hold her at arms length and study her face. As though unsure of what he saw there, he gave her a quizzical look. "Where shall I sleep?"

For answer she took his hand and led him to the door.

She frowned as they entered the hall and made for the stairs. "Just a moment, Blake." She opened the kitchen door and switched on the light. There seemed to be nothing untoward; floor and surfaces were still spotless from their earlier scrubbing.

He moved to her side. "What is it?"

"I thought I heard something, a sort of scraping sound."

"The one you hear at night when in bed?"

She shook her head. "No, much softer, more of a rustling. There – listen!"

He froze for a moment then shook his head. "I don't hear it."

Jo shrugged thinking she must have been mistaken, but as the door was closing caught a whiff of the musky perfume and heard the sound yet again. She paused and frowned, trying to place it whilst Blake walked impatiently to the foot of the stairs.

Jo stubbornly remained where she stood, listening for sounds that lay just beyond the threshold of physical hearing. So many times she had been aware of a solitary whisper, or an incoherent dialogue, or heard muted conversations that streamed past consciousness like the chattering of the beck in the garden, or the secret autumnal whispers of feet shuffling through drifts of dry leaves. And because they were her experiences and seemingly hers alone, they set her apart.

"Are you coming, Jo?"

She half-turned her head, said over her shoulder: "In a minute."

If only she could make Blake understand.

There was always movement at Twilight Cottage, she reflected, leaning against the wall and staring unseeingly at the kitchen door. Ruffles in the fabric of normality. The creak on the stair for example, as though a foot and invisible weight had descended upon it causing the ancient timbers to shift. More worrying still were the shadows; the dark and indistinct shape that shifted at the edge of her vision, then disappeared the second she attempted to focus; or the half-movement in a shadowed corner, the tremble and shift of reality that lasted less than a second but kept her looking over her shoulder the rest of the day. Oh yes, it was all real. But how to convince a man like Blake? Of a presence that defied sensible detection, was as fleeting as a bat on the wing, as ephemeral as life itself.

With a sigh she turned and walked down the hall and saw that Blake was still waiting about half way up the stairs.

"You're overwrought."

"Yes, that must be it," she agreed tiredly. Then the sound she had heard downstairs clicked suddenly into place and a shiver ran down her spine.

"What is it?"

Looking up as she climbed the stairs, Jo saw the concern in Blake's eyes.

"Nothing. I'm fine." She looked down to hide her expression.

The rustling suggested the hem of a heavy skirt sweeping a stone floor.

FIFTY-THREE

~

They had caught up with her in a clearing in the forest, a bare quarter mile or so from the ruins. The place, St. Clair reminded himself, where she had lain half-naked with her lover. It was necessary for him to do so if he was to proceed with the plan: she looked pitiful enough now held between two of his soldiers, men handpicked for the job and loyal to him – but also to Scotland. And in his possession were documents to prove each man's guilt, which meant they could never talk about this night; not without losing their lives and placing their families under threat, should he ever reveal those papers to King Edward.

Almost, for a second, he contemplated having her run through. Cleanly and quickly – instead of the death he had so elaborately prepared. But no, there could be no pity for a wife who played the whore. Not so haughty now, my lady, eh? The fear was stark in her face. But still she refused to cringe and beg and this more than any other thing hardened him in his resolve. Her beauty still moved him though; especially that chestnut mane, now dishevelled and framing her white face. But the defiant tilt of her chin as he entered the clearing was frost to any bud of compassion. He had loved her once to distraction, but now felt only hate.

He stopped a mere couple of feet from her. He could see her breast heaving, and her dilated pupils as she stared him out with forced defiance. From somewhere within the wood the blackbird resumed its song. There was nothing to be said; she knew she was about to die. He drew back his arm and struck her a sharp blow to the head. Soundlessly she crumpled and sank to the ground. He looked around. The clearing lurked at the end of a rough sheep track well back from the lane. "This will do," he rapped to the waiting men at arms. "Fetch the cart – and start digging."

That's right. Not next to her lover, as she would wish, even that comfort would be denied. His face implacable he looked down at her still form.

Let the bitch lie where she fell.

Any awkwardness vanished once Jo and Blake were together beneath the quilt. Never had Jo thought to be here with Blake in this room, the scene of so many fraught and miserable nights. For once she could appreciate the simplicity of whitewashed walls and low ceiling, the intimacy of nooks and crannies, and the way the oak beams striped the moon-washed floor with deep shadows. He pulled her to him and kissed her first with lingering tenderness then mounting passion. Jo sighed and her exhaled breath caught on something suspiciously like a sob. Blake paused in caressing her and searched her face as though expecting to find rejection there. "Okay babe?"

She nodded and smiled, unable to speak. Seemingly reassured, Blake lowered his head again and gently nibbled her lip. It wasn't at all like her, to be constantly on the verge of tears and she closed her eyes so that Blake could not see the intensity and confusion that must surely be mirrored there. Not that she was ready to compromise, she told herself; it signified nothing more than her exhaustion, the trauma of facing the possibility that she had killed a man. It was also, she reluctantly admitted, reaction to the excruciating loneliness of the previous weeks.

"You with me babe?" Blake murmured into the hollow at the base of her neck.

"All the way." She allowed herself to respond to his touch as his lips brushed lightly over her breasts, then gave a little cry as his teeth gently nipped.

"I'm with you, I'm with you!" she cried from somewhere between laughter and tears.

His deep throaty laugh brought a rush of emotion, and her legs and arms encircled him as though clinging to the past and afraid to hope for the future.

"Don't worry Jo; we'll sort something out," he whispered as though picking up on her insecurity.

"Whatever tomorrow brings Blake – I want you right now."

"That's it. Just go for now – and enjoy."

He was right, Jo decided abandoning herself to the moment. His body was warming hers, and his tongue and lips on her breasts were telling her that there was at least one person in this world who cared whether she lived or died. That realisation alone was sufficient to bring her close to tears, but of joy this time and gratitude for his presence.

"Touch me."

His whispered entreaty was unnecessary; her hand had already found and encircled him, and she secretly smiled on hearing his sudden intake of breath.

"Like this?" The way he moaned deep in his throat told her better than words.

"More, more."

"No I want you now!"

She raised herself above him, lowered herself ever so slowly and smiled again at the power as he moaned and moved his head to and fro on the pillow.

"Oh God I've missed you Jo – missed *this*."

"You only ever wanted me for my body," she teased whilst moving on him.

"Too true."

He opened his eyes and she saw the love lurking behind his amusement. She smiled in return, then the laughter died in her throat as the intensity burning in his eyes seemed to scorch her soul.

"You know," he said as she froze, poised above him, "I think I'd rather kill you than let you go again."

The fact that it was said quietly in a conversational tone made his utterance all the more chilling.

"Don't say such things Blake."

He made no reply, but in one fluid movement pushed her aside so that she rolled onto her back, and mounting, towered above her in dominant pose.

"I mean it Jo."

In the muted light cast by the bedside lamp his eyes glittered with malice. He drove into her then as a man dying of thirst might dive into a crystal pool in the desert.

"Blake?"

"I love you Jo."

Reassured, she matched his rhythm then faltered on catching a flicker of movement in the shadows.

"What's wrong my love?"

She frowned: an odd expression for Blake, too flowery. "Nothing," she said, not wanting to put him off his stride. "Trying too hard I guess."

He grunted and pushed down again.

She tried to concentrate, to match his rhythm but the atmosphere was slowly changing. The cold from the window was creeping inside, the chill of death and the dank earthy smell of the grave. A prickling sensation crept over her flesh like minute electrical charges.

Antony Antony

Jo peered over Blake's shoulder to the furthermost corner of the room. *He was there.* At first she merely sensed his presence, but then became aware of a dark form. There was nothing wraith-like or transparent about it, she found herself thinking with a sense of detachment; the figure was seemingly solid and real. Body armour gleamed dully in the light from the landing that filtered through the partially open door, but the face was cast in shadow, the features slightly distorted like her image when mirrored on the screen of her lap top before it was switched on. The emerald set in the ring on his hand flashed as he raised his hand and beckoned. There followed a pulling sensation at the centre of her forehead as though her psyche was being drawn out.

Then nothing but darkness, and the tunnel. She was whirling through the tunnel again, just as on the day of the accident. This cannot be happening a part of her mind protested. Doubt, like rain on a window, distorted her vision: she was no longer in the bedroom of the cottage with Blake, but with *him* in a candle-lit chamber where swords, axes and shields were hung on the walls.

Tapestries too: a rampant unicorn that was somehow erotic particularly claimed her attention. His armour gleamed in the light shed by the torches in the wall sconce and her eye was drawn to the hawk sprawled across his breastplate. His hair was as dark as Blake's, but the eyes that watched her from the bold-featured face were as green as the emerald on his finger.

I would die for this man.

"Antony," she breathed.

He held out his hand; she walked in slow motion towards him. As she moved, the hem of her silk gown whispered over the stone floor.

Naked, she lay with him in the great bed, her hair a copper cascade on the pillow. Her gown lay discarded on the stone floor, a pool of silk and satin rippling in the light of the candles and sconces. Stripped of his finery he looked younger but no less imposing. With his taut muscled frame, dark tousled locks and emerald eyes he could be one of the Fianna, the warrior-heros so beloved of the Celts; or even perhaps the great CuChulainn himself, the demi-god whose exploits were recounted and revered by Cormac her husband's Irish bard. Her eyes shadowed with fear as thoughts of St. Clair darkened her pleasure.

"No sadness tonight, Madeline."

As though he had been privy to her thoughts, she marvelled. But then they were that close. "Then make me happy, my love."

"Like this?"

She smiled then laughed aloud as his fingers intimately teased, and his tongue tasted her secret flavours. He was suddenly very still, poised above her and watching her face with the intensity she had come to dread. "We could be happy always," he said quietly, his eyes searching hers for the answer he craved.

Breathless from laughter and passion she did not for a moment speak, then repeated his own words. "No sadness tonight, Antony."

"We could go away . . ." He looked about to argue further, then nodded and smiled the wistful smile she had come to love more than life itself. "You are right, sweetheart. Whatever comes we shall have this night to remember."

He loved her then, with a passion that stole her breath and left her bemused. "Antony, Antony my love," she murmured into his chest as he came down on her with a force that was almost demonic.

"Shall you always love me?" he demanded, pausing above her, his hair dishevelled, his eyes hard with challenge.

She met his gaze without flinching. "How can you doubt it?"

For answer he drove down on her hard. Moonlight streaming through the casement set the coverlets awash with silver, a tide of heraldic argent that roared in her ears and swept her up and carried her to a paradise-land of shining blue seas and apricot moons where they could live and love without fear of others. Riding the storm of passion she abandoned herself to the moon's tidal pull, to its inexorable suck and control of her life blood, the ebb and flow of her bodily fluids. Her lips parted to release the ultimate cry, but the sound came not from her own but Antony's throat, or so it seemed as they clung and shuddered together in the final paroxysm.

A white-owl screeched beyond the casement jolting her back to reality. As she opened her eyes the magic fled: moonlight washed over Antony, bleaching his face and body of colour and imparting the waxy pallor of lilies and death. Except where a moonbeam streamed through the stained glass casement. It struck the ruby tint of the hawk family crest, casting a livid bloodstain over his chest. She shivered as if with premonition, as though an icy hand had laid itself over her heart.

He raised his head from the pool of moonlight where he lay sated and submerged. "What is it, my love?"

She gave a little shake of the head in denial. As though for once misreading her meaning as lovers in their intensity are prone to do, his expression darkened and he wound her tresses around his fingers and pulled. "I would kill you rather than have you leave me."

"Don't say such things Antony," she whispered, her voice hushed by superstition. She winced and he slackened the grip on her hair, his hands sliding instead to her neck. "Then leave him Madeline," he entreated. His fingers caressed the delicate skin of her throat: "Leave him and come with me."

Come away, with me; come away . . .

Away, come away, away, away . . .

Whirling, whirling through time and space. When she opened her eyes the bedroom at Twilight Cottage seemed unchanged, the corner was empty; nobody stood in its shadows.

Because the strangeness is here in the bed.

Overcome by the sudden intensity of emotion, Jo moaned and nibbled Blake's lower lip with her teeth. He laughed, then reared above her – like the unicorn in the wall-hanging, a spontaneous thought that filled her with confusion – and plunged deep. She cried out. Never had their lovemaking been like this, it brought tremors of both terror and excitement. He shuddered and held himself rigid above her, the muscles of his chest and arms knotted and glistening with sweat, the veins of his neck twisted like cords. He closed his eyes and cried aloud as though in the throes of death. She felt the scalding spurts as he released his seed and his body went limp.

At length he opened his eyes and Jo, disturbed by the oddness of his expression, paused in raising her hand to caress his cheek.

"Blake?"

"I love you too much." His hands slid around her neck, his fingers caressing the tender skin gently at first, then she felt the thrill of fear as his thumbs began to press against her wind pipe.

"Blake – what are you doing?"

"It would be so easy," he said softly. "Then I would never have to fear."

"Let go, I can't breathe." Her head threshed to and fro on the pillow as she struggled to escape. She ceased and was still as he tightened his grip in warning.

"If you ever betray me, I'll kill you," he whispered.

She swallowed and spoke with difficulty: "What's got into you Blake?"

"Do you understand? I'll love you forever . . . but *I will kill you.*"

Jo gasped: in the light from the landing Blake's eyes were a clear emerald green.

FIFTY-FOUR

~

Louise Costello threw down her pencil and pushed aside the manuscript she had been editing. *Jo Cavanagh get out of my head!* Rising from her seat at the desk she poured herself a small and far-too-early gin. Okay, one more try. Moving back to the desk she picked up the telephone receiver and dialled. As on numerous previous occasions, nothing except that awful crackling and buzz on the line. Frustrated she slammed down the receiver and inadvertently pressed the intercom button.

Her assistant's voice came over. "You want to dictate, Ms Costello?"

"No, no it's alright, Karen; a mistake," Louise said flicking the switch to 'off'.

Why fret and fuss like a mother hen? Jo would be just fine.

Owning the cottage, Louise reasoned, didn't make her responsible for Jo's welfare. Jo was a big girl now. *But there's something wrong with the place.* There, it was out. Something she'd never admitted to herself before. And Jo was out there on her own. However it did seem likely she wouldn't be alone for long: Blake had telephoned asking for the address, and she didn't mind betting he wasn't about to write a letter. In fact he was probably on his way up there right now. He still had it bad for Jo: it had been there in his voice, disguised of course as men do, but he couldn't fool an old campaigner. A momentary sadness disturbed her habitually blasé expression. There had been lots of men, and all on her terms, but Blake Durante was something else. He could have kept her by his side for good – had he wanted to, she mused. But then along came Jo, as the song goes. A smile of self-derision spread over her flawlessly made-up face. But that was history; no point in crying over turned pages. Besides, she was genuinely fond of Jo, the relationship was closer to friendship than the usual author/agent deal. She had tried 'phoning her several times during the past couple of days, but had heard nothing except crackles and white noise.

It might, she thought finishing her gin and replacing the glass, be interesting to see how Jo reacted to Blake after the break. Not that they'd want her around, but hell, it was her bloody cottage. She didn't want them to split up of course; nor was it a case of her being there to pick up the pieces, if Jo rejected him and Blake fell apart. Thoughtfully she tapped the rim of her empty glass with a scarlet fingernail and grinned at herself in the art deco mirror above the cabinet. London was dull just now, prior to the Christmas countdown. She looked out of the window at the overcast sky, but saw no sign of the snow that was forecast. Why not motor up there, break the journey at a country house hotel for the night? It would be a change, would dispel this bloody boredom and sense of dissatisfaction with life. Yes, that's what she needed: a little spice and adventure, to see her through until Hank came over again. She pressed the intercom button. "Karen? I'll be away a couple of days. Have you anything booked?"

"There's Leo Rand in the morning, and that new author the following afternoon."

"Make my apologies to Leo, he'll understand. I'll contact him when I return. You can see the new author yourself."

"Very good Ms Costello. Have a good trip."

"Thanks, Karen."

Louise flicked the switch. A good girl Karen who would make an agent herself one day. She hesitated then picked up the manuscript and stuffed it into her briefcase. Might as well do some reading whilst out of town. The sense of freedom was exhilarating and her step lightened as she walked out of the building into the noise and bustle. A watery sun was struggling through the clouds as she drove out of London.

But that was this morning. Dusk was now falling, and London

and the Midlands were now well behind and the windscreen was dotted with snowflakes. No problem at present but it might get worse. That sky, she thought leaning forward to peer out of the windscreen, looked pretty damned full. Maybe it would be better to stop off for a meal then keep on driving instead of stopping over. Being snowed-in at a north country hotel wasn't her idea of 'adventure' or 'spice.' And she wasn't tired; the new Merc ate up the miles without effort. Making up her mind, she drove on for another hour or so then pulled off the motorway and into the forecourt of the South Lakes Hotel.

Louise, you go through life making all the wrong decisions she told herself wryly as wind-driven snowflakes whirled across the dual carriageway in ever denser patterns. In her private life that was, she qualified, because she was a damn' fine agent – probably the best in London and therefore must be doing something right. Only she wasn't in London right now, she thought grimly, and more's the pity. It seems it would have been sensible after all to stay put at the hotel. And despite her reservations the dinner was good, she admitted begrudgingly. The potatoes *dauphinois* were enough to turn Pierre at the *Coq d'Or* green with envy. However she hadn't stayed and now had no choice but to carry on. Unfortunately the meagre daylight was fading fast and the worst part of the journey was yet to come.

To compound her worries, the feeling that all was not well with Jo intensified. Louise's attempts to contact her via the hotel telephone had failed so obviously the line was still out of order. No, it was a damned nuisance, but she had to look after her investments, she told herself, refusing to accept concern or partiality on behalf of one of her authors as the motive. Hard-headed Louise that's me, she thought switching on the radio. Minutes later the Alan Bennet play was interrupted for 'severe weather warnings' for the North of England. Louise gave an exclamation of disgust and turned it off. Panic-mongering was the last thing she wanted to hear.

Three quarters of an hour later mild irritation was replaced by serious alarm. The boisterous wind was piling up drifts at either side of the narrow road, creating blizzard conditions. The pass over the mountains had been out of the question from the start, but even via the coast road – twice as long but less of a roller coaster – the journey was still a nightmare. Had Blake got through? she wondered, leaning forward again to peer through the windscreen at the white-speckled night. He would be handicapped by not being familiar with the route, in fact it would be a miracle if he found Twilight Cottage.

She slid a cassette in the player and music reassuringly filled the car. The theme from *Officer and a Gentleman* brought back memories of her brief affair with Blake. For a time she amused herself with a fantasy in which she was marooned in the snow and Blake happened by to rescue her, and they ended up together in the bedroom of some cosy inn. *Hell Louise, that's the pits!* she thought with a grin. As bad as any formula romance off the slush pile! Unconsciously she had relaxed her vigilance and her foot pressed down harder on the accelerator. *But fun.* She grimaced at herself in the mirror, laughed and recklessly pressed harder. The chuckle died in her throat as a figure appeared on the road ahead, one hand raised as though in command. "Oh, God!" Her mouth went dry. The figure loomed closer, filling her vision; the Merc' skewed across the road.

Frantically she pumped the brake and wrestled with the steering wheel. The back end swung round as she tried to pull out of the skid and regain control. She cried out in alarm as the car nosed through the drift at the roadside, the wheels whining and spinning as, panic-stricken, she hit the brake hard. The bonnet tilted and the car plunged into the ditch. The twin beams from the headlamps bounced and dipped, manic strobes in a nightmare disco sending tree shadows careering across the snow.

She screamed as a tree trunk loomed ahead. The impact knocked the breath from her body. As the car swerved she was thrown sideways and her head made sickening contact with the side window. The white world outside suddenly turned to black.

"Help!"

Her own voice sounded weakly from somewhere beyond herself. "Help!" There it was again. Her head felt muzzy and everything was spinning. She closed her eyes tight, perhaps she was hanging upside down? She opened her eyes a fraction. No, gradually the world was stabilising so thank God, the car must be the right way up. Her head throbbed and she remembered actually seeing stars on impact. Her hand reached up to feel for the damage and came away wet and sticky with blood. "Oh God!" *Don't panic* she told herself. It hurt yes, but instinct told her it wasn't serious. Cautiously she looked to left then right; her head moved from side to side so her neck wasn't broken. Panic threatened again as attempts to move her body were unsuccessful. *Stupid cow*! Not paralysis or something sinister – just the damned seat-belt. Her hand searched for the release catch and her wet fingers fumbled and slid off the metal. At the second attempt there was a clicking sound and the constriction across her chest was released.

She sat still for a moment then opened the door and groaning with pain, eased herself out. Nausea rose in her throat and red hot hammers pounded inside her head as the world spun sickeningly then stabilised. Ice crystals in the air cut like tiny invisible razor blades, but also helped to revive her. Tears of loneliness, shock and distress threatened, but she cleared her throat, sniffed angrily and forced them back. There was nobody here to help so she bloody well had to help herself. "Go girl! – it hurts but you can do it," she urged herself in a jocular not-a-bit-scared sort of voice. The climb up the bank was somehow accomplished, albeit at the rate of one step forward and three back as her soles slid on the slope of a miniature bob sleigh run. "Okay, Louise, you're doing just fine," she muttered, heaving herself upright as she reached the road.

Frowning she looked around her expecting to see at least a maimed figure and maybe even a corpse, but the road stretched away, white silent – and empty. So where was the weirdo who had stepped in front of the car? She looked down, saw the skid marks made by the Merc's tyres, then her stomach did a double flip: there were no footprints. Fear gripped her then, one that was very different from the anxiety of being alone in a comparative wilderness.

This fear belonged to the world of childhood and nightmares; to the unexplained and unknown, the type of fear that brought the flush of a sudden sweat to her face even in sub zero temperatures. *The same thing happened to Jo.* The thought slipped into awareness before she could stop it, but was quashed with the ruthlessness of the born survivor. Start thinking that way and you've had it, she warned herself. Whatever the explanation it made no difference now.

She tried to walk and almost fell, and was reminded of her first visit to the skating rink as a girl when each step on the ice meant the instant ignominy of sitting upon it or lying flat on her back. There was comfort in the memory, safety in the nostalgia and normality of it, being removed as it was by a thousand light years from her present bizarre situation. She tried a couple more steps and stifled a cry as pain twisted hot tight bands around her shoulders then streaked down her spine. As she paused to recover an unwelcome realisation dawned: there were no lights showing in the valley, no friendly glow dotted here and there, reassuring travellers that at least *somebody* lived in this benighted desolation. The lamps of the Rigby place should be glimmering over there, and further down on the other side the vicarage should be shining a beacon of hospitality from its windows. For a brief second she looked wildly around, doubting her position. Was she in the wrong valley? Fear gripped her innards at the prospect of being abandoned in some uninhabited wilderness, but then common sense took over. Of course, there must be a power failure. It normally didn't take much, so was inevitable given tonight's appalling conditions. So come on girl, the cottage is within limping distance, and you are at least wearing boots and a fleecy jacket. Taking a handkerchief from her pocket she wiped the blood from her forehead and struggled on. Everything will be hunky dory, she told herself; as long as you don't do something stupid like fainting or giving up.

She dragged herself across the road to the lane and couldn't help comparing this to her last visit here. The memory of herself and Callum walking hand in hand in the snow brought a lump to her throat. Dear Callum, she missed him sometimes. Which was simply the predictable result of a nostalgic journey to the area; that and self pity arising from her present predicament, she told herself sternly. Her hand clutched at the dry stone wall as she reached the far side of the road. I must, she thought swaying on her feet, have been mad to come. A crazy game concocted from the safety and sophistication of London, a world that had nothing whatsoever in common with this primitive place.

As she left the lane and started down the track for Twilight Cottage, a handful of snowflakes still blew in the wind but it seemed the worst of the fall was over. The silence, apart from the crunching of pristine snow beneath her boots, was absolute. The moon appeared through a break in the cloud lending a magical bluish cast to the whiteness that blanketed tree, wall and fell. The solitude, the purity of it all was up-lifting, almost mystical, she thought with a sense of surprise, putting such uncharacteristic reverie down to shock and alcohol-withdrawal. Here both snow and silence were deeper and more profound.

As she limped along a pall of unease settled over her shoulders. Reaction, she told herself, relentlessly plodding on, and her goal was almost in sight. Nonetheless her pace quickened, so that every now and then her feet stumbled over a hidden rock or branch and each time pain tore through her in tortuous flashes. She jumped as a screech ripped a hole in the silence, then heart uncomfortably thudding against her ribs, realised it was just an owl.

Nonetheless the hush, rather than inspiring reverie now brought a creeping sense of dread. Jo must have come unstuck too, she thought coming across the snow-covered car and slumping thankfully against it for support. There was a sort of comfort in the realisation that Jo had walked from here to the cottage too. Stupid really, but again it lent a touch of normality to the bizarre. Louise frowned over a set of larger prints, then her brow cleared. Blake must have got here despite the weather. Well, well, so it was to be a cosy threesome after all. A slow smile of pure mischief spread across her face. What a shame to have to disturb their slumbers – or whatever else they may be doing.

The overhang of branches was so weighted with snow that it almost touched her head as she passed beneath. But it didn't matter. The claustrophobic tunnel had lost its power to enthral. Jo, Blake and blessed normality waited at the end. And with a bit of luck some fun too. Louise smiled to herself again, imagining the look on Jo's face upon seeing her agent in the back of beyond and in the middle of the night. And Blake's too; his embarrassment would be something else. Her lip curled in a sardonic smile. How ironic that in the past he had declined her invitation to Twilight Cottage, and now they were all to meet up there in a classic *ménage à trois*. That delightful prospect urged her on when pain would have stopped her in her tracks. How silly to have let herself be a prey to worry and fear. It was all a bit of an adventure, now that Blake and Jo were waiting to sympathise and succour her wounds. She was still smiling when a sense of not being alone made her swiftly turn. Nothing moved in the moonlit snow-scene, and she shrugged and struggled on.

The cottage could not now be far away, yet her recent euphoria was evaporating fast. Something, a sense of creepiness at the nape of her neck maybe, made her turn and glance over her shoulder. Nobody there, nothing disturbed the oppressive stillness and silence. As Louise limped along the presentiment grew. Another glance over the shoulder – and yet another, and this time a shadow moved at the edge of her vision. Her heart began to thump: someone was following her through the tunnel of trees.

She stopped dead and turned round as a dark shadow flitted behind a tree. "That you Blake?" she shouted, pausing for an answer and moving on again when none came. "Blake?" A hush settled once more on the wood. "Jo?" she tried next, and as she walked on fear paced at her side.

Love Hate

For no apparent reason the words echoed inside her skull.

She wasn't quite sure how long before realisation dawned: Oh God, this isn't somebody real. Real people don't move through a wood in silence, they tread on twigs or rustle through leaves and don't generate this awful aura of hatred and anger. It was palpable, crept up from behind and touched her with evil. An image came to mind of a swarm of bluebottles buzzing around a rotting carcass. What on earth made her think that? An icy coldness numbed her from the inside and a voice in her head whispered death and despair.

The sense of a presence grew stronger. Her heart missed a couple of beats: something was right behind her now. One thing for sure – she knew now why the man in the road had left no footprints. Could a ghost kill? There came the soft *plop* of snow falling from branches, and fear dripped along her spine like melting ice.

Hate Anger Forever

The words arose again in her mind, but louder this time, if that was possible, given that they were unspoken. The branches were spinning overhead, pain flashed through her and nausea rose in waves.

She turned and glimpsed the figure of a man, the features contorted in fury, mouth twisted and cruel. Hate and anger pulsed from him like blood from a severed artery, and spiralled towards her along the tunnel, gripping her with a malevolent vice. Cries escaped her as her feet slipped on impacted snow and her ankle turned on a ridge of frozen mud. Keep going, must keep going. The cottage couldn't be more than a quarter mile away now. Her foot caught in a raised root; she pitched forward and sprawled in the snow. The breath was knocked out of her and tremors of pain and shock coursed through her body. She lay still, her will and resistance ebbing, then sensing his presence struggled to rise, the sobs catching in her throat.

A shadow fell on her and she cried out. A deathly cold was creeping up from her feet. *I'm dying*, came the thought. Her blood was turning to ice, and there was nothing else in the world but this terrible aching cold that paralysed her limbs and evoked the grave.

Hate Anger

She could have sworn the breathy words came from somewhere outside her head.

Summoning all her remaining strength, Louise struggled to her feet and began to limp towards the cottage. *Oh God help me.* She wasn't going to make it. Her body was seared by white hot pain, nausea rose in her throat and the snow-laden tunnel spun around her. And he – whoever he was – remained with her, was still in pursuit. At first it had sounded like wind soughing through the trees, a whispering of nature. But the sound of breathing was now unmistakable, and the whispers were not of the natural world. A cold clammy sweat broke over her until she thought she must faint. The breathing was louder, the whispering close enough to paralyse her with fear.

Anger Hate Forever

The words clawed at her brain.

Pushing aside the strands of spruce and winter-bare larch that whipped across her face she staggered into the clearing. A sob of relief rose in her throat: the squat grey shape of Twilight Cottage had never looked so beautiful. But the whisperer may reach her before she could rouse its occupants. Panic assailed her as she limped closer, constantly looking behind, expecting a hand to reach out and grab her. Nothing moved in the shadows. She paused, shoulders hunched with tension, stopped in her tracks by pain and something else, a subliminal awareness of absence. Head to one side she tasted the air for sound and found it lacking. The sense of a presence was no longer with her. The whisperer had gone.

Thank God. So great was her relief that her legs all but gave way. Her hand clutched at a branch for support, dislodging a shower of snowflakes. She remained still a moment longer, swallowing draughts of mountain-cold air delicious as any wine: the taste of freedom, of continuing Life that a moment ago had seemed forfeit, and so now was doubly precious. Another glance over her shoulder confirmed that she was alone. Better still the glade *felt* empty; no unseen hand waited to grab her, no phantom breath chilled her neck.

No need to rush. Time now to recuperate before knocking at that door and entering the next phase of the game. Taking a deep breath she threw back her head in a timeless gesture, scanning the silent stars and gazing upon the face of an enigmatic moon. Resisting the urge to run for the door, she inhaled the silence and peace of the night. Nothing had really followed her, it was all down to the shock of the crash. That and finding herself in this god-forsaken place at dead of night without any lights. It was also, she convinced herself, down to the rumours about the place, the silly stories of country folk with nothing better to do. Jo's disclosure had obviously preyed on her mind too. Whatever else was wrong with Jo, it had nothing to do with spooks.

She was still blaming her imagination when a high-pitched squeal split the night. Before she could even cry out, a wave of indescribable fury billowed up and around her throwing her to the ground. Snow disturbed from branches splattered her body as a commotion raged overhead. Rolling onto her back she saw the arrow-head stark against the moon. It hovered there, shrieking and clawing the air. Her scream as she struggled to her feet mingled with its screech as it dived. Louise, gobbets of snow dropping from her coat, ran for the cottage and hammered at the door with her fists. She paused to protect her head with her hands as the hawk wheeled overhead.

FIFTY-FIVE

~

Jo shot upright in bed as somebody pounded the front door. "Blake!" She had been lying sleepless next to him, and now shook his shoulder. "Blake! she repeated urgently.

"I'm awake!" He sat up and swung his legs out of bed and cursed beneath his breath as the racket downstairs continued.

Jo became aware of the trembling of her limbs. "Seth!" she whispered, her eyes huge.

Blake stood up and leant over her. "Seth's dead Jo," he said slowly and with great deliberation. "He's *dead:* do you understand?" he repeated whilst stroking her hair. Gradually her terror subsided. "Yes," she said dully, pushing her hair back from her face.

"God in heaven! Who is that anyway?" Blake grumbled, reaching for the lamp. "Shit! The power's off. Torch? Candle and matches?" he shot at her over his shoulder, suddenly the professional with a job to do.

"There's a torch on the window ledge."

The beam sent shadows leaping up the wall and across the ceiling. "Stay there!" he ordered fastening his pants whilst heading for the stairs.

Jo was already out of bed.

She caught him up in the hall.

"Okay, okay I'm coming!" he called irritably. "Who is this anyway?" he added, standing behind the door but making no effort to open it.

A woman's voice shouting something unintelligible was followed by renewed banging. "Somebody in one helluva hurry," Blake muttered drawing back the bolt. The door swung open; Blake focused the torch beam on the threshold. There was an upsurge of feathers and an ear-piercing screech. Jo screamed as a bloodstained figure fell into the hall.

"Louise!" Jo stared at her agent in disbelief.

"Bolt the door! Don't let it in!" Louise Costello screamed, dragging at Blake's arm. He had been looking at her as though stupefied, but now slammed and bolted the door. He turned again and trained the torch on their visitor. Jo took in the bloodstained face that was white with exhaustion, Louise's dishevelled appearance and complete lack of cool, and felt she must be dreaming. "Louise, what is it? What's going on?" she asked, helping her along the hall to the sitting room.

Louise paused and glared up at Jo "A remake of Hitchcock's *Birds* at a guess," she said with characteristic aplomb.

"But what were you doing here in the first place?" Blake chipped in from behind as Jo guided Louise to a seat.

"Tell me!" Louise groaned, sinking onto the easy chair. "Because for the life of me I don't know."

Jo watched as Louise breathed a huge sigh then swallowed the last of the brandy that Blake had placed in her shaking hand. Jo lit the last of the candles she had brought from the kitchen and eyed her critically. "That head wound needs cleansing," she said, taking one of the candles and heading for the bathroom. Shadows slunk away from the flickering light and skulked in corners.

What else can go wrong? she wondered, pouring Dettol into a dish of water that was still tepid although the fire had long since died. The door was open and she could hear Blake asking Louise about her injuries, and gathered from the reply that Louise had crashed the car. She found it unsettling, Jo admitted making her way back to the sitting room with cotton wool and the bowl, Louise being here with herself and Blake. Which was silly, because Louise was history as far as Blake was concerned.

"Okay, let's have a look at that," she started to say, then stopped abruptly and hovered on the threshold. Blake was positioned behind Louise and his hands ran expertly over her neck and collar bone before sliding along her arms. "Flex your wrists for me. Fine, now clench and unclench your hands," he instructed, his thumb gently feeling along each bone. "Now your fingers – can you move them all? Good."

"As good as any doctor," Louise murmured, glancing slyly from the corner of her eye as Jo advanced with the bowl.

Blake didn't even look up as Jo set it down on the table. A fact which afforded her a degree of comfort: had there been any intimate undercurrent he would scarcely be so laid back, she reassured herself. Blake ordered Louise to sit forward, then ran his hands expertly down her spine, then over her thighs and down over her shapely calves to her ankles and feet. "There's nothing broken," he pronounced pulling his sleeves down again. Jo chided herself for a mean possessive bitch. It made no difference; she didn't like Blake touching Louise one bit. Especially when Louise smiled and simpered 'Thank you doctor," in that stupidly arch way.

Once Louise was cleaned up and a dressing applied to her head, Jo made coffee and they huddled around a fire kindled by Blake.

"What made you come, Louise – and in this weather?" Jo demanded, condemning as unworthy her suspicion that Louise's visit was somehow connected with Blake's reappearance.

Louise gave an elegant shrug. "I was bored, honey; you know how it is, London's dead just now."

"So you come *here*," Jo exclaimed, disbelief written over her face.

"Okay, so it's not exactly the cosmopolitan metro of the North." Louise stirred her coffee then sighed and scowled up at Jo. "And you, of course. I came because of you," she admitted.

"But I don't understand –"

"I was concerned, for God's sake! I've been trying to reach you for days."

"Jo says the telephone's been playing up. I'll check it out," Blake said moving to the hall. "Still off," he reported on his return.

"Anyway, I am very relieved to see you are alive and still in one piece, Jo," Louise said severely as Blake took her cup and refilled it with coffee. "I was convinced something **awful** had happened. Then when that thing out there –," She shuddered, made a derisory sound in her throat and shook her head, as though in disbelief of her own experience.

"What exactly did happen?" Jo pressed, leaning forward on her seat.

"Now are you less sceptical," Jo demanded of Blake as Louise finished her chilling account.

"Not really."

"I'm almost sure I saw a man following me," Louise said stubbornly.

Blake raised an eyebrow. "Almost?"

"Okay I'm not certain, but are you saying I made up that crazy bird?" Louise challenged in an ominously quiet voice.

"It won't wash Blake!" Jo chipped in.

"Now just hold on here." Blake held up a hand in protest. "All we can be sure of is that Louise was attacked by some kind of raptor. It's rare but not unknown for birds of prey to act out of character and attack during extreme weather conditions. It doesn't prove the existence of ghosts!

"Okay – and what about that Katrina woman I told you about, and Colin too?" Jo's mouth took on a stubborn line. "It's not exactly an isolated incident."

"Hey what is this – what don't I know?" Louise demanded setting down her cup.

Briefly Jo told her how they had read the report of Katrina's death, and about the attack on Colin.

"*Three* attacks are *not* coincidence," Louise exclaimed as Jo concluded her account. "And," she added thoughtfully, "I'm not sure about this, but I doubt hawks are nocturnal."

Blake scratched his scalp then pressed his hand to the nape of his neck. "I don't know," he confessed. "But that did cross my mind too."

"And what if Louise *was* followed – are you saying there's more than one madman stalking an isolated place like this?" Jo scoffed, sensing her position had strengthened. "It couldn't have been Seth – he's dead remember," she added echoing his earlier words.

Louise looked up from her coffee, plainly startled. "Seth Rigby? So how come he's dead?" she demanded.

Blake and Jo exchanged looks; Jo shrugged. What was the point in concealing the truth? Picking up on her signal, Blake related the story, and finished with obvious reluctance with a description of the events that took place in the graveyard.

"*Christ Almighty*, what have I walked into here?" Louise exclaimed, holding her head and making theatrical gestures with her other hand. "And you say you've just left him there – and that woman's corpse too?" she added, her face drained of colour.

Blake shrugged. "There's nothing to be done until morning; the roads are blocked and the telephone lines are down."

"Hark at Cool Hand Luke," Louise said with a loud sniff.

"I'll sort it out tomorrow Louise," Blake said in the tone of voice that told Jo he was holding hard to his temper.

"*You'll* sort it?" Louise mocked.

"Remember Blake works for –," Jo began, but was silenced by a warning look from Blake. She flushed and quickly said instead: "You two don't know about my research do you?"

"What research is that?" Louise politely asked, obviously feeling obligated but patently uninterested given the night's events.

"The story of Antony Chase and Madeline St. Clair – and her husband Justin."

"Sounds fascinating, do tell," Louise sneered in her old manner, with a quizzical look at Blake who raised his eyebrows expressively and gave her a half-grin in return. Incensed by this show of disloyalty, Jo frowned and stared at Blake who, refusing to be drawn, returned her look with one of blandness.

"Come on then, Jo – do tell," Louise prompted, settling back on her seat with a customary elegance that defied her ruined make-up, bruised face and dishevelled appearance. So Jo related her part of the story, including the inscription at Barrowburn Castle, her trips to Lancaster and Durham Universities, and her subsequent conversations with her sister Barbara and her colleague Deirdre Spencer.

"And the rest you know," Jo finished, refilling their cups and sitting down again.

"That's some story," Louise commented, the mocking tone no longer in evidence. Blake pursed his lips and nodded, but remained silent. Jo felt a prickle of unease as he watched her with an odd expression on his face. He had looked and acted normal until she had uttered Antony Chase's name. Now she could almost be back in that dream-chamber. She could see the flicker of fire and candle light reflected from shields and weaponery on the walls. *Could almost hear the rustle of her silk over-gown as she moved.* She shook her head in a gesture of denial and suppressed a shiver. The wood in the grate belched thin plumes of sulphurous smoke rather than burning cleanly as before. As though reading her thoughts Blake leaned forward and placed a log on the embers. A flame spurted and burned with a sickly bluish light that afforded little heat.

Even the candles are struggling Jo worried, noting the spluttering wax and wildly dipping flames. Louise shivered but said nothing; Blake cursed and picked up the poker which he used to abortively prod at the smouldering pile in the grate. He bent over the fire and in its subdued light his appearance changed: the normally jet-black hair where it fell across his forehead glowed with amber lights; his profile became sharper, the cheek bones more prominent and the nose more delicately moulded imparting a touch of arrogance and breeding. *Antony*

The name arose spontaneously to her mind, bringing with it a confusing *mêlée* of love, anger, longing and fear. Jo looked at Louise wondering if she had noticed, then back at Blake, who now looked his normal self once more.

Nobody is voicing what we're all aware of, Jo thought leaving her coffee untouched. There was no doubt about it: the temperature had dropped and the atmosphere had turned distinctly sinister since she had voiced the legend.

Antony Antony. Jo looked round. The breathy whisper had sounded right beside her. She looked from Blake to Louise but they carried on talking animatedly to one another and obviously had heard nothing unusual.

"Come on Blake, there has to be something in it," Louise was arguing, leaning forward to make her point then wincing with pain.

"Balls!" Blake said unequivocally.

Jo tensed, sensing a deterioration in the atmosphere as voices and tempers rose. Somehow she must convey this to them, despite Blake's scepticism and Louise's tendency to fall in with him. "I guess where we're going wrong is in trying to make sense of this thing via logic."

Blake gave a sigh of exasperation. "And how else are we to proceed?"

"But this thing *defies* reason," Jo persisted. "It's like trying to measure human emotions say, with precision laboratory equipment. It doesn't pan out."

Blake scowled. "Don't start pulling Wittgenstein on me Jo. I had more than enough rammed down my throat when you were writing the book."

Louise, spotting a breach, swiftly abandoned pride and principle and jumped into bed with the enemy. "Poor Blake," she murmured, leaning forward to pat his knee and forgetting this time to wince. "It can't have been easy for you."

"And that's enough from you Louise," Jo snapped in response to Louise's treachery. Which wasn't very smart, she immediately realised as shock waves jolted the air. There was something not very nice in this room, and she was helping to feed it with her resentment.

"Well, I must say!" Louise was spluttering with indignation.

"Sorry Louise; I guess we're all a bit stressed out," Jo broke in quickly for the sake of their mutual safety. Thank God for that, she thought as Louise subsided into an injured silence and fractured air-waves healed.

"As I was saying," she continued with a warning glance at Blake, "We have to approach this with open minds. It occurs in response to emotional triggers provided *by ourselves*." Blake's sigh of impatience caused her to hold up a hand in protest. "No, hear me out," she said firmly, striving to ignore the mocking look of sympathy that Louise gave Blake. "Somehow our feelings create the right atmosphere for this thing to feed off and thrive. At times St. Clair's anger manifests, at others Antony Chase's despair. And sometimes, like tonight, both are active and we all get caught up in the energy-crossfire."

"Neat, but why should these remnants of personalities cause disruption rather than spreading sweetness and light?" Blake scoffed.

"Don't put words in my mouth, Blake," Jo retorted, still sore from the Wittgenstein jibe. "I'm not necessarily presuming *personalities* here, but *emotions*. And if there is anything in the theory that intense feelings can be absorbed and stored by the environment, then surely we can expect the old conflicts behind them to still be played out?"

Blake shrugged and look unconvinced; Jo challenged him with a look but he lapsed into silence.

"I may buy that; but what about the bird?" Louise demanded.

"A symbol," Jo replied promptly. "of his anger and frustration, at a guess. I don't know precisely how it works," she confessed, "but we know as a matter of historical fact that the hawk was the emblem of Sir Antony Chase."

"Okay, but why should these things be disruptive just now?" Louise argued.

"Precisely," Blake chipped in with a glance of complicity for Louise.

Jo hesitated, reluctant to admit Louise into their privacy. "There are – strong feelings, conflict between – well, I'm sure you know," she said haltingly, stung into speaking by Blake's look of triumph.

"She means the break-up with you Blake," Louise provided with relish. "In fact if we're talking past tense here, we're quite the little threesome, aren't we?" she added with a smirk. "Enough angst around here to literally wake the dead!"

"Give it a rest Louise," Blake growled but Louise's smile grew broader. Jo watched Blake with a worried frown, and tried hard to believe her own argument. No personalities: just torn fragments of feeling from the past, yesterday's debris with no significance for today. Fine, great. She blinked hard to dispel the memory of a unicorn rampant and ripples of satin on a stone floor. But one image resisted all her efforts, that of Blake's face, his eyes glowing green in the light from the landing, and she knew her theory was incomplete.

She blinked and roused herself as Blake's voice penetrated her reverie. "Anyway, sounds good," he said with a forced grin and an obvious attempt to lighten up the proceedings. "I mean, there speaks the author!"

Louise's eyes gleamed with sudden excitement. "Sweetheart – what a book it would make! A Field Study of Paranormal Phenomena, I can just see it!" she gushed, leaning forward to briefly grasp Jo's hand.

"Then you write it darling!" Jo mocked, mimicking Louise's camp style. "Just bear in mind the narrator's likely to get bumped off!"

Louise hitched herself up on the cushions. "There's no need to flip darling."

"Well that's our Louise, isn't it?" Jo said, unable to stem the resentment any longer, "ever on cue for a book. The only problem is inconsistency."

Louise gathered herself in an attitude of disdain. "I can't imagine –"

"I mean you change your mind as fast as your lovers!"

"Well!" Louise gasped, and for once seemed too taken aback to reply.

"It's true. One minute you claim you were followed, the next you take the piss out of me and every damn thing I say. You're refusing to take any of this seriously." Jo turned from Louise to glare at Blake "And you seem to have little idea of what is happening to you." As he opened his mouth to protest, Jo forestalled him. "And how can you, Louise, make light of what happened out there?" she demanded, pointing at the door. "You weren't exactly amused when we let you in!"

Louise removed an imaginary hair from her lapel and refused to look Jo in the eye. "Okay, I was scared out there in the dark and snow, then when you started on your theories – well, you got me all confused, sweetie."

"Bullshit!" Jo said without ceremony. "That bird was no delusion! Blake is your compass – you follow wherever he points."

Blake, pretending to act as referee, held up a hand. "Okay, girls, break!"

The look of amusement was wiped from his face as two of the four candles spluttered and died.

They sat quiet and unmoving for several minutes. "Good God! What's that smell? It's like a mortuary in a heatwave." Louise wrinkled her nose in disgust. Jo, who had been deliberately ignoring the nauseous odour in the hope that it would fade, rose to her feet. "I'll check out the kitchen," she said with reluctance, picking up one of the two surviving candles. Before Jo could move, Louise suddenly clapped her hands to either side of her head.

"What is it?" Blake frowned and looked distrustful as though fearing another display of histrionics.

"Those words, the same as out there," Louise said, wincing as though they caused her actual pain.

"What words?" Jo asked carefully.

"LOVE – ANGER – HATE."

Jo drew in her breath sharply. It was Blake not Louise who had spoken.

Even before reaching the kitchen door, Jo heard the buzzing of the flies. "Oh, no," she murmured, unaware that Blake and Louise had followed her out of the room. Her hand hesitated on the latch; taking a deep breath she opened the door. The scene by the flickering light of the candle was reminiscent of Dante's depictions of Hell. "Oh, God!" The miasma floated out to meet her in sulphury yellow streaks. She clapped a hand over her nose and mouth and heard Louise retching from the vicinity of the doorway. A column of bluebottles rose and fell steadily above the centre of the stone floor. The sound of their buzzing grated along Jo's nerves and made her want to scream. But flies and smell were nothing compared with the rest. The flagstones oozed green slime and putrefying toadstools, and mould clung to everything: a bluish green fuzz mottled drainer, work tops and the legs of the table, and the carpet square was furred with obscene white pile. Jo looked upwards, seeking the source of a repetitive sound. Decomposing fungi dripped slime from the ceiling with a steady *plop plop plop* onto the floor. By the combined light of the candle and reflected moonlight on snow from the window, she saw the customary piles of earth. They littered the floor like giant worm casts.

She whirled round as someone elbowed her roughly aside.

"Oh, shit!" Louise whispered, staring into the room and grasping the lintel for support. Her face registered horror and disbelief. Then, as though it was all too much, something appeared to snap and she began to scream. It was a terrible sound, wild and primitive and it hurt Jo's head. On and on it went, shrill and insistent until Jo struck her sharply across the cheek. Louise gasped then crumpled; Blake and Jo caught her before she sank to the ground.

"Take her up to the spare room, Blake," Jo commanded, suddenly strong. Perhaps something aimed at debilitating her had been using Louise as a channel. But there were more practical concerns to worry about. "There's spare blankets and pillows in the airing cupboard," she added as he picked up Louise as easily as if she were a child. "I'll make a start down here."

Blake shook his head emphatically. "No! Shut the door tight on it and leave it until morning."

"But the flies! The smell –," Jo protested.

"Are unreal, aren't they?" he challenged. "If they are the result of paranormal phenomena, then no amount of cleaning will solve the problem."

Jo stared at him, unconvinced but unable to counter his argument.

"And I think we've all had enough for one night," he added firmly. "It's freezing, we're shattered, and if we're to fight this thing, we need sleep."

Reluctantly Jo shut the door on the stench and the buzzing flies. At least he's half way to accepting what's going on, she thought, following Blake as he carried Louise upstairs.

That night the scratching awoke her again, was more frenzied than ever before. Blake lay beside her, his regular breathing telling her he was asleep. She tried not to think of the scene in the kitchen or admit her secret fears. The room felt like an ice storage unit. She shivered beneath the quilt and hunched up closer to Blake for warmth and comfort. He grunted and stirred but did not awake.

Antony Antony

The cottage breathed his name. It felt alive: something prowled its rooms with a palpable energy. There was a movement at the other side of the door. She raised her head off the pillow to listen, her back and stomach muscles aching with the tension. There it was again, a sound like silk rustling along the floor.

Jo pressed closer to Blake and tried in vain to sleep.

When sleep finally came, she found herself wandering in a world of desolation; a landscape of rotting carcasses and putrid decay. She screamed as a hand shot up from the ground, fingers clawed as though grasping at life itself. The flesh was grey and stinking of death. She awoke with a start, her body filmed with perspiration, even though her breath smoked in the icy temperature of the bedroom.

Let me be wrong, she silently prayed; please God, let me be wrong.

FIFTY-SIX

~

By morning the outside thermometer on the porch window was showing one and a half degrees above freezing: warm enough for more snow. It fell in fat silent flakes that mottled the windows and draped the world outside in silence. It made Jo feel they were cut off from normality and the rest of the world, she even found herself wondering if anything more existed beyond the cottage and the enclosing fells.

Louise had not yet surfaced. When Jo had poked her head round the guest room door, she was still sleeping. But fitfully, and every so often she made whimpering noises and her head moved restlessly on the pillow. Her face was deathly pale and the dressing, Jo had noted with concern, was dark with seeping blood.

The robin she had befriended fluttered at the porch window asking for food. Glancing out she saw a flock of chaffinches, blackbirds and goldfinches huddled miserably and in silence among the bare branches of trees. Moved by pity she made her way along the hall to the kitchen for some scraps, was about to open the door, but recoiled and withdrew her hand. For a moment she had forgotten the events of the previous night. Now nightmare images of slime and decay flooded back. Unwilling to check out the room on her own – Blake had gone to fetch logs from the shed and kindling to start the fire – she slipped into the sitting room and took three biscuits from the pack of digestives left from the previous night.

Standing there in snow marked only by tiny bird-arrows and a single trail of footprints to the shed, afforded Jo a blessed few moments of normality. Knowing what might lie in waiting within the cottage, she gave herself to the momentary pleasure. The robin, already tame but emboldened by hunger and drastic conditions, hopped repeatedly onto her hand for morsels of biscuit. Chaffinches, no longer silent, chattered, dived and pecked as she scattered crumbs on a space cleared in the snow. Blackbirds *chic-chic-chic'd* as they scolded, scurried and vied for food. A female lowered her head and charged, scattering the quarrelling males: an avian Boudicca in her chariot routing the Roman army, and making Jo laugh as she watched. Scattering the last of the crumbs, she stamped the snow from her boots and reluctantly went back inside.

She joined Blake in the sitting room where he was lighting the fire.

"Hi." He turned round as she entered, then frowned. "You okay, Jo?"

"Yes, didn't sleep too well. Does anything stop you sleeping?" she asked, attempting a note of levity.

He swivelled round on his heel and grinned. "Nope! Something kept you awake?"

"I had a nightmare." She shuddered at the memory. "A hand striking up out of the ground at my feet. Horrible. And it didn't make sense."

"Well they do say dreams are the answers to questions we haven't yet got round to asking."

She gave him a thoughtful look. "Yes, they are, aren't they?" was all she said.

"Have you tried the telephone this morning?" she asked minutes later. He nodded. "Still off. So is the power. Thank God for Calor gas – at least we can still make coffee."

"That rather depends on the state of the kitchen," Jo said dryly.

"We'll check it out in a minute."

"Louise needs a doctor."

"I'm going to walk to the village later and see what can be done from there," he said holding a match to the newspaper, then throwing it down and shaking his hand as the flame burned too low. "There must be a spare Land Rover somewhere."

"Don't leave us here alone, Blake!" Jo cried looking alarmed.

Blake was saved from replying by a knocking at the front door.

"What now?" Jo said with a groan, making her way down the hall.

Five minutes or so later, Jo returned with her visitors who had by now divested themselves of their snow-encrusted anoraks, scarves and hats. "This is Colin and Finola," she said to Blake, "And Dr. Cahill from the hospital," adding when Blake showed surprise at this last introduction: "apparently she arrived at Throstle Garth last night. Her car's stuck in the snow."

"*Roz,* please – I'm off duty!" Roz Cahill smiled and rubbed her hands together before holding them out to the fire which was now under way. "Hi, pleased to meet you," she added offering her hand.

"Hi, Roz. And Finola." Blake returned her greeting, and seconds later Finola's, with a nod. "Blake Durante," he supplied, adding with a wry smile, "Guess we all got caught out – my car's had it too." but Jo noted the suspicion in his eyes as he looked at Colin. "You must be the sculptor, the guy who rescued Jo the day she ran off-road."

Colin shrugged self-deprecatingly. "It was nothing."

"You were wonderfully kind," Jo protested. "I don't know what I'd have done –,"

Blake broke in without letting her finish. "Anyway – thanks mate."

Colin raised an eyebrow, as though tacitly questioning Blake's right to thank him on Jo's behalf.

"I'm grateful; you see Jo and I are a serious item," Blake said evenly.

"Oh, I see." Colin wiped his mouth with the back of his hand and turned away.

Boy talk! Jo thought with a sigh of exasperation, resenting the way Blake had so crassly staked his claim.

This was all very cosy but as yet they hadn't checked out the kitchen, she thought with an unpleasant buzz of adrenalin. Jo was about to devise some excuse for not offering tea or coffee, and therefore forestalling the need to go in there, when Finola took her by surprise.

"Jo, we've told Roz about what's been going on here," she volunteered.

"Yes. You see, I've been concerned that something was wrong from the day we met at the hospital," Roz admitted. "In fact, I was on my way here to talk to you last night when I got stuck."

Jo eyed them both in silence for a moment. "Well in that case," she said slowly, "there's something you might as well see."

She looked at Blake and he nodded; Jo led the way to the kitchen.

The mayhem within may have been due to psychic phenomena but it was all too tangible when she inched open the door.

"Shit!" Blake exclaimed, contorting his face in disgust. The odour that greeted them was truly obnoxious and akin to rotting meat on a hot summer's day. The bluebottles droned incessantly, and more had hatched from a wriggling heap of plump white maggots on the stone floor.

"Oh, my God!" Finola looked around the room, her eyes huge behind her glasses. She pressed a hand to her mouth. The colour drained from her cheeks and she rushed back along the hall. They could hear her vomiting in the bathroom.

"Has this happened before, Jo?" Colin asked, muffling his nose in the crook of his sleeve.

Jo hadn't missed the look of annoyance that flitted across Blake's face at Colin's familiarity. *Men, really!* As though things like that mattered in the face of this. She nodded. "Several times, but this is the worst."

Roz Cahill pushed up the sleeves of her sweater. "Okay. Let's get this mess cleared – then we talk, okay?"

"You don't have to –," Jo started to protest.

She smiled grimly. "I'm a doctor remember. Strong stomach – and I did my stint in the mortuary!"

Jo stared at her, visibly taken aback.

"Much worse smells than this," Roz explained as though to a child.

"Oh, yes of course." Jo smiled and shrugged apologetically. "Okay. If you're sure – well, thanks. No, not you Finola. You go and tend the fire," Jo added kindly as Finola reappeared and hovered, green round the gills, in the doorway.

Thankfully Finola nodded and disappeared.

"Bastards!" Blake marched into the room holding a rolled up newspaper and advanced upon the bluebottles. After flinging the window wide he set about the buzzing swarm. Fat black bodies dropped beneath the blows of the expertly wielded paper; survivors buzzed angrily at the window, crowding it in their eagerness to escape. Fungus and slime still dominated. Jo rolled up her sleeves and resigned herself to yet another scrape-up-and-mop session. Roz Cahill had already found a shovel under the sink, and was depositing her first load of dripping fungal decay outside the back door. Colin was scraping toadstools off the rug with a metal dust pan from the shelf.

How was all this going to end? Jo found herself worrying. The sensible thing would be to say this was not her problem and walk away from Twilight Cottage never to return. Yet even as the thought crossed her mind, she knew it wouldn't happen that way.

At last they were through. The kitchen was spotless again. Only a slight lingering odour lurked beneath the mask of disinfectant and air freshener. Nervously, Jo opened up the bread bin. Miraculously, no mould decorated the loaf within and soon they were all eating toast and drinking tea round the coffee table in the sitting room. At least all of them except Finola. She still looked pale and likely to throw up again at the slightest provocation. On Jo's orders she was propped against cushions on the sofa, sipping weak tea liberally sweetened with sugar, imposed upon her by Roz and with the stern instruction to get it down her – 'doctor's orders'.

"I feel such a bloody wimp," Finola fretted.

"No, just ultra-sensitive – there is a difference," Roz had consoled her; "The price I'm afraid for that exquisite art you produce."

Duly consoled, Finola sipped her tea and gave Roz a smile of gratitude.

"Oh my God – Louise!" Jo exclaimed suddenly so that everybody except Blake stared at her in amazement. "Ros, we have a woman upstairs in need of a doctor," Jo explained, guilt-stricken at suddenly remembering her agent. Briefly she gave Roz an account of Louise's car crash and injuries. "I'm sorry, I should have told you earlier," she apologised. "How awful: I actually forget her in that frenzy of cleaning!"

"Understandable!" Roz said dryly then stooped and picked up her bag which she had deposited beneath the table. "I'll have a look at her now."

"I'll take you to her," Jo offered, leading the way into the hall.

"Incidentally, how goes that hand of yours?" Roz inquired as she climbed the stairs behind Jo.

"Oh, on the mend," Jo said over her shoulder. "Leastways, it must be – I'd forgotten about that too!" she added with a sense of surprise.

"I'll take a look later," Roz promised as Jo tapped, paused and pushed open the door of the guest room.

"Louise." Jo touched her on the shoulder and Louise opened her eyes and looked at her in a dazed sort of way. "There's a doctor here. Her name's Roz Cahill. She's going to check you over, okay?"

"Hi, let's have a look then shall we?" Roz took Jo's place at the bedside.

"I'm okay – fuss about nothing," Louise protested, pulling herself into a sitting position.

"Just a precaution as they say," Ros said cheerfully, opening her medical bag. "Roz knows everything, Louise," Jo said from the doorway.

"Yep, spooks and all," Roz quipped unfolding her stethoscope. "Only it isn't funny, is it?" she asked, watching Louise intently.

"No." Louise glanced furtively at Jo, then swallowed nervously before moistening her lip with the tip of her tongue. "No, it isn't."

"Okay. Talk to me."

Jo left them to it and made her way back downstairs, wondering as she went how Louise would play it today – as believer or sceptic.

"Right – council of war," Blake said grimly, pushing aside his cup. "It seems we're all in this now, so I'd better fill you in on what's been happening here. Then Jo can tell her side. Okay?"

"Fine by me," Roz entered the room and sat down after Jo patted the seat of an adjacent chair.

"How's Louise?" Jo asked tensely before Blake could begin.

"She'll be fine. I've cleaned the wound and put in a couple of stitches. I've also applied a fresh dressing. You two did all the right things though last night," she said looking at Blake then back at Jo, who let out a sigh of relief and poured some coffee before handing Roz the cup. She poured tea into another cup and placed two slices of toast on a side plate. "I'll just take this up to Louise – if she's allowed that is."

"Fine by me. She's shocked more than anything," Roz added stirring her coffee. "I've told her to rest up for today. I suppose she told you what happened last night?"

Jo paused in the doorway. "Yes, she did."

"You believe it?"

Jo nodded. "We've all had bizarre experiences Roz."

"Which brings us back to my suggestion of a de-briefing session," Blake said, looking inquiringly from one face to another.

Everyone nodded or verbally agreed to his proposed plan.

Blake waited for Jo to return, then proceeded to relate Seth's pursuit of Jo and his subsequent death. As he finished, Jo noted the way his eyes held the gaze of Roz Cahill. It seemed she understood some tacit message and made no comment about Seth's death or the exhumation of Maud.

"How awful," Finola whispered, reaching for Colin's hand.

"What happens to him now?" Colin demanded, addressing the practicalities.

"I'll take Roz down to the church yard; she can certify the death." Blake said smoothly.

Roz looked about to speak, but as Blake gave her a hard stare, desisted.

"What about the police? And won't there have to be a coroner?" Colin persisted.

Blake ran a hand through his hair and sighed. "With the 'phones still out, we have to make do with what we have – which is an in-house doctor," he added wryly.

"Shouldn't somebody let the vicar know about poor Maud?" Finola looked round at them all. "He might walk down to the church and get an awful shock."

"Come off it Fin!" Colin protested.

Dear gentle Finola! Jo suppressed a smile, and was nearly undone when Blake caught her eye and Roz made a comical grimace. She could just imagine telling John Penrose about the open grave and his dead parishioner, and imagine his expression of horror, hear him saying: *I knew you were trouble the day we met!* On a serious note, did Fin have any idea of the danger they all still faced? In fact had it occurred to anyone other than herself that they were marooned here, at the mercy of psychic energies? Anything might happen once darkness fell. "I shouldn't worry about the vicar Fin, we'll sort something out later," Jo said reassuringly, whilst Colin looked up at the ceiling in exasperation at Finola's innocence.

"I'll walk back to Throstle Garth for the Land Rover," Colin offered. "And I can call in at the police station whilst I'm at it," he added with a defiant look at Blake.

"Do nothing please, until we get back," Blake said shortly.

Jo recognised the Conflict Resolution Officer speaking, the voice he used over the telephone when dealing with a recalcitrant party. He rose to his feet, effectively bringing discussion to an end.

"Why? Why is all this happening to us?" Finola asked, shaking her head.

"I may be wrong, but I have the feeling," Jo said thoughtfully as Blake and Roz moved to the door, "that we have been brought together for a purpose."

"Like what?" Colin asked bluntly, his feathers still ruffled from Blake's rebuff.

Jo hesitated, feeling it might be time to voice her worst sus-picion, then deciding against it simply said: "I don't know, Col. I don't know."

She had the feeling however that they would soon find out.

FIFTY-SEVEN

~

The turbulence as they walked through the front door caught Blake by surprise. When he and Roz had looked out from within the cottage the trees had hardly been moving, now they lashed the air with their limbs like Solti conducting Wagner's *Ring*. "Oh!" Roz exclaimed in surprise and clutched at his arm as they were rocked on their feet. The snow had stopped falling, but gave the illusion that it hadn't: the hurricane-force whipped it up and tossed it into the air like confetti. It whirled around them sticking to their clothes and eyelashes, blurring their vision. Blake grabbed her and they clung together waiting for a lull. The wind howled as though in rage, and branches whipped with a sound like metal flails, sending snow cascading in all directions. It brought to mind *Clash of the Titans*, a film he had seen when a boy. After thinking about it a moment he realised why: this tumult resembled a clash of wills. He could actually feel the conflict between two opposing forces. Fear, absent on the Bosnian battlefields, now crawled around his innards. No amount of scepticism would come to his rescue today, this wasn't Jo's account but his own experience. He could feel intent, *personalities* even, behind the elements, rather than blind Nature. He had no option but to believe.

Roz broke away then turned round to shout something to him, but the wind snatched away the words from her open mouth.

HATE ANGER FOREVER . . .

The wind screamed words of its own. A grating sound above his head made Blake look up in time to see slates hurtling down the roof. "Roz!" he yelled. The wind drowned his words. He leapt forward, arms outstretched and his hands struck the middle of her back. She gasped involuntarily and pitched forward onto the snow with Blake on top. One of the slates thudded into the snow end-on, embedded to the half-way mark at the exact spot where Roz had been standing. He rolled off her back. She turned and gave him a startled look, but on seeing the slate, one that also said 'Thanks, mate' before struggling to her feet.

"Somebody doesn't want us to leave," he mouthed. "Feel it?"

Ros shrugged and spread her hands; her words were whirled away in the maelstrom.

"Shall we try and make it back inside?" he shouted.

Roz shook her head emphatically and pointed down the track in the direction of the lane.

He gave the thumbs up sign, admiring her courage as he did so. Head down and shoulders hunched against the blast, Roz inched forward and Blake followed.

The mini-blizzard was localised thus confirming his analysis that something or someone wanted them confined to the cottage. Once clear of the building the wind mysteriously dropped and snow was no longer whipped up like flakes in one of those glass domes when they are shaken. In fact a sinister calm had settled over the countryside. It was too still, too quiet. Waiting. That's how it felt, Blake decided. There was an understated air of suspense and something waiting around the proverbial corner.

"I've heard of micro-climates but this is ridiculous!" Roz joked, indicating the tranquillity of the trees as they turned from the track into the lane. He saw her look of speculation as she glanced at the rucksack on his shoulders, but she did not question him, and he didn't volunteer an explanation.

As they came to the lych gate Blake placed a hand on her arm. "Look, I know you're a doctor – but just be prepared," he warned her quietly.

"No problem. You wouldn't believe the things I've seen." She opened the gate and led the way. The crunch of crisp snow under-foot was the only sound to be heard. The yew trees watched in snow-laden silence as they passed beneath.

Even so she winced but did not look away as they stood by the grave. The crows had not wasted time. Seth's empty sockets stared up at them from a face encrusted with dried blood.

"Okay?" Blake asked, touching her arm.

Roz nodded. "At least the intensely low temperature has halted decomposition. Now," she turned to face him squarely. "It's time you told me what you have in mind."

Blake shrugged. "I think for now we should settle for cosmetic measures."

"Such as?"

"Moving Seth into the church for a start."

"He shouldn't really be touched," Roz said severely. "There'll have to be a post mortem and enquiry. Suspicious circumstances and all that."

"We don't know how long the 'phones are going to be off, or the cold snap is going to last." Blake reasoned. "And it'll freeze again tonight. Even if we summon help, no-one will get through. And we won't be able to move Seth without breaking all his bones."

Roz's eyelids flickered, her sole concession to distaste. "Colin reckons he'll get through in the Land Rover."

"He can try."

"You don't think he'll make it?"

Blake ruffled his hair with his fingers. "Who can say? I don't know anything any more. We're not dealing with ordinary forces here. In the meantime, this is pretty obscene. I suggest we get him out and you as a medical officer certify that he is dead. Then we put him out of the way before the rest of the local fauna come to the banquet," Blake finished dispassionately.

"What about a coroner."

"Leave the coroner to me."

"And the police?" Roz by now was looking distinctly suspicious.

"Leave them to me too."

Roz folded her arms and confronted him with a stubborn look on her face. "I have legal and moral duties and don't want to find myself struck off!"

"You won't be; you have my word."

She surveyed him for a moment through narrowed eyes. "Ok, so just who are you Blake?" she demanded.

Wordlessly, he put his hand into his inside pocket and drew out an I.D. card.

Roz's eyebrows went up. "In with the Big Brass, eh?"

Blake shrugged. "So let's get this over with. It's pretty dam' ugly," he indicated the open grave and its two occupants, "– and unnecessary. Jo has been through enough. She can do without police crawling over the cottage and their interminable questions. So can I. Seth walked down here *after* she hit him. Jo didn't kill him. And they're hardly likely to be able to prosecute whatever did," he said dryly.

Roz was regarding him with a dubious expression. "You could have *this little lot* kept quiet?"

"You'd be surprised what governments will cover up when it suits them," Blake assured her with a cynical smile. "Remember Roswell?"

She frowned. "That was the U.S. – not a no-nonsense British Government!"

"No difference when it comes down to it," Blake replied cynically.

"There's no aliens involved here."

"No, just a phantom hawk that attacks and kills, and a cottage that stinks and spontaneously sprouts mushrooms overnight," Blake taunted.

Roz sighed. "Okay. Even if that's true, why should they cover up this case?"

"I'm on a couple of day's leave from Bosnia. My brief is to keep a low profile. Can you imagine the headlines if this got out? *Grave Robbing and Satanic Rites in Lakeland Backwater – Top Bosnian Mediator Now Being Questioned: Girlfriend on Murder Charge.* They won't want me within fifty miles of Bosnia after that. No my dear Roz," he concluded satirically, "they won't want me at the hub of any sensational media hype – there's too much at stake in terms of world peace. And with talks underway, for the moment I'm indispensable."

"Well, this is hardly a 'low profile vacation'; I should think your

Big Brass won't be very happy with you anyway!" Roz said with smile.

He gave her a sidelong look. "They never are."

"Then how come you still have so much pull?" Roz demanded.

"I'm good at my job," he said simply.

Roz was silent for a moment, then gave a sigh of resignation. "Okay – I'm probably risking being struck off, but let's get this thing over."

He gave her a look that said *Thank God for that; lady – you're hard work,* and slid the rucksack from his shoulders. He sensed her curiosity, felt her gaze on his back as he unbuckled the straps and pulled out the waterproof sheeting, portable stretcher and leather straps.

"Ah. I did wonder – thought you were planning on a hike," she quipped as he straightened up. Her eyes met his and Blake smiled.

"Pot-holing is more in my line," he said, glancing at the hole that gaped at his feet.

Amity was restored.

His face devoid of expression he eased himself into the grave, carefully placing his feet at either side of Seth's body and wedging them against the rim of the coffin. He forced himself not to dwell on Maud's macabre grin of welcome as he bent to grasp Seth's shoulders. Good, he wasn't yet frozen to the ground, and thanks to the cold the stench was bearable. After some painstaking manoeuvres the dead man's feet protruded. "Grab his ankles and heave on the word," he instructed.

Roz bent and did as he bid. A small sound escaped her as Seth's sightless and mutilated face appeared at the edge of the grave.

"You're doing just fine," Blake encouraged.

Thankfully he replaced the lid on Maud's coffin and climbed out.

Some ten minutes later they had Seth wrapped in the sheeting and secured with the straps. Blake unwrapped the portable stretcher and raising his hand indicated he would only be five minutes or so. He returned with two stout branches which he proceeded to strip of twigs before running them through the loops on the stretcher. "Okay, take his feet again."

They eased him onto the stretcher and between them, carried him into the church.

"That feels better," Roz said with a sigh of relief as Blake closed the door of the church.

"Maud's grave now, then we can make our way back to the cottage." Blake said, leading the way.

"Shan't be too sorry," Roz muttered as she followed. He turned; she was shivering and her breath stained the air white as it rose. Despite their recent exertions he noticed her lips were turning blue with cold. "You've earned yourself a large whisky when we get back," he said with an encouraging grin.

"Aye, cap'n." Roz raised her hand in mock salute.

The spade, half buried in snow, was still lying where Seth had dropped it on the night of his death. Blake dug it out with his hands and prepared to replace the mound of earth removed from the grave by Seth. "Another freezing night and we'd have no chance," he remarked, spade poised to strike.

He brought the spade down and it rang against the hard red earth beneath the snow. The shock of impact buzzed along his arms, up his legs and through his spine. Simultaneously a shrill scream sounded from the yews and a dark arrowhead streaked their way.

Roz screamed and the shrieking reached a crescendo. Blake raised the shovel again and prepared for a second strike. The hawk swooped at his head, its wing tips grazing his forehead. Roz leapt forward to fend off the attack.

"Bastard!" Blake swiped at the bird which swerved with ease. The screeching rose higher and the beating of wings sounded in his ears. Blake slashed at the air with the spade; the bird swooped. A yellow eye flecked with black met his in challenge. The beak gaped, so close that he could see the pointed red tongue and livid throat. It hovered, apparently without moving and the gaze of that yellow eye bored into his brain. Time stood still. The shovel dropped from his nerveless fingers. The hawk rose on a powerful downbeat and swerved back into the yews.

Blake became aware of Roz. She was trembling and her face was ashen. "It's okay," he soothed, taking her arm and pulling her to him. He held her shaking body close to his until he felt the tremors receding. "Okay?" he said again, holding her at arms length and scrutinising her face.

She nodded and managed a bleak smile. "God, what a wimp you must think me!"

He shook his head. "Remember what you told Finola!" he admonished. "I was shit-scared myself there – only a fool wouldn't have been."

Roz placed her arms across her chest and hugged herself; he wondered if it was to do with the cold or something else. "I guess."

"I know so. In fact I've had enough; let's get back to the cottage."

"Thanks for being kind."

"Bullshit."

Their eyes met briefly.

"Jo's one lucky lady," Roz said softly.

"Do me a favour – tell her!" He squeezed her arm then released her.

Roz smiled. "She probably already knows. But has things she must do. I know – I've been there."

He shrugged. "I guess."

They walked from the grave in silence.

Roz turned to him at the lych gate. He saw that her eyes were troubled.

"What is it?" he asked gently.

"That bird. It didn't want us to fill the grave," Roz said in a low voice.

Blake said nothing, but as they stepped into the lane, cast a look back.

A dark speck perched at the top of the largest yew watched them depart.

FIFTY-EIGHT

~

A thin plume of smoke curled into the air filling the glade with its pungent peaty aroma. Justin St. Clair's face was implacable as he watched them wrap his wife in the pitch-coated shrouds. An inner one, then an outer one just to be sure. Her body was limp, her eyes shut. He held up his hand. All activity stopped. He stood perfectly still, looking upon her beauty for the very last time. He lowered his arm. A fold of the shroud was laid over her face. His chief man-at-arms looked across at him for confirmation. He nodded for him to proceed to the next stage.

The men lifted Madeline and placed her in the coffin. A cruel smile twisted Justin's lips. They had been forced to flex their muscles when they brought it down off the cart and onto the metal straps. A heavy coffin. One made of lead. He watched as they heaved the lid into place. He nodded again, and the blacksmith kneeling by the hastily kindled fire approached with the soldering iron. Justin thought then that he would never forget the smell of molten lead as the smith sealed the joints. It must always for him mark this instant, resurrect for him not so much his wife's eyes, the sound of her voice, the mane of chestnut hair – but the moment they were sealed off from him and the world for ever. He lifted his hand one more time. The men moved forward and carried the coffin to the freshly-dug grave. He nodded, and they lowered it down by the strips of metal, their faces red with exertion as they strained against the weight.

He stepped forward then and took a shovel from his captain. Digging deep in the pile of displaced earth, he dropped first soil on Madeline.

"Fill it in," he commanded, throwing down the shovel.

Still he couldn't leave. Not until the mound was completed, then covered with brushwood and dead leaves.

Then and only then did he mount his horse and ride like a demon from hell.

Back to Barrowburn Castle.

Back to his new love. The woman who would soon be his wife.

Jo glanced at the clock and felt a surge of anxiety at the pit of her stomach: Blake and Roz had been gone some time. She rubbed her forearm.

"Worried about darling Blake and our attractive young lady doctor, sweetheart?" Louise jibed from the couch where she now regally reclined.

"Don't be silly." Jo denied the urge to go to the window and look out yet again.

Louise really was being a pain in the backside. But then tension was mounting all round, she worried. Colin was still complaining to Finola about what he described as Blake's high-handedness. She could hear him now from where he was lounging in the corner by the window, threatening to go for help in the Land Rover.

"I can be there and back before that domineering bastard even shows." His whispering had risen in volume along with his indignation.

"How do we know they'll be back?"

Jo glanced at Louise and noted the look of anxiety flit over the other woman's face. "Stow it Colin," Jo commanded. "You know Blake said to do nothing – and he *will* be back!" The very air in the cottage prickled her skin, she thought uneasily.

"That guy has an attitude problem," Colin said darkly.

"I doubt it: it's his job not to have," Jo snapped back.

"Yes well he's off-duty now."

"Don't be childish, Col."

To Jo's surprise it was Finola who had spoken.

"They're here now," Colin begrudgingly reported about five minutes later. "Just coming up the path."

Jo gave him a look that said 'told you so' and was waiting in the hall as Blake opened the door and entered the cottage followed by Roz. "Are you alright?"

Blake nodded and gave her a brief kiss after stamping the snow from his shoes on the mat.

"All taken care of," Roz said in a too-hearty manner.

"Yep," Blake added, "Seth's in the church; the coffin is covered."

"Buried again you mean," Jo said looking relieved. The whole business of that open grave had worried her since it happened.

Blake shrugged. "Well not exactly – but we did replace the lid. And the others don't need to know the details," he said in an undervoice.

"Especially Finola," Roz whispered, looking at the sitting room door as if she thought Finola might hear. "It may prey on her mind."

"So why didn't you –?" Jo stopped in mid-sentence, noting their expressions. "What happened?" she added swiftly.

"It seems somebody didn't want us to fill in the grave," Roz added.

Jo grabbed his arm in alarm. "What's been going on Blake?"

"The hawk," he said laconically. Then added as Jo opened her mouth to fire more questions at him: "Again, least said and the better, I think. Now shall we go in? I've promised Roz here a very large whisky."

They all had one. Blake laced their coffee with it and they sat huddled around the sitting room fire whilst he gave them a very expurgated version of how they had arranged things down at the graveyard.

"I still think we ought to try and get the police," Colin said stubbornly, rising and going into the hall. Jo guessed he had gone to check the telephone. Sure enough she heard him drop the receiver noisily back on its cradle. "Damn' thing's still off," he complained on his return. "I'm going to get the Land Rover."

"I'd be careful out there, if I were you," Blake said, rising to his feet. "Something seems hell bent on stopping us from leaving. In fact, I'll come with you."

"Don't bother," Colin said rudely. "I can manage."

Jo glared at him. "Colin, what's got into you?"

"Male ego, darling," Louise drawled from the sofa, where she was intent on dragooning 'Dr. Blake' into stroking her temples. "Must be very edifying for you!"

"Oh shut up, Louise!" Jo snapped, exasperated.

Louise subsided on her cushions with an injured air, and gave Blake a martyred look.

Colin banged the door shut behind him and trudged off down the lane. There. Nothing had tried to stop him. What a load of bollocks; the whole thing was getting out of proportion. He for one wasn't wholly convinced about this 'restless spirit' nonsense. He just didn't buy it; ten to one there'd be a rational explanation.

His optimism and mood of pure bolshiness were reinforced when he reached Throstle Garth and the Land Rover started first time. There, no problem. He peered through the windscreen, taking a moment to appreciate white-latticed trees, crags sculpted in ice and noble foothills draped in ermine, the tops of dry stone walls tracing the broken black edging. Bloody inconvenient this weather, but the beauty of it was something else. In fact it was giving him ideas for a new set of winter sculptures. Yes, about time he got back to work, instead of brooding on all this mumbo jumbo. The fantasy-bubble that had briefly contained Jo, beautiful woman and famous writer had burst. Enjoyable whilst it lasted, but it was hard to convincingly fantasise after seeing the way Jo looked at Blake Durante. Lucky bastard. He throttled up and guided the Land Rover onto the lane, the wheels crunching over the pristine snow, the smoke from the exhaust staining the air with a faint trail of blue.

He was tempted to carry straight on, out of the valley and to the main road, but decided he had better return to the cottage and ask if supplies were needed whilst he was out. Besides, it would be good to crow a little over that big shot Blake Durante; let him know he had made it, was on the road – and that "he who has jeep is Top Dog!" Thank God for four wheel drive, he thought as the vehicle made light work of the snow-covered lane.

He parked outside the cottage, looked up as he walked across the snow to the front door. There was a strange sort of stillness in the air. It was too quiet. The sort of feeling that made your neck tingle just above your collar. He glanced up again. Odd. No crows, no rooks circling the trees. No wind bending their branches either. That had dropped as if by magic: the thin plume of smoke rose straight from the chimney and hovered as though held upright on an invisible string before dispersing. No snow falling. No movement of any kind. Just this sense of waiting. But perhaps he was just being fanciful, he thought, opening the front door.

Colin saw the flicker of annoyance pass over Blake Durante's features as he announced his plan. "Does anyone want anything from the village store then?" he asked for the second time. Jo looked about to speak, then glanced across at Blake and fell silent.

Blake looked deceptively pleasant, but Colin knew he was fuming by the way he ruffled his hair in that gesture of irritation.

"It's not a good idea to go to the police, Colin," Blake said in a tone that implied he was doing his best to control his temper.

"There's a local man dead down there, for God's sake! And an open grave! Maud isn't exactly at peace, is she?"

"I've told you: Seth is decent and inside the church; Maud is not on display."

"That's hardly the point!" Colin shouted.

"Precisely. The point is I've asked you not to interfere," Blake snapped.

"And who in shit's name do you think you are then?"

"Look, I'm in a position to deal with this; I'm not at liberty to say more."

"Bullshit! I'm going for the police right now! It's ridiculous being held here – prisoners of our own imagination."

Before Blake or the others could stop him, Colin marched back along the hall to the front door.

He was aware of Blake watching him from the sitting room window, of Jo standing at his side. Silly cow, he thought angrily, what the hell did she see in him? His breathing came quick, and his heart thumped in response to the surge of adrenalin. He checked his pace, momentarily taken aback by the violence of his feelings. He walked on down the path to the Land Rover, his hands clenched into fists as he imagined punching holes in Blake Durante's confidence, cool bastard that he was.

He frowned and quickened his pace. He could feel his anger swirling around him, a tangible thing with a force of its own. It writhed free of his body in coils, a black serpent that poisoned the air, choking him with its venom. At the same time a wind arose, and struck as though summoned by a shaman's staff. It howled and shrieked around him, tugging at his clothes and almost tearing the hair from his head. Snow was falling again. Fat white flakes swirling and eddying, blown into fantastic shapes by the wind. He hesitated, unsure of what to do. The Land Rover was thirty yards or so away, the front door of the cottage less. But Blake Durante was still watching from the window, and he would look a fool if he backed down now. No choice but to go on.

He reeled as the wind and driven snow buffeted him, first tugging then pulling, like a living thing in conflict, unable to make up its mind. He staggered towards the Range Rover then stopped. Nothing less than a blizzard was raging now. It whirled snow in a spiralling column that shifted and seemed to take on substance as he watched.

LOVE . . . KILL . . . FOREVER

The wind screamed words that hurt his ears and scrambled his brain. The column of snow rose, subsided a little then changed shape yet again, bringing to mind those transparent lamps with blobs of wax that metamorphosed in response to heat. He gasped and felt the shock of adrenalin coursing through his body as the shape became briefly fixed. As in a Turner painting, the form was blurred at the edges but the features were distinct: the straight nose, the square chin and the angry line of the mouth. And then eyes like green chips of ice that watched him with unblinking stare. "*Christ!*" Colin had a brief impression of a red hawk on a white tunic before the snow swirled again and the figure disappeared.

Simultaneously he noticed a trickle of blue smoke had begun to seep from beneath the Land Rover's bonnet. He started forward, his shoulders hunched and back bent against the blast. The smoke increased and turned black. A tongue of flame licked from beneath the bonnet. He watched fascinated as it flickered and grew, knew he should move but found he could not. The explosion was deafening. The force of the blast threw him into the air and onto his back.

FIFTY-NINE

~

Blake had reached the front door even as Jo returned to the window. "Oh, my God!" she cried, causing Finola and Roz to rush to her side.

"Col!" Finola screamed, her hand going to her mouth.

Roz snatched up her medical bag and dashed to the door to join Blake. Jo watched from the window as he ran, sliding and slipping, across the snow to Colin's side. She pushed Finola down on the settee with terse instructions for Louise to 'look after her,' and followed the others outdoors.

"Stay back!" Blake yelled, turning to address her over his shoulder.

Jo held her breath as she watched from a distance of several yards. Placing his forearms beneath Colin's armpits he dragged him clear of the blazing Land Rover. Roz reached his side and knelt to take Colin's pulse. "He's still with us," she breathed, pushing back on the balls of her feet and rocking to and fro with relief. Raising her hand to Jo she gave the 'thumbs up' sign.

"Thank God! But is he badly burned?" Jo asked anxiously, joining them and staring down at Colin's blackened face and singed hair. His eyes were closed and he lay unmoving.

"I suspect not. But I'll know better once I take a proper look," Roz answered. As she was speaking she scooped up handfuls of snow and placed them over the exposed skin. "It's vital to cool the skin immediately," she explained, seeing Jo's questioning look. "I'm pretty sure the damage is superficial, but surface burns can be painful, and intense pain can result in shock, which can be fatal."

A voice reached them on the clear air. "Oh God, what's happened?"

Jo spun round to see Finola clinging to the door jamb and looking distraught. "Col? Col! Finola's voice was rising, balancing on the edge of hysteria as she began to flounder towards them.

"Look, go and reassure Finola will you?" Roz said tersely.

Jo hurried towards her and placing an arm round Finola's shoulders turned her round and led her indoors. "Don't worry Fin," she soothed. "Roz will sort him out."

Roz stood up and turned to Blake who had cracked the ice which skinned the water butt and was busy dousing the Land Rover. "Let's get him inside."

Between them they carried Colin into the cottage.

"He's going to be okay," Roz assured a distressed Finola, whilst gently sponging Colin's face with a lint-free cotton cloth rung out in ice water. "His pulse, heart rate and blood pressure are all fine. And thankfully, this scorching is superficial, caused by heat-blast rather than contact with actual flames. The blackening as you see, is mostly smoke." She held up the stained cloth for Finola to inspect. Nonetheless, patches of reddened and shiny skin appeared on his forehead, nose and right cheekbone.

The pain of her ministrations must have penetrated his consciousness because he winced and his eyelids flickered open. "What the –?"

He tried to rise, but Roz eased him back onto the cushions of the settee, graciously vacated by Louise.

"It's alright, Col – take it easy."

He looked at her with a dazed expression. "What happened?"

Roz grinned as she rung out the cloth again in the iced water. "You blew up the Land Rover with your temper!"

"Oh, very humorous," Colin grumbled, wincing.

"Hurting?" Roz asked, holding the wet cloth over his forehead.

"Just a bit," Colin said ironically.

"Good!"

"Gee thanks!"

"It means the burns are superficial, not deep. No damage to the nerve endings. If there was, you wouldn't feel anything," Roz explained whilst carefully applying a colourless gel.

"What's that?" Finola asked, leaning forward to look.

"Aloe Vera gel." Roz said over her shoulder, then turned back to address Colin again. "Wonderful stuff. It heals quickly without pain."

"I'm all for that," Colin sighed, briefly closing his eyes.

"Have a couple of sips of water, then rest. You've had a shock."

"I'm alright" Don't fuss *doctor*."

Roz grinned. "You'll do. Finola, take my place; you'll feel better if you're doing something. Give him frequent sips of water, okay?"

She relinquished her seat and Finola sat down.

"Bad jokes apart, what *did* cause the thing to explode?" Colin asked, looking up first at Roz then at Blake who had entered the room with a tray of coffee.

"I've no idea," Roz said, patently uneasy.

Blake shook his head, put down the tray and shrugged. "Sorry, mate – can't help there."

Colin went to stroke his forehead but being painfully reminded of his burns, winced and dropped his hand. He frowned and looked past them as though striving to piece together a mental jigsaw. "I remember now. It was *him*," he whispered. "I *saw him*. I actually saw him this time," he said raising his voice and becoming agitated. "He did it. I don't know how, or why – *but he did it*."

"Okay, honey. Rest now," Finola soothed, taking his hand.

Colin let his head fall back on the cushions, but didn't close his eyes.

Jo poured coffee and handed around a plate piled with slabs of bread and cheese. After taking a cup and a sandwich to Finola, and one to Louise who was now ensconced in the easy chair by the fire, she sat down at the sitting room table with Roz and Blake. "That's all the vehicles out of action. And both Louise and Colin too, by the look of it," she said in an undervoice.

"What are you two whispering about?" Louise called petulantly.

"We're just discussing the weather forecast, and our stock of provisions," Jo lied unashamedly. The last thing she wanted was a panic situation. No good would be served by everyone running around like headless chickens.

"You're telling me porkie pies!" Louise accused, leaning forward on her chair. "You don't have newspapers delivered and there's no power for radio – so how the hell can you get the weather forecast?"

"I have a small portable radio upstairs; it runs off batteries," Jo said quickly, glancing out of the window at the lowering brownish sky. "And there's more snow on the way."

This masterly piece of deception earned Jo amused and admiring glances from Roz and Blake. Louise snorted and went back to drinking her coffee.

"So what do we do?" Jo asked, looking to Blake for guidance.

"I go on foot for help, I guess."

"You won't be allowed to," Jo said simply.

Blake paused, coffee cup halfway to his lips. "What?"

"Haven't you got it yet? He has us all back here again. We won't be allowed to leave until we do what he wants. And don't," she said fixing him with a hard look, "insult me by asking 'who'. All of us here now know the score – whether we choose to acknowledge it openly or not."

"Okay, so what is that? Just what are we expected to do?" Roz intervened.

Jo looked down at her cup. "That joke of yours – about Colin's temper causing the Land Rover to explode," she evaded, "well I don't think you were far off the mark. I think our energies are being used by the psychic entities involved. Especially our anger and other strong emotions."

To her gratification, Blake instead of decrying her idea, nodded in agreement. "We're feeding them, both Justin St. Clair and Antony Chase."

"But for *what*?" Roz repeated, looking exasperated.

Jo shrugged. "My guess is that Antony Chase wants to keep us here for some purpose, but one that doesn't suit Justin St. Clair."

"But have you any idea what this thing might be?" Roz persisted with a frown.

Jo pushed back her chair and stood up. "I need a breath of air," she said quickly to avoid answering.

"Where are you off to?" Louise's voice demanded as Jo went to the hall door.

"Just stretching my legs." She had felt an initial stab of annoyance at Louise's patronising attitude, but then recognised the fear lurking beneath her words. She saw too the way her fingers – scarlet nail polish showing unprecedented chips and white specks of nail at the tips – continually plucked at the blanket which covered her knees.

"I'll come with you," Blake said, preparing to leave the table.

Jo raised one hand to forestall him. "No thanks. I need to be alone."

She left the room before he could argue.

Jo shivered despite having donned her boots and duffel coat with a fleece-lined hood. Her body grew warmer as she climbed the fell at the back of Twilight Cottage. She stopped on the ridge from where she had watched Maud's funeral cortège. And now Seth too was dead. His mutilated body was lying down there in the church behind that screen of dark yews. And more perhaps to come before the night was out. "What do you want of me, Antony?" she said softly. "Stop being angry for a while, and tell me."

A dark speck circled the chimneys of the cottage below.

She watched for a moment then breathed deeply and looked about her, freeing her mind of the claustrophobic atmosphere of the cottage. Always isolated, the surrounding fells and valley now seemed desolate in their emptiness. The sun, a huge red disc about to dip behind a bank of sepia cloud, scored snow-covered fields with livid bars of orange and crimson. Like bars on a shield, or a stained glass window: the thought arose spontaneously in her mind. A window adorned with the jewel-tints of heraldic device. As she watched the last sliver of sun slip behind its shroud, a haunting cry tugged at her heart. Instead of aggression it conveyed a terrible yearning. Overhead the hawk circled, and in its slow motion arcing and soaring, the occasional wing-stroke of air currents, the lonely tilt of body, Jo sensed the same desperate pathos, the same heart-rending plea.

By the time she reached the garden, the first stars had been tossed like tinsel from a careless hand and arranged by fate into perfect symmetry. Standing there alone, Jo felt the pull. Her head swam, and she swayed on her feet as though to some timeless rhythm, pulled by currents more powerful than any she had previously known.

The wood, the cottage, the garden with its back-drop of fell all exerted their presence, made known to her their indescribable mystery and sadness. She wandered through a crystal maze, tracing the path of the beck which even when skinned with ice, seemed always to murmur his name. Pain lurked with woodlice under boulders; betrayal hung from limp leaves and the frosted spines of the Judas tree in the shrubbery. Anger smothered the stagnant pool, oiling its surface with petrol blues and greens, reflecting the tear-streaked sky of the dying day. But there was unbearable tenderness too. Love languished in aching shadows and begged for her intervention.

"Alright Antony: I'll try," she whispered, having known for some time what must be done. Absurd, that she should also feel this twinge of envy, a spurt of jealousy towards an unknown wraith called Madeline St. Clair. Overhead the hawk mewed, a soft note of supplication, a sound more fitting perhaps to its prey. A sound that found its echo in Jo's heart.

As she made her way to the back door, the first snowflakes speckled the night.

SIXTY

~

It was dark. Pitch black. Why was there no chink of light? Never had there been darkness like this. So dense was it that it stuck in her throat and choked her lungs. Slowly Madeline came to her senses, became aware of a clinging sensation over the skin of her face. Something covered her head. Still stunned, she tried to raise her arm to remove whatever it was but failed. Something was restricting her limbs, preventing her from moving. The darkness was suffocating, the lack of sound unnerving and absolute. An unnatural silence. The silence of the grave.

"NO!" Her cry was strangled in her throat, muffled by her bindings – her winding sheet – as the realisation hit her with the physical force of Justin's blow. "NO!" Even he could not be fiend enough for this. Fear crawled over her then, a living breathing thing with fingers of ice that plucked at her flesh.

An explosion of fear and energy lent her the strength to rip the linen and claw her hands free of the shroud. Oh Dear God! Her nails scraped along the metal lid as she tore the cloth from her face and screamed. She thought of the earth pressing down upon her, felt its weight and screamed again. And she had failed to save William! She would die this terrible death in vain. Some other woman would rear her son. Better that William too had died, rather than have his love poisoned over the years by his mother's murderer and his wench. It was all horribly clear to her now. She had let Antony die thinking she had betrayed him in order to save a son whose soul was already lost She screamed until there was no more air.

Her frantic clawing slowed then stopped. Her fingers were warm and wet, her nails jagged and broken. Her breath came in gasps, like that of a landed fish on the deck, tore at her chest like a grappling hook. There was nothing else in her world now but pain, that and the fruitless fighting for breath. Let Death come soon; nothing could save her now. And a curse on you Justin St. Clair. May worms eat your body whilst you still live, and maggots writhe in your head as I writhe now in my pain. And may they bring torment and nightmares to feed your worse fears until we meet again. Then I shall see you in hell.

But there was not long left and her soul should not leave in bitterness and fury. Her tortured thoughts returned to her dead lover. Oh how we loved; and how much I love thee still. Would his spirit ever forgive her? Would he ever know the truth?

"Antony."

She sighed his name with her last breath.

Jo entered the cottage and stripped off her outdoor clothes. The snow beyond the windows glowed with a bluish-violet tinge. Someone had lit a night light and left it in the hall beneath a glass globe for safety. Something made her turn. Shadows crept down the stairs and pressed against her back. She paused before the kitchen door. It was shut. Noiselessly she pushed it open. The glow from the night light filtered in, sufficient for her to see that the room was as clean and normal-looking as they had left it.

She shivered and hugged her arms: there was a cold spot in here. Was she mad? she worried contemplating what lay ahead. A shadow rustled in the corner, which was crazy of course because shadows can't *rustle*. But this one did, and there it was again. The swishing of silk or some other material. Her gaze swept the room. Nobody there, just a shadow lurking and watching.

Antony Antony

The breathy whisper crept around the hall.

She gave a little cry and spun round, heart thumping as the door to the sitting room opened. Candle in hand, Colin stood on the threshold. "I was just about to come looking for you." He was holding the candlestick low, and lit from beneath his face took on an ugly look. As Jo watched, the features changed.

Justin Justin

His lips twisted in a cruel half-smile. "Come here."

Fear crawled over her skin. "No!" she backed away from him until her spine was pressed against the wall. The cold was such that it penetrated her sweater and chilled her shoulder blades.

Colin slowly advanced. "Where have you been?"

He was blocking the way to the sitting room where the others were gathered. Not for a moment taking her eyes from his, Jo edged along the wall to the front door. I have to get out of here, was all she could think.

The temperature in the hall had plummeted; her teeth were chattering with fear and cold. Colin was smiling as he advanced but the smile didn't reach his eyes. They were cold and hard, the eyes of the sadist. This wasn't Colin, she realised; this was a stranger who even smelled different, a sort of woody musk of a scent that emanated from his clothes as he moved. A scent that she had never detected on Colin. One that contained oils brought back from the Holy Land by a crusader? By Justin St. Clair? She tried to scream but it came out as a whisper. "Stay away from me!" The urge to flee the cottage became overwhelming.

In slow motion she reached for the latch.

"Stop!" He put the candle down on the hall stand and the shadows leapt grotesquely over wall and ceiling. "You've been with *him*, haven't you?"

Jo only just heard the words, he had spoken in a malevolent undervoice.

"Colin, don't be –," she started to say.

"You have, haven't you," he interrupted in that same sibilant whisper, "go on, admit it."

"Colin?" a male voice demanded. The door opened revealing a wedge of light that spilled into the darkened hall. "Or is it you Jo?"

Blake stood framed in the doorway. Colin spun round, snarled like an enraged beast, then lunged as though to grab Jo by the throat.

"Leave her alone you bastard!" Blake launched himself at Colin.

Jo screamed as Colin turned and they grappled like Cumberland wrestlers, then Colin drew back his arm. The sound of his fist making contact with Blake's jaw made Jo cringe and again cry out. Blake staggered, then recovered and grabbed Colin by the throat.

"What the hell's going on here?" Roz cried, bursting into the hall. Finola and Louise appeared in the doorway next, faces white with shock. A painting crashed from the wall, and a vase toppled from the window sill and smashed on the ground as the two men fought.

"Stop!" Jo yelled, as realisation struck. "Stop it! Can't you see you're being used?" Leaping forward she rescued the candle that was in danger of falling and shoved it into Roz's hand. There was another crash as a blow from Blake's fist sent Colin sprawling over a chair and onto the floor.

"Stop it! Leave him alone!" Finola threw herself at Blake and flailed him with her fists.

Blake muttered a curse and caught hold of her arms. "Fool! He's trying to kill her – don't you understand?" he snarled, pushing her roughly aside. Whirling round he confronted Colin who, about to take advantage of the distraction, was wielding a heavy glass dish above his head. Finola regained her balance and stepped between them. "*No* Colin!" she said with surprising firmness, pushing hard against his chest with her outstretched hands. Colin bared his teeth in a grimace of rage and brought down his arm. Wrenching Finola away in the nick of time, Blake grabbed Colin by the wrist and smashed his knuckles twice against the door jamb. Colin grunted with pain and the dish shattered in pieces on the floor as Blake's hands went around his throat. As the grip tightened Colin's face turned puce.

Louise cried out and Finola screamed. Jo hurled herself on Blake's back and grabbed him by the shoulders. Finding this to be of little effect, she dug her hands into his hair and tugged, hanging on with all her weight. He swore, and releasing Colin, swung round so that she fell sideways and sprawled on the floor.

"Blake! Don't let Antony Chase use you! *Blake?*" She held his gaze as he loomed over her, saw with relief the dawning of recognition in his eyes.

"*Christ*. What am I doing?"

Shaking his head he let his hands to hang limply at his sides. He knelt then and kissed her murmuring "Sorry Jo; forgive me love," before pulling her close to his chest.

He went to Colin next, who was massaging his neck and taking in huge gulps of air. "All right, mate? Sorry." Blake held out his hand in peace, but Colin had no chance to take it.

"Bully! Bastard! You could have killed him." Finola raged, suddenly turning on Blake and hammering at his unresisting body with her fists.

"No Finola, STOP!" Jo commanded, running to her side and taking her arm. "No shouting, no anger," she said urgently. "You'll start it off again."

Finola stared at Jo, her face blank, then her shoulders sagged and she nodded. "Okay, I get it now."

"I'm sorry Finola. I didn't hurt you?" Blake said contritely, running a hand self consciously through his hair. He turned to Colin as Finola shook her head. "Sorry mate. You all right?"

Colin nodded. He grasped the outstretched hand and gave a lop-sided grin. "Same here, mate – and yes, sorry everyone," he added looking round at the others. "Not like me at all."

*   *   *

They retired to the sitting room and Blake poured everyone a generous measure of brandy. Roz took hers, swallowed it at a gulp, then handed the empty glass back to Blake and carried on swabbing Colin's face and cut lip.

"I really am sorry, mate," Blake said, looking devastated. "As if your burns weren't enough!"

"Don't fret, Blake. If Jo's right then you weren't yourself!" Colin said then added generously: "Besides, I started it."

"Yes, well you seem more clued up than the rest of us, Jo – so how about telling us what you know?" Louise piped up from her armchair, her spirits and colour much improved by the brandy.

Jo stood up and paced about the room then sat on the arm of

the sofa where Colin was lying. "As I see it, Justin St. Clair came through Colin – as he has done before of course. He wanted to scare me into leaving the cottage."

"Okay. I can just about get my head around that," Colin said wincing, as Roz smoothed gel on an eye that was already turning purple. "If only because nothing else would make sense. You see I'm no fighter, too worried about these." He flexed his hands and winced. "Sculpture is my bread and butter, not to mention my life. But what happened to Blake?"

"He was a channel for the energy of Antony Chase," Jo said quietly. "He was used to stop me leaving."

Everyone looked at her in silence, the only sound being the sharp *click* of Roz's medical bag closing.

"Any more of that brandy going, Blake?" Louise said nervously, brandishing her empty glass.

"No!" Jo said sharply, checking Blake as he reached for the bottle.

"Oh come on, darling – no need to be mean with the drinkies!" Louise snapped.

"No more alcohol – for any of us," Jo said firmly, ignoring Louise. "We don't know what the night has in store."

"What better reason for a drink," Louise muttered.

"Wouldn't it steady our nerves?" Finola ventured.

"Alcohol lowers inhibitions; unruly emotions let nasties in," Roz stated succinctly.

"Precisely." Jo threw her a grateful look.

"Fair enough. None of us want a repeat of what happened out there," Finola agreed. "But there's something bothering me, Jo."

"Me too," said Blake, giving her a direct look.

"Finola first."

"Well, I want to believe what you say, Jo, really," Finola said looking awkward and fidgeting with the fringe of her shawl, "but why should this Justin St. Clair want to drive you out of the cottage?"

"Because there is something he doesn't want me to divulge."

"And what's that?" Colin demanded, craning his neck to look up at her.

"More to the point, why does Antony *want you to stay?*" Blake interrupted before Jo could answer.

She held his gaze for a moment then looked away, wondering if he had begun to suspect. She stood up and looked at each of the faces before her in turn, then spoke directly to Blake. "You said, *dreams are the answers to questions we haven't yet got round to asking,* remember?" She continued as he nodded: "Well, I got round to asking." The candles flickered and almost went out. She felt a cold breath upon her neck, an ominous presence at her back, but refused to back down.

Blake held her gaze. "Go on."

"The question is –," Jo started to say then stopped.

An icy wind howled through the room, banging the door shut and extinguishing all the candles.

SIXTY-ONE

~

Justin St. Clair shuddered as he stepped outside and closed the door of the hunting lodge. He breathed deeply of the fresh pure air and walked towards his horse without looking back. Over fifteen years had passed since that night. He had two more fine sons and a bonny daughter, yet still he had to return. He would go for months, sparing himself the torture, then would have to ride out to the clearing in the wood. Partly to enjoy his secret, partly from dread. Maybe it had been a mistake to build on that unholy ground. At the time he had given way to a superstitious impulse; it had seemed one way of keeping her down. He shook his head at such folly.

He mounted and walked his horse to the edge of the clearing. He looked back then, once. As he always did, and as always the smell of molten metal burned in his nostrils, so that once again he imagined the scrape of her nails on the coffin lid, heard her weeping and muffled screams. As he rode towards home his eyes held a hunted look. He was getting old; one day soon they would meet again.

The curtains were drawn; darkness and silence were absolute. *Like the grave.* Jo shuddered at the words which repeatedly went through her head. For the initial two or three seconds everyone had been stunned; nobody moved or made a sound. Now pandemonium broke loose. All around her were cries of "Oh, God!" and "where's the matches?" and "For *Chris'sakes* – let me out of here!" There was the sound of a muttered curse followed by the crash of books hitting the floor as someone stumbled into the table.

The fire had also perished in the rush of wind that had died as mysteriously as it had risen. The room was now like ice, with that unnatural chill that Jo had learned to recognise. He was here. Here in this room. "Don't harm us, Antony," she whispered, staring hard into the darkness, waiting for the next threat to manifest. "Hurt us, and I won't ask them to help."

"What? What the hell are you mumbling at Jo – you're giving me the bloody creeps!" Colin's voice sounded irate and irrational in the darkness.

"Sorry Col, it's nothing."

Had Antony heard? she wondered. More to the point would he pay heed?

"Be still! I'm lighting the candles – *now*." Blake's voice, peremptory but calm, brought an end to the undignified scuffle for the door. With relief Jo heard the sound of a match scraping the box and a second later saw the reassuring spurt of flame.

"Okay, now let's sit down and talk calmly about this thing." Blake blew first on the match and then on his fingers as he lit the last candle.

"Oh do lets; after all there's only some bastard ghost intent on killing us all before the night's out!" Louise said sarcastically, her voice teetering on the edge of hysteria.

"Okay, Louise that's enough." Blake tempered the harshness of his words by pushing her gently down on the easy chair and adding just loud enough for Jo to hear: "It'll be alright, Lou. Don't worry. I know I can rely on you not to panic the others."

Louise simpered and offered no more aggression.

Does he manipulate me that easily? Jo found herself wondering, then abruptly stopped. Was that thought her own, or had it been planted? A chilling notion, that she was a possible channel. And even if not, negative emotions were an invite, ammunition to be used against them to set them quarrelling amongst themselves. She mustn't allow herself to be used in a war of subtleties. Resolutely she cleared her mind of doubts about Blake and concentrated on what he was saying. A natural leader, he had once again taken control.

"There's no point whatever in running away. It's freezing out there. We are much safer in here. It was scary," he was saying, "but none of us are actually injured or under threat now, agreed?"

There followed a second or so of unrelenting silence, then Louise piped up reluctantly: "I suppose," followed by Colin who stoutly declared that he wasn't in the least bit scared. "I was," Finola admitted, earning a smile and an affectionate wink from Blake followed by: "So were we all sweetheart."

"But shouldn't we try and do something about it?" Roz volunteered. "It seems we're stuck here, and I for one need to be away pretty soon, or I'll be looking for a new job!"

"Join the club," Blake said ironically with an apologetic look for Jo. He stroked his chin with the ball of his thumb and stared unseeingly at her face.

"What is it Blake?" she asked.

"The question," he said at last. "The one you are ready to ask but didn't get chance to tell us just now."

"You know what it is." It was a statement from Jo, not a question.

Blake nodded and Jo remained silent.

"Then do you mind informing the lesser gifted amongst us what conclusion your superior intellects have divined," Louise said sarcastically, so that Roz sniggered and turned it into a cough.

Jo shrugged. "Just a hunch, Louise. I think we should be asking: where is Madeline St. Clair?"

"So what now?" Finola said.

"We start looking," Jo said with conviction.

There was really only one place to look. Jo mentally stepped back, tried to see the scene in the kitchen as a stranger might: the snow mottling the black shiny window pane, the candlelight and oil lamp, the latter found outside in the shed along with a container of paraffin; the rug rolled up and placed on the table which along with the chairs had been pushed back against the wall. The group of people contained within the yellow circle of light, their breath rising in white smoke, their shadows leaping up the walls, the flickering flames of the candles creating alter-egos out of shadows and imbuing them with a life of their own. They worked mostly in silence these people, their faces set and serious. The only sounds were the clink of crowbars against stone, the shuffling of feet and the groaning of each slab as it gave way. A bizarre scene indeed. Suddenly Jo was assailed by self-doubt. What if she was wrong? What a prize idiot she would look if that turned out to be the case.

"Grab this, Jo."

Blake's words shattered her reverie. Automatically she moved forward to take the first bucket of soil. Once again, God help her, she was a participant on the macabre set, rather than impartial observer. There was about the whole thing an air of unreality, of the mundane side by side with the impossible. They formed a chain, herself, Finola, Louise and Roz, and systematically passed buckets and piled earth onto a plastic sheet. Roz took a few minutes out to put the kettle on the stove. She then went to fetch the coffee pot from the sitting room where they had left it earlier. Blake had tried to prevent Colin from working, saying he should be resting. Colin had pulled off his sweater, rolled up his shirt sleeves and set to alongside Blake. Now his face was red and sweating with exertion, so that his burns looked even more livid. Jo watched as he prised up the last of the slabs from the centre of the room, exposing the bare earth. He picked up a shovel to help Blake with the digging. They worked in silence for the next hour or so, except for the odd sigh or grunt of effort.

Sensing a movement Jo turned to find a white-faced and hollow-eyed Louise at her elbow. "Why here, Jo?" she asked, her expression a blend of curiosity, scepticism and distaste. "What made you decide to search here?"

"The toadstools?" Finola piped up, slipping over to join them.

"Clever girl," and Jo smiled as Finola flushed with pleasure. "Those and the scratching noises which always seemed to come from down here."

"I still don't get it," Louise complained. "This place is only three hundred years old – your knights must be more than twice that!"

"But it's not forced to be a virgin site." Blake had obviously overheard and was now resting on his spade watching them.

"Okay, explain," Louise demanded.

But Blake never got the chance.

It happened in an instant. Colin had paused for a moment, the spade poised ready to strike. Something about his stance alerted Jo. She frowned and tried to catch Blake's eye in warning. An icy current was swirling around the room. Colin flung down the spade and turned on Blake. "This is insane! Absolutely insane!" He whirled round to confront Jo. "And you – you'll have us all as crazy as yourself!"

Blake turned from Louise to confront Colin. "Hey, now just a minute here – Jo isn't crazy. If she genuinely feels we should do this, then we should show a little faith."

Jo gasped as she watched Colin's face change. His eyes had turned almost black, his lips compressed and cruel. "You would say that though, wouldn't you?" he said in a voice so low it was almost a whisper. The flames of the candles danced and curved as though bent by a fierce wind. The air was thick with hostility; Jo could feel it creeping along her skin.

"Col?" Colin pushed Finola aside as she went to take his arm; the two men faced each other across the trench they had dug in the floor. Jo saw with dismay that Blake's features were blurring, melting and reforming like hot wax.

"What do you mean by that?" he said silkily.

Foam flecked Colin's lips and he almost snarled: "You know full well. You've still not given up, you bastard."

"Nor will I! So dig!"

"You're an arrogant dog, Chase!" Colin stooped to retrieve the shovel and brandished it at shoulder height. "You stole her from me in life; now you stalk her in death. But I'll see you in hell before I let you have her."

Blake moved like lightning and picked up the crow bar. He stood in classical confrontational pose, legs apart, feet splayed and head thrust forward. With a sense of alarm Jo saw the vein at his temple begin to throb and pulsate. As he raised his arms higher his shadow reared on the wall behind.

Jo felt the waves of fury and violence emanating from his person. Colin tightened his grip on the shovel and held it across his body. Blake brought the crowbar smashing down and Colin raised the spade just in time to parry the blow. The ring of metal on metal reverberated around the walls. Jo stepped forward in agitation: could they not see what was happening? "Stop! You're being used again!" she cried. The two men acted as though she had not spoken. Colin raised the shovel again to strike; Blake brandished the crowbar in readiness. Hatred crackled between them. Jo ran forward and with outstretched arms thrust them apart. She cast an agonised look at the door as it opened and Roz appeared on the threshold. Pray to God Roz didn't blow it, that she had heard enough before entering to know how to act.

She needn't have worried. "Jo's right," Roz said calmly as she advanced. She gave Jo a warning look then placed her hands on Colin's shovel. Jo lowered her arms and stepped back. "Have a rest *Colin*," Roz said, emphasising his name. "Would you like a drink, *Colin*? I've just made some coffee, okay – *Col*?"

He looked at her as though dazed, then lowered the shovel.

Jo turned to Blake. "*Let him go, Antony*," she whispered on impulse, then spoke softly to Blake, emulating Roz by saying his name over and over. She heaved a sigh of relief as he let her take the crowbar.

"I think we could all do with some of that coffee, Roz," she said wearily, resting the crowbar against the wall.

It was now clear to Jo that each time the two men were used in this way, it took its toll of their energy. She watched them surreptitiously as they sat around drinking scalding coffee. Colin had dark smudges beneath his eyes and his movements were slow and heavy; Blake's face was white and drawn with fatigue. They were all under threat; Louise was also giving her cause for concern. "Louise, why don't you go and lie down for a while on the sofa?" Jo asked, noting the increased pallor of her cheeks and the hollowness of her eyes.

Louise emphatically shook her head. "And miss the climax, after enduring this far?" she said with a theatrical gesture that made them all smile. "No thanks, darling. I'm in to the death, as you might say."

They all groaned and Colin blew a raspberry. But the incident had served to lighten the atmosphere, Jo noted with relief.

Ten minutes or so later they recommenced work. The tension was palpable now, the lack of conversation pronounced. As the night ticked away, the candles burnt low and wax formed and dripped in fantastic shapes. Outside the snow had ceased to fall, but lay over the countryside in a thick blanket of silence. The muscles of Jo's arms ached from lifting and emptying the buckets of soil. Weariness overcame her in waves. "Why are we doing this anyway? Col was right, what's the point?" she said slumping back against the wall. Her limbs felt leaden, her eyelids drooped. "It's stupid, digging up the floor like this. It isn't as though we've found anything to account for the toadstools and slime." Col and Blake stopped work to stare and Louise looked uncertainly from one to the other.

"Carry on Col – and you Blake." Finola's voice rang out with surprising strength.

"No, they must stop. They're making fools of themselves!" Jo cried, pushing herself upright again. She must tell them, they would listen to her. "Stop digging you fools, do you hear me – stop digging!" she rushed forward to grab the crow bar from Blake.

"Ignore her and carry on!" Finola cried, stepping forward to grab Jo by the arms and drag her away.

"Are you alright, Jo?" Louise's pain-ravaged face filled her vision.

"Jo?" Sharper now, her voice cut through Jo's weariness like a spade through newly-dug earth. *No, must tell them not to dig.*

"Jo – don't let that St Clair bastard get to you!"

Jo gasped as her head was flung to and fro on her neck. Her eyes opened wide. Louise was shaking her like a child.

"Jo – if you go under, we've all had it!" Louise was saying firmly. "Fight him! Think about it: we must be onto something if he's getting to *you.*"

"She's right Jo," Finola said sharply, "so kick the bastard into touch."

Gradually their words began to make sense, to penetrate the fog. Jo even managed a weak smile at Finola's new-found drive and aggression. Good old Finola, she was behind the cause. But what was the cause? What were they doing, digging up floors in the middle of the night? Jo ran her fingers through her hair then pressed her knuckles against her temples. *Madeline.* That was it, must find Madeline. "Antony?" She whispered his name, felt a warmth surround her, the strength return to her limbs.

It was at precisely that moment that Blake's spade struck against something other than stone.

SIXTY-TWO

~

Antony rose on the wind. Like the hawk that was his anger, and which sometimes tore free of his breast to soar and claw. But the girl, was helping him with her mind, helping him understand. At times she talked to him, aloud or through her mind, asked him the reason for his anger, and to help her if he could. He saw the images that came to her dreams and when she sat quietly thinking. Terrible pictures that mirrored the woman's own fears; fears about what had happened to Madeline. Pray God she was wrong on that count. Yet if she was right, there was hope too amongst the pain.

He had been so confused whilst waiting on the outside of Time and beyond Grace. Waiting to take his revenge. On St. Clair of course, but on Madeline too – when he could find her. He had thought to have done so, when the girl's soul had briefly left her body to join him. There were similarities: her recklessness, intensity and courage. Was she aware that he had been close to destroying her? By mistaking her for Madeline and thus believing she had betrayed him.

"Madeline! Why, oh why?"

His anguished cry echoed down the centuries.

Love, hate – it had got that way he couldn't tell one from the other. His hatred for Madeline was just his love betrayed and pain unmasked. He loved her still, but that bitter destructive twin, his hatred, kept him from her. He was weary of wandering the winds alone; maybe he should give the young woman a chance to plead and prove Madeline's case. But did she possess the courage to do so? And if so, had she also earned the right to pass through the threshold of light? And if, as the woman believes, Madeline was murdered by Justin, there was still the matter of her compliance, her failure to warn him.

We shall see. If she fails, or is wrong in what she believes, then his vengeance would be dreadful indeed.

And if she is right about Madeline?

Then St. Clair would pay a terrible price of her suffering, he would see to that.

And pray God my sins be forgiven and I find her at the last.

At last the thing lay exposed.

"Jo, you were right," Finola breathed, her eyes enormous behind her gold-rimmed glasses.

"Well we've found *something*," Blake said cautiously, "but we don't yet know what."

"To think Callum and I – all those months – and never guessing, right here," Louise shook her head and gabbled incoherently as she peered down at what appeared to be a wooden chest.

"Well done, Jo," Roz said warmly. "I must admit to being sceptical at the outset."

Yes, it is well done.

Jo started at the echo. The words went round and round in her head and a glow that was becoming familiar suffused her heart.

Colin scraped away the remains of the soil with the side of his shovel. "What do you think is inside?"

"Only one way to find out. Straps, Jo!" Blake said in a business-like voice, bringing her down to earth. She stared at him blankly for a second, then realised he was referring to the straps constructed of metal mesh he had produced earlier from his rucksack, with the words: 'If I'm right, we'll be needing these.'

"You okay Jo?" Colin asked, looking up at her with concern from were he was standing in the hole they had dug.

"Fine, thanks." *It's Colin who looks in need of care,* Jo worried as she handed the straps to Blake. Some of the blisters which had formed on Colin's face had burst and looked raw and painful. In fact he looked just about all in. At the last coffee break, Roz had

given him a shot of antibiotic to guard against infection. She replaced a couple of guttering candles with new ones.

"How come, after all this time, the wood hasn't rotted away?"
Finola asked as Blake and Colin worked and manoeuvred.

"It's not wood – it's made of lead." Blake panted, straining to
shift one end sufficiently for Colin to slide the first of the metal
bands beneath. "Which is why it's so bloody heavy."

"That's odd," Finola said frowning.

"That's *interesting*! I think we might be in for a surprise," Roz
said enigmatically, but could not be persuaded to say more despite
the promptings of the others. She's guessed, Jo thought noting the
suppressed excitement and tension in her face.

At last the straps were in place and Colin and Roz positioned at
one end, with Jo and Blake at the other.

"Will they take the weight?" Roz asked eying the straps dubiously.

Blake nodded. "No problem. Tungsten-steel alloy."

"Okay?" Colin asked, looking at each of them in turn.

"Then heave on three but not before," Blake instructed. "If we
don't pull in synch. we lose it."

Jo felt as though her arms were being wrenched from their
sockets.

"Hold it!" Blake commanded, the veins in his neck standing proud
like ropes. "Just one more folks! Don't let it slip now, one two three
– and go for it!"

The chest began to rise until it was level with the brink of the pit.

"Here she comes!" Blake cried triumphantly.

At last their burden rested on the kitchen floor.

Jo, pale and tense, stepped forward then stopped. Which one?
she worried, which one had they found? And had the others guessed
yet? It took some time to break the seals and begin to prise off the
lid. At last the cover began to slide beneath the combined efforts of
Blake and Colin. As though at a given signal both men paused,
reluctant it seemed, to make the final move. As she stood perfectly
still watching with the others, Jo's nails bit into the palms of her
hands. Now that her suspicions seemed about to be confirmed, she
almost wanted to leave things as they were. It seemed sacrilegious,

to look upon something that had lain undisturbed for some seven hundred years. And again – which one had they found? Had she only been partially right? Better to leave well alone, to put the thing back and cover it over again.

Somebody else it seemed had different ideas.

Love . . . Love forever . . .

"Antony?" she whispered.

She could feel him close. He was there with them in the room.

But so too, she thought with growing alarm, was a less benign energy. The chill was creeping out from the corners to wrap itself around them. She saw Finola frown and look over her shoulder, and Roz instinctively shiver. Louise was aware of something too; she constantly licked her lips as though her mouth had suddenly gone dry. Blake was staring at her, his eyebrow raised in query as he tacitly asked permission to proceed. Jo was suddenly consumed with awe: this was an historic moment. As though picking up on her thoughts, Roz looked anxious. "You know, really we ought not to proceed any further until this thing can be reported," she said, looking first at Jo then across at Blake. "It's a find that belongs to the nation."

"But we don't even know what's in there yet!" Finola complained.

"It doesn't take much working out!" Roz said scornfully, looping strands of her hair behind her ears.

"She's right, you know." Colin stared belligerently at Blake. "I vote we leave well alone and get the thing taken from here."

A warning bell sounded inside Jo's head. *Here we go again; the battle's not over yet.* "No," she said firmly, feeling the stirring of the air about her, sensing Antony's agitation. She looked across at Blake who was still regarding her with a quizzical look. She nodded, suddenly sure. "Do it!"

"You heard her Colin – move!" Blake commanded.

Colin stared him out, seemed about to rebel again, then subsided and seemed to revert to his normal self. He and Blake bent to the task.

There was a stunned silence as the lid slid off the chest and the contents were exposed.

SIXTY-THREE

~

Justin St. Clair sighed and the flame of the candles below bent, sickened and almost died. They had not met in death after all, he and Madeline. There had been no reason to fear the curses she must have laid upon him with her dying breath. Nor had he been consigned to Hell, forced to hear her scratching and screaming her way through eternity. But he had been trapped. Snared ironically not by Madeline but by Antony Chase's hate and incarcerated in oblivion. But first the unsuspecting man, and now this stupid woman had set them all free with their meddling.

It was Antony Chase, not Madeline who waited in the shadows for his revenge. Well he was ready. His hatred was as fresh today as it was when he stuck Chase like a pig, and sent Madeline to her living grave. He had crushed them then, and would do so again. Justin sent a cold tremor around the room and two of the candles guttered.

He knew what Chase wanted. But he would not have her, even in death.

"*Madeline!*" Jo breathed. Following the first exclamations of wonder and disbelief, they surveyed the contents of the coffin in stunned silence. The brown eyes of Madeline St. Clair looked out at them after seven hundred years. The expression captured within them bore witness to her fear and agony as she died. The skin had not discoloured, was stretched across high cheekbones that were a testament to her timeless beauty. Perhaps most striking of all was the tumbling mane of hair, the russet of autumn chestnuts unfaded after the long winter of interment. With a shudder Jo recalled reading somewhere that hair continued to grow for a short time following death. But not retain its colour and richness like this. The woman lying before her resembled a person who had only recently died.

A gasp of air like a huge sigh rose from the coffin. It hovered there, slightly opaque, then dissipated. At that precise moment a shape darkened the window. A second or so later there was a sound like an explosion and glass showered the air in a shining arc. Stunned, Jo watched the myriad pieces fall as though in slow motion, winking as they passed through light shed by the candles. An arrowhead of feather and muscle hurtled around the room, skimming the ceiling. The women screamed; Blake and Colin swore and shouted curses and made wild gestures with their arms. The air was filled with a terrible screeching and the flapping of wings.

Candle flames wavered and dipped, and the oil lamp flared then subsided.

Madeline!

The anguish of that cry brought tears streaming down Jo's cheeks.

As she watched, stunned and unable at first to move, a dark shadow seemed to be moving across the room. It's passage was like an eclipse. It left in its wake darkness, dankness and lack of hope. She backed away until her spine was pressed against the wall. The stain spread over her, darkening her soul. *Justin Justin* The hawk screamed overhead, its wing-tips fanning her face. The pain was blinding; her head felt to be splitting in two. She screamed and fell writhing to the floor. She was being torn apart. Two fragmented souls were fighting for hers, and Justin St. Clair – the dark shadow – was winning.

Blackness, the blackness of evil, was seeping into her soul. She moaned and felt herself being drawn out as the two entities fought for possession.

Mine. Mine.

"No, no," she muttered, feeling consciousness slipping away.

JUSTIN JUSTIN

HATE FOREVER

"No!" Jo screamed inside her head as she whirled along a pitch-black tunnel.

ANTONY

LOVE, LOVE FOREVER

Hope had all but died when the disc of light appeared at the end of the shaft.

Warmth enfolded her, the golden warmth of that first meeting. He stood before her, resplendent in mail and a white surplice. But no red hawk adorned his chest.

Justin St. Clair's screams of pain and rage echoed along the tunnel.

She risked a backward look. The hawk hovered, claws and hook of a beak gorged with blood.

"Jo! Jo!"

Blake's voice tore at her mind and hauled her back.

The hawk careered around the walls, hitting them, bouncing off, imprinting them with the blood of impact. Brown and bluish-grey feathers drifted down, mimicking the snow flakes which had begun to fall outside.

"No! No!" Jo screamed, abortively trying to follow the bird's course, arms outstretched to prevent this orgy of self-destruction.

She cried out as it smacked into the opposite wall and slid motionless to the floor.

Bury my anger.

Jo started out of her misery, jolted by the clarity of the words. She looked around her at the grey and white shocked faces in the light of the remaining candles. None of the others appeared to have heard.

Bury my anger . . . with her.

Trembling, Jo crossed the floor and knelt by the mangled and pitiable heap of blood and feathers. She picked it up, it's head lolling on broken neck, and walked to the coffin. Nobody spoke. Had they done so, she would not have heard. For the first time she noticed Madeline's hands, how they had clawed their way free of the pitch-covered shroud. She winced and briefly closed her eyes. Those hands told their own story. The nails were ragged and torn, the fingers encrusted with dried blood. She saw too the scratches on the inside of the discarded lid. How this woman must have suffered for her illicit love.

Briefly Jo held the dead bird against her chest and with one finger gently stroked the broken neck. "Rest well and be angry no more," she whispered.

Tenderly she placed the hawk on Madeline's breast.

Stepping back, she tried to ignore the idea that arose spontaneously to mind. But it persisted, nagging at her conscience like the aching of a bad tooth.

"Are you alright Jo?" Blake watched her with patent anxiety, but made no move towards her as though sensing intervention now was unwelcome and prohibited.

Unable to speak, Jo nodded. It had to be done, but giving it up would not be easy. In the end it would be the only tangible evidence, the sole proof that any of these bizarre events had happened. It was not hers to keep; yet it was the only thing that could validate her experience. And so went the internal arguments. Remote from the others in the room, Jo fought her solitary battle. At length a sigh escaped her, and her expression was one of resignation. Still without speaking she went from the room and returned a moment later.

Nobody had moved. Blake watched her, his face working with emotion but he refrained still from interference. Kneeling by the coffin Jo opened her clenched hand. In the palm nestled the ring, emerald eye winking. Even now it was a struggle to overcome her reluctance. She took hold of one of Madeline's poor mangled fingers, third one, left hand. To her amazement the joints were still supple and the ring slipped over the knuckle with ease. It had to be right, now that the hawk of Antony's anger was laid to rest. Surely this was where it belonged? On the hand of the woman Antony once loved.

SIXTY-FOUR

~

Blake blew on the small pile of kindling and the glow at its heart burst into flame. Instinctively Louise leaned closer, as though its meagre heat might warm away the chill of their find, the eternal coldness of the body awaiting them in the kitchen. "I still don't understand," she complained stretching out her hands to the glow, "how she came to be buried here when this cottage is only three hundred years old."

"But Jo said weeks ago that she thought Madeline's husband had murdered both her and her lover," Finola contributed, flushed with excitement.

"So?" Roz pressed impatiently.

"Well say he caught them together – here in the woods. What better place to dispose of her body?"

"Oh yeah, and this cottage just happened to be built over the exact spot!" Louise sneered so that Finola blushed a deeper shade of red.

"Nice try, Fin – but it's asking too much of coincidence," Roz added kindly, obviously regretting her earlier sharpness.

"I guess." Finola sighed and lapsed into silence.

"Blake, you said something back there about a virgin site," Louise persisted.

"He was meaning there could have been a building here before the cottage," Colin chipped in.

Blake turned from his ministrations at the fire and nodded. Spot on, Col." He eased himself up and sat on the nearest chair. "Have you seen the deeds to this cottage, Louise?"

Louise half closed her eyes and sat for a moment in thoughtful silence. "You're right you know, Blake," she said excitedly. "Now I think of it, these woods were once part of the Barrowburn Castle Estate. The land once belonged to the St. Clair family!"

"And I don't mind betting," Blake said nodding, "even though Land Registry documents probably won't go back that far, that a building of sorts was erected over the spot by Justin St. Clair."

"But why should he do that?" Jo asked.

Blake shrugged. "Who knows. Maybe he couldn't resist marking the site, secretly crowing over his crime. A summer house, or small hunting lodge maybe. And when centuries later it crumbled into misuse, a local landowner maybe used the stones to build this cottage."

"But wouldn't they have found her when they dug the foundations?" Jo asked with a frown.

"There are none," Colin supplied promptly. "None at Throstle Garth either. None of these old cottages and farmhouses had foundations as we know them. No Building Regs. in those days," he finished with a smile.

"That's right, the ground would simply be cleared," Blake added. "But the question now is," he said leaning forward to place a few larger pieces of wood on the fire, "Is what are we going to do with her?"

He sat back and waited, surveying them all with a critical eye.

"Inform the authorities surely. It's an intensely valuable find," Roz said emphatically, sipping fresh coffee.

"No!" Jo pushed herself up on her elbow: Blake had laid her on the settee and covered her with a tartan rug to recover from her ordeal.

"But It's amazingly well preserved," Roz persisted. "The tissues are soft, the skin colour good, and the joints still supple. Even the eyes are intact, though granted they'll decompose with exposure to the air. There's only been about half a dozen such bodies found in the whole of Britain; I wouldn't mind betting this is the best."

Jo shook her head with equal emphasis. "I don't care. This is one the rest of the nation will have to do without!"

"How come you know so much about it, Roz?" Colin asked, holding hands that were blue with cold out to the struggling fire.

"A few years back, whilst doing a stint in pathology, I compiled a dissertation on embalming. Which is basically what this is: the resin-coated cloths and sealed lead coffin provide a water and air-tight environment. Over time, the body virtually embalms itself."

"Is that why you said we were in for a surprise when you saw the lead coffin?" Finola asked.

"Precisely. I did have some idea – but never expected so perfect a specimen!"

"She's not a *specimen* – she's Madeline St. Clair," Jo objected, sitting upright.

"Sorry if I was insensitive," Roz said tartly. "But she has been dead for some seven hundred years! Let's not get over-involved here Jo."

"That doesn't deprive her of her identity – especially under the circumstances," Jo argued heatedly. "But I suppose we're conveniently forgetting all that has led us here and the anguish of Antony Chase."

"Is that the royal 'we' – or is it aimed at me personally?" Roz snapped, two bright spots of red appearing high on her cheek-bones.

"As you please!" Jo returned with asperity, flinging off the blanket.

"Take it easy, Jo," Blake warned, frowning.

"No way! Look, I've gone through a lot for this." Jo rose from the couch and paced the room. "You and Roz have only just come in on the action, but are wanting to run the show," she complained, turning to face them.

"No-one wants to do that Jo. It's been a very stressful night, so now let's all chill out," he said in an even voice before turning to Roz again. "Just how does the body embalm itself?" he asked, in an obvious attempt to diffuse the tension.

"The lack of air reaching the interior of the coffin causes a chemical reaction to take place," Roz explained. "A substance called glycol, a potent preservative, is produced in the cells."

"But why did St. Clair do it?" Finola said, holding out her cup for more coffee.

Roz shrugged. "Who knows? A sick mind: the beauty which

enslaved him surviving death but unseen by any man? I'm sorry Jo, but we really must report this and let the authorities do a full post mortem examination – as soon as possible too, before further deterioration sets in," she concluded with an apologetic look for Jo.

"No."

"Jo –," Blake started to remonstrate, but Jo held up a peremptory hand. "I said NO, do you all understand me?" she blazed.

Finola stared at her nervously, as did Louise; whilst Colin, Roz and Blake looked around the room as though expecting the candles to dip and the shadows move. "You needn't worry. St. Clair won't worry us ever again. Neither will Antony, as long as we do what he wants," Jo said, resorting without conscience to emotional blackmail.

So she was as shocked as the others to hear sounds coming from behind the kitchen door.

"What's that? Finola whispered, turning white.

Jo moved stealthily to the door and the others followed. They crowded into the hall and listened. "There it is again," Louise whispered.

"Shh." Jo leaned with her head close to the door. But she had already identified the noise. The swishing of a heavy silk hem over stone, a sound she had heard several times before.

Heart thumping, Jo pushed open the door. The scent of cedarwood and musk arose evoking vague memory. Roz who was pressed against her back gave an audible gasp.

Antony! Antony! The whispers reeled around Jo's brain.

Madeline St. Clair stared up at them, her eyes dimmed by contact with twentieth century air. Nobody spoke, but fear stalked the cottage once more.

They had, Jo recalled with a *frisson* of fear, replaced the lid of the coffin before leaving the kitchen.

She turned and faced the others. In the glow from the two candles on the hall stand they looked a weary and frightened bunch. Except for Blake who was used to the rigours of war and was therefore wearing well. He was watching her with a detached and slightly puzzled air, as though seeing her for the first time. Jo addressed Louise. "There will be no peace in this cottage until we do what they want," she stated.

"Listen honey – they can have the damned place! I won't exactly be counting the days until I return!" Louise sparked with a flash of her old bolshy humour.

"We have to get away from it yet, before any talk of coming back," Jo cautioned.

This seemed to be the decider for Roz. "Oh, what the hell. Public conscience apart, I can't afford to risk my job by staying away any longer. Okay, you win, Jo – do what you want with the bloody woman!"

"What does everyone else think?" Louise asked, surveying their faces one by one.

"That," Blake said raising an eyebrow and looking sternly at Jo, "rather depends on what Jo has in mind."

Jo looked at the coffin. "It's simple. We take her down to the churchyard. We have to bury Madeline with Antony's remains."

"You can't do that!" Roz said turning on Jo with a scandalised look.

"Just what do you intend doing with Maud Bickley? There isn't room for both!" Blake said sarcastically, running his hand though his hair in desperation.

Jo looked at the faces before her, judging by their expressions they thought her completely mad. "Yes there is," she said with a faint smile. "Madeline is wasted now, tiny enough – without that coffin.

She challenged them all with a look.

SIXTY-FIVE

~

Madeline sighed and floated free. Free – after all this time, after being held captive by her own need, her own desire for vengeance. Antony too had claimed his revenge and now, please God, Justin St. Clair would leave them in peace. She was still afraid to believe it. And was it foolish to hope that Antony now understood? That he knew she had not betrayed him? During the conflict she had dared believe so, but maybe her desperate need had coloured her judgement. Had love for her fired Antony's spirit, or only his hatred for her husband? Surely the love they had shared could not be so easily extinguished? Albeit a love unsanctioned by the Church, but one nonetheless which – on her part at least – had survived death and seven centuries. He must now be aware of how she had died – but did he also know why she could not have warned him of the ambush? Or did he still think himself betrayed?

She hovered on the wind, watching the little procession pass beneath on its way to the graveyard. Her coffin had been carried by cart once before, though before she had occupied it. They had thought her totally insensible, but she had seen them trundle it into the glade before finally losing her senses.

The young woman understood, knew they must be laid together if they were to rest. Then, God willing, Antony would cease to be destroyed by his grief. He needed to witness that final ritual, to know that her physical self rested above his remains. Then her body would be released from enforced preservation, would be allowed to melt and their essences mingle. His spirit, freed from the anger of the hawk, could then soar with hers and they would be forever united. If he so wished it. If he forgave her for sacrific-

ing his life for William's, as he surely must once he knew. Centuries of hate and anger had blunted his perceptions, muddied the waters of his soul. The cycle had to be broken, the fissure healed at source – which depended upon the courage and love of the girl.

Would she be equal to the task?

Jo was adamant, and at 2.35 a.m. they were making their way down the lane to the churchyard. Colin had brought a cart from Throstle Garth, the one he used for moving masonry destined for his carvings or dry stone walling. Between them they loaded the coffin onto it and began their bizarre journey.

Jo knew she would never forget this time. The snow silvered by moonlight, the breathing hush of the night; the solemnity, the expectancy and yes, the sheer practical difficulties as well. In the deep snow the cart was difficult to navigate; the wheels seemed to have a will of their own and at times slid off course with a heart-stopping swerve, or had to be dug out of a drift with the shovels Blake had brought. Progress was sure but necessarily slow. Dips and ruts had to be negotiated, the coffin steadied by nervous hands. Nobody spoke. One wheel squeaked incongruously at each revolution, a sound that would stay in Jo's memory for ever. The fells brooded beneath the stars and as the cart turned down the lane, the yews at the church stood to attention against an indigo sky.

Prior to leaving the cottage Jo had told the others what had to be done. At last they were in the churchyard and without words, the plan was put into action. Blake and Colin lowered themselves into the open grave and placed the straps around Maud Bickley's snow-topped coffin. For the first time since her arrival in Cumbria it seemed to Jo, Fate oiled the wheels and the operation went smoothly. In no time at all, the coffin was lifted and placed at the graveside.

The next stage was more traumatic. Blake took the shovel from the cart and began to dig below the level of Maud's existing grave. The iron blade rang on the hard earth and, it seemed to Jo, must be audible miles away. Blake grunted with effort and felt the sweat turn ice-cold on his forehead, but declined Colin's offer to take over. "I'm okay, thanks mate," he said, and Colin nodded amicably.

Jo directed the beam of the torch over the newly dug area. "Any-thing?" she asked tersely.

"Not yet, but can't be far now." He paused to wipe beads of sweat from his face with his sleeve.

He moved carefully now with his spade, scraping away the red earth instead of digging for fear of smashing the thing he sought. "Here. Shine it here."

"Antony," Jo whispered. She felt a lump rise to her throat and the torch trembled in her grasp.

Caught in the pool of light, white bones showed stark against the earth.

She and Blake climbed onto the cart. Colin and Ros waited below to receive the precious bundle. Louise and Finola watched lending their silent support. Blake removed the lid. Before leaving the cottage they had rearranged the shroud to cover the body. But loosely enough, Blake had instructed, to allow the circulation of air so that natural decomposition could take place.

"Ready?" he asked now, giving Jo's hand a quick squeeze.

She nodded. With great care they lifted Madeline St. Clair from the coffin and lowered her into the arms of Colin and Roz.

Blake and Colin then set about reinterring Madeline, placing her body directly over Antony's bones. Watching, Jo felt oddly dis-oriented and unreal. She took a backward step from the proceed-ings, both physically and psychologically, to survey the bizarre tableau. It was all going well. *Too well?* The qualifier arose spon-taneously and made her frown. Then awareness dawned. For one thing Colin and Blake were too polite and friendly to one another.

"Sorry mate, did I move before you were ready?"

"You're doing just fine."

"Thanks mate."

"No problem."

Snatches of their conversation drifted across the ether which separated her normal self from this other being; the one capable of standing back to dispassionately observe. For another, the intense cold had taken on another dimension, was penetrating her clothes and skin to numb the core of her being. She turned up her collar against the freshly risen wind and drove her hands deeper into her pockets.

"*Well done, it's almost there.*"

"*Agreed. An inch or so lower your side, I think.*"

So it went on. The phrases of false politeness, that rang as hollow as a grave-digger's shovel on unforgiving rock. Jo saw that Finola was shivering and that by the light of moon and torch her lips were blue. Louise had shrunk deep into her hooded coat.

Hate Kill the wind moaned, but Jo turned a deaf ear to the sibilant hiss. That was all over, finished back there by the hawk.

"God but it's cold." Roz stamped her feet on the impacted snow.

"Hang in there girls," Colin paused to encourage, his breath writhing white serpents that rose when he spoke. "Almost finished."

Jo shivered; his expression was somehow at odds with the solicitude of his words.

Yes, almost finished – and this time for good.

The thought, and accompanying flush of aggression, caught Colin unawares. Yet not really. Not when he thought about it; he had every reason to feel aggrieved, he decided watching Blake straighten his back.

"That's it. Let go of your end of the strap."

"Okay, mate."

As he complied the ball of resentment in Colin's stomach swelled and threatened to overspill in violence. Just who did he think he was? Coming here and fouling his chances with Jo. And she was as bad. He turned his head slowly like a stuck bull and glared in her direction. *Trollop. Whore.* The rising wind took up the words and tossed them high above the yews before flinging them back in his face. Like a bitch on heat she was, whenever that bastard looked her way. Panting and all but slavering in her haste to be served.

Someone was turning the screw, wracking his guts with unbearable tension. He watched Blake raise his arms and strike the hard earth, stoop to pick up a handful and pause, before dropping first soil on Madeline. His lips were moving as though in a prayer – or a protestation of love. Would he never give up? The screw turned another two revolutions.

"Col?"

The name penetrated the mist of his anger, "What?"

"You okay?"

Blake was peering at him in concern, his face elongated and distorted as though viewed through the bottom of a glass.

"The shovel, for God's sake. Take it."

Colin remained immobile, hands at his side, and stared.

Blake thrust out the implement for him to take. "First earth, man. You know."

Colin grasped it, splaying his feet to stand against the wind that tore at his psyche. His fingers tightened on the shaft of the spade. The wood felt reassuringly hard and smooth beneath his hands; well-used and who knew for what dirty work? The urge to raise it above his head and smash the other man's skull became almost too much to resist. And in that second he knew. *That bastard St Clair is using me, using guilt and hatred to get his own way.*

But could he be blamed? After all, he had been wronged had he not? His wife had betrayed him with a lover. And he, Colin, knew what that felt like, could sympathise with him in his fury. Jo was not his wife of course, but it was a similar case. She had been warming to him; all he needed was time. Who knows what might have developed if that bastard had not returned. The arrogance of it. Anger arose to choke Colin as he thought of how Blake had deserted Jo, then walked back into her life when it suited.

"Col – are you alright?"

He started as Finola's voice penetrated his madness.

"Col, what's wrong?" Finola's fear caused the pitch of her voice to rise.

"Yes. Yes. All right," he muttered, using the back of his hand to wipe icy sweat from his upper lip. *Finola. There lay reality.* Part of him knew the fantasy of himself and Jo had been a lie from start to finish. A part of him cringed with shame as he looked across at

Finola and sensed her distress. That aspect of himself was aware of being used – yet another wanted to be.

His eyes narrowed and his hands tightened their grip on the spade.

At the same time that awareness struck Colin, it also illumined Jo. The sinister changes were not, she realised, due to imagination. The yews bent and swayed ominously, their branches scourging the air with an angry whiplash motion. The rumble of the river emerged from the background to roar with menace from long ago.

"Blake?" Her voice held a tremor of fear before his name was snatched away by the wind. He paused, lifted his head and looked her way. Jo froze at the naked hatred visible in his face.

HATE KILL

This time she could not ignore the malignant whisper. As though her intervention had been some sort of signal, the two men stopped work and faced each other in open confrontation.

Jo blinked and slowly turned as a voice pierced the veil of her helplessness.

"What's going on Jo?" Roz repeated.

She had moved to Finola's side and had instinctively placed a protective arm around her shaking shoulders.

Jo spoke without conscious thought. "The final conflict."

Because now there could be no doubt. Justin St. Clair had not been finally vanquished by the hawk.

SIXTY-SIX

~

"I'm scared Jo."

There was a note of appeal in Finola's voice, as though she thought Jo could avert the disaster they all now thought to be imminent.

"Buck up Fin! At least we're safe from that bloody bird!"

Louise's attempt at heartiness and Finola's response were lost to Jo. They, and Roz too, faded from perception. She was watching the two men with focused intensity: the scene before her had changed, had a surrealist air about it. In the background the yews still flailed; the wind screamed and hissed around buttress and bellhouse, and an owl-cry ripped through the night. Yet within the circle of moonlight stillness and silence held sway. Nobody else existed, only herself and the two men. "Blake! Colin!"

In half-crouching stance, they circled one another like cats in slow-motion.

She screamed as Colin brandished the spade and Blake slipped on the snow.

Jo shouted once more then fell silent. The world around her was retreating, becoming ever more remote, her body more awkward, her movements more difficult to co-ordinate. The sole reality lay within that circle of light. The men now seemed deaf to her cries, yet strangely she could sense if not physically hear, their words:

"Bastard! You think you have her now, don't you?"

Instinctively Jo's hand moved to her mouth. The voice which had issued from Colin's lips was not his own, resembled more the snarl of a dog or the growl of a maddened bear.

"She IS mine."

Blake's voice too was changed, yet it struck a chord in her heart.

"She never loved you, St. Clair."

"Fornicating bastard! Dog spittle!"

"Let her go."

"Never! Her wolf-slit will never enfold you again!"

"Befoul her once more, St. Clair, and I'll rip out your tongue."

Powerless, Jo listened to the escalating conflict, knowing at any moment hell would erupt. Colin lowered the spade slightly, used it to gesture at the grave in which Madeline's body now lay.

"Did she lie atop you in life, Chase?" he taunted, and Jo heard the inward suck of her own breath. His demonic laughter sent a chill down her spine. *"Did she ride you like a favourite stallion? Well,"* he took a couple of steps to the brink of the grave, *"she won't lie atop you in death!"*

He bent as though to tear Madeline's body from its resting place. Jo recoiled in horror as Blake threw back his head and loosed a terrible howl on the night. "Blake! Blake!" she screamed, but he seemed not to hear. She watched in disbelief as a geyser of cold blue light spurted from the ground at her feet and shot around the perimeter of the circle, effectively sealing it off. As the two ends joined the resulting flash was blinding, and Jo was forced to close her eyes. She reopened them and looked on a changed and terrifying world.

Shadows were stealing across the sward and congealing in the ruins behind the two men. "Blake!" she screamed, and bats fluttered in alarm from the crumbling tower, but the man within the circle gave no sign of having heard. Neither was he the man she knew as Blake: a red hawk with splayed talons sprawled across his chest. Moonlight reflected dully on the clasp of his cloak, and gleamed on the blade of the sword in his opponent's hand. "Why can't you hear me?" she sobbed rushing forward, intending to run to his side. Collision with an unseen barrier knocked the breath from her body and brought a shock of pain. Volts of energy burned her hands and coursed up her arms as she pushed in vain against the invisible shield. *And why did he not draw his sword? Why this apparent reluctance to defend his life?*

Because it is no longer worth living.

His pain reached her across the barricade.

Then she knew why he could not hear, and also what had to be done. *"Antony!"* The force of her cry carried her across the cordon of light and into the circle. Her satin gown trailed in the mud as heedless she ran towards the two men. "No!" she cried, reaching out to grab her husband's arm as he drew back his sword to strike. With a sound that was more of a snarl than a human cry, he whirled round and caught her a back-handed blow. The ruins spun in slow-motion about her head as she fell. Dazed, she struggled to her knees. There was the taste of salt in her mouth. She wiped her lips on the back of her hand, and the white pointed cuff of her gown turned scarlet with blood. "Antony draw your sword!" she urged, but it was already in his hand.

The clang of metal on metal, the sound of muttered curses and insults brought her to her feet. Heedless of her own safety she stumbled towards the battle. The blood was pounding in her temples, her gown torn and impeding her progress. Antony's face swam before her, and her heart was squeezed dry by the pain and hatred she saw in his eyes. With a supreme effort she reached his side. "I didn't betray you Antony," she panted, clutching at his free arm. "He had William! Don't you see?"

For a second his attention waived from St. Clair's weapon to her face. The green eyes searched her own for the truth. Only a second of distraction, but long enough for St. Clair's sword to strike with the speed of an adder. She screamed as blood splashed her face and Antony's left arm opened up to the bone.

"Bitch!"

St. Clair thrust her aside and went in for the kill.

The ring of metal on metal filled Madeline's ears as fear filled her heart. Antony's wound was flowing freely now, and twice she saw him slip and falter in his own blood. "I love you Antony! I'll always love you," she cried, as her husband slashed and hacked in a blind rage. "Shameless whore! Watch your lover die – *then* join him!" St. Clair panted, slashing with renewed fury. She saw Antony's head fractionally turn her way, and instantly regretted her intervention. But she had seen the brief nod with which he acknowledged her words, and felt the return of his love. St. Clair raised his sword and lunged. Antony side-stepped and dropped to one knee, and seeing the opening, struck upward and obliquely with terrible force.

Blue lightning flashed round the glade, throwing the ruins into sharp relief. Screams filled his ears and the roar of the river drowned everything with its thunder. The yews threshed their grieving heads, bats squeaked and fluttered on the wind and a tide of blood cleansed the earth. St. Clair staggered and dropped to his knees as the blade was swiftly withdrawn. The screams stopped, were replaced by an ineffectual gurgle. So they were together after all. His last sight of this world was of her running into her lover's arms.

It no longer mattered. A shaft of ice had pierced his heart, leaking his life-blood and killing all feelings of love and hate. He could no longer recall her face. Even her name had faded, along with that of the man he had sought to kill in revenge. What a waste of a lifetime and beyond, but there was comfort in letting go. Nothing now but this creeping cold, spreading in healing ripples from where his heart had once been.

"Col! Col!"

The heartrending cry reached him across the wasteland of his life, but meant nothing.

Sobbing openly now, Finola knelt by his twitching body.

"He'll be all right."

Blake pulled her upright from where she knelt in the snow and passed her gently to Louise. Slipping off his coat he laid it over Colin and rolled up a scarf to cushion his head. "He'll be all right, I promise," he repeated as Roz anxiously bent over his now still form. "Give him a few minutes to recover," he added before moving over to Jo. He pulled her protectively to him and held her close. "That's the end of St. Clair. He'll cause no more trouble."

Jo pulled back slightly, raised her head and looked intently into his face.

"Who are you?" she whispered.

He looked down at her in silence for a moment. "The man who loves you," was all he said.

Jo blinked. For a moment, the moonlight had turned his eyes to green.

SIXTY-SEVEN

~

All was restored to normal in the graveyard. The tiny church looked much as it always had, oblivious to a dark past and the ruins upon which it was built. The yews stood dark and inscrutable, with never a fingering of their needles to break their stillness. Every now and then Jo stretched out a hand, half expecting to see the blood-stained point of a white satin sleeve, but saw only the prosaic cuff of her Barbour jacket. Blake nursed his arm for a time, and when asked by Jo in an undervoice, admitted to deep-rooted pain. Jo demanded he roll up his sleeve and gasped aloud as a livid mark was exposed.

"Just a shadow. It will fade," Blake assured her, covering it again. And given his previous scepticism, Jo marvelled at his new under-standing.

Colin was still subdued and remote, but recovered sufficiently to help Blake cover Antony's bones and Madeline's body with several feet of earth. They then lowered Maud Bickley's coffin to rest at the original level of her grave as dug by Seth. When this was done Blake, with one look at Colin's ashen face, insisted he rest on the cart. Blake then filled the cavity with soil, aided by Roz and also Jo, who despite her ordeal rejected Blake's advice that she should rest. Finola was dispatched to fuss over Col, and Louise who was also looking decidedly grey, was ordered to join them.

"I've been such a fool – can you ever forgive me, Fin?" Colin was heard to say.

Once Maud was safely reinterred and Blake had recited a simple service learnt on the Bosnian battlefields, all of them stood for a moment in silence before filing away into the night. Snow had been softly falling throughout, and by the time they reached the postern gate, a white mantle lay over the mound rendering it unremarkable.

"Did you want to go into the church?" Blake asked, pausing at the gate.

Jo thought of Seth lying in there and shook her head. "There's no need. We've done everything necessary out here. They're free now – and so are we."

"Come on then," Roz sighed. "I'd be ruined for life if this ever got out."

On hearing her words Jo was content, knowing her secret to be safe.

One backward look at the peaceful scene, then they trundled the cart to the snow-banked river.

All that now remained was to dispose of Madeline's coffin. The roar of the falls increased as they approached. Spectacular against the snow-scene they cascaded down in a curtain of foam, ethereal in the moonlight. The pool into which they spilled was green and deep. *Like his eyes*, and she pushed the dangerous thought aside. It was very deep; and thick with water weed and secrecy. They slid the lead coffin in first. Water rushed in and it immediately sank without trace. Then the lid. Nothing now remained; it was, Jo thought with a pang, as though the whole thing had never taken place.

"The beauty of it is, this church is known to be built on an ancient burial site. Should it ever be found, no-one will think it the least bit odd," Jo said, satisfied as they watched the water race and eddy on its way.

"Thank you – all of you," she said warmly before turning and walking away.

She thought then of Madeline and Antony, separated by centuries but now reunited. She tried too to reconstruct the strange events of the graveyard, which even now were fading from her grasp. The forms were hazy, the details indistinct like a child's painting in which the colours have run. How much had really occurred, and how much had been played out only in her psyche? And in the end, what did it matter? Who was to say what was 'real' and what was not. "My thanks most of all to you, Blake," she whispered on reaching his side.

He turned and placed both hands on her shoulders. His eyes as they searched her face were river-dark with passion. "Forgive me, my love. I should have known you could never betray me."

Jo, deeply moved by his pain, wondered who had spoken.

Antony? Blake? Or maybe both.

Gently, almost reverently, he kissed her forehead and taking her by the hand, led her back along the lane.

SIXTY-EIGHT

~

Jo sighed and watched from the window as the last of the snow dripped from roof, hedgerow and branch. So now it was all over. The local garage had fitted Louise's car with a new windscreen, and Blake's vehicle was freed as the drift melted. The day before Roz had driven off back to the hospital and Col and Finola were back at Throstle Garth. The power was back on, the telephone working, and Blake had exercised his diplomatic powers. As a result Seth's body had been removed from the church with minimum fuss and his family had been informed. Blake and Colin had replaced the flags in the kitchen and all was back to normal. Even her hand, she thought eying the pink and healthy new skin. So why this feeling of discontent, of something missing? The complete absence of presence maybe.

It was simply a question of time, she told herself watching the robin and a host of chaffinches pick at the scraps deposited on the grass. It would take a while for her feelings to settle, to realise the horror was truly at an end. As yet it didn't seem real, and she still paused nervously at times before pushing open the door to the kitchen and stepping inside. But since the night of Madeline's burial, nothing so far had disturbed the peace. Was that the problem? she mused, gazing beyond the garden to the backdrop of brooding fells.

Soon Blake would be going too. Her eyes clouded with pain at the knowledge of this. Yet her heart was lighter; the enactment of the scene in the churchyard had in some strange way rekindled their love, served to remind them how precious their bond. They would work things out somehow, he had assured her last night, whilst holding her tight in the bed upstairs but at the same time refusing to make love. No thanks, he had said with a laugh that didn't ring true when she had felt for him beneath the covers. "It's all quiet now – let's not push our luck," he added whilst stroking her hair to rob his words of any hint of rejection.

"Coffee darling?"

Jo turned from the window as Louise spoke from the doorway. "Lovely, thanks."

"Then I'll have to be on my way, sweetie," Louise said, placing the tray on the table then straightening up to give Jo a speculative look. "You'll be okay?"

Jo nodded. "No problem."

"I thought I smelt coffee," Blake said entering the room.

"Trust a man," Louise joked but the glance she gave him was pregnant with meaning and tension.

"Look folks, I know what you're thinking – but I'm not leaving with you," Jo said firmly, taking a steaming cup from Louise. "I need time to collect my things before I go."

"And your thoughts?"

Jo was uncomfortably aware of Blake's speculative expression, and the knowledge that he understood more than he ought. "Something like that," she said lightly before turning pointedly to Louise. "I hope the thaw continues until you get back to London."

Louise shrugged her elegant shoulders. "No problem darling."

"What is it Jo?" Blake asked quietly as the three of them sat by the fire with their coffee.

Jo looked at him and Louise, saw the anxiety in their faces and knew it wasn't fair to dissemble. "Oh, anti-climax I guess. It's taking time to adjust."

Blake gave her a teasing look. "I suspect you're missing him."

But Jo saw the steel behind his eyes. "Rubbish! Thanks – but I wouldn't want to go through that again."

"Maybe not." He smiled, but the unspoken words hung in the air between them: *no but you mourn his passing on.*

"It's not that," Jo said as though he had actually spoken. "It's, well, unfinished business."

He frowned and set down his empty cup. "What do you mean Jo?"

"Well, historians still have him down as a traitor: we know now that it isn't true, that St. Clair set him up."

"So why not tell them?" Louise demanded.

Jo choked on the last of her coffee and Blake rose to thump her on the back as she spluttered and coughed.

"Gee, I'm flattered your poor old agent still has such dramatic effect!" Louise commented dryly so that Jo had to laugh which made her cough again. She rose, and aware of being closely watched by both Blake and Louise, paced round the table then sat down again. "It wouldn't do," she pronounced regretfully. "There's no proof. Historians and academics would dismiss it as fantastic speculation."

"Of course they would," Louise agreed, nodding her head.

Jo saw that Blake had slumped on his seat and was looking bored with this cul-de-sac discussion. "Louise this is not the time for one of your –," she began with a withering look.

"A *novel* darling," Louise interrupted with a sweet smile of triumph.

"What?"

"Think about it: you could write a convincing novel."

Blake sat upright and joined in again with renewed interest. "Louise could be right: you have the power to set the record straight, clear Chase and his family of disgrace."

"But will anyone take any notice?" Jo said doubtfully. "Anyone with influence that is."

Louise jumped in before Blake could reply. "You bet they will – *now!* You have the 'name and fame' – all thanks to me of course darling," she added patting her coiffure and throwing Jo a mischievous look.

"Critics have awesome powers," Blake contributed leaning forward. "You need only put a question mark over the history books to start a buzz. Louise is right."

Louise leaned forward, her eyes shining with enthusiasm. "Of course I am! People want a good story, not a lecture for God's sake! They remember the Arthurs, the Guineveres, the Tristan and Isoldes, the Hero and Leanders – the all-time lovers of our myths – not the dry data of historians." Patently sincere and carried on the wings of her own rhetoric, Louise leaned forward to take Jo's hand. "Tell his story Jo – get *the people* on his side!"

Jo chewed her bottom lip, tried to quell the spurt of excitement that leapt up inside. Blake's support was generous, his lack of self-ishness impressive, but how would he cope with this, her all-time *obsession*?"

"Anything's better than this mealy-mopey stranger you've turned into," he said with an ironical smile, reading the thoughts as they flit across her face.

"I'd have to stay here," she said uncertainly.

Blake's eyebrow rose. "You don't exactly seem in a hurry to leave."

Jo wavered. "I don't know."

"There could be a film in it honey," Louise tempted. "Convince her Blake!" she appealed, watching dreams of financial security fade.

He shook his head. "This one has to be up to Jo."

"I'll give it some thought," Jo promised, standing up as Louise glanced at her Cartier watch indicating she had to leave.

Louise rose, gathered up her overnight bag and pecked Jo on the cheek. "The cottage is yours as long as you want it."

At the front door she turned to give Jo one of her no-nonsense 'I'm your agent Goddammit' looks. "Do it Jo!" she commanded and swept out into the thaw.

Is *this* the reason I was brought here? Jo wondered, watching the wheels of Louise's car spray tides of slush as it moved away.

Later that day she had to watch Blake leave too.

"I do have to go," he said apologetically.

"I know."

"When I'm through in Bosnia?"

She nodded. "We'll talk."

He shook his head. "No, we'll work it out – and we'll *love*," he corrected firmly.

They kissed and held each other as though neither could bear to part.

She was frowning slightly as she looked directly into his eyes. "Take care, Blake."

"Don't worry – I'll be back."

She watched until the car disappeared round the first bend in the track.

That night the cottage felt curiously empty. Blake was right, she admitted ruefully, towelling herself dry from her bath. She did miss Antony. Not his cruelty and pain, but the man at the end of the tunnel, the man with green eyes who had loved so deeply before wrath had taken hold. She lay in bed listening to the beck running through the garden. Tonight it was loud, swollen with the thaw. Her mind mulled over Louise's proposition. Could it work? Could she handle it in emotional terms? Doubts crept in and she was on the verge of shelving the project when watery sounds began to intrude. There was, she thought drowsily, a voice in the beck, behind the gurgle and grumble of the flow.

Tell them. Tell them for me.

Jo smiled and closed her eyes. The cottage no longer felt empty. She would receive help enough in writing the book. Sorry Ruskin – maybe some other time. She would telephone Louise in the morning, tell her she was ready to make a start. Let her know she was staying on at Twilight Cottage.

EPILOGUE

~

And they are gone: aye, ages long ago
These lovers fled away into the storm

'Tis dark: quick pattereth the flaw-blown sleet:
This is no dream, my bride, my Madeline!
                                        Keats: Eve of St Agnes

The first time she had vomited on rising, Jo had thought little of it. A stress reaction, she told herself. It was only after the third morning of running to the bathroom that she began to worry in case there was something seriously wrong. Then when it continued, and nausea frequently struck during the day and certain other signs manifested, she started casting her mind back in panic. Leafing through her diary, she recalled the bizarre events of the night Blake unexpectedly showed up at the cottage, the strangeness of their lovemaking. After counting again, she finally had to admit the truth. This definitely had not been on her agenda. Nothing that a decent house, shared chores and a good nanny can't sort, a delighted Blake had said when told the news.

And of course he was right. They had talked, reached agreement about her career, found a workable compromise. She thought of all this now, nine months later and smiled down at her son. A reward? Maybe. After the first shock had passed pregnancy had enriched her as a writer; Louise, and later her publisher, had raved over the finished manuscript. *Antony's story*. Blake's roses bore a card telling her he was on his way to the hospital. What would he make of the baby? She leaned over to stroke the infant's cheek with her forefinger as he awoke, and for a second he seemed to return her conspiratorial smile.

After all, it was a shocking combination: the jet black hair and those green eyes.

434

Also available in Pendragon by Nina Green:

DARK STAR

(ISBN 0 9530538 06) £6.99

Direct Orders: **Pendragon Press Ltd., Testa Teres House, Copse Road, Fleetwood, Lancs., FY7 7NY. Tel: (019253) 772788. Fax: (019253) 773359. Price: £6.99 + £1 P&P.**

Reporter Darcy West, separated from her husband, reluctantly takes in her orphaned nephew Alisdair, who finds a strange meteor on a lonely Lakeland fell. It falls into the hands of a psychotic physicist and disaster strikes. Darcy battles against greed and corruption, aided by Mr. Ambrose, a hermit with supernatural powers.

Dark Star by Nina Green weaves a splendid web of bizarre and chilling incidents around the globe. A five star story, with excellent characters, that never flags.
Bolton Evening News

Nina follows her star – it packs in a lot of research . . . everything from quantum physics to theories about afterlife, plus murder, environmental mayhem and emotional chaos. *Manchester Evening News*

Take Scully – add a little bit of Louis Lane – and you may be close to the heroine of this new novel by Nina Green. A nail-biting conclusion . . . a book to fuel the imagination. *Lancashire Evening Post*

Dark Star relates a battle of opposing forces – Science against Nature, Good versus Evil, husband against wife. It conjures up haunting images of what could happen if these forces collide. A thoroughly enjoyable, if at times disturbing, read. *North West Evening Mail*

Author Nina Green puts a chill into the hearts of readers with *Dark Star*. The novel – and you have to keep remembering it is a novel – explores what happens when scientific discoveries are abused for greed and personal power. And there is of course, a love angle . . . an easy-to-read compelling book.
Chorley Guardian

A compelling novel . . . *Blackpool and Fylde Coast Gazette*

. . . the result: a New Age thriller called *Dark Star*. *Publishing News: London*

. . . *Dark Star* is perfect bedtime reading . . . On one level the book is a straight-forward thriller with enough murder, intrigue and short chapters to keep today's short attention span readers enthralled and wanting more. On another it asks pertinent questions about the nature of the cosmos and life after death, the biggies that most of us encounter at some point in our lives.
Cumbria Life Magazine

Coming next in Pendragon by Nina Green:

IMMORTAL DUST

A Darcy West Mystery

Reporter Darcy looks back to when she first met Brant Kennedy and
the beginning of their tempestuous relationship . . .

The telephone rings in her office at the *Manchester News*. It is her old
friend Caro Stevens: they were students together at Hilldean University.
Still employed on campus, Caro is now a lecturer in the Archaeology
Department. Her team – up in the English Lakes on a routine dig –
have found a preserved body.

"There's a scoop in it, Darcy. Eight hundred years old – and his blood
is still fluid!" There is a pause at the other end of the line. "Oh and
Darcy –,"

"Yes?"

"His eyes are still green."

Darcy is hooked.

Whilst investigating St. Gildas Man as they have named the body,
Darcy meets Brant – an astrophysicist working from a remote obser-
vatory on the cliffs. After a stormy start, they call a truce to investigate
the case of the long-buried knight. The trail leads Darcy into deadly
danger, betrayal and deceit. Is Brant all he claims to be, or is he really
a part of the conspiracy to murder and steal? And if she learns too
much or stands in his way, would he be willing to kill her too? Blocked
by Government Departments, betrayed by her editor Frank Kelly,
and finally victimised and discarded by the *Manchester News*, Darcy's
world is beginning to crumble. Worst of all, Caro is in mortal danger.
Afraid to trust anyone, Darcy goes it alone.

From solitary knight to a powerful monastic Order, she is led to the
secrets of Alchemy. Predictions, heavenly constellations, bizarre symbols
and magical arts weave a maze of coincidences and contradictions.
Her quest takes her from medieval monastery to Nazi Germany and
a war criminal's lust for gold. It doesn't end with a madman's memories:
a series of chilling clues leads her to a present-day secret society with
a sinister plan to control the western world.

Mythical gold? Or was there once a secret known only to a powerful
few? The quest for precious metal? Or immortality symbolised by gold
dust? *Or both?* Moving through a nightmare world of illusion and the
supernatural, Darcy's faith and her love for Brant must pass through
the alchemical fire.